CW00741852

Lightfall

Lightfall

Book One of
THE EVERLANDS

ED CROCKER

ST. MARTIN'S PRESS
NEW YORK

This is a work of fiction. All of the characters, organizations, and events portrayed in this novel are either products of the author's imagination or are used fictitiously.

First published in the United States by St. Martin's Press, an imprint of St. Martin's Publishing Group

LIGHTFALL. Copyright © 2024 by Edward Crocker. All rights reserved. Printed in the United States of America. For information, address St. Martin's Publishing Group, 120 Broadway, New York, NY 10271.

www.stmartins.com

Map artwork by L. N. Bayen

Library of Congress Cataloging-in-Publication Data

Names: Crocker, Ed, author.
Title: Lightfall / Ed Crocker.
Description: First edition. | New York : St. Martin's Press, 2025. |
    Series: The Everlands trilogy ; book 1
Identifiers: LCCN 2024029782 | ISBN 9781250287731 (hardcover) |
    ISBN 9781250287748 (ebook)
Subjects: LCGFT: Vampire fiction. | Fantasy fiction. | Novels.
Classification: LCC PR6103.R59 L54 2025 | DDC 823/.92—dc23/eng/20240712
LC record available at https://lccn.loc.gov/2024029782

Our books may be purchased in bulk for promotional, educational, or business use. Please contact your local bookseller or the Macmillan Corporate and Premium Sales Department at 1-800-221-7945, extension 5442, or by email at MacmillanSpecialMarkets@macmillan.com.

First Edition: 2025

10 9 8 7 6 5 4 3 2 1

To Grandad
You would have liked this
Thank you for everything
I miss you

The important thing is not how long your life is but how long it seems.

Terry Pratchett, *Truckers*

Lightfall

Prologue

Neuras Sinassion

First, imagine a continent. Let's call it the Everlands. A continent full of immortals. Vampires. Werewolves. Sorcerers. No humans here. These immortals live forever if they are careful (or, in the case of the vampires, if they drink the right blood), but they can be killed. They are immortal, not invincible, as future wars will firmly and bloodily attest to.

Next, imagine they are mindless beasts, roaming the land. One day, in an act many future scholars will smugly call the *Great Intelligence,* these beasts develop self-awareness. Become civilized. The first tribes are formed, then villages, then towns. A few centuries later, the first cities go up. Vampire cities. Wolfkind cities. Sorcerer cities. Civilization thrives.

The pinnacle of this civilization is Lightfall, the great city of the Centerlands, the first city where all three immortals mix. It has a vampire name, but then that's vampires for you. Always hogging the nomenclature.

Life is good for a period. Then the Twin War comes. The kind of existential war that all civilizations face after a while. Miraculously, these immortals do not wipe themselves out. Their weapons are not yet advanced enough. Life is even better, with the lessons learned from the shadows of war. Another century passes.

Then, almost a hundred years ago to the day our story begins, the Grays appear. Imaginatively named for the gray cloaks that hide their features, they decimate the immortals with impossibly powerful weapons. The cities of the Centerlands are no more—even mighty Lightfall.

The surviving immortals flee to their homelands in the corners of the continent, leaving the Centerlands to the Grays. The sorcerers stay in the Desertlands, the wolves in the eastern forests, and the vampires remain north in the first—now the only—vampire city.

A century passes. Our tale . . . or *my* tale, as you will eventually see, begins.

I have told you the *what*. The *why* will take a little longer.

PART I

The Gray Race

Ashes to Ashes

To die in normal circumstances is traumatic enough for the family of a deceased immortal, given the loss of so many potential centuries. For a wolf or a sorcerer, it is galling. But for vampires, there is not even a corpse to mourn over. It is a vivid representation of the permanence of death: one minute they are there, the next . . . Or to put it another way, there is grief, and then there is the grief of ash.

Cardinale Ciani, *Reflections on Eternitie*

First Lord Azzuri

My son is dying, and there is nothing I or anyone else can do about it. There are five bullet wounds in his slender frame, but the bullets themselves have long since dissolved into his blood and sealed his fate. Bright purple veins stand out on his face and arms. His skin softly glows; I put my hand to his forehead and find it boiling to the touch. Soon the poison inside him will do its work, the same as if he had stood before the sun.

They found him not far beyond the city just after nightfall, not long after the day watch handed over to the night. A watchman spotted him in the flickering light of the torches that stretch out a hundred meters from the city walls, and the Scout Guard went out to inspect—a dangerous mission at any time, but they hoped he might have been a corpse of one of the Grays, the reason we have the sundamn walls in the first place. That would have been a first. Instead they found an Azzuri, slowly dying beneath a tree. Now all I can do is stand here and think about what I am going to say to his mother and his sister and his older brother. And how many of them will care.

Suddenly his skin seems to glow even stronger, a bright, searing pulse. Then noiselessly he explodes, leaving nothing but a pile of ash-gray dust.

I stand there a few more moments. Then I turn to my first man, Redgrave. "I am going to speak with my family now. Then I want to know why my son died."

"Yes, First Lord," he says, avoiding my gaze.

"Oh, and don't ring the alarms yet. Not until we know if this is a prelude to an attack on the wall." I go to leave.

"First Lord?"

I turn back to my counselor, my friend. "Yes, Redgrave?"

"You . . . ah, you have some . . ." His words trail off and he points to my shoulder.

I look. I have some of my son on me. I brush the dust off and walk out. It is going to be a long night.

Sam

Finally I have it. Standing in front of the bookcase, I hold the vial of blood between my thumb and forefinger and inspect it. It's red. Same as all the other blood. A little darker than you'd expect, maybe. A little tingle on my nose, my senses dulled from a life of blood poorer than this. But you still wouldn't know it was different from any others. Different from the cowblood me and the rest of the servants have to live on.

Still holding the vial, I steal a quick glance behind me at the palace library. I'm fairly sure I'm still alone—there's an hour until nightfall, and vampires like their sleep, or at least they're not that fond of the day—but it can't hurt to check, given I'm about to do something that would have me tied to a stake and burnt to cinders before the morning sun if I was caught. My floor, which circles around the entire library, is lit well, so I can see all before me, even with the eyesight of someone on the worst blood for decades. The glow of the desertmold in glass sconces that adorns the walls—show me torches or oil lamps in a library, I'll show you a moron—gives me a good view of the lower levels. Bookshelves line the perimeter, stretching to the tall oak doors of the entrance and, in the center, a vast expanse of reading desks. Fixed ladders connect the lower floor to the uppers. These are for the servants, as Midways or Lords can clear the levels with a quick bound on their blood.

Above it all is the great dome of the library, on which are painted grand frescoes of vampires building First Light, my city. In Lightfall— the old vampire capital, dead for a century—the palace library was glass roofed, giving a perfect view of the night sky. Mechanical wooden shutters covered it during the day. I never saw this myself, being born thirty years ago, or seventy years after the mysterious Grays made their feelings clearly felt about the cities of the Centerlands. This is the only place I know. But like a lot of things I read about Lightfall, it sounds nice.

Convinced I'm not about to be caught, I turn back to my task. The next step in my freedom. The section of bookcase before me looks no different from the rest on this level. It's a mix of fairly new and reasonably old; hard-backed volumes in good condition, some with gemstones ensconced in their covers (a sign of real wealth), are mixed with slightly older, rougher, animal-skin-backed volumes.

What is different, though, is the raised dais in front of it, a little to my left. Tall and bronze, it reaches up to my waist, and atop it is a circular indentation, in the middle of which is a small hole for something to be poured into. I open the vial, and for a second I catch a proper scent of the blood within, and my body feels alive, like a flash of lightning has shot up my nostrils and singed my brain.

Wolfblood. The blood of the wolfkind. The king of bloods.

It took me a while to find this. I've been searching for a vial of this stuff in the rooms of the Lords I clean almost all my ten years here. Even the Lords are not allowed to take wolfblood anymore. The blood that gives you wings and the strength of fifty. That right is reserved for the First Guard only. They say they need to keep the wolfblood for the fight against the Grays, whenever that is. They hoard it. Of course I know this can't all be true, as I found this vial in the palace guest rooms of Lord Beryl. Maybe he stole it. Maybe the Lords give themselves a secret treat now and then. I wouldn't put it past them.

I could catch this scent all day, and for a moment I want to down it. Fly far from the palace. But where would I go? How would I hide? They don't let servants start new lives. Hence, this bookcase.

With the determination of someone who's been cleaning Lords' chamber pots for the last decade, I quickly upend the vial into the hole atop the dais and allow a small trickle of the blood to fall in, making sure it's just a trickle.

Then I wait.

There's no sound. I don't know how it works, but I'll wager there's some kind of tiny mechanism designed by the Kinets. Of all the five sorcerer types, the vampires love the Kinets the most. Once they moved whole mountains, but now that kind are gone. These days, either they are engineers or they have turned their focus to moving tiny things. Some people think they put magick into objects. That's a misunderstanding.

Sorcerers use their magick *on* things, but they can't put magick *into* anything. Kinets simply change the way tiny things are structured. Shortly before Grayfall, some Kinets worked out they could use their powers of moving the tiniest matter to make blood stronger. Magicked blood. It's been a real turning point. The strongest bloods are now made even stronger. They're so effective that when the vampires fled the Centerlands for here, the First Lord made sure to bring a group of them with him, leaving many of his own class to die instead. Now, other than a small group of Neuras sorcerers used by the First Lord to communicate long distance with the other kingdoms, they are the only sorcerers who live in First Light.

Suddenly I hear it. A slight sound of something moving within the walls. One side of this section of the bookcase hinges open, turning the bookcase into a door, which slowly opens to reveal blackness within.

The first things I'm hit with are must and damp—old parchment and the decaying scent of centuries. There are old books in here, my nose tells me, long before my eyes have their go. I don't hesitate; I stride in.

The dark hits me. I wait for my eyes to adjust, but this is proper dark. All-consuming. No lamps here. I'm sure the kind of vampire that waltzes in with wolfblood to spare is used to drinking the noble bloods that give you perfect night vision. Whoever built this wasn't thinking of palace maids. I'm not going to do this on cowblood. I consider taking a trickle of wolfblood from the vial, but that would be madness. I need to save it for the return visits I'll need. And all I need is night vision, not the wings and super strength that comes with wolfblood.

So I reach into my petticoats and draw out my emergency vial, one I found when cleaning Lord Sapphiri's palace guest rooms several months ago. It was concealed under a couple of broken ones from his antics the night before when I found it, so I knew he'd never miss it. It's only fox, a Midway blood, but it's lightly magicked, which means it's a little stronger—good enough to see perfectly in the dark for an hourglass at least. I quickly down the whole vial—I'm sure Sapphiri will have another piss-up at some point and gift me with more—and the pitch-black becomes a glowing gloom.

You think you get used to the different effects of blood after a few decades, but you never do. Especially when you're not used to them. There are three types of vampire class, defined by the blood we take. Worns, the poor of the city, get cowblood. It doesn't stop your aging—hence our name. After a couple of centuries your skin is saggy and wrinkled and your strength is sapped; few live much beyond that. I'm only thirty years, barely into adulthood, so I've got another few decades before the first hint of a line arrives. The signs that signal my place even more than my poverty.

The Midways get better blood, such as fox, boar, crow. Makes you stronger, more alive. Stops your aging. Even better now after the sorcerers have started to magick it. Not strong enough to make them challenge the nobles, of course. Just powerful enough to make Midways work well as administrators. And the nobility? They get the best. The noble bloods. Whale, snaptail, bear, hawk, stag, mountain cat . . . The ones that make you punch through walls should you want to. But only wolfblood, elusive, restricted wolfblood, gives you wings.

The lines weren't so fluid back in Lightfall. A lot of things were better, or so I'm told. No, not told. No one tells me anything.

That's why I read.

My eyes fully adjusted, I inspect the large circular room in front of me. It's nowhere near as big as one floor of the main library, but big enough to house what look like a couple of thousand books. In the middle is a solitary reading table. I suppose not many people come here. I move to the nearest shelf; I touch it, feel it. It's redoak. I can't see the red shade in my night vision, but I can feel the toughness of it, the quality. Better than the reinforced crestwood shelves of the main library. These shelves cost a pretty penny. I take the nearest volume to me and blow away a light film of dust. It smells slightly fragranced, like it was bound in the desert south. The animal hide that binds it is soft, velvety. I inhale it, not minding the dust or the smell.

I love books too much. What began as a survival plan turned into obsession, I suppose.

The title of the book is embroidered onto the skin, with jewels encrusted into the stitching. It winks at me in the gloom. *A Studie of the Effects of Wolfblood in the Worns*. I gasp. This is definitely not the kind of title a Lord would want lying around. I replace it and move down the shelf, feeling the rough and smooth touch of old vellum on my skin. A volume at the end is parchment, poorly tied together with what looks like reeds. There is no writing on the cover, but instead a faded sketch of a figure next to a mountain, a hand outstretched toward it. A Kinet. The mountain movers don't exist anymore. More prohibited knowledge. The next one is bound in the dark green scaly hide of a snaptail, which is a bold choice, and the faded ink on its spine tells me that it contains *Theories of the Great Intelligence.* The time before civilization no one talks about, when the first immortals were simply beasts.

I was right, then. These are the books of forbidden knowledge or ancient disputed history or suppressed information. The kind of books that will tell you how to fool the nose of the wolfkind, so they can't hire one to hunt me down when I escape into Worntown. The kind of books that will tell you the full powers of all the bloods or the concealed real family histories of the oldest Lords, so when I make myself a new life, I can be a Midway with knowledge people find useful—and pay me for in better blood.

I wasn't meant to be a servant. And I won't be one forever.

Click.

The sound carries all the way. The foxblood in me has amplified it, and now I hear a different sort of clicking, one of shoes on marble stone. Panic grips me, tight and hard, but I didn't get here by freezing up in its clammy embrace, so I shake the terror from me like dead leaves and sprint out of the forbidden library, hoping that somehow the door mechanism closes automatically. I am right; the bookshelf swings shut behind me (a mechanism you step on? Not now, Sam). But my relief is short lived, because the ladder to this floor shakes a little and I hear footsteps climbing. It's not a Lord, then. Or a guard. That's good. But it could be a valet. That's bad.

I freeze again. There's no point in running; they would see me in a moment and it wouldn't look good. But there's no reason for me to be here. And if they know where I am, where they had to come in the library to find me, then that means they have me exposed anyway.

Fight it is, then.

As I stare at the ladder, the footsteps nearing, time slowing, I think. Maybe it's the Midway blood in me, the fox so potent compared to cow, or maybe I'm just always angry. But it comes easily. I think of my father, burnt before the sun for protecting my mother. I think of my mother, taking her life from grief, leaving me and my sister orphans before either of us was a decade. I think of my sister, barely eighteen, desperate to work at the palace, tired of the streets. I think of the accident during her palace-joining ceremony. Burnt to a crisp in the sun. I think on the Lords picking me instead. An easy replacement. A servant at the First Lord's palace, a *privilege.* A job you never leave voluntarily. I think of all the things that have been done to me, and I ball my fists and try and extend my fangs on the little blood in me. I find, to my delight, that I am not afraid. The rage triumphs.

Here we go.

"Evening, Sammy. Thought I'd find you here."

My fists uncurl and my fangs retract and I stand there, gawping. It's Beth. Just Beth. My chambermate, my only friend, grinning as though she's stumbled on me at a Worntown dance. She adjusts the ribbon on her day gown, pulling the rough linen tighter.

"Climbing that ladder was not my idea of fun, by the way," she says, panting a little.

I smile, all my rage turned to relief, with just the nervous energy in my veins left to remind me of it. "It helps if you're not on cowblood when you're doing it."

"I bet it does, you sneak." She stares behind me at the bookcase. "So you found the wolfblood then. Have you been in yet?"

I stare at her, gawping. "How . . ."

"It's not exactly blood magick, Sammy. I woke up. You weren't there. Sneaking in the library as usual, I assumed. But then I thought about your excitement the previous night. You wouldn't say why, but I know you. Why else would you be excited in this life of ours if you hadn't found the thing you'd been looking for? A nice little shot of the good stuff, get you access to all the forbidden nonsense. I don't mind you didn't tell me. You know I'd tell you not to be a bloody fool."

Beth has never read a book in her life. But oh by the twin hells is she clever sometimes.

"But why did you come?"

Beth shrugs, her tight bun bobbling as she does so. Within that bun is long, flowing, golden-hued hair. Far removed from my own drab shorter brunette locks. She gets to unfurl it only in her chambers or at the end of the week on Hallsday. It's a waste. Like a lot of things here.

"Because there's less than half a glass before everyone wakes, and I knew you'd lose track of time, and as much as I would quite like the whole room to myself, I've sort of got quite fond of you in our ten years together, and I don't really want a new chambermate, although since you spend half the time sneaking around this musty pit, I'm not really sure why."

"Oh, Blood Gods, is it really that time?"

"Yes, it is. Honestly, Sammy, I think you want to get sunburst some-times." She nods behind her at the bookcase. "Was it worth it? Find any-thing good in there other than dust and spiders?"

"I've only just started looking. But there is proper knowledge in there. And I reckon I've got enough wolfblood in this vial to give me access to it a good twenty or so more times. I'll spend the whole day there next time."

"Or you'll be caught and have a short walk to the cross and a face full of sun."

I laugh, despite myself. "Or that."

Beth's grin fades and her wide blue eyes look at me pleadingly. With her rosy cheeks (for a vampire) and her button nose and large lips, in an-other life, she would break hearts. "Is it worth it, Sam? Worth the risk?"

"Beth, the knowledge in there will teach me how to run. And stay hidden. From hired wolves, from the First Guard, from anyone who comes looking. And then it will teach me things I can use. To become a Mid-way. Knowledge to barter. To start a whole new life in a better class. Begin again. Drink the better blood. You know all this, Beth. You know I want this better than anyone."

"I know, Sammy. But isn't it good enough? Being a Worn? Being one of us?"

I look away from her, turn my eyes up toward the library dome. It's an old, tired conversation. Ten years in the same space will do that to a friendship. "Why should I age and die when others live forever?"

"Would it be so bad aging with me?" asks Beth, looking down at the floor.

I move closer and touch her arm gently. "Beth, that's not what I meant."

"I know. I wouldn't try and change you for the world. You're like a storm, one of those charged ones that make your skin feel all funny. In Lightfall, you would've been something. You shouldn't be here. It's like putting lightning in a cage."

I grin. "I'm fairly sure lightning would just go through the bars of a cage."

"I'm fairly sure I came here to save your life, not take your jests."

"And yet here we still are, nattering away."

"You think you're very witty sometimes, don't you?" She turns toward the ladder. "Let's do this."

We exit the library at full speed and bound down the stairs. Four flights, straight down to the servants' entrance. The busts atop the corner banisters, one for each flight, are of various First Lords of the vampires, five centuries' worth. I wonder if there are more First Lords than staircases, and how they choose who to leave out if so. This is the kind of thing you think about when you're running for your life. Halfway down, I signal wordlessly to Beth, and we hide behind a cabinet case of bloodflutes and carafes on the landing. After a few moments, the footsteps I heard on my better blood are loud enough for Beth to hear, too, and then a palace guard on the day shift strolls past, his red and blue tabard ill-fitting on him. The day guard never get the best uniforms. A shit treatment for a shit post. He's obviously ready for his post to be over and for the ignominy of sleeping during the evening, because he's barely paying attention to anything around him, head starting to droop. We probably didn't even need to hide.

When he's rounded the corner, we race down the remaining staircases and are about to slip into the servants' quarters when we hear the quiet tread of an early rising valet coming round the corner. We have nowhere to go. I freeze and turn to Beth, who's equally rigid with horror. On my magicked fox, I smell the first drops of evening cologne on him. A senior valet, then. I hear his harsh breaths, so close to me I fancy I can feel them, too.

Then, at the last possible moment, he stops and sighs. We hear him go back the way he came. Gods bless whatever thing he forgot.

Our chamber door is near to the entrance of the maids' quarters, so the final bit is easy. We slip in, and for a moment I allow myself to breathe. The familiar quarters of ten years. A third of my life spent here. Half of that literally in this room. Two beds, wafer-thin mattresses on rickety malderwood bases. Two dark brown dressers, made of barely better gelmwood. Two wardrobes for our slim collection of dresses—day dress, cleaning garments, and one "nice" dress for Hallsday, our one chance a week to see the outside world.

There's no window—as if Worn servants would be allowed thick sun blinds. So no starlight, but no oil lamps or desertmold lights allowed here, either, just candlelight. Not a problem if you're on better than cowblood, but for us, we're condemned to a life of shadows and gloom.

We can't even keep books or writings in here, lest on the random checks the head valet makes he thinks we're in league with the Worn rebels. Not that there are many left after Grayfall and the following century of tightly controlled life behind First Light's walls. Only Worns up to no good would need books, clearly.

The only sign of color, then, of personality, of *us,* is the pendants we each hang from the knobs of our respective dressers. Beth's is a kaleidoscope of color—tightly woven rainbow threads with a small pearl on the end, an heirloom from her mother. The only thing of any value she has. She keeps it in her petticoat when she's not in this room.

Mine doesn't need hiding. It's just white thread with a small wooden block at the end, crudely carved into something approaching the letter *S,* if the letter *S* had been involved in a fairly bad accident. Made by my sister, for me. Of all my family, this is all I have left. I never wear it. I don't carry my pain. I don't need to. It follows me always, second only to my ambition.

Our short-lived peace is suddenly broken by heavy footsteps padding down the corridor. Heading our way. They can belong to only one woman. We glance at each other, then jump into bed. I hope for the footsteps to pass, but instead they stop outside and a loud knock follows.

I jump out of bed, making sure I'm loud enough to indicate I was in it, and I open the door to see Phylis, the first maid, standing there, with a scowl on her face so wide it carries on around to the back of her head. Phylis is by far the oldest of the palace maids, almost fifteen decades, I hear. She was maid to the First Lord in Lightfall. Deep wrinkles have begun to ring her eyes and mouth, and her hair is more than tinged with gray; a few more decades of this kind of aging and I fear for her future. Lords don't like to be reminded in their own home that it's only their access to the finer blood that staves off the face of time. To me, her wrinkles make her face more interesting than the indistinct averageness of most of the maids. But if I tried to be that nice to her, I doubt she'd take it either sincerely or well. Her loss.

Underneath her sky-blue gown she's wearing her day dress. She was obviously woken herself. "I'm to pass a message on to you, girl," she begins. "From the first valet himself. The First Lord's son is dead."

"What?" I reply, all my tension from the previous hourglass forgotten.

"The youngest, that is, not Rufous. They found him outside the walls. Killed by the Grays, I'm hearin'."

I try and piece this information together. I don't have much to go on, so I don't try for very long. "Why aren't they ringing the alarms?"

"Drain it all, Samantha, do I look like the First Lord? That's their business. I should hope it means the Grays aren't invadin' and it was just an accident or something."

"And what's this got to do with me?" I say, trying to speed up this conversation as quickly as possible. It's not that I'm unaffected by this news. I like the young Azzuri, though I've rarely seen him. He's the rebel of the Lord's family, estranged from them and hardly ever in the palace. It's said he spends his time among the Midway or even among my kind. He sounds like the least deserving of the Lords to get a one-way trip to the Bloodhalls. But first maids are not the kind to take emotion well. They are chosen for their ruthlessness. To keep the maids under them in line. Show emotion and they will use it against you. You may as well put a weapon in their hand.

"You're to go to his room," says Phylis, pointing a thin wrinkled finger at me. "Clean it. Shouldn't be hard, he's not lived in it for decades. But make it spick-and-span just in case, free of anything . . . untoward. Suggestive of his life beyond the palace. Before his grieving mother chooses to look at it. Now. It can't wait till first bell."

"Why me?" I ask.

"Why not?" She grins. There's a moment, then, a truth spoken between us. We know that I'm reliable. She doesn't know why—that I have to be, to allay suspicion, allow me to live my double life in the library these last ten years. Reading. Learning. Or to get access to the good rooms to clean; the Lords' rooms, where I will find the good blood. So she knows I can be trusted. But she also knows that this means there's a stake at my back; for if I do a bad job, if the late Lord's mother finds something bad in there . . . I could see the sun the next morning. The fact this makes her grin says all you need to know about her.

"Fine," I say, slowly edging the door shut. "I'd better get ready, then. They won't like it if I'm late."

"No," says Phylis, unwilling to lose her lizard grin. "They won't."

2

A Room with a Clue

I envy you being born after Grayfall, sister. You cannot remember Lightfall. But I? I cannot stop with the memories. The sundamn things fill up my dayhaunts and enter my nightdreams when I should be doin' something else.

Katrina MacLachlan,
in a letter to her sister Mary

First Lord Azzuri

It has been one hourglass since my youngest son burst into dust in front of me. It may as well have been one year.

My wife reacted with a long-drawn-out wail; she had never lost faith he would return to the family properly, and in that scream I heard where such faith gets you. Now she is more composed, though she has a glassy quality to her; she imbibed a large quantity of the new calming batches of magicked whale blood and has retreated to her quarters. Whatever the sorcerers have done to it, there is no doubt it has quite an effect.

Rufous reacted to his sibling's passing exactly as I expected: great, demonstrative anger, promises to scour the city until he found the truth. Plans to raise an army against the Grays far ahead of schedule. I quashed that idea pretty quickly. I know where his performative anger comes from. It certainly doesn't come from grief for his brother; his comments dismissive of him have been even stronger than mine in the past, and I suspect the truth behind all his fury is simple: he gets to cause a little mayhem in the protective cloak of this minor emergency and round up some Worns.

Now I sit in my study, where things are quieter and clearer, and I catch up on the affairs of the city. My son may be dead, but my duties continue. In front of me sits my desk that has served four generations of Azzuris: darkened quacian wood from the Wolfland forests of the east, with panels on the side that, when pressed on, reveal a cutaway shelf for blood flutes and vials. On the desk lie a pile of the latest reports, covered with the scrawled, often illegible handwriting of the various Midways responsible for the recordkeeping of the latest bloodstores and the even more indiscernible scrawls of my watch commanders. I am still coming to terms with the fact it is all written in blood. Only cowblood, so it is hardly distracting, but still. Once the First Light sorcerers worked out how to reduce the clotting effect of blood, it was pointed out by a particularly ingenious summaster at the Crownbank that using some of the vast and almost worthless excess of cowblood instead of ink would save a tidy little sum for the city every year.

I am pulled from my thoughts by a knock at the door. Redgrave walks in, slightly hunched over, as if the efforts of the last couple of hours are already weighing on his back.

"I have sent a message to both the Archmage and Ashen Ansbach via the Neuras, First Lord," he begins. "I thought it best it get to the sorcerers and wolves instantly, given events. I hope I wasn't being, ah, presumptuous."

"Not at all, Redgrave," I reply. "No point having Neuras mages on our books if we don't make them actually use their shockingly expensive mind powers every once in a while, is it? Anyway, I promised Ashen and Vespassion that the next time a vampire falls by Gray we would let them know, in case it was the start of some coordinated attack on us all. There's no evidence in these hourly reports from my commanders that this is what it is. But the hours are young." I clear my throat. "Let's get to it, then. What do we know, Redgrave?"

My first man doesn't reply straightaway, but strokes his moustache, anxiously pulling on the corners. Only Midways wear moustaches. But no one wears one quite like Redgrave. It is waxed and curled upward, and one end is thicker than the other. An old style, long gone. He is one of the oldest vampires left in the city; at least six centuries—he pre-dates the founding of First Light and the era of cities, surely. I have never had the bad manners to ask him how old exactly.

"No one saw your son leave the city walls, First Lord," he replies.

"There are five hundred Wall Guard," I note. "Oh, don't be so surprised, Redgrave," I add, having observed his ever-so-slight raise of the eyebrow. "I do actually read these bloody reports . . . My point is, I find it difficult to believe that no one saw him."

"We can always ask . . . under duress, First Lord."

"No," I say, raising my own eyebrow with a lot less subtlety. "I don't think torturing our own guards would help matters, much as my eldest son would like it."

A tired voice in the back of my head points out he's not my eldest son anymore. He's my only. I stand and walk over to the window. The view onto the western gardens of the palace is peaceful compared to the commotion at the front. A fountain spews carelessly, and under its waters I spy a mosaic of First Gods, the city's biggest prayhall. Perhaps I should be there now, praying and bleeding to the Bloodhalls for the safe care of my son. He won't like them when he gets there. That's if he's even allowed into them.

"To leave by one of the main gates he would have had to have the gates opened for him," continues Redgrave behind me, "and no one would have done that without the highest orders, even for one of your own blood."

"The secret exits?"

"All covered by the Wall Guard, now, First Lord."

"Then how, my old friend, did my son end up outside the walls?"

"I . . . I have a theory."

"I thought you might." Redgrave's mind works quicker than a wolfblood shot to the eyeball, as my valet is fond of saying.

"There is a vial of wolfblood missing from the emergency store, First Lord. That's enough to give him wings, though only for a very short period. But long enough for a quick flight over the mountainside where the city meets the Fang Tips, where someone could be lost in the mountain shadow and not seen by the Wall Guard if they flew high enough. We don't watch the sky, after all."

"Yes." I nod. "The Grays don't fly. Yet, anyway." I turn from my view of the fountain to face my first man, resisting the urge to grab a bloodflute from the recesses of my desk and down it in one. "So what you are saying, Redgrave, is that my son, one of the few who had the access and knowledge to steal wolfblood, did so in order to fly past the city walls undetected and to his death."

"I believe that this is the most likely option at present, First Lord, yes."

"That is the how, then. But what of the why?"

Redgrave pauses, and I can see on his face the flicker of disgust at not having the information to hand.

"We will need more time for that, I am afraid to say. There are no tracks to or from the spot where he was found, which would suggest a Gray was responsible, not that we need more evidence for that."

"Quite. The five bullets lodged deep within him were enough proof, I fancy."

"But as to why he was there in the first place, and whether the Gray attack was random or planned, I am afraid you will have to wait a little longer for such answers. We are still gathering his . . . associates . . ."

Freaks, he means.

"—and we hope they may provide us with answers."

I nod and rub my forehead, where a vein is pulsing. I feel its pounding rhythm; I listen to its tune.

"The only vampires to have been killed by Grays, at least since Grayfall itself," I say, "are those who chose to leave the city or were exiled from it, those who tried to enter it but did not quite make it, and scouts who ventured too far past the city gates. But no scout party has been attacked as close as my son was. Nowhere near that close."

Redgrave does not say anything. He has learned when to listen and when to speak. Lords can spend centuries finding a first man who has that wisdom in him.

"I have lived a long time," I continue. "Not as long as you, old friend, but long enough. After the fourth century, you begin to learn patience. But, Redgrave," I add, hoping that my face is composed, because I will not show him that side of me, old friend or not, "I have never felt impatience like this."

My first man nods. "I understand, First Lord." He clears his throat. "There is something else, actually."

"Is there?" Redgrave looks anxious, an expression most would not spot, as it involves a slight twitch of the moustache. But it's there.

"Your son was, ah, associating with a clerk in the Blood Bank."

I think on this. "I assume by *associating,* we are not talking about platonic friendship."

"Not as such, First Lord."

"Or innocently friendly conversations."

"Not particularly, no."

"Is this relevant? When I tasked you with keeping abreast of my son's . . . activities, I told you I did not want to be concerned with the who or the why unless it became a matter of danger to him or embarrassment to us."

"Which is why I have not mentioned it until now, First Lord. But it accords with the other thing you have tasked me with."

"Explain," I say, feeling the beginnings of dread creep across my countenance.

"The bank vault. The one Saxe is in charge of. That you tasked me with discovering the contents of. The bank clerk your son was . . . associating with is one of the clerks responsible for its administration."

"Are you suggesting this thing that has befallen my son—blooddamn these euphemisms—my son's *murder,* is connected with Saxe's plans?"

"It may be a coincidence, First Lord."

"In the two centuries you have served me, has anything ever been a coincidence?"

"Not that I can recall, First Lord."

"No. We do not live in that kind of world, worse luck." I pour myself a bloodflute from the desk after all, only briefly savoring it before it goes down my throat.

"Very well, Redgrave, here is what we will do. Outwardly I will turn all the handles of the city and the guard to discover the truth of my son. Let Saxe do his work, too. But you and I, we will engage in our own investigation. We will presume that our suspicions of Saxe and my son's death are linked, and we will pull the threads wherever they go. At this point, I cannot trust any of my First Council enough to confide in them. It will be me and you."

"Just like the old days, First Lord."

"Yes. Just like them." I have fewer fond memories of the old days than Redgrave, but I wisely let this pass. "If I must make visits through the city, we will do so under the pretense of honoring my son and where he lived. Maybe this will become obvious, but I am beginning to be past caring."

"That is fine, First Lord. I am capable of doing the caring for both of us."

I glare at him. "Now we have a secret mission, I see you have found some wit about you, Redgrave."

He lets that one go, wisely.

"Can I trust you to make the arrangements? We will commence at once."

"Of course, First Lord. Is there anything else?"

"There is. Tell the commander of the Scout Guard to expect me. I wish to see the spot where my son was attacked."

Redgrave is caught off guard, for the first time this meeting, if not this month. "I'm sorry, First Lord?"

I raise my eyebrow. "I think my statement was fairly clear. I wish to see where my boy was shot."

Redgrave reaches one hand to his moustache and pats it down a little. For him this is a sign of stress, equivalent to an attack of the faints for anyone else. "But, First Lord—"

"Yes, yes. I haven't been outside the city walls since Grayfall. We could be attacked. But I will be surrounded by the most well-trained men First Light has to offer short of the First Guard themselves. More to the point, these reports say my son was found on the cliff overlooking the valley; the last point before Gray territory officially begins. A mere half mile from the wall, a place where scout parties regularly go to observe the valley floor beneath. Not a dangerous spot."

"It was a dangerous spot for your son, First Lord," Redgrave replies, wisely avoiding eye contact as he does so.

"This is not a negotiation, Redgrave, unless recent events have abrogated my title as well as my family. I will not be denied my investigation, outward at least, into the circumstances of a direct attack on an Azzuri. I must be seen to lead."

"It may be seen as reckless, First Lord."

"Good. My recklessness will distract those watching from our bid to uncover answers. Now are we done, or must I down another bloodflute to get me through this conversation?"

Redgrave nods and leaves, taking all our past secrets and the ones to come with him.

Sam

The first thing I notice about the rooms of the late Azzuri the Younger is that they're enormous. I'm used to cleaning the rooms in the East Wing that belong to the extended family and those Lords in the inner circle who frequent the palace; I know their stains and habits and stenches by heart. But in my ten years as a maid here, I've never so much as set foot in the West Wing rooms of the First Family.

The dining quarters are almost as big as those for all the palace maids put together, and there's enough bedding on his four-poster monstrosity to cover half their mattresses. If you used the fabric from the huge sun-blinds that cover his windows, I reckon you could dress them, too.

Aside from the size, I notice something else. There's no sign of life here. That is, there's no sign of the *living*. No portraits are hung, no blood bars stocked. No extravagant rugs with family crests stitched into them are draped before the fireplace. It's almost like the First Lord's dead son didn't think of this as home. If the rumors are true, he didn't stay here long enough for it to be considered as such. It's neat, ordered, loveless. I feel a little bit sad in here.

I'm beginning to think he did, too.

I scrub and I clean, which given the near-abandoned state of the rooms essentially means wiping dust off everything and giving it a shine. Much easier than what I'm usually faced with in a Lord's room: the broken glass of blood vials, bloodstains from spilled carafes, and various types of fluid I make blooddamn sure to never think about too closely.

It's when I'm almost done that I see it; next to the dresser, on a non-descript crestwood table, is a small chest. But it's not a normal chest. Not at all. It's a chest made of castaray wood, from the trees that grow across the Southern Sea on the other continent, the Ashlands—the one that no Everland immortal has set foot on for a century and a half. I walk over to it and stroke it; the wood is a brown so dark it's almost black and smooth to the touch. Castaray wood is a strange thing. It doesn't weather, and it doesn't scratch.

I feel a thrill of excitement. I've spent many a happy hour reading about the city this chest is from, even more so than Lightfall. Last Light, the miraculous vampire city on the northern shore of the Ashlands, that held out for centuries against the dangers in that unexplored southern continent until its fall last century. Everything from there is strange, in one way or another. And most things from there have secrets.

I open the chest. There's nothing in it. I don't care. A memory of a vellum-backed, emerald-encrusted tome on Last Light fills my head. Most volumes on the lost city are filled with conjecture and rumor, as the few survivors who made it back aren't in a hurry to reveal its secrets. But some of the items found their way to our continent along with a few of its citizens, and these chests were one. I'm sure I've seen a picture of them and read how their emptiness is meant to deceive.

Without thinking, half-wrapped in this memory, I fumble around the underside of the chest, not entirely sure what I'm looking for. A secret latch, perhaps? A clockwork mechanism?

It's then I hear footsteps coming down the corridor to the chambers. I'm back on cowblood for the moment, so I can't get much of a sense of who or what class it is, but it's a fair gamble they'll be checking on me and my cleaning. I only have a few moments. My scrabbling gets more desperate, and I consider simply throwing it to the floor in the hope the secret compartment is revealed. But being killed for a sudden surge of curiosity would be a pretty stupid way to go out, even in this city.

I'm about to give up when my finger catches on a tiny sharp piece of metal protruding from the base, drawing blood from my finger. I gasp, and then I gasp for a very different reason when I see the blood absorbed into the wood, followed by the soft clicking sound of a mechanism inside. Blood magick. Just like the forbidden library.

The footsteps are almost at the door now, and in moments I will be caught red-handed in the most real sense, but I'm trapped at the mercy of that soft whirring and what the chest will reveal to me.

Then as the double doors to the chamber are pushed wide open, the floor of the chest shoots across, revealing a hidden compartment with a thin piece of parchment in it. With the speed of someone who's not sure if their hourglass has run out, I thrust out a hand to grab it, then pull it out, closing the chest lid as I go and stuffing the parchment down one of the several layers of my petticoat.

No sooner have I done so than the visitor to the chambers is standing before me. My mind, geared to survival, switches on instinct and I curtsy before them.

"Lord Azzuri," I say, careful not to look at him directly until my curtsy is over.

The eldest and now only son of First Lord Azzuri, Rufous, appraises me. His hair is long and golden and flows freely around his shoulders. It frames a soft, youthful face, full of all the contours and good skin you'd expect from (almost) the best blood all your life. His eyes are round and his face is oval, giving him a slightly baby-faced look. I know what's beneath that seemingly angelic face, though. Rufous is not his late brother. The Young Azzuri was kind to Worns. Rufous is whatever lies on the far side of *kind,* deep in the darkest shadow.

"A maid," he says, having taken his look of me. His voice is high and reedy. Each syllables drips with his breeding. "I did not expect his room would need cleaning. He was never bloody in it. Annoying." He glares at me then, and I take in his attire. He's wearing a red silk shirt beneath a slim sleeveless waistcoat, also silk, which is blue with gold trimming, along which small red rubies wink at me. No jacket. Very underdressed for a lord. For a second, I panic that his annoyance at me seeing him so will turn into something very bad for me. But then he turns away from me and examines the room. And smiles.

"While I'm here, I may as well inspect your work." He strides across the room, running a finger along the surface of any furniture he encounters. I thank the Blood Gods and any other kind watching that my cleaning was done before he entered. After a little of this, he looks at his finger, disappointed. I'm not sure what he would've done if he'd found it dirty, but the dungeons beneath the palace lie testament to the smallness of the crimes paid to receive his attention firsthand.

"Hmm. Well, I suppose cleaning is all you do," he says, manhandling my victory into nothing. "Ah well, piss off now, so I can breathe in my brother's room one last time." He stays turned away from me.

"Yes, Lord Azzuri," I reply, before moving my legs as fast as they've ever been driven to get the twin hells out of there so I can breathe again. I'm at the entrance when his high-pitched noble drawl comes at me again.

"Hold on, girl."

I turn, wondering what oversight has kept me from my freedom. He stares at me, one hand rubbing his clean-shaven round chin. "I recognize you."

I leave that unanswered, hoping for a follow-up sooner or later.

"How long have you been here?"

"Ten years, m'lord." He does not ask for my name. It would not help, of course; the idea of him knowing our names is beyond madness.

"Ten years . . ." He thinks for a second. His whole face scrunches up as he does so. It would almost be comical if the consequences of his thoughts weren't so potentially shit for my immediate future.

"Aha! I have it. You're the one who braved the sun. The crazy bitch who tried to save her sister in the palace joining ritual. I'll never forget that. Those rituals are rather dull, but not that day."

"Yes, m'lord." I keep my hand behind my back so he can't see my fists clasp and unclasp.

"Still, you got to join the palace in her place. A good deal for you. I'll bet you bless the rotten piece of roof that sealed her doom."

I look down. To show anger now would be exactly what the bastard wants. His words are waves, and I let them wash over me, soothing my fire.

"What was it like, seeing your sister turn to ash in front of you?" A small smile creeps across his face, but he stares intently, and I realize that he actually wants to know as well as to torment me.

"It was the second-worst moment of my life, my lord."

His thin smile breaks into a grin. "Oh really, maid. Well. And what was the first?"

"Finding my mother dead by her own hand soon after my father was sunburst."

"And why was your father sunburst?" Rufous asks. "What was his crime?"

"He refused to let a Lord who had taken a shine to my mother come into our home and take her away," I say, finding my way through this surreal conversation. "My mother couldn't handle the guilt and the grief, so she let the sun take her, right outside our house."

Rufous laughs, high and giggling. "A grim tale, indeed. Poor luck, to find your family whittled away like that, one by one. But you are alive and in our care. Do you not feel gratitude?"

"Of course, my lord. Every day. Mostly as I am emptying pisspots."

For a moment I realize I've gone too far. Time slows down; I feel goose bumps.

"Ha!" He laughs suddenly, bending over to cackle, and slaps his leg. "Hmm. I wish all Worns were as entertaining as you. You give good wit, girl. Perhaps you should be in my maid circle." He stares at me for a while longer while horror slowly seeps into my chest. Then I see the moment his face loses interest and privileged boredom returns. "Off you go now. We've had our fun. Go do more . . . whatever it is you do."

Then he turns away, done with me, and I escape from those chambers like the sun is rising on my back.

3

The Lies That I Tell Them

Lord Skye: Can you explain, Spymaster, why we are so ignorant of the Grays when it has been a century now since their appearance? Why do they not settle in the Centerlands, though they prevent us from passage through it? Why do they not attempt to invade, either here or the Desertlands or the Wolflands? I could go on . . .

Lord Saxe: I am surprised you do not.

Lord Skye: I beg your pardon?

Lord Saxe: We know the most important thing, Lord. That we cannot ever be complacent against them.

Minutes from the 485th Meeting of
the First Council on Knowledge

First Lord Azzuri

The great stone doors of First Light swing open, and the world beyond the city lies before me, such as it is. I am reminded of the story of Sangre Cabalti, the founder of First Light, first of the Red–Blue nobility, who rode into this very valley to wipe out the wolves who had laid claim to it, too. Except I have never led a battalion of soldiers and have seen little action in war, unless you include the great exodus from Lightfall, fleeing the Grays and their weapons of death, which included a great deal of action but very little war.

The air out here is cooler than in the city, thanks to the wind always whipping its way between the mountain peaks First Light nestles between. The ridge my city sits on, overlooking the vast valley below it like an eagle squatting on its treetop nest, seems to draw in the currents. I am on magicked stag, however—two flutes full—so I hardly feel it; the same as the rest of the Scout Guard who, unique to the city's militia, are always given such strong blood on patrol. There are some who say all scouts should be on wolfblood given the dangers they potentially face. But it is not necessary, as the two-winged guard high in the night sky above us, burning through our precious stores of the stuff, should warn us of Grays far before they would ever reach us.

Ahead of me, even on stag, all I really see is the great line of torches stretching out into the valley, relit at the start of every watch, giving light enough for those on the wall not on the best blood. The flames burn with a mixture of sulfur and lime and rosewood, allowing them to last the course of the night. I take one last look behind me as the great doors swing shut and see two members of my personal guard there. I forbade them to come with me out of respect for the Scout Guard. Out here they are the ones in charge, and I need no protection if they do their duty.

"Upon your call, First Lord," says Commander Tenfold, the Midway leader of the Scout Guard, and for the first time in a long time, not the supreme authority beyond the wall. He is tall, much taller than me, and his shock of red hair—quite a sight for a vampire—almost seems to glow in the night. The four blood droplets stitched into his black tabard give away his status as commander. As a Midway he does not age, yet there is something about his stern, granite-hewn face that bestows a reassuring sense of experience upon the onlooker. Or perhaps I am being conde-scending to those beneath me. It is hard to tell sometimes.

"Thank you, Commander," I reply. "Let us proceed. I defer to you for instructions from here on in."

He nods and calls out to his men, a fifteen-strong company garbed in black-and-green tabards. None of the red of the Blood Guard for them. Over their tabards is armor, unheard of for vampires prior to Grayfall but necessary for anyone outside the city now. It won't stop a direct hit of a Gray bullet; the armor you would have to wear for that would restrict all movement, even on the best blood—at least that is what my Lord of War claims, and I trust he has tested this—but at the very least it gives them a chance should they be attacked.

The men themselves all wear grim expressions, like they have seen it all and allowed it to wash over them. You must have to have a strange bearing on life to be able to constantly venture out to see the world as it was and still is but cannot be again, in most ways, at least for now.

"Onward, march. Ring around the First Lord. Unrelenting to First Point," Tenfold barks out, and we begin, me within a circle of my bodyguards—scouts of daring I have reduced to merely a protective guard. But if you ever feel guilty about such things, then your time as First Lord is surely over.

We march halfway to our destination with no event. I can see through my stag-borne, almost pure night eyes our goal approaching a quarter mile ahead, the tree-protected cliff edge looking out over the valley. That is where my son was killed, at a point where Grays are never normally found. Below, tantalizingly out of sight for now, is a vast swath of woods and grasslands and small peaks. The valley is technically part of the Centerlands, and thus where Grays roam, but really it signals the beginning of the northern mountains true.

I breathe it in. I will soon have my first sight of this valley floor for a hundred years. I feel something lift from me; a lightness descends in turn. A feeling of being hemmed in, gone; an appreciation for the vastness of the world and a feeling that it could be mine again. For a second, I feel like running. Screaming.

"Halt!" cries Tenfold then, before we can sight the valley. I feel a mild panic before I realize he is waiting for the signal of the winged guards above. They fly so far I cannot see them, especially thanks to the clouds scuttling across the moon. But then I see them sweep down to give the signal of the all clear: a single beat of their wings, the black leather curvature outlined against the night.

We continue on, and finally we are almost at the copse of trees on the cliff. I prepare myself for the sight of my son's fall and the sight of the valley below it.

Thunk.

The first bullet hits a guard to my left. I know it is a bullet because through the slight gap in my phalanx I see it ricochet off his breastplate. A moment later, I hear another sound of metal on metal to my right, and then the call goes out.

"*Grays!*"

"Retreat! Protect the First Lord. *Do not break phalanx.*" The voice of Tenfold is steel, piercing the night, and if there is any indication of fear, he does not show it.

Through the small gaps in my guard, I cannot see much, just the trees up ahead and the night beyond and around. No shapes in the dark. I listen out, my hearing acute thanks to the magicked stag in me, and I hear the whine of bullets through the air.

"Incoming!" shouts a guard to my front, and then I hear a whole barrage of bullets hit. The Grays must still be too far away, as none pierce armor, and by some miracle, none pierce the unprotected limbs, either.

The guards pick up the pace back to the city, as do I, all trapped in the same rhythm, the quick march of retreat. It tastes bitter in my throat, but we came here to scout, not to fight.

It is then I see a guard on my left raise his arm and point. "Gray!" he shouts. The phalanx tightens around me and I cannot see it myself; there are no longer any gaps to see through.

I hear the bullet, closer this time, and I hear the soft damp noise of flesh being hit. A guard to my right roars out in pain and collapses to the floor.

"Close phalanx!" shouts the commander, and as it does, I briefly glimpse the fallen guard on the ground, the bullet lodged in his unprotected forearm, the purple veins of his doom already spreading out. His face is a rictus of pain so great he can only silently scream. Then his place is taken and I see him no more.

There is only a third of a mile to go now and I can see how close the city walls are; if I squint, I can even see the small movement of archers preparing to shoot any Grays that come close. I wonder where the winged scoutguards are, and then I see them both, shooting down through the sky, aiming at a place about forty feet beyond my ring of flesh and steel. There is a loud thump of wolfblooded vampire. I wait for them to rise up again, having taken care of a Gray or two. But then I hear an array of bullets, all at once, and a surprised cry cut short, and then I hear them no more. So much for wings.

"Pick up the pace!" screams Tenfold.

We retreat at speed now, my phalanx and me, matching me step for step, even as their doom flies past them. I hear the telltale impact of bullet on flesh again, and a guard to my right collapses. This time the bullet is in his eye. In the brief moment before he is left to die on the ground, I see his eye socket is smoldering, burning, the disgorged fluid of his eye leaking across the crater of the impact. Then a guard to my left falls, legs caved in beneath him by the force of two bullets, one in each shin. As he buckles and recedes into the distance I see the purple veins of his end shoot up his leg like some fast-moving ivy.

More bullets bounce off breastplates. More go into limbs. My phalanx is reduced and there are now gaps in its protection. I feel outrage. How dare the Grays attack this close. How dare they make me run. A bullet grazes the air beside me and lodges into the guard in front, into the back of his neck just above his armor. The impact half explodes the flesh around it, leaving the rest to quickly turn a shade of dark violet as he collapses. More debris for the journey, a living corpse who will turn to ash before a quarter of a glass has gone by.

There are more gaps than men now, and I hear the final calls through the air of those bullets seeking me out. I brace myself for the pain, for the force of it.

But I get an open door instead, and the cries of two hundred men on the vast wall above me and the screams of "Shut the gates!"

I stop finally, on the right side of the wall. I am not exerted, not on this blood, but my breath comes sharp and quick. I turn to see the remains of my guard. Twenty are now twelve. A rout. The faces of the men, trained faces, are fixed, their mouths only moving slightly. The violent force of the stag blood pumping through their bodies stops them from betraying the drama that has unfolded.

Redgrave arrives, the beginnings of a panicked look on him. "First Lord, I—"

I wave him off. "I am fine, Redgrave. I had worse than that every day during the Twin War." He goes to speak. "If you are about to say anything that suggests that you were right to counsel me against this, I will forget the centuries we have known each other very quickly." He decides against this.

There is a period of uncertainty as the guards atop the wall keep watch. Some of the torches along the route have gone out; they will stay unlit for a while. I remain within the barracks cityside of the wall as guardsmen race around me and my personal guard, giving us a wide berth. A captain offers me a flute of magicked bear and bades me sit in the officers' quarters. I reject the wine and remain standing in the main barracks area, where I can observe the commotion. Finally we get the call that there is no sight of Grays anymore. They are not breaking the habit of a century to actually attack the wall. Instead, they have slipped into the night as suddenly as they arrived.

Commander Tenfold approaches. His face looks paler than it did a half glass ago, but he keeps his composure and his voice retains the same tone.

"Are you hurt, First Lord?" he asks.

I check myself cursorily. But I am free of bullet wounds.

"No, I am fine."

Tenfold nods, his expression the same but his tone quieter. "I lost eight men, First Lord. The first since Grayfall."

I nod. "They did their duty. The Day Guard will retrieve what remains of their ashes. They will be honored. Their families will be lauded. They will be legends in the Bloodhalls when they arrive there, Commander."

"That is what I will tell their families, yes," says Tenfold slowly.

"Commander, I do not like the tone of your—" begins Redgrave, but I wave him off.

"Commander Tenfold, do you know what it is I do, every day?"

Tenfold waits.

"I keep everything from chaos. You remember chaos, yes? You were there at Grayfall, marshaling the exile. Instrumental in our survival, as Gray bullets flew past us and condemned all those they hit—Worn, Midway, and Lord—to the Bloodhalls sooner than they deserved. You also served in the Twin War. With distinction. Only a captain, but I remember you. So you know chaos. And you know that it lies right beyond these walls, and perhaps inside, too, if we do not keep the city together. So I will not explain myself for the deaths of those who willingly undertook to save this city. I will do what I must when I must to ensure this city endures. Do we understand each other, Commander?"

"Yes, First Lord," he says, but his eyes don't give me thanks; they do not give me outright recrimination, either, but I have seen that look before in the faces of those forced to give their men up to their fates.

For a second I want to explain to him. Explain why I had to go. Why I had to be at the place where it ended for my boy. Explain my anger I feel toward my son for his actions; explain that there is something else beneath it, something else driving me forward, I know not what. For a moment I want to ask him if he is a father, too. Ask him if he has ever known the frustration of it, and then later the pain, blinding you if you let it.

But I am not here to explain myself to those beneath me, nor have I ever been.

The lies are my duty, and I give him the full force of them.

Sam

After I take my midblood I have some time before the next rooms to be cleaned, so I rush back to my chambers, the leaf of parchment from the chest in the late Azzuri's quarters burning a hole in my petticoats. Beth is there, changing into a fresh gown after what looks from the bloodstains like a particularly difficult cleaning session.

"Sammy!" she cries as I walk in. "Sammy, have you heard the news?"

I stare at her eyes, wider even than normal now.

"No," I say, confused. For a second I wonder if she somehow knows what I've found already.

"The Grays have attacked," she continues. "It's all everyone's talking about in the palace. Suns, Sammy, what have you been doing these last few glasses?"

"Cleaning, Beth, like you," I say, sticking my tongue out. I don't add that I keep away from the other maids and valets when I'm doing so. I can cope with one good friend. I don't need others. This isn't my world. Or at least it won't be for much longer. All my news I get from my books. The rest? Beth will fill me in.

"Well, if you'd had your ears open, you'd know that the First Lord went outside the city. To see where the Younger was killed. But the Grays attacked. Killed some of the Scout Guard."

"Was the First Lord killed?" I ask, trying to parse the news. I have no desire to see the First Lord come to harm, unlike his sadistic eldest son, but given that he is the figurehead of this shit excuse for a city that currently has me enslaved, I won't cry if I hear he's ashes.

"No," replies Beth. "He wasn't. But they're saying he's furious. First Scout Guard to be killed since Grayfall. The Grays have never come that close to the city walls before."

I shrug. "Maybe they're coming for First Light, too. They want more than the Centerlands."

Beth gapes at me, openmouthed. "Sammy! Don't say that!"

"Why not? Not like it could get any worse." I sit down on my bed and stroke my calves. This work is killing for the legs. A little Midway blood, even some magicked cow, and we wouldn't feel it as much. But who cares if servants ache a little?

Beth clumps down on her bed, glaring at me. "Yes it could. We could die. A lot of innocent people would die as well as these bloody nobility."

I think on a retort, but I let it go into the air. She's right. It could be worse. I've read the accounts of Grayfall fairly widely. Historian sorcerer Atmos Regardis wrote volumes on it. When the Grays came suddenly to the cities of the Centerlands, with their bullets of death that killed wolf, vampire, and sorcerer alike, thousands of families were butchered in the space of one day. The word *massacre* doesn't cover it. "You're right, Beth, sorry. You know I get a little grim sometimes. I had an encounter with Rufous earlier. Just me and him. Probably hasn't helped."

"Wait what? That skull-addled devil? Are you okay, Sam?"

"Yes, don't worry. He just came to the young Azzuri's room when I was cleaning it. He said he remembered me from when I came to the palace. My sister. He enjoyed talking about it."

Beth reaches her hand out to mine, clasps it. "Whatever he said, remember you're better." She shivers involuntarily. "By the Halls, he's a creep."

"But that's not all, Beth." I pull the piece of paper out and show it to her. She stares at it as I explain how I found it. "Go on, then," I say after I've finished. "Tell me what's written there." She looks at me, confused. "You mean you haven't looked?"

"No, Beth. I've been cleaning rooms. After Rufous walks in on you, you tend to get a little nervous."

"Okay, well, it's just . . ." Her face crumples in confusion. "A list of names, I think?"

I take it back off her. Beth barely had any scholaring when she was young and can't read well. My patience goes only so far. I inspect it. "The first line just says Commander Tenfold. The second says Bank Clerk Keepsake."

Beth stares at me, wide-eyed. "We know the first name, Sammy."

"*Everyone* knows him."

There is a final line at the bottom of the page. I read it out. "*I think I know who the Grays are. Tonight I find out for sure.*"

"Sammy, this is . . ."

"It's a clue to his death, Beth, is what it is. Look at the ink in the last line."

"You're sounding like a bloodguard now. An inquirer, even."

"Well, I've read enough of their books. But the ink, Beth. It's less faded than the others. Newer. Really new. I reckon it was written on his last night alive. Which means that he's talking about why he went out past the city walls. Which means that when he died, he was probably trying to test this theory. Of who the Grays were. And he got killed for it."

Even as I say the words, I realize that I've jumped a lot of lines of reasoning. I'm trying to spin this into something. But I've been waiting ten years for any kind of thread, so I'm not going to beat myself up for the weaving I'm doing now.

"Sam," says Beth quietly. "If anyone knew you had this they'd . . . take you. You'd be tied to a stake in front of the morning sun before you can say *sunburst*. And me, too, just for reading it."

"But they don't, do they?" I reply. "They don't know."

"Sammy . . ."

"I'm going to find out more," I say, grabbing both of Beth's hands. "I've got this, and I've got the forbidden library section now, too. There's no stopping me. I'll flee, and they won't find me, and whatever I find, it'll help me start a new life, whether through knowledge or blackmail I don't care." Beth starts to protest, but I'm already shushing her. "It's okay. It's okay. I won't leave you. I'll take you with me. We'll escape this life and never look back."

"You're raving, Sam," says Beth, more serious than I've seen her in a good while. "They'll kill you."

"Then I'll die. And I'll go to drink in the Bloodhalls. Or serve the drink, knowing this lot."

Beth turns away from me then, and I see that this is too much, even for her. But I can't stop myself. It's always been my problem. I can think of worse to have. "Aren't you tired, Beth?" I ask. "Tired of this life? Aren't you tired of being afraid? Treated like we're nothing? We're better than them who we serve, and I know it burns you like it burns me."

Beth stays quiet. I wonder if I've broken her. It must be tough living with me and my need for more. Maybe after a while, the energy to put up with me simply goes, like a torch starved of fuel.

Beth speaks up eventually, voice low. "Do you remember when we met, Sam?"

I do. I remember talking about when we met as well. The same conversations tend to come up when you've known each other for ten years. I don't know how some vampires manage centuries.

"I do. Like yesterday," I reply.

"Do you remember what you said to me? And what I said back?"

I smile at the memory, despite myself. "I do. I told you I couldn't bear to live anymore, not with my sister gone. All alone in the world. I told you my fire had gone out. And you grabbed me and you said that you'd only just met me, but you could tell I had more in me, and it would never go out."

"Yes, I did. Might be the most poetic thing I ever said." Beth gives a quiet chuckle. "I can't stop you, Sam. And maybe I shouldn't." She turns back to me. I thought maybe she'd been crying a little. But her eyes are dry. Maybe she's tougher than I ever seek to give her credit for.

"The Leeches," she says suddenly. "Get them to help you."

"What?"

"You heard me, Sammy. That's what they do, isn't it? They find out things."

"They're just a rumor, Beth. Something to give us hope, like the rebels."

Beth laughs properly then, and that's how I know she's back. Fuel burning, never dimmed.

"All that book learning, but you don't know the streets, do you? That's why you need old Beth."

"I'm not sure I need her if she's going to refer to herself in the third person."

Beth ignores this. "There was a Lord not so long ago, I forget his name, who would beat his maids badly if they left any bloodstains, and well, with his parties there were always stains. One of them was a friend of Misabel, who works down the stables. This maid got in touch with the Leeches and told them about how this Lord was paying a visit to another Lord, a married one, late at night to do the kind of things their wives would scarce believe, let alone accept . . . Anyway the Leeches put their moves on him and suddenly he wasn't so quick to put his hands to his servants."

"How do you know all this?" I ask Beth.

She smiles. "You read, I listen. I listen to what the maids are saying. Everyone knows someone who's been helped by them. No one knows who runs them, though. The Queen Leech of the rumors—whoever she is, she keeps herself well hidden."

"But I still don't know how to contact them," I say, choosing for now to go along with Beth. She has an advantage over me here. Gossip, the events of recent years . . . These aren't in the library books. For once I might have to swallow my pride and accept that I know less than she does. It's a bitter taste.

"Ask around, Sammy. One of the maids in the palace will know how to find them, surely. I'd wager the Leeches have someone in the palace, after all." Beth smiles triumphantly. She thinks I'm impressed. I am.

"There's nothing for it, then," I reply, the rest of the night's cleaning suddenly seeming much more appealing than a moment ago. "I'm going Leech hunting."

4

A Kind of Magick

Get sorcerers of the four active magick types together and ply them with drink and see the battle rage over their superiority: the Kinet claims prowess, as who can argue against the sight of a great object flying toward you? Ah, says the Neuras, but I need fear no physical attack if I can read your mind. Yes, notes the Cloak, but there is no situation a good illusion cannot get you out of. The Atmos speaks not; he simply sends a thunderbolt flying in the middle of the company, which is a useful argument settler. At least they can all agree on one thing: Thank Light they're not a Quantas.

Cloak Kilfastion, *The Five Magick Types*

Sage Bailey

I stare at my would-be assassin, noticing in particular the barrel of fire powder that hovers in the air beside him.

It is a common barrel in most respects: made of southern whiteoak, painted dull red as a not-so-subtle nod to the explosive contents within, and reinforced with thick metal bands.

"A hundred pounds of fire powder?" I ask, rubbing the sleep from my eyes.

"Thereabouts," replies the assassin.

"I see," I say. "Yes, from this range I suppose that would kill me. Not enough to destroy the temple, though I'm lacking certain of the parameters I need to make this calculation completely accurate, I fear."

The assassin shrugs and idly brushes some sand off his robes, which are puce-red with light orange stripes running down the front and sleeves—standard Kinet colors. "They don't care if some of your temple remains. They consider it enough to kill you."

"Dare I ask *why* they want to kill me?"

"You are the leader of the Cult of Humanis. They want to get rid of the Cult of Humanis. If you go, the cult goes with it." The assassin smiles. "By the way, your temple defenses are poor. I've rarely had it so easy."

"We have guards."

"Barely a handful. I threw them against the wall before they could do anything. Although I'm curious to know what sorcerers who can't do magick would be able to do anyway."

"We have our ways." I sigh. "Did you kill any of them?"

"You can't kill a sorcerer just by throwing him against a wall."

"Depends on how you throw him. For a Kinet, you're not really aware of your powers, are you?"

"I'm an assassin."

"Yes," I reply. "So you keep saying. But here I am alive, and here we are, talking."

The assassin grins. "It's been a long ride. You live so shading close to the northern border we may as well be in the Centerlands. I got bored. Nothing wrong with a bit of conversation."

I sigh and stare up at the sandstone walls of the temple, a hundred feet high, supported by thick gray columns in the Distoric style, topped with elaborate patterns. There are small gaps in the walls made in battles past, through which I can see the stars in the clear night sky.

"I know who sent you," I begin. "And I know why. And I can disarm you with *one word*."

"Disarm me with one word?" he says once his belly laughs have subsided. "Oh, I doubt that. What's your cult motto again? Something about dreaming? You're not exactly known for your combat skills."

"There are worlds beyond mine and things I have only dreamt to touch," I reply, stepping back a little, the assassin stepping forward in kind. "Not that you could comprehend its meaning. And I stand by what I say."

"Go on then, funny little *Quantas*. Show me how clever you are."

I don't bridle at the derogatory use of my sorcerer class. I am used to his kind, after all. He is the classic overmagicked bully I have dealt with all my life. To him a sorcerer who cannot perform magick cannot be a threat. His lesson will be learned hard.

"First, let's start with who sent you. You are not, I'm afraid, a high-level assassin. I might not be having this conversation if you were. If a Neuras, Cloak, or Atmos had been sent, then I would have been dead already, I imagine. But Kinets tend to be on the brutish, obvious side."

"I'm thinking I might just end this conversation and introduce you to the contents of this barrel, you little Quantas prick."

"No, you won't. Curiosity has got the better of you. It's written on your face. Anyway, the fact that you're not a master assassin leads me to the conclusion that it is one of the lesser sects who hired you. So the question is, who would find us so offensive that they would hire a second-rate assassin?"

"One more insult and I'll—"

"Carry on listening to me? Yes, I thought so. Do stop interrupting, now. Anyway, it has to be a Kinet. Smaller sects stick close to their own kind. Narrow ambition breeds narrow-mindedness. They wouldn't trust a non-Kinet. So that leaves us with twenty sects it could be. But to narrow down the *who* further, we have to specify the *why*."

The assassin just stares at me. He is pretending not to be interested, but his eyes and the twitching of his mouth tell me different. I step back again, the same distance as before, as if I'm slowly retreating, and once again the assassin steps forward a little to meet me.

"You know, it's funny," I continue, "no one ever challenges us out of fear. And why would they? We are a cult entirely composed of, as you so pithily put it earlier, funny little Quantas sorcerers. We're the ones who believe in the mortals. We're the ones who believe the children's stories and are mocked for doing so."

"You forgot you all give yourself Worn vampire names. We make fun of you for that, too. Sage Bailey sounds like a damn herbjuice. Although, to be fair, I understand why you don't want to be reminded of your limp-cock mage class."

"So when they send their assassins," I continue, ignoring his goading, "and they do come, every few years, like clockwork . . . they come for other reasons. Neuras Sunkallion, he was sent to rob our rumored coin stores. He read my mind almost to the moment of my death. Almost. Atmos Rasbastion? You may have heard of him. The Cloud Maker. His lightning bolts seemed threatening, though his knowledge of the dangers of metal and conduction were not so. His corpse is still smoking. Cloak Krespatarion, sent by one of the western Cloak sects who, frankly, just like killing other sects, was a little better. His illusions were very convincing. Not many people know, however, that there is always a tell in an illusion. He certainly didn't."

For the first time, as I give him the illustrious list of his failed forebears, I sense a little hesitancy, a little softening of his all-weather grin.

"So, my little Kinet friend," I continue, "who sent you?"

I think for a moment, but more for the sake of a dramatic pause than anything else. I've known the answer since he first confronted me.

"It is the Linklassion Sect, is it not?" I say eventually. The assassin gapes at me. It is an expression I am familiar with. I'm not as clever as his expression would indicate. It's just many sorcerers have become lazy over the years. If you let your magick speak for your brain, then soon you don't have much of either.

"How can you possibly know that?" he asks.

"Because it's not about us at all. You Kinets do like to squabble. The Linklassions are being forced out of their temple land by the Laspassions. They need a new home. I stay abreast of minor sect intrigue. Always a good idea, when you're seen as a soft target for any sect with a few coins. Furthermore," I add, pointing to his brown leather desert sandals, "you still have some reddish orange sand from the Dunehills on your shoes. The Linklassions are the only minor Kinet sect from there."

The assassin looks down at his feet and grins. "Well done, *Quantas*. I admit I'm impressed. At least the Light of Luce gave you a brain to make up for not giving you any powers. I'm sure the ladies prefer your brain to actual magick any day. I bet you're drowning in bloods and cubs here in this temple. I can't see any, though. Maybe they're all washing their hair?"

"Very droll. I've met my match in this conversation. If only I'd bought some funnier quips to my assassination."

The barrel starts to shake threateningly, and I can see my time in parley with him is almost up. A shame. Most of the sorcerers I live with roll their eyes when I spin out my reasoning. But here I have a captive audience.

"I notice you haven't told me the one word you need to disarm me." He grins.

I glance down quickly at the assassin's feet, then look back up at his barrel, which is raised high now, ready to lower at me.

"Wait . . ." he says, unsure, having noticed my glance. He looks down at the thick woolen rug he is standing on, a frayed affair, a study in scarlet and blue. It is the only piece of real ornamentation in the antechamber.

"Oh . . ." he begins, and then quickly hops a couple of steps back to the stone slabs that lie before the rug. "You almost got away with that. The old trapdoor trick. Not bad for a Quantas. I'm sure that worked for the others. Not so for a Kinet. We're made of sterner stuff."

I look at the second-worst assassin I have ever encountered for a few final seconds, standing now exactly where I want him. Then I say the word.

"*Now.*"

A ripple of confusion spreads across his features as the stone slabs beneath him give way, followed by a rictus of terror, and then he is gone, followed shortly after by the barrel. I wait a few seconds as his screams descend in volume. Then I hear a distant splash, followed soon after by a large explosion. I look down beyond the trapdoor, into the cave system that stretches far beneath our temple. As I'd calculated, the underground lake my assassin fell into has contained most of the blast. Then I turn to Jacob, my deputy, who has been concealed behind a pillar at the far end of the antechamber the whole time, hand poised next to a lever set into the wall.

"That worked well," I say, scanning the rest of the area around me in case the assassin had a compatriot. But there are few places here they could hide. This is not a room for activity; it's a place to pass from one point to another, from the temple surface to the catacombs beneath, where another assassin's corpse now lies.

"Easy for you to say," he replies. "You weren't the one waiting patiently for you to stop boasting so I could get rid of the man trying to kill me."

"Well, technically, Jacob, he was trying to kill *me.*"

Jacob stares at me.

"But I see your point," I add diplomatically. Jacob pulls a little on his short, neatly sculpted goatee, which is how I know he's genuinely annoyed. His facial hair, shaved head, stocky muscular frame, and obsidian-black skin is in stark contrast to my floppy brown fringe, lighter umber complexion, clean-shaven face, and tall, skinny frame. It's only the green robes we both wear that give any indication we are of the same sect. It's a good job the assassin didn't see us together; he would've made some tired remark about us resembling a stagetale comedy pairing, and the level of wit in the place would have fallen even further.

"We were never in any danger," I reply eventually. "He was en route to the catacombs when we intercepted him, no doubt planning to explode it there and then flee before the resultant fire blast consumed the whole temple. He was hardly going to release it here and risk his own life, was he?"

"And you know that for a fact, do you?"

"With people as easy to read as him, yes, it may as well be."

Jacob scowls. "Still. It was a risk. We should have just fled."

"As someone who has spent multitudes of hours designing a series of traps throughout the temple for all the numerous assassins who have graced us over the years, that seems an odd thing to say."

"Well, I'm very attached to my life, Sage. It's done well by me, and it's all I've got."

"And yet you chose the Cult of Humanis."

"I seem to remember you chose me. *Come join the cult,* you said. In a temple in the middle of nowhere. Far from women, wine, or mead. Remind me why I agreed again?"

I smile. This is a common game we play, and we have done so for a hundred and fifty years.

"Because you love it, Jacob, more even than you love your wine, though you'd scarce admit it. You love knowing what came before. You have that feeling I have, that feeling of needing there to be more, and needing to know for sure that there is."

Jacob grins. "I wasn't asking for a clichéd speech, but I'll take it. Although I feel obliged to point out that we've not been finding or knowing much of anything since Grayfall. Sort of hard to do our job when we can't travel beyond the Desertlands."

"Unless my theory is correct."

Jacob pulls a face. "A fact we will never find out, because I like my body alive and free of Gray bullets. I'm very fussy like that. I'm known for it." He yawns. "Why do assassins always attack in the middle of the night anyway? Just rude, if you ask me."

I'm about to ask him to reflect on his last statement when we are interrupted by one of our cult brothers, peering hesitantly around the door leading back to the surface temple.

"It's okay, Brother Finlay," I say, smiling at him and then nodding to the trapdoor. "Our latest visitor is in a great number of pieces a great number of feet below us. How are the guards?"

"Bruised, First Brother. Their egos, mainly."

"I see. Thank the five magicks for that." I stare at Brother Finlay, who is tall and gangly-limbed. His face is obscured by the light green hood he wears, a hood attached to a cloak free of any patterns or sigils, unlike other cults or sects. We in the Cult of Humanis don't wear our

Quantas signs for all to see. We see no reason why we should advertise the magick type that never did anything for us, that failed to give us the bare minimum of magick itself. I sense the brother's stress, hood or not.

"It's Mikael, isn't it? I don't think we've been properly introduced yet."

"It is, First Brother."

"Sage, please. I think we can dispense with the cult formalities for a moment, given the day we're having. How long have you been with us now?"

"A decade, roughly."

I pause just long enough to consider that I probably should have found some time to introduce myself to him a little earlier. Ten years is not *too* long when the cult you founded has fifteen decades under its belt, but people skills should perhaps not be left until assassination attempts. "And how many assassins have been sent our way in that time?"

"Ten, I would say, First—I mean Sage. One a year."

"And when faced with how many want us dead, do you regret your choice of sect? Do you regret joining the cult?"

Mikael thinks on this a little. "No. The consistency with which we dispatch them instead makes me realize I made the right choice."

I smile and turn to Jacob. "Well, look at that. Your recruits do turn out right in the end."

"Of course they do," Jacob replies, winking at Mikael. "If they can hold their drink, they can hold their own."

"Ah, if I may?" Mikael holds up a small piece of parchment. "News from First Light."

I raise my eyebrow. "Not direct, I assume?"

"No," he replies. "It came to Luce through the Neuras at First Light, straight to the mind of the Archmage, who then passed it straight to *my* mind through his Neuras. I'm not sure why it came to me and not yourselves . . . I think, I mean it *felt* like it was done in a rush. I managed to write it down before it left my memory."

Jacob scowls. "By the five magicks! First the assassin, now the Archmage wants something. I'm going to have to sleep through the day at this rate."

I stare at him.

"What?" says Jacob. "I'm not missing out on my sleep. We've talked about this."

"The news is of First Light," Mikael adds, deftly ignoring my deputy.

"Well, it came from First Light, so I imagine it's about First Light, don't you?" Jacob continues.

"Please ignore him," I say. "He's worried I'm trying to get him killed. As if I don't have easier ways to do so. Out with the news, then."

"It's Azzuri," says Mikael. "I mean the Azzuri the Younger. The First Lord's youngest."

"What about him?" I ask, the warmth of my recent victory draining out of me.

"He's dead."

"What?" I feel empty now. I reach for my careful, chosen words, but the cupboard is bare. "I . . . how?"

"It's . . . the message is not completely clear . . ."

I grab the parchment from him, suddenly impatient. I read, and then read again.

"It doesn't make any sense," I finish. "He was killed by Grays. Earlier this very night."

"What in Light's name?" asks Jacob. "Grays got past their walls?"

"No," I say, trying to piece together a puzzle made solely of corners. "He was killed outside the walls. They found his body there. They don't know why. At least, that's what they sent to the Archmage."

Jacob's face pales. "Shades . . . of all the Lords to die. He was a good one. I liked him."

"He was . . ." I am lost again, groping. "He listened to us." I cast my eyes up at the temple pillars holding up our home around us; I stare at the reliefs on the friezes. Leaves around a knot. Wrapped tight, holding everything together. For no real reason, I try again. "He listened to *us*." My words sound fainter.

A memory takes over.

ONE HUNDRED AND FIVE YEARS AGO
FIVE YEARS BEFORE GRAYFALL

I am meditating in the herb garden when Jacob disturbs me.

"We have a visitor," I say.

Jacob squints at me. "Let me guess. I walk in a certain way when a stranger is near or something."

I restrain a smile. "No, I was more thinking that visitors and emergencies are the only reason I ever wanted to be disturbed from my daily mindvisioning."

"Oh," says Jacob. "I'd actually forgotten that, to be honest."

Now it is my turn to squint. "Forty-five years as my deputy brother and you haven't yet learned the art of listening to me, have you?"

Jacob shrugs. "We live in hope. By the way, *mindvisioning* is a stupid word to use when *meditation* will do."

"It is a type of meditation, Jacob. It is a present-orientating . . ." I stop myself. "Let's not keep the visitor waiting, then. Are you going to be inclined at any point to tell me who the person is?"

"I've no idea," Jacob says. "They didn't tell Brother Wragg his name. He's dressed in plain desert robes. He's on his own. Could just be some wandering madman. Probably is, to come all the way out here. He's in the eastern antechamber. Brother Bressinger is keeping an eye on him."

"Is he keeping an eye on his bottle, too?" Not all new brothers make it. Life is difficult out here in the desert outerlands, as we are one of the stranger cults.

"One way to find out, Sage."

I sigh and stand up. This will most likely be a waste of time. We have been a cult for only forty-five years (at least in our current incarnation; I try to forget my prewar attempt). This time frame is nothing for sorcerers, and we still have that sense of newness about us which attracts random waifs and strays. Some are acceptable candidates, who believe in the idea of seeking out relics from a mythical race most believe to be legend. Some are opportunists or worse.

When I enter the antechamber, the newcomer is studying the detailed art along the stone columns. The carvings depict a great light, surrounded by sorcerers bowing to it. They are not as intricate as the ones in some of the other cult temples, but then we are hardly the largest, and our home has seen better days. Torches line the long thin antechamber in which we stand, though there's not much for them to illuminate, apart from the art he is currently stroking.

"This is beautiful," says the stranger. He is a vampire, I see that immediately (annoying that this detail wasn't conveyed to me; my chain of communication needs work evidently). He has long dark hair, dusty and sand-covered but clearly normally well kept. His face is classically handsome: a long aquiline nose and well-defined cheeks, but instead of the austere eyes you would expect from his bloodline, his are rounder and softer, taking away some of the intimidation of that face. As Jacob said, he is dressed in plain brown desert robes and sandals; no jewelry or ornamentation in sight. An interesting puzzle, but one I solve fairly quickly.

"It is not our work," I reply. "This temple was originally home to the Cult of Light, as that decoration suggests. They all died in the Twin War, to a man, and so when I founded the Cult of Humanis shortly after the war, I . . . adopted this abode."

The stranger nods but keeps his eyes fixed on the decoration. "I find the creation myths of the sorcerers fascinating," he says, "so very different from our kind. You believe in something called the Light, yes? A source of sentient power that formed magick, from which the five kinds of sorcerers came? The same source which they say produces every sorcerer, fully grown at birth, in that chamber somewhere in your capital Luce?"

"Precisely," I reply. Normally I would love to engage in a theological debate with a stranger, but given how many assassins and rogues we get, I would rather press on with business. "But you did not come here to speak of our origins, did you, Lord Azzuri?"

He turns to me then, shocked. Then he smiles. "Ah, you have seen a portrait then. I thought I was drab enough in appearance to be deceiving!"

"I have seen no such thing," I reply.

"Then how?"

"Your facial structure clearly gives yourself away as a Lord. Even if it did not, from the shine of your skin, you are clearly used to being on the blood of nobles. So the question is *which* Lord." I move closer to him, refining my deductions even as I say them.

"You have clearly come here alone," I continue. "I do not yet know the reason, but the lack of concern for your safety in the Desertlands combined with the plainness of your robes suggests that either you are running from something or you do not care for such things as propriety. It must be the latter."

He smiles, brushing his long hair from his face. "And why is that?"

"Because no one who was running from something would think it a good idea to come here. So I think to myself, which Lords are known for being, shall we say, un-lord-like? Rebellious. And although I do not keep up enough on the politics of the Centerlands, I know enough to hear that the First Lord's youngest son, despite the levity of his years, has already shown a little rebellion. A sympathy for the Worns. A willingness to encourage the blurring of the classes that is proceeding apace in Lightfall."

The young Azzuri laughs, a soft laugh that nonetheless carries through the antechamber. "That is impressive. A gamble, though. You could not have been certain."

"All such deductions are gambles. Despite what you read of the best of the inquirers in our capital, no one can deduce such things with complete accuracy."

"You should know, Sage Bailey. You were an inquirer once, yes?"

I pause, taken aback. I am not usually so thoroughly known, especially by vampires. He takes advantage of my stunned silence and continues.

"I have read about you. It was not easy, but in the great library of Lightfall, almost all things are recorded. Like all your cult members, you are a Quantas. You resided in Quantile for a while, aiding your fellow kind. Then your talents were noticed and you were made an inquirer in Luce, the first Quantas sorcerer to be so. Despite your lack of magick, you solved every sorcerer crime you were put on. Then the Twin War happened. After that, you changed pace completely; you became obsessed with the legends of the mortals, and whether evidence of their mythical civilization could be found in our lands. You founded the Cult of Humanis out here for this purpose, far out in the desert, away from all the other sorcerer towns."

I nod. "It is strange to hear my achievements stated so plainly by one in such power."

Azzuri nodded. "I do not care for power. All the people I know who do care are not particularly nice to me. My family already hates me for my uncaring, I can tell. It is not a nice thing to be hated so early in your life by the ones meant to love you." He looks away, having given away too much to a man he has just met.

"Can I interest you in some blood?" I say quickly. "We keep some for vampire visitors. We can retreat to the guest chamber if you like. It's not massively different from here, but you can sit, and there is a mildly reduced amount of sand."

He shakes his head, smiling. "No, thank you, First Brother."

"Sage, please."

"Sage it is. I must be quick. I suspect my father has sent people after me to keep an eye on my exploits. As you can imagine, it did not go down well that someone of my *station* . . ."—here he pauses, letting the affect on the word make its mark—"would leave the Centerlands on my own for a tour of the Desertlands. I do not want them knowing I came here."

"And why did you?" I ask, increasingly fascinated by this unusual specimen of nobility before me.

"Because I want to tell you something," he says, running his hand along the craftwork of the mages who lived here before me, "and maybe seek your help. I have always had an active imagination. I love myths. I love legends. And perhaps to my detriment, I often find myself believing them. Whether they were the mortals of the children's stories or something else, I believe there were others before us. I have and seen and read enough of this land to believe that."

"I wish others would see it that way. We are mocked in sorcerer society."

He raises his eyebrow. "And I imagine you care as much for their opinion as I do for that of my own society."

I grin at that. I am beginning to like this specimen a great deal.

"Which brings me to my pertinent point," he continues, pushing his shining hair out of his face. "There was something large found in the ground just outside of Lightfall six months ago, during the depths of winter. Buried deep. It was transported from the burial site to the Lightfall Blood Bank, and from there to the Blood Bank of First Light, which these days is considered even more secure."

My mouth grows dry. I feel anger that vampires should find something, instead of me, but I quell it. Anger is rarely of use, and even when it can be, it is only as a ruse, even to oneself. "Do you know what it was?"

"No. It was explained away as a sorcerer trove of minerals, from before the founding of Lightfall. But I have enough connections still with several Lords on the Councils that matter to know it was something important enough to be kept secret. Under the care of Spymaster Saxe."

I nod, understanding. Saxe is a legend, even to the other races. The Lord whose web of knowledge keeps the Worns down. As much as progress is being made in Lightfall to break down the old class divisions, it would be going at a decidedly faster rate were it not for him and his litany of deception.

"This is quite something, Lord Azzuri."

"Red, please."

"Red? I thought your choice name was Vermillion, like your father."

"I am Red to my friends."

I pause a little at this. "I am hardly your friend."

"But you're hardly my enemy, Sage. And right now, that's good enough."

I can't fault his logic. "Something though it may be, but I'm afraid I do not see what is to be done. As you say, Saxe has it in the securest of locations."

"Let's say you were right. The mortals existed. Do you want people like Saxe or, dare I say it, my father, to have such knowledge of the old ways?"

I shake my head. "My existence, the cult, proves that I do not."

He nods. "Neither do I. Tell me, have you ever found something that definitively proves their existence? The mortals? Something that sheds proper light on them? Books, records, weapons, crafts, temples, anything?"

"No," I say, nodding and hoping he cannot read faces the way I can. "We have only found ancient relics, not quite determinate. Some could say it was of immortal kind if they wanted. But that will change one day."

"I have no doubt. From the meeting of you, you are impressive enough that I have faith. But these mortals you believe existed, then surely they may have had weapons and tools of great destruction, beyond imagining?"

"I believe so, yes. I believe the stories of them, the myths, are formed from some innate knowledge of when we, or at least the few of us still alive from that time, were beasts. Before the Great Intelligence and the beginning of immortal society. I believe the answers lie in the semi-truths passed down. And these truths tell us these were powerful gods, despite their mortality."

"I see." He thinks on this. "Then if there is a risk that Saxe and his Lord friends have found something like that, then it is important that we know, yes?"

"Very."

"Excellent!" He throws his hands in the air, and for a second I think he's going to dance a jig on the spot. I can see how, if the rumors are true, he acts in the Lightfall stagetales in secret. He is certainly performative enough.

"Then I will be your eyes and ears in Lightfall," he continues, "and in return you will tell me what it is I have found, so we can at the very least improve the knowledge of the land and if necessary prevent the Lords from amassing any more power."

It is such a bold proposition that for long moments I stand, mouth slightly agape. I am not used to reaching for words. I am even less used to such directness. So I put my words aside for once and I reach out my hand instead, and a thin beam of moonlight from a broken temple roof up high crosses where we shake.

PRESENT DAY

The memory lingers in me, and I wonder how something so far back in time can assume such clarity. I nod to Mikael. "You may go now. Thank you. If you could start preparing our things for a journey."

"Of course. How long is this journey?"

"Two weeks, if our horses are fast and we ride all of the day and a good deal of the night."

Mikael looks alarmed, or at least as alarmed as a mage with a hood over his face can look, but he nods and leaves. I turn to Jacob, who is staring at me like a man who's just heard how temporary his stay of execution is. He will take this hard. But he'll get over it.

"You are not serious," he says.

"You're the funny one, not me," I reply, "as you like to tell me at every opportunity."

"Sage, this isn't a jest. We can't go to First Light. I know you think this had something to do with what Azzuri was doing for us—"

"It most likely has everything to do with it."

"But we can't get to the city. No one can. We will be killed by Grays. It's what happens. It's what's been happening for the last hundred years. I can draw you a diagram, if you like. Us on the road to First Light, being shot and killed. Me making a very explicit gesture to you in my last moments."

"If my theory is correct—"

"Damn your theory, Sage! It's madness."

"Oh, really!" I ask, feeling a little anger in me, my calm rationality slipping now that I have no small victory to look forward to. "Is it? As opposed to what? This sane shading world we live in?" I begin to pace up and down. This is a time for pacing. "Read the situation. First

Lord Azzuri sends word to the Archmage that his son has been killed by Grays. He uses Neuras. Fairly rare, that, and fairly expensive, so only used for urgency. We can therefore assume that it was a warning, most likely in case the Grays are planning something here, too, that his son's death was merely a prelude to. With me so far?"

"Aren't I always?"

I wisely let that slide. "The Archmage received word earlier tonight, according to his message. Then he uses a Neuras himself to tell us before the night is out. *Us*. The strange cult far from everyone else with no powers and little respect. Why do you think that was? Because he's keen to keep us in the loop for political reasons? Come on, Jacob. He's remembered what I told him. My theory. He knows only I can get to First Light. He wants sorcerers there he can trust to assess the situation. He wants us."

"Does he say this in the message?"

"No, but why else would he—"

"Hold on there, quickmind," says Jacob, slumping down to the floor and lying against a pillar, legs splayed out. He takes his sandals off and idly massages his sand-dusted feet. "I could do with a drink right now. Why do we have so many empty antechambers without places for drinks? I really should have been here when you moved in."

"Jacob . . ."

"Yes, all right. I'm still with you. So we're mages of import and in the Archmage's circle now, even though he ignored you the last time you droned on at him. He trusts us, though not enough to explicitly say so, apparently. But why would Azzuri expect us?"

I shrug. "We will be diplomats, come to pay our respects at the funeral. He'll be surprised someone made it in one piece. Suspicious, maybe. But we will act the polite visitor while we find out what happened to his son."

Jacob puts his hand over his face and groans quietly. "We'll never get there, you cocktender. We'll die."

"No, we won't. My reasoning is good."

"And if it's not?"

I shrug. "Then you will have had a good long life, full of womanizing and drinking, and occasionally pausing from both activities long enough to help me run this place."

"True, but not helping."

"Fine. Then I will go on my own. But if Azzuri died because of us . . ."

Jacob grimaces. "You don't know that."

"But I have to suspect it. Based on the letter he sent me not three months ago. We have to be prepared for the possibility that he had finally discovered something definitive about the find and was murdered for it."

Jacob's face betrays his skepticism, his left eyebrow almost levitating off his head. I press on. "He was . . . he was gentle. He wasn't like the rest of them . . . And now we have no one left in First Light who can help us. No one who knows if the Lords really did find something of the mortals under the earth. Only we know what that could mean. Just how irrepressibly terminal that could be for all of us."

I can see Jacob wavering, but not enough. I go for the jugular.

"When I found you, you said anything was better than how you were living then."

Jacob smiles, but it's not really a smile in the way I know it. "I said a lot of things back then. I was just relieved to have a fresh start."

"Good," I say, nodding, knowing I have him now. "Then remember that relief and carry it with you, old friend. We've got a long way to go."

Sam

There's a loud knock on the bedchamber door. I sit up in bed, already alert, and push aside the rough wool blanket that suffices for a bedsheet, straightening my hairnet and blinking my half-closed eyes alert. I wasn't going to sleep anytime soon anyway. I was thinking over my failed second half of the night, all the conversations with maids that had gone nowhere. I'd been careful about it, dropping the Leeches into conversation like I was bored and wanted to lark about with some gossip, but all I'd got for my care were shrugs. If there were any Leeches in the palace, they weren't going to show themselves to me.

Beth wakes up. We glance at each other. It's unusual to get a knock so late, half a glass after lightfall. Outside, the sun is rising. I can't feel it; but I can sense it. Sense its presence. All vampires can; maybe it's survival instinct. Only bad things happen in the palace when the sun is up.

I jump out of bed, pick up the blue Hallsday shawl from the floor, and throw it into the wardrobe so no one can accuse us of being slovenly. I scan the room, looking for anything else that might receive ire; I see some mold has crept into the wood paneling on the side of the wardrobe, but we can hardly be blamed for that, I hope. Then I open the door to Phylis again. She's still in her nightclothes, not yet dressed for bed, which might explain the scowl on her face, although since her scowl is ever permanent, it might just as well not.

"You're to go to Lady Hocquard's estate in Northeastfall," she says. "Tonight, at first bell."

"What?"

"You heard me, girl. Lady Hocquard. She needs extra maids for some ball she's got planned. She asked in particular for maids with a bit o' thinking about them. So naturally they chose you. All them words you say finally getting you a change of scenery, it seems."

"Why does she need extra maids?" I ask.

"Well, I'll be drained if I know, girl, gods' sake! A carriage will be waitin' for you after nightfall, soon after first bell, that's all you need to know. So don't dally when you wake."

After the first maid has left, I turn to Beth, whose eyebrows are raised. "Lady Hocquard," she says. "I think I know her. She puts on kindcoin balls, money to the poor of Worntown, all that stuff."

"She sounds like one of the good ones, then," I say, quietly. "By the sounds of her name, she's not one of the Red–Blue Nobles, anyway. They're normally the worst." It's a good rule to go by, that. If you meet a noble called Scarletia Cyania or, appropriately enough, Rufous Azzuri, then you will do well to keep out of their way if you like your life long and fruitful.

"Don't speak too quick, Sammy. She's high up with the highest of them, all part of their party society. She probably just does the kindcoin so it looks like they're helpin' us. Help the Ladies turn a blind eye to what the Lords are up to when their backs are turned."

I smile. Beth is full of surprises, even though I have known her for two decades. Sometimes I forget she's not stupid. She just acts like it a lot of the time. "You're probably right, Beth," I say approvingly. "How come you always know about such Ladies?"

"You have your books, I 'ave me maid gossip," says Beth, winking. "It's good to see a grin on your face, Sammy."

She's right. I am happy. This makes up for my failure to uncover any Leech knowledge. "This could be good, Beth. If this Hocquard isn't one of the bad ones, then she'll take a shine to me and request me permanent. Especially if she's as high up as you say. I'll charm her first maid and I'll bring you with me. It's got to be better than here."

"Constantly planning, Sammy. Constantly scheming. I can't hardly keep up with you sometimes."

"Don't be silly now, Beth. You're the only one who can. We're the schemiest maids who ever did nick some blood vials hidden in a lord's underwear drawer." I wink at her and we both laugh.

"Tell me a story, Sammy, to help me to sleep. Tell me one of your tales." I sigh inwardly. I want to tell her I'm too tired, but she knows she has me because I'm swanning off to a Lady's mansion after nightfall.

"What story, Beth?"

"You said the chest in Azzuri's room was from Last Light. Tell me that story."

"Suns, Beth, I must have told you that a dozen times." More like a hundred. Telling Beth the history of the land in daytale form is my penance for reading up on it in the first place. Although sometimes there is fun to be had in the recounting of it.

"Yeah," says Beth. "But I like it, Sammy. It makes me feel far away. You can understand that, right?"

I can't argue with that. I put on my story voice, half talecaster, half parent, and I begin.

"Around three hundred and fifty years ago, four noble vampire families left their homes, each from the biggest cities of the continent: one from Shadowfall, one from Lightfall, one from First Light, and one from Dawn Death. They said they wanted to explore where no one had gone beyond— the Ashlands. To brave the legends of the banshees that roamed it and the other horrors there that prevented anyone from crossing it. Thousands of curious explorers followed in their wake. They crossed the Southern Sea and made camp on the northern shore of the Ashlands. But the expedition south of that never happened, for instead they founded a city. No one knows why they had a change of heart. But they did. They built the walls high, and whatever lay beyond them could not get at them, and they named this new city Last Light.

"And there the city thrived for two hundred years, and not a single soul on our continent ever heard from any of them. No honegulls, no messengers. No one came from the city across the sea. Last Light was separated from the world, but rumors grew. Of a city of legend and myth, of spies, of found things and secret things, of forays beyond the city walls, and of feuding—great endless feuding between the four founding families. Of betrayals and murders and marriages and back-stabbing and more.

"And then, barely forty years after the Twin War had caused such ruin on our continent, Last Light fell. No one knows why, but it did. You could see the flames from the southern Swamplands. Some made it over the sea, but only hundreds out of the many thousands of the city. The survivors of Last Light live among us now, keeping their secrets safe and their stories untold. Some say that they carry the deepest secret of them all, whatever that might be."

"Hmm," says Beth eventually, her words half tumbling into her dreams. "We'll go there one day, Sammy. See the ruins. You and me. You and me in Last Light."

She always does this. Dreams of a future we will never have. I normally say yes to this, but over time it gets harder. The longer your life goes on without change, the more your dreams curdle in the hearing of them; the more they start to mock you and grin at you, your failure reflected harshly against their white smiles.

I start to reassure Beth anyway, the lies heavy in my mouth, but her eyes are already closed.

5

They Can Hardly Get Worse

I have spoken to many a Lord of the issue of the Leeches. It is a common point of conversation among us Midways, and even more so for the Worns. No Lord will take it seriously, though. When we say female collaboration, they think of gossips and such frivolitie, not actual machinations. They cannot imagine Worn women ever capable of more. I wonder if they should.

Redskin Sliptide,
A Pamphlet on the Rumors of First Light

Sam

I wake half a glass before first bell and leave Beth to finish her dreaming.

I dress quickly, putting an orange shawl around my standard sky-blue maid gown, because it's been cool this week and because I want to look as dressed up as I'm allowed. This is the only extra outdoors clothing we're allowed to wear, save on Hallsday, when we're likely far enough away from the palace to be risking ruining the carefully coordinated look the Lords demand from their servants. It's a good-quality shawl, finest wool of a fang-tip ram, given to me by a second maid in an unexpected act of kindness when I was going through my period of sorrow in my first few months at the palace.

After a quick glug of cowblood in the maids' bloodhall, I hurry to the carriage waiting for me outside the servants' entrance. The wind is up tonight and the air is cold, worse than usual in the early weeks of Green-death, so as I settle down for the ride I wrap my shawl around me a little tighter. One of the many gifts weaker blood bestows upon you: when the summer starts to wind away, you really *feel* it.

As the carriage moves off, I think on my destination. The First Lord's palace is in the proper north of the city, Northfall, about halfway between Centerfall and the northern mountain line, whereas Lady Hocquard, according to my driver, lives in the southernmost stretch of Northeastfall, almost on the border with Eastfall, where the Lords' estates give way to the Midways' townhouses and smaller acreages. The land is low from Northeastfall southward, so if her mansion is big enough, then on a good day she might be able to see all the way across the Midway part of town to Southeastfall and the Worntown streets I grew up on. Maybe that's what makes her so charitable. Or maybe, like Beth said, it's just a way for her to play the society belle. It's not often Beth is so cynical, despite what she's been through. I almost hope she's right.

As the carriage forks left onto the main road to Northeastfall, the imaginatively named Lords' Way, I see that the roads are already teeming with carriages, Lords and Ladies coming past me on their way to the palace or south to Centerfall, perhaps to see a stagetale or to bet at the Blood Markets. The moon is almost full tonight and there are no clouds, so I get a good view of the carriages as they pass me by, full of the great and the good and those who wish they were both. I get glimpses of what the Ladies are wearing. Their dresses interest me little; boring variations of red and blue, the colors the nobles obsess over.

But it's their necklaces I'm fascinated by, for this is where the detail's found: each silver necklace shaped in the animal of their traditional family blood. The real wealthy ones wear a stag, a hawk, a bear, or a whale; I see other noble animals, including an eagle, a snaptail, and a greatshark. I know from my reading that some have historically had wolfkind necklaces, but I imagine these have been carefully hidden away in some family vault somewhere now that we're at peace with the wolves. I'm sure that makes the wolfkind feel much better. Gemstones function as the animals' eyes: the richer the family, the larger or better the stones. Rubies and sapphires are popular, given the dreary predictability of the color scheme, but I see topaz and emeralds, too, and a decent smattering of pearls. Just one of those could keep me in Midway blood for a good decade, I would wager.

A half glass of this nosiness later, and the flat stone and concrete of the King's Way has given way to the smaller paths and bridleways that link the mansions of the nobles of First Light. This deep into Northeastfall, the sounds of the city retreat and the relative silence of the valley's countryside descends. Off in the distance, across fields and behind small clumps of trees, I spy the mansions of the nobility, imposing themselves on the landscape as only vampires know how.

As I watch these homes from afar, Atmos Rastrillion's brick-sized tome *Vampire Builds Across the Ages* comes to mind. I spent a good couple of weeks of library reading on that one a few years back. And so I know they used to be castles, these homes of the well-blooded, far before my time. Great fortresses in the style you now find with the wolves only, Grosshunt, all grandiose arches and flying buttresses and creepy wassergoyles staring at you, water pouring out their mouths.

But then the Twin War happened, and suddenly there wasn't much need for the protections of castles. The eastern border seemed a lot less scary when the wolves beyond it had lost half their number in the most brutal five years of known history. So down went the castles and up went mansions and villas in the Old Mage style, classical sorcerer buildscaping, already used in some of the great buildings of Centerfall. Towering columns, domed roofs, perfect symmetry. A new postwar vampire age, a style we didn't come up with ourselves but were blooddamn well going to make our own. Vampires in a nutshell, that: little original thinking, but as mimics we can't be beaten.

Interesting as this is, I'm lulled into sleep by the steady rhythm of the carriage, and I'm wakened only by the crunch of the carriage wheels as they ride over the small pebbles of a long driveway, at the end of which is a building that, even by the lofty standards of this side of the city, is impressive. In classic Old Mage style, it has a portico over the entrance, made up of four great columns supporting a domed roof. With the thrill of a true bookmind who's lived more in the library than in the real world for years, I recognize the columns are in the Revellic style, topped by a scroll design. The rest of the mansion was clearly designed by someone clinging to the idea of symmetry like it was their last blood: dozens of windows all equally spaced, stretching out across five stories, each window framed by its own columns and domed pediments, all under a flat roof.

But there's a twist that separates this from the fancy clone buildings I've seen one after the other on my drive, for the columns of the portico over the entrance are scarlet red in contrast to the white of the rest of the building, giving it the unnerving impression of bloody teeth. Then there's the fact that vines and other growers have been allowed to climb up the first three stories of the mansion, some blooming with thorny red roses despite the season. The lady likes her flowers, it seems. I wonder what else she likes.

The carriage rolls up to the front and stops.

"Out you get, then," calls the driver.

"This is the main entrance, not the Worns' entrance," I reply.

"My instructions were to drop you off here." He laughs and rubs his fat jowls. "Maybe they've mistook you for a Lady."

I get out of the carriage, confused, and watch as it drives off. There's no one here to greet me. I can't see anyone in the windows; the ones facing me are dark and unlit. I trace the path of the vines above, and I see no light in the upper-floor windows, either. There's no one looking down at me from the top-story balustrades. I stare at the portico above me and I see the frieze running along its roof: a series of foxes in various states of running. I suppose I know the Lady's blood animal, then. Fox is usually considered a Midway blood, though. Another strange thing to add to the growing collection.

Rousing myself to knock, I stare at the front door. As entrances go, it's as imposing as the house itself. Revellic pillaries, mimicking the columns that support the front, frame it. It's red, too, a throat I'm about to jump down.

Before I can actually do the knocking, the door opens, and I'm greeted by a maid. She must be a first maid, I reckon, because of her outfit; her gown is made of fine-looking linen, not cotton. Also, I can smell a faint bottled scent on her, an aroma of lemons. Exactly the kind of touch you'd get on the most important maid of the house.

Her face, though . . . She has her long brown hair tied back in a neat bun, yes. Her face is clean with no makeup, yes. Nothing unusual there. But there is something in her eyes. And her arms . . . they're thin, but even under her gown, I can sense they'd have some strength to them if it came to it. In short, she doesn't look like most prim and proper first maids I've ever seen. She looks like she could break your nose without a sweat. And as vampires go, she's practically tanned. I wonder if . . .

"Are you going to keep gawkin' at me like that or are you comin' in?"

That accent . . . there can only be one place she's from. My curiosity gets the better of my manners.

"You're from Last Light? I've never met someone from—"

"Right off you're not askin' *who I am,*" the maid interrupts. "You're askin' *where I'm from.* Sign of a nosy one, that." She winks at me. "I think we're goin' to get on." I relax at the wink. I shouldn't have. A second later a knife is at my throat and that thick accent and lemon scent are at my ear. "But we're goin' to get on in the cellars."

As I follow the maid with the blade into the mansion, fear and curiosity competing for power over me, I try to figure out what might be happening, but I don't try for very long.

Blade now at my back, she pushes me at great speed through a domed vestibule that could fit five servants' bedchambers in it; I have time to look up at a sparkling cut-glass chandelier before I'm taken through to a long corridor. To the left, it leads off to fine rooms that by the looks of the doors would challenge the entrance hall for its pomp, but she turns right instead and stops at a worn gelmwood door that has seen better days, and even those weren't that good.

Beyond the door is a pantry, and for a second I wonder if she means to finish what I was worried she wanted to start at the front door. But then she pulls aside the mops leaning against the back wall of the pantry and presses hard on a slightly loose piece of stone that I would never have noticed myself, and the back wall swings open to reveal a narrow stone staircase that winds down, corkscrew-like, into the basement.

The basement level is not like the floors above. The corridor at the bottom of the staircase is cold stone, more castle than mansion, with torches instead of the oil lamp braziers of the house above. It doesn't take a quickmind to work out that these are the lower realms of the old castle, the mansion built on top of it. I follow the first maid down the corridor; it branches out into three, and she takes a left and follows it to a worn malderwood door at the end, which makes the pantry door seem modern. She unlocks it with a rusted key spirited from her gown; beyond is nothing but a small crestwood side table and a tall chair made of redoak, where she bades me sit. Someone has placed a rug on the floor, perhaps in the hope it will make the room seem less of a dungeon. I'm not sure their hopes have much going for them.

The first maid from Last Light plays with her blade as she stares at me. It has a blade curved inward, almost like a small scimitar. Its handle has small green jewels inset into it. I've never seen its like before, that's for sure. I wonder what she might do with it. You can't kill a vampire with a knife. Not without a lot of effort and a very sharp blade. But I imagine there are lots of other things she could do to me.

"Has anyone ever told you you need to work on your people skills?" I try to put some confidence into my shaking voice. "Look, either tell me what's happening or hurt me." A little better. I don't feel any better, though.

A few more seconds pass and she lets out a loud cackle. I've never heard a laugh like that. It's like she's just been told it's the last laugh she'll ever make. I'd be surprised if the Grays couldn't hear it. "You're brave, girl, I'll give you that," she says. "I thought you'd be quiverin', you spendin' so much time in the library and all, but you've got a brave way about you. The courage of a codswopper."

I stare at her, trying to work out what thing or animal a codswopper might be. Then I realize the meaning of what she said. "How do you know about that? Only Beth knows about that."

"There's more peepers in the palace than you know, Sammy girl."

I twig, then. I curse myself for not seeing sooner. "You're a Leech!"

She bows. "Alanna, at your service."

"But how did you know I was looking for you?"

"You weren't very subtle askin' your questions. In the future I advise a little more of the tiptoes about you, Sammy."

"But that was only last night! And the invite came a few glasses later!"

"We can be quick when we want to, girl. Quicker than a sharp point in a dark alley. Anyways, if you want your questions answered, then the one who'll do so draws near."

Sure enough, I hear the sharp clicks of light boots on the stone pavings of the corridor, a Lady's boots, I would wager. Then the door is swept open and hasn't even swung shut before the Lady herself launches into her opening. "Well! I am Lady Hocquard, Sam, but call me Daphnée, please. I lead the Leeches. It's very good of you to come, I must say. Not that you had a choice, I imagine . . . I am sorry for keeping you in the dark, but then that's rather the nature of our operation. I hope Alanna didn't scare you too much. She hasn't stabbed you anyway, which is more of an achievement than you realize, my dear. And I suppose I should also apologize for your surroundings, but as you might have gathered by now, my home is something of an artifice, a lightshow that comes on when we have guests, but otherwise is the mere front to what happens down here in the basement level. Anyway, that's quite enough of my rambling, I am sure you have some questions, Sam, so do fire away."

I know she's expecting an answer, but I stare at her a while longer anyway. She has long dark brown hair, styled in intricate braids that turn into cascading curls down to her shoulders, as is the fashion for noble ladies. Small white flowers of the kind I couldn't be bothered to guess at are pinned among it. Her eyes are large and oval, accentuated by thin black kohl, and her face is long and attractive, her skin having the un-weathered, perfect pale glow of a noble vampire who's had (almost) the best blood around since she arrived into this world. She's wearing a long scarlet dress that touches the floor, small white gloves, and a thin blue scarf stitched with rose patterns, which is wrapped tightly around her neck so it doesn't obscure her fox-shaped necklace, with large rubies set in the fox's eyes. It would be difficult to imagine a more appropriate look for a countess. She certainly doesn't look like she runs a secret blackmail ring of coingirls and maids. She looks like she should be at a ball some-where telling everyone in hearing distance how her garden is doing this season.

At some point, it becomes obvious I've not spoken. I summon words.

"You're . . . you're the Queen Leech? A Lady?"

She and Alanna exchange amused glances.

"Yes, dear, I did introduce myself as that a few moments ago. You'll have to keep up. Things move rather quickly around here." She pauses, then pats her dress, looking for something. "I tell you what, Sam darling, even for someone with such promise as you, I can see we might have thrown you in the deep end with your daydress still on, so to speak, so have some of this to perk you up."

She takes out a small blood vial from her dress and hands it to me, and as she does, so I smell the strong scent of roselily on her wrist. I down the vial immediately, my body taking over from wherever my brain has gone, and it hits my veins immediately, much quicker than I'm expecting. I gasp a little and feel a tingle spread throughout my body as I feel my mind expand.

"That should bring you out of your little state of shock, my dear," she says, carefully watching me.

"I'll say, m'lady," says Alanna, staring at me from the corner of the room with a smile I'm trying not to pay attention to. "It hits all the spots."

"It feels incredible," I say when I've recovered the ability to speak.

"It bloody well should, my dear," says Lady Hocquard. "It's magicked stag."

She notes the even more shocked expression on my face and smiles. "Oh, don't worry, it's not enough to last that long. And I would wager that as a maid in the palace, you've come across your own opportunities to indulge in a little high-quality blood in your time. I'd be rather disappointed if you hadn't," she adds, winking.

I nod, while the best blood I've ever tasted jams its fingers into the corners of my brain and applies lightning to its roots. Short of wolf-blood, it doesn't get better than this.

"Right," says Lady Hocquard. "Now you're sufficiently jolted back, why don't we start again. Ask your way into answers."

I think, properly this time. "Why is a noble Lady running an organization that targets her own classes?"

"Ah! A better question!" She smiles. "I am not going to give you my past in the first glass of knowing you, Sam, dear. But I will tell you that I was blind. Not by sight but by the life I lived. I pretended I didn't know what happened when we noble Ladies weren't around. Then I met Alanna here, and she showed me what was being done in the shadows, and how you could cast a little light into them, using all the tricks she had learned in Last Light. Alanna gave me the knowledge and the know-how, my dear, and all I had to do was supply the money and the safe locale and a little sense of order at the heart of a rather big network."

"I . . . I understand," I reply, still getting used to the tiny amount of stag, resisting the urge to manually rip the arm off the chair just to see if I could. "Why . . . why are you telling me all this? Why have you told me who you are? I assume, m'lady—"

"Daphnée, please," she interrupts, with the carefree manner of someone who doesn't realize that I've never in my life been asked to call a noble by their choice name.

". . . that other than your first maid here . . ."—I point to Alanna—"and perhaps a select few, none of the . . . night ladies and maids who pass you information know who you are. You've met me now for the first time, and you've no reason to trust me with such information. All you know is that I've been asking about you. I could hurt you with it, but you've given it away without a thought."

Lady Hocquard turns to Alanna. "I'm seeing it now," she says to her first maid. "She has a quickness of mind about her and a little confidence as well. You were right."

"I often am with such things, m'lady, if you want some honesty," replies Alanna.

"To answer your question," continues Lady Hocquard, "you are wrong to say we have no reason to trust you. The truth is, Sam, that Alanna and I have kept an eye on you for a while, pondering whether to bring you into our little web."

"Swamp, m'lady," adds Alanna. "That's where you find the Leeches, not in a web."

"Why, thank you for pointing out my mixed metaphor, Alanna. I do so appreciate it."

"Anytime, m'lady."

"If you know anything about us, Sam," continues Lady Hocquard, "then you should not be surprised to hear that I know everything there is to know about you, at least that which you haven't kept secret in your heart and in your mind. I know about how you joined the palace and what happened on that remarkable day. I know what happened to your family. I know you read in the library every moment you can, I assume to plan your escape from that life of palace drudgery. From all this, I take a little confidence that you are someone who could be of great assistance to the Leeches."

I am taken aback by that last comment. "I'm sorry, my lady, but how can you possible know that?" I realize my pitch has suddenly got louder, and I fear offense, so I add, "I . . . you must understand that if it was known I was in the library to do anything other than clean, I would be punished, perhaps fatally."

"Sam, we have Leeches everywhere. They know how to look. And not be seen. The maid who follows your library habits would no doubt have picked up on them straightaway. We are formidable, in our way. But do not fear, they would never tell a soul—aside from me, of course. We exist to support your class, not to betray them. And your secrets are safe with me, and if they are not, then you most certainly should not stay in my vicinity any longer."

"I understand," I say, but I feel what little color is in my cowblood cheeks draining away anyway at the thought of my forbidden forays into the library being carefully recorded as just so much extra information in a web of spies.

"But before we go on," she continues, "I am ignoring the most pertinent question: why you suddenly took a turn of curiosity about us, after so much reading and never choosing to look into us."

Before I reply, I savor this moment. To be spoken to like that by a noble . . . it feels good. I have the sense of being caught on a wave, one I know will surely come crashing down soon. But until then, I'm going to ride it out, and to the twin hells with the consequences.

"I . . . I think I found something important," I begin. I take the young Azzuri's note from my petticoats, show it to them, and explain where I found it.

There's a silence. Lady Hocquard looks at Alanna. Their expressions don't seem to change, but I can tell they're so close that they communicate not with expression and not with sound. I feel a pang of something. Maybe one day I'll find someone like that.

Lady Hocquard turns back to me. "Yes, I can see why you thought this important. That line about the Grays, knowing who they are. And the names on this list. Take the first one. Do you know who Commander Tenfold is?"

"The commander of the Scout Guard," I reply. "Was the old commander of the Lightfall South Watch. A Midway, four hundred years old or thereabouts. Fought with great distinction as captain of the Second Battalion in the Twin War."

Alanna grins at her lady, then raises her eyebrow. "You get that from your book learnin' or have you heard that around?"

"A little bit of both, if I'm honest," I reply, and I let myself feel appreciated for once. It could catch on, this feeling.

"Well, that settles it, then," says Lady Hocquard, clasping her white gloved hands together. "There is no turning back now, Sam dear. I rather fear you're one of us now."

I gasp. "Just like that?"

Alanna cocks her head at me, and something that might be a frown or a grin flashes across her face. "I rather think this girl wants a ceremony and water and belts and candles and blood and such, m'lady," she says. "I could take her down to a room myself and arrange somethin' a little unusual to make sure she's satisfied enough."

Lady Hocquard coughs a little and avoids eye contact with her first maid. "I'm sure that won't be necessary, Alanna, not that that stops you asking every time we take in another girl."

Alanna shrugs and sticks her tongue out at me. I don't know whether to fear her or laugh at her.

"Anyway," says Lady Hocquard, gesturing around her, "what happens next, Sam, is that you will return to the palace. Then, in good time, I will request you again and you will continue to investigate with us what you have begun here."

"In good time, my lady?" I ask, my impatience overtaking my manners.

"Yes, Sam. The First Guard have only just taken all known associates of the late Azzuri into their custody. They caused rather a stir, but that is to be expected from such men, I suppose. It could be a very inauspicious time to start seeking out people on this list to ascertain their connection with Azzuri. Let Saxe and his underhanded creatures cool. Then I promise you we will work together to see if this scrap of parchment you gave to us is either a little bit of nothing or something that we can use to light a fire under this city."

"A fire?"

"Yes, dear. You don't think we want to do what we do forever, surely? If you have any doubts or you get scared, remember something, Sam. Remember where you live right now, and remember that there are things happening that are good, and that these things need a little bit of help sometimes." She takes her scarf off as she speaks, hot from her talking, and I see her neck is even paler than her face. "Somewhere in the city, there is a Lord who is being told that if he hurts the girl who cleans his bedchamber one more time then his wife will be told about the coingirl he sees every Hallsday while his wife is at First Gods, the one who he chains to his bed before he uses her in ways that would make his wife faint before you even finished the sentence. Thus a little good is done. Somewhere else in the city, a member of the Blood Council is planning his day, and on his schedule will be a meeting with the First Secretary of the First Council itself, and in this meeting, the former will propose to the latter that some of the Worns be offered some of the Midway animal blood that is more widely available at cheaper prices now, rather than simply cow or worse. He will be denied, no doubt, but at least he tried. And the idea will be planted." She pauses, and I can see that her pale cheeks have reddened slightly, like a small blood spill on a snow-covered field.

"You see, Sam, what we do is just a part of something. It is a fight for a soul of a city. Maybe I am tired of keeping the fight small. Perhaps this gives us an opportunity—a small one, and maybe nothing at that—but it is a chance to see if we can speed up the process. Maybe I am tired of working in the system. Maybe . . . oh, I don't know," she ends, flustered, "maybe I am just tired."

"I think," says Alanna, "that what m'lady is trying to say is that one day you wake up and you're tired of fuckin' with the Lords one by one, and if you see a chance to fuck with them all, it's a wise decision to take it, by and by."

Lady Hocquard's eyebrows rise at Alanna's free cursing, but she doesn't look unhappy.

"Do you really think things can get better?" I ask my new employer.

"Well, darling," she replies, "I don't need to tell you this, but they can hardly get worse, can they?"

And then she's gone.

Lady Hocquard

I watch Samantha's carriage roll away from the parlor window. I hold a bloodflute tight in my hand. It is hawk, nonmagicked but still a powerful blood I would not normally waste on an idle drink. But the conversation with Sam unnerved me, more than I hope I let on. Not in a bad way, but just the kind of conversation with the sense of a storm running through it, of something happening. I rarely meet someone like Sam, in the Worns anyway. My Leech girls, of course, are incredible—braver, smarter Worns you could not meet. But there was something in Sam's eyes. Something that spoke of futures to come. Or perhaps I am being overly dramatic. I often am, I fear.

"A barter for all of your idles, m'lady?" says Alanna behind me. I take a moment to work out what she means. Many of the Leeches who work closely with Alanna find it hard conversing with her sometimes. I never tire of it.

"My pardon, m'lady," she adds, seeing me pause. "I mean a blood-crown for your thoughts."

I smile and take a moment to take in her face: the long aquiline nose, the thin eyes, and that strange tan—almost as if she has been suntouched but not scarred. I knew she was a Last Lighter the moment I met her decades ago. Everything about her is exotic, of farther climes. I am sad that she lost everyone when Last Light fell. But selfishly, it brought me to her, so there is some gladness in me of the events, too.

"Ah, I see, Alanna. I am just concerned that I was a little too open with this Samantha. I confess I may have got a little too excited at the thought of recruiting another palace maid, especially one like her."

Alanna shrugs. "I liked the gist of her, m'lady. She dealt with my blade in her face better than most, which shows she has a strong heart as well as a strong head, and that is rarer than fur on a fish, m'lady."

I squint at her. "That is a strange saying, Alanna."

"Not in Last Light, m'lady. Fishes had fur there, but it was very rare, so it is a very accurate saying in that way."

"Right . . . But yes, I agree. She was impressive. Perhaps we should have given her a chance when she first arrived at the palace rather than waiting all this time. I am just always wary of that place. It is a nest of vipers and forktails, and I worry what an environment like that does to someone's head."

"Can't be worse than my head, m'lady."

I stare at Alanna, as you can never tell whether she is being truly serious. I don't detect a grin. She looks sad, if anything, and that is rare. "You're an unusual creature, Alanna, but I won't have you say anything about your head. I am rather fond of it, in all honesty."

She grins then, a grin that flashes wide across her face, from serious to wild in a second. I want to reach out to her.

But I do not.

6

The Son and the Spymaster

If you wonder why some vampires follow the red–blue naming tradition—first name a shade of red, the second name a shade of blue—while others do not, it is because such nomenclature was a whimsy many decided on when Lightfall was founded. The most prominent families changed their own ancestral names to celebrate the first vampire city of the Centerlands (as it was then, before it became a home to other immortals, too). An exercise in ego, perhaps, or a show of faith in a new future. This is not a hard rule, but if you meet a noble who follows such naming conventions, then there is a good chance that they will be in power, or craving of it, or both.

Quantas Quistile, *A Sorcerer's Guide to Vampires*

First Lord Azzuri

"That did not go as I planned," I begin, reports of the watch commanders once again spread out on my desk, a flute of bloodwine to my side. The blood is magicked snaptail, a seven-year vintage. Not one of the finest tasting if you're drinking for pleasure, as the ones bred in the animal farms of the city don't grow into the same strength as those from the Swamplands south of Dawn Death that used to be carted to Lightfall. But it is calming, and Blood Gods know I could do with some calm after the failed foray behind the wall of the previous evening. And unlike what happens with whale blood, the calm does not affect the attention span—a useful quality if you are an anxious commander.

"It did not," replies Redgrave, standing in the same place he was when he advised me against the trip out of the city.

"I thought Tenfold was going to punch me, Redgrave. Those men will take that hard."

"They know the risks, First Lord. They are men dying to taste some excitement, which is why they chose the Scout Guard. If this wish should be taken literally by the gods, then they can hardly complain."

"Perhaps now is not the time for that famous wit of yours, Redgrave."

History will be denied Redgrave's deadpan response, however, because there is a knock on the door, and my spymaster enters. Lord Saxe is nothing if not predictable: his usual black velvet doublet is covered by his black cloak and, imaginatively, black breeches and black shoes. If he wishes to convey his life in the shadows, however, he would do well to work on his face—a wide smile combined with an untidy mess of blond hair. He is hardly sinister, at least at first glance. His eyes make up for this somewhat: small and currant-like, they suck all the warmth from his amiable grin, so if you are looking for it, you can spy his true nature easily enough.

"First Lord," he begins.

"Now, Cinibar, I am too tired for protocol. Call me Vermillion, please, unless you have no news for me, in which case no formality in the Everlands will satisfy me."

That was a little harsh, but there has always been something about Saxe that has unsettled me. Perhaps that is the nature of such men.

"I have no news as such, Vermillion," he replies, settling himself into the chair opposite like a crab inhabits a new shell, "but the certainty of news to come."

"It's too early for riddles," I note, offering him a flute of bloodwine, which he rejects.

"If you recall, Vermillion, you asked me to watch your youngest when he . . . grew less close to you and your family after Grayfall. And in so doing, my whisperers have gathered a long list over the century of those he has . . . made acquaintances with. Midways and Worns. Stagetellers, musicians, artists, scribers, and others of more dubious affiliation."

"Speak plainly."

"Coinboys, Worns of criminal intent, those who have been flagged as rebellious in the past . . . and persons he may have been associated with in a more-than-immodest fashion."

"Cinibar . . ."

"Men he has taken for lovers."

"I see." I refill my glass quickly, avoiding Redgrave's expression. "I did suppose that you would be keeping records. Although I note you have not shown me these records in the eighty years since I first tasked you with this."

Saxe shrugs, stretching his legs out in a manner suggesting far more comfort than my austere study furniture should allow. "I assumed you would not want to know. I assumed the knowledge that he was being watched would be sufficient."

I have no energy to argue, so I do not press the point.

"So," continues Saxe, "it is my belief that when this . . . prodigious number of your son's associates are brought to be questioned, we will devise a pretty picture of the circumstances up to his death, prettier at least than some of them will end up looking, ahem."

Despite my distaste at Saxe's words, I cannot deny it is a good plan. I look to Redgrave, who gives a quick nod. "Very well," I say. "But I want this to be done delicately. These people are not under suspicion. My son was many things, but he was not a criminal. The people he associated with—those few I know, anyway—some are Midways or Worns who may have some standing. I do not want to cause commotion or disquiet among various groups in the city, especially after what just occurred beyond the wall."

"Of course, First Lord." Saxe nods. "Delicate as always."

"Speaking of which," I add, "we must keep my eldest out of this. He is not of a delicate nature and is looking for something to take his anger out on."

"Ah," says Saxe, his eyes darting anywhere but to me.

I put my glass down. "I do not like the sound of this *ah,* Cinibar."

My spymaster draws his legs in and paints himself a serious expression on that charade of a face. "I should tell you, Vermillion, that I may have encountered your eldest on the way here, and not wanting to hold back or dissemble to someone whose rank is, I may respectfully remind you, technically above mine, I may have . . . told him of the list."

I feel a cold chill creep down my spine, and no amount of calming snaptail can hold back the disquiet of my stomach.

"Told him of the list, Cinibar? Or given him a copy?"

"Ah. . . ."

I go to say words I will regret, but I remember Saxe and his nature, and I remember what he did to his predecessor, and I hold back. Such self-control is how First Lords survive centuries, after all.

"I must see Rufous now," I say, standing up a little too quickly and almost spilling my vial. "Before he takes action into his own hands."

"You won't have to go far, First Lord," says Redgrave, whose hearing has always been better than mine. And, sure enough, my eldest son bursts through my study door at that moment, pushing his long blond locks out of his face as he does so. He is wearing his red and gold First Guard tabard, which I take to be a bad sign. Though he is the captain of the twenty-strong elite company of my personal guard, he rarely bothers with its uniform in the palace unless something dramatic is happening.

"Rufous," I say. "Good. We are planning our strategy now."

"I have saved you the time, Father," he replies, all booming voice and toothy smile. "It is already being executed."

I study him for a moment, waiting for my panic to subside. He has his mother's eyes, big and wide, and a long, well-defined face, always clean-shaven, with full lips. The ladies cannot get enough of him. Very little of me is in that face. My likeness was in his younger brother, though not much else.

"Rufous," I reply at length, "what do you mean by that?"

"The list, Father. My First Guard are taking care of that as we speak."

"They are not *your* . . ." I stop, aware of my audience, and begin again. "Tell me what you have done."

Rufous points to the window, to the palace garden, and now I have a very bad feeling indeed. "I think you should probably see for yourself, Father."

I walk to the window and look to the sky, well lit by the moon tonight. My study faces west to southwest, so I can see across the city to the distant points that signal Westfall, and beyond that, Southwestfall. Tonight, however, I see an added sight: the entire First Guard flying toward me. The First Guard are the only ones besides the flight regiment of the city's Blood Guard who are allowed wolfblood to give them wings outside of emergencies. And there they are, all twenty of them, flying in perfect formation, veined leather wings expertly turning to adjust for the currents. This is not unusual.

What is unusual is what they are carrying. Each of them is holding one person in each hand, the strength of wolfblood making it look easy. I see Worns in their grip, and even worse, I recognize—by the clothes and the hairstyles and the better complexions—that there are a few Midways, too.

As I watch in muted horror, they bank left slightly and are out of sight; I know they will be landing at one of the balconies on the southern side. Slowly they all disappear from the skies, and then, moments later, my worse fears are confirmed when I see them all reappear, faster now without their cargo, returning to Westfall to, I assume, take more bodies with them. I try not to imagine the sight in Westfall as people are plucked from their homes with no explanation.

I turn back, every drop of the snaptail doing its blooddamn best to calm me out of my nascent apoplexy. I look at Redgrave, who has been eyeing Rufous with a carefully blank face that might conceal his amusement or his distaste, it is impossible to tell. Then I turn to Saxe, who has his usual jovial smile, which could mean anything of any shade of dark. "Please," I say to them both. "Leave us. Now."

Once we are alone, I finish my flute in one gulp, and I resist the urge to pour another one.

"Rufous," I begin, "what in gods' name do you think you are doing? You cannot just snatch people in such an unsubtle manner, all at once. *Especially* Midways."

"But, Father, I'm sure Worntown won't notice a few wrongbloods going missing."

I wince at his description. It is not language I use myself. It is not that I care for them, but I know what my son was, and if that is what they are called, then that is also what my son is—was—and I do not care for that at all.

"There are more than a few, Rufous," I add. "And not all of these are . . . Some were just his friends. And Midways. And those prominent in the Westfall arts scene. This is the kind of thing that makes them rebel. I do not know how many times I have told you over the years. If you treat them too badly, you stir a white stripe's nest."

"And what of it?" Rufous shrugs. "There have been few attempts at any kind of rebellion for forty years. And the last one, I seem to remember, consisted of fifty bloodvatters high on barely magicked boar blood. It was hardly the riot of the century. Well, I mean technically it *was* the riot of the century, but you know what I mean." Rufous grins. To get him to take something seriously is an achievement I have never mastered. My dead son was too serious and my live one is too frivolous. Such is family.

"Rufous," I reply, "you do not understand the city. The balance we must maintain."

"The balance?"

"Yes. The balance. Things are not like Lightfall, where we controlled them with the illusion of freedom. In this post-Grayfall age, in this smaller city, we must do things differently. To control them, we need them to fear us, and in doing so, if they hate us a little, then that is acceptable. If they fear us, they will not try to disturb the order of things. And though they may hate us, they do not hate us more than they love their families, whom they would put at risk if they try and seek a better life or a better blood for themselves through force. But if they fear or hate us *too much,* then they may think that the risk is worth it, or perhaps they may not think at all. Then you will discover, Rufous, that though fifty vatters is something to be laughed at, fifty thousand Worns is not, and to anger a whole city would be to doom us, wolfblood or no wolfblood."

"Father," replies my son, running a soft hand through his hair, "if it ever came to it, I would cleave through them all myself, with one hand tied behind my back. I met a maid in my dead brother's room last night who had more steel than all the Worn rebels put together."

"I would not be so sure it would be so easy. You fight for sport, Rufous. And you have not had to fight for much else since the war. I rather think they would be fighting for their lives and their souls, and so the fight in them would be fiercer than yours."

Rufous does not know what to say to this, so he scowls. Unlike his dead brother, he does not always have the wit to keep up with me when he disagrees. I realize I have never thought of it like that. I used to hate the arguments with my youngest, at least back in the days when we still talked. Now I wonder if I miss them.

"So you disapprove of my efforts, then, Father?"

"No. It is done. I wanted them, just not in . . . that obvious a manner. Saxe will interview them, and only then—and only if it is warranted—will you have at them in your . . . ways. Do I make myself clear?"

Rufous looks sullen. "As ever, Father." Then he turns and stalks out.

I beckon Redgrave back into the room. "Who is worse, old friend, my spymaster or my surviving son?"

He wisely lets that go.

"Well, if we are correct about the connection to Saxe and my son's death, then his handling of the investigation can be presumed to go nowhere, and the less said about my eldest's contribution, the better."

I sigh and put down my flute, having had enough of the snaptail's calm. "This distaste for the Worns," I begin. "This loathing of them, rather than seeing them as part of the balance of the city. I see it so much now, not as extreme as in Rufous but increasing in the other Lords. We have never had so much power over them, certainly more so than in the last days of Lightfall, yet the more control we exert, the stronger the distaste becomes. I wonder, you know, if we erred when we made the pact with the wolves so soon after Grayfall."

"First Lord?" asks Redgrave, no doubt surprised to hear me take such a detour.

"We were so scared then. We still thought the Grays might press on beyond the Centerlands, try and invade First Light. We knew that wolf-blood and the wings it gives us was our only hope to defend ourselves. Hence that hasty little agreement. I thought it so clever at the time. They send us their criminals. We drain them. We store the blood until we one day have sufficient quantities to attack the Grays, a whole airborne army. Yes, fine. As a deal it made sense. But then we promised them we would not go beyond the Borderlands into their forest lands. We would contain ourselves to First Light. And now look at us. The wolves have the entire eastern coast, all the lands from the edge of the Centerlands through to the forests. We are confined to First Light, the impassable Fang Tip mountains our only escape. Our population is vast compared to theirs, too. And in our haste to confine ourselves, we forgot what happens to a people trapped in one city, who must contend with themselves. We forgot how much we hate our own."

"These are interesting thoughts, First Lord."

"By which you mean if anyone was to hear them, they would think me a Worn sympathizer."

"Not what I said, First Lord."

"I've known you five hundred years, Redgrave, I can parse those dry comments like I can taste the finest wine. The funny thing is, I am hardly that. I was as alarmed as the rest of us at the Worn progress in Lightfall, the opening up of the Blood Markets, their power. I am no anarchist. They must have their place. But we need not hate them for it."

Tired of my soul-searching, I reach into my desk store for a different drink; I pull out a carafe of magicked hawk. It is the opposite of snap-tail's calm, all agitation and intensity, but good for thinking, albeit of the hurried kind. "Enough of this, Redgrave, I am falling into musings. We must proceed with our work quickly."

"I agree, First Lord. I have some ideas."

"I daresay you do, but our next stop is my own decision. I saw—or at least tried to see—where my youngest son died. Now I must see where he lived."

Sam

Lightfall is almost upon us, the last of the night ebbing away, and all I want to do after my meeting with the Leeches is collapse into my rough sheets and sunken bed, but Beth is keen to tell me all about the events of the night that I missed. And by events, I mean the same kind of things I've heard all ten years of my time at the palace. Lamia has a new dress she wants to wear on Hallsday, almost Midway quality. She's not sure where she got the fine linen from, and she's worried the Lord will notice and disapprove. Ceri has been getting extra vials of blood from one of the valets and she thinks that means he has an eye for her, and some have said there might be more in those vials than cow.

It's the cost of having a friend as bubbly as Beth, a constant tide of gossip that I could never quell even if I wanted to.

"Anyway, enough about me, Sam. I've been blabberin', haven't I? What was Lady Hocquard's like? It must have been a proper old digs. She's rich as Cyania, that one. I heard she had a ball last year where even the Midways were given refills of magicked stag."

I smile at Beth's wonder. For a few seconds the boredom is gone. I prepare myself to tell her the truth, of Leeches and secrets below vine-covered mansions. But I don't. Something holds me back. Some instinct urges caution. Is it because I knew Lady Hocquard would be disappointed if I told her, even though I can trust Beth with anything? Or is it that, when it comes down to it, I can't? Sorry, Beth. I'm not as good a friend as you think I am. I'm not even as good a friend as *I* think I am.

"Truth to tell, Beth, I didn't see much in the way of anything while I was there. They had me cleaning in preparation for her Greendeath ball."

"What? So all that talk of asking for a maid of learning was rubbish, was it?"

"Yes, afraid so."

Beth gives me her best exaggerated frown. Every expression of hers is outsize. "Oh, I'm sorry, Sammy. Well, they don't know what they're missing. You could run rings around them if they gave you a chance."

My head reels. Don't be nice to me, Beth. Don't do that.

"Thanks, Beth." I can't take it anymore. "Going to have to say good night, I think. I'm properly drained."

"Yeah, you look it. It's okay. I'll fill you in in the evening. Ain't no escaping me gossip, you know. If I don't tell you, I end up talking to meself."

I put my head on the pillow, closer to my freedom than ever and feeling more alone than I ever have.

7

Powerless

They tied me to a slab, you see,
Born of Light, no family,
They told me straight, all woe, no glee,
A Quantas I shall always be.

Anonymous sorcerer ditty

Sage

There are numerous excellent ways to test a theory, but putting your own life on the line is not my preferred choice. The Grays have seen us, and now I'm either right or we're dead.

Up until now we had spent the journey unseen. Or at least if we were seen, then the Grays weren't informing us of this fact. The first part was simplicity itself. Fifty miles north through the desert, from our temple up to the edge of the sands, where the Grays have never strayed beyond. Granted, yes, we can never be completely certain about that, but the evidence strongly suggests they keep north of the desert line. In a hundred years, nobody has ever been killed by one or observed one venture into the Desertlands, just as none have ever ventured into the Wolflands or attempted to breach the walls of First Light. Or to be more exact, there are no reports of this happening, which is not, of course, the same thing. Whoever they are, though, they appear to have a greater respect for borders than the other races of the continent of the Everland have ever shown.

It was when the greenery of the Centerlands began that the tension really ramped up. The southern Centerlands are vast plains of flat grassland, with occasional spinneys of trees and very occasionally even a wood. Some of the grass is wheat, a reminder that much of this land was farmed by Kinet clans pre-Grayfall. Most sorcerers eat little, and the vampires and the wolves clearly weren't fighting over bread or other nonmeats, but the Kinets stuck to agriculture for several centuries, as agriculture was practice for the smaller Kinet arts and no doubt helped them develop the relatively new art of strengthening and changing blood for the vampire Lords, a far more profitable enterprise.

I have quite enjoyed this part of the journey. The temperatures are still fairly high here, but the sharp drop from the desert is noticeable, and the dry air feels refreshing and cool on my body, which is used to extreme heat. The rain is frequent and welcome. The sky is a vast canvas of blue and cumulus white that, unlike the sand-whipped skies of our home, can be seen stretching on for miles.

Jacob has not enjoyed the journey as much.

I turn to my deputy and whisper, "Now we find out."

"Yes." Jacob nods. "I can't wait. I have some last words prepared. Some basic jeers at myself, then some standard insults at you. I'm going out in style."

The Grays have gathered beyond the tree line ahead of us, standing stock-still beneath the tall oaks and shorter crestwoods that make up the wood we had begun to cross before we ran into them. We are crouched behind some bushes, which is absurd, because they know we are here, but I've got bigger things to worry about right now than our dubious logic. All I can make out of them is the outline of their cloaks; the shades of the woods are obscuring anything else. They seem slight, almost ephemeral. If we were in the desert, I would call them mirages, the illusions that came to sorcerers of old who got lost in the desert during the Twin War, and who had used too much magick to see the world the way it is anymore. These illusions, however, are very real.

"So what do we do now?" asks Jacob, and I hear the fear straining his voice. But not as much as I had thought. Long ago, before my current obsession of the best part of two centuries, I would study the way people's bodies reacted aside from their words. I called it secret signs, the indications of how we really are that go with the words we say. There is a sorcerer, another powerless Quantas like me, who studies it now, somewhere east of Luce. He calls it body talk. I think I will stick with my name for it.

Jacob's eyes are not wide, and he is neither avoiding my gaze nor holding it obsessively. Conclusion? He is not really as scared as he makes out. He really does believe in the rightness of my theory. I feel proud. And a little guilty that I am not so sure of it myself.

"What we do now, Jacob, is we wait to see if the Grays make their next move. Or not."

"By next move, you mean killing us."

"Quite, yes."

Jacob thinks on this. "Do you have any more proactive strategy," he says eventually, "than waiting for the bullet? Or even better, a plan for what happens if you are wrong and they try to kill us?"

"No."

"Oh, good." Jacob rolls his eyes. "Good conversation as always, Sage, thank you. If you need me, I'll just be dry heaving in the grass."

The Grays have moved forward a little now. I can see ten of them in total, all dressed in the same tight gray cloth the continent has come to fear. They even have a gray cloth mask tightly fitted around their face. They are still too hidden to see anything more than this. No one has ever got close enough to them for that. They are all equally spaced out, I notice. About ten feet between each one. I realize, with a deep disquiet, that I didn't actually see them move forward toward us. They must have done it while I was talking to Jacob. But that would suggest . . .

"By the five, Sage!" says Jacob, and points to one on the left of the group, who has pulled something out from somewhere in all the gray. The dying light and the shade of the trees and the semi-camouflage of the Grays' outfits conspire to prevent me seeing exactly what it is, but it has the vague outline of a weapon, short and cylindrical.

"They're teasing us," says Jacob. "We're prey. You've made us prey." His eyes are wide now. The fear he lacked before is there in spades.

"There is no evidence of that," I reply. "Just wait."

And we wait. The spectral figures in the woods wait, too. The seconds tick by, and soon the minutes, and I realize with what might be panic or a thrill that it's been a long time since I have felt such true suspense or peril. I was not affected by Grayfall in any meaningful way and, with one very important exception, I did not see much action in the Twin War a century before it. I was looking for evidence of a mortal civilization while the current immortal one tried to wipe itself out. I have to go back to my beginning for any real tension, back to my birth. All sorcerers are born as adults, through a process we know not. We emerge from the birth chamber and are tied to a stone slab in case we were born mad. Then the Guardian of the Chamber tells us what kind we are.

I have such a vivid memory of the moment. I knew already *what* this world was. The knowledge was already there in my head. I remember trying to sense the answer of *who* I was inside me. Do I feel like a Kinet?

An Atmos? A Cloak or a Neuras? I remember how cold I was; never since have I felt so. I remember being confused and clearheaded at the same time. It was my first and perhaps only true moment of ignorance. I remember the low hum of something behind the door I had come out of, the memories of what caused the hum fading quickly if they were even there. Most of all, I remember the expression on the guardian's face as he told me who I was. Told me I was powerless. A Quantas born, and a Quantas ever shall I be. He didn't try to hide his pity. It was a harsh way to come to know yourself.

I'm shaken from my reveries by a sudden movement. Every single Gray in front of us takes a step back at once, their movements eerily coordinated. Then they take another step. Still watching us. Still silent. Another step. And another. Finally they are swallowed up by the darkness of the wood, and it is as if they were never there.

We wait an hour, just to be sure. We barely talk. We are not sure what to say.

Then Jacob, who has never shown such patience in his life, finally stands up. He winks at me. "You were right, old friend." It's the first time he has smiled since we began our journey. I allow myself a smile, too. "You know what this means, don't you, Jacob? Now we know for sure the Grays won't touch us?"

"What?"

"We're not powerless anymore."

I shake the leaves off my robe and start to walk on, on toward First Light.

PART II

Endless

8

The Stroke of Midnight

If you're bloody stupid enough to find yourself hunted by a wolf, do yourself a favor and make sure it's not Raven Ansbach on your tail.

Chestnut Gevaudan,
Lessons of a Pack Life

Raven Ansbach

As I lie in wait for my prey to arrive, I focus my senses on the scene not far from me.

One minute the clearing is calm, the only noise the pounding rush of falling water. Then a distant thrashing can be heard—the sound of something racing through the forest. The next moment a brown blur bursts forth from the trees and races toward the cliff edge. For another second it seems to slow down, as if pondering its next move, but then it leaps off the cliff edge and plunges into the depths of the waterfall: a graceless, desperate lunge into the fast-moving currents.

The wolf emerges downstream, sodden and bleeding. A normal wolf would have been smashed to pieces on the rocks. But this wolf is merely weeping from a dozen wounds. It gives one frantic look back, eyes mad with terror, then carries on downstream, racing down the riverbank and keeping pace with the current. It comes to a fork in the river and, bracing itself, leaps back into the water, climbing out the other side moments later and sprinting into the wood beyond.

Minutes later it emerges into another clearing and pauses to get its bearings. It sniffs the air for a moment and allows itself a moment of breath; then it careers toward the slope of the hill at the edge of the clearing.

I can smell him strong now. I can smell his sodden fur and scent of fear. Fear is metal, sharp and fierce. Its steel tang fills my nostrils.

As he passes the line of trees at the slope's edge, I detach myself from the nearby branch that has been my hiding place this last half glass and dive through the air, tackling the wolf mid-sprint and tumbling with him across the grass. He is momentarily dazed, and that gives me the moment I need to jump onto his chest and pin him to the ground. He reacts in a frenzy, kicking the air and trying to bite my muzzle. But it is no good. After a few seconds, I tire at his pathetic attempts and snap at his throat, uttering a deep growl that bounces off the hillside and around the clearing.

This has a singular effect on my prisoner. One minute a dark brown wolf is pinned to the ground; the next, the air shimmers and the space around it seems to move at a speed faster than the rest. There is a flash of skin and bone and what may be cartilage, and then a naked man is lying on the ground, blood pouring from three large torso wounds. He coughs and spits blood onto the grass.

"I don't understand. I took the shortcut," he mumbles.

I back off a little. Then I, too, seem to vibrate at a frequency different from the air around me, and suddenly my dark fur becomes tanned brown skin and I stand before him a naked woman, pushing my jet-black hair out of my face.

"If you have to jump off a waterfall . . . then it's not a fucking shortcut, is it?" I reply, edging toward him. He is short in person form, reasonably muscular but stout as well, with a thick mane of auburn hair that falls across his shoulders and carries on down the back. The impression of strength you get from his body, however, is let down by the face: scrunched up behind a thick beard, like a gerbil trapped in a rug, beady eyes looking in all directions. I feel revulsion looking at him, and I resist the urge to end him now.

"You can't make me go back there," he says, a little blood coming out with his words. "I may as well be a barn animal. Letting the vampires bleed me whenever they want. It's not *right*." He glances down at his wounds again. "Look at me. I'm bleeding quite a lot now."

"And mewling a lot as well," I reply. "More a cub than a wolf, aren't you, Tawny Stubbe?" I half spit his name out. "A silly little cub out of his depth."

"Look, Lady Ansbach—"

"I'm not a *lady*. Don't put that vampire shit on me. I am *Raven* Ansbach or am I nothing."

"Look, *Raven,* I know the rules, but you don't understand what it's like."

"Then tell me."

"Er . . . well . . . it's awful. I'm a prisoner, effectively."

"Effectively?"

"I mean I have quarters, but I can't simply wolf-run. And they hate me, you can see it in their eyes. And the bleeding . . . it's constant. A century of this, Raven! It's not *right.*" Tawny tries to emphasize the last word, but his voice sounds faint and feeble under the open sky.

"Are you alive?"

"Yes, but it's not—"

"Yes, I heard you. *It's not right.* But neither is slaughtering any of the wolfkind outside of a hunt. But that didn't stop you, did it, Tawny? Your sense of right has a fleeting quality to it, I see."

"Fine! I committed a crime! Then punish me properly, as one wolf to another!"

"Oh, I intend to, I assure you." His scent is finely balanced now. Fear and anger compete for attention. The strong metal tang curbed by a sharp citrus aroma, one of bitter lemons. I wonder which fragrance will win out.

Tawny runs a shaking hand through his mane. "There was a time when handing over our own to the vampires would've been an outrage. When did we start pandering to the bloodlords?"

I smile, a smile so wide my lips pull back to reveal my pearly canines. This always starts off a smile. But it rarely ends that way.

"*There was a time,*" I begin. "That's an interesting way of putting it. Up there with *Back in the day.* Of course you don't remember that time, because you're a beta wolf from Pack Stubbe. Not a single member in your youthful set pre-date the Twin War, correct? And yet you all claim to know so much about the prewar years. You're practically fucking past-scribers on the topic. And you're always the first to remind all the other packs how wonderful it was when we still counted vampires as the enemy. Maybe you should take a deep breath, count the moons, and try talking to a wolf who was there."

I lean over him and my hair falls across my face so that only my eyes and smile are visible. I didn't expect to feel this rage. You could grow a lemon tree from my perfume alone. "And as for pandering to the Lords, I've killed more vampires in my time than your entire pack and half a dozen others, so don't fucking talk to me about pandering, you dogskin, or I'll rip your throat out before you can blink."

Tawny does not reply to this. I go to say something else, but I stop. It is pointless. There are many wolves who do not like the pact that came after Grayfall. We wolves send our worst criminals to the vampires to be kept for fifty years and bled. To build their stores of wolfblood. Once they have enough, they promise, they will have an army of vampires who can sustain wings long enough to take the fight to the Grays and give us all back the Centerlands. I cannot say I am thrilled at the idea, either. But there are other forests in the world I would like to run through one day, and I cannot see many other ways to do so.

I turn away from him and sit down on the grass. Out here in the hinterland between First Light and the Wolflands known as the Borderlands, where the mountains have given way to green but not yet forest, the sky is a deep sapphire blue. It calms me, even during a hunt. If I focus hard, I can ignore the rotting emotions around me and focus my nose on the river close by—fresh, with a hint of mineral and sulfur. Eventually I pull myself back and I speak.

"You Stubbe Pack, you'll never understand. You've known only the idea of immortal war, not the living of it. You'll never understand the joy of running through miles of forest, because you never had it almost taken away from you. At the height of the Twin War, we couldn't run free. Whole swaths of the forest were not ours to roam as we pleased. And now it is all ours, all the forest east of the mountains. Vampires have but First Light, while we have the whole Wolflands. And all we have to do is give them a little of the blood that fuels their mad dreams of war against the Grays." I pause, breathless. I cannot remember a time I have spoken so much. "You speak of rights?" I continue. "You speak of dignity? I can't touch these things. I can't feel them on my face. I know only the feeling of racing through the forest north: five days, then ten, then fifteen, barely stopping, barely breathing. I come to the northern coast and I take a breath—and then I turn around and I do it again. And as I do, I think: All this is mine. All this is *wolf*. And ever will it be so." I turn to Tawny. "And a whining cub like you won't put an end to that, that much I can fucking promise you."

I shrug. I am myself again. "Now, where were we? Let's see. General pack law states that fleeing a term with the vampires—"

Tawny mutters under his breath, "It's not *my* pack law."

". . . makes you forfeit to a serious penalty of permanent pack exile.

However, your original crime was slaughter. So your punishment is death."

"Fuck you, you bitch."

I sigh. This is vampire talk. To call a wolf a bitch is stating the obvious, and it sounds ludicrous from another wolf. The implication of inferiority is even stranger. There are no sex slurs in the wolfkind because an alpha is an alpha, regardless of whether they birth the cub or contribute to its birthing. These words are symptoms of a vampiric virus, and one day, perhaps, I will rip all their throats out to salve it.

Tawny spits on the grass. I smell the fish from his last desperate meal. "They call you the Midnight Assassin. But you're just a tool. You're no freer than when the forest was taken from us."

I smile, ignoring his baiting, and sniff the air. "It's going to rain," I say. "May as well get this over with."

Tawny stands up, wincing from his wounds. He turns so the setting sun is on his face. "How does it work?"

"I rip your throat out. It's fast. Almost painless. I'm maybe the only wolf who can kill one of our own so quick."

Tawny growls. "Lucky me." His eyes flicker toward the hillside for a moment.

I shake my head. "It's too late for that," I say. "Your wounds may have stopped bleeding, but you still wouldn't make it ten yards."

His head drops, and I smell the beginnings of tears. "It's not fair to kill one of your own. Great Wolf, it's not fair to kill *any* of the immortals. There's centuries, maybe *millennia* more for me to see. And now it's all gone." His voice falters. "It's not fair."

I stand next to him and steal some of the sun for my own face. "It's never fair. Do you think death is better if you've had more of life? If death came for me today, I would not welcome him with open arms, little cub. I would fight and snarl and aim for the throat. Death is death. It's always unfair. You've just had your slice of unfairness a little earlier than mine."

"But *you* might live forever."

I shake my head. How little he knows. "I'm not immortal. Nothing is endless, Tawny Stubbe. It's the great lie." I laugh. "Ha! Listen to the shit I'm saying. A good sunset always makes me philosophical."

Tawny's face falls. He is a beaten wolf. "Just get it over with," he says.

"As you wish." I step back at first, but as Tawny closes his eyes and waits for the end, I am suddenly behind him. I put my lips to his ear.

"Just one more thing, Tawny," I whisper, soft and languorous. "I forgot to mention one little detail. The wolf you slaughtered—he was my nephew."

"Oh no," begins Tawny, but this is as far as he gets before the air itself moves behind him and a great growl fills his ears. He turns in time to see the sky turn black, midnight black, and then I fall upon him. I pin him down, savoring the moment, and then I give him agony. First I bite his hand off, and then his nose, and just as his screams begin to hit my ears I bite his tongue off, giving a new timbre to his shrieking. Choking on his own blood, pieces of him rapidly falling onto the grass, he gurgles his cries of anguish as the seconds drag on. Somewhere in all his orchestra of pain he finds the strength—even as I am busy tearing his cheek open—to lift his head up and stare directly into my eyes. Does he see a wolf in there, or does he see a person? I do not know.

Then I rip his eyes out as the sun sets behind us.

9

How the Game Works

Vampires never quite have enough of the blood they want. It is what drives them, when you get right down to it. You see it in their main religion. The Bloodhalls. What are the Bloodhalls? They are a place, literally above them, far above in the heavens, where the Blood Gods, their alleged progenitors, feast on the best blood, the pureblood. If you follow the Blood Gods and you bleed for them in the prayhalls, then when you die—if you die—they will let you sit with them, sit with your own gods and have the best blood for eternity. An entire religion founded on neither morality, nor mystique, but a never-ending supply of blood.

Kinet Levillion, *Religions of the Continent*

Sam

I wake and go through the motions. Same motions of a decade. Dress, ablutions, then first evening cowblood, drunk from tired wooden cups in the Worn serving quarters. We sit on low rough malderwood benches, mostly splintered, staring up at low stone ceilings, no windows to give us even the distraction of a moonlit sky. The glum silence of a room full of maids who know that they have the same rota of cleaning ahead of them that they have had six days a week for gods knows how many years on the kind of blood too weak to help them get through the drudgery.

Except today is slightly different. Today is the funeral of the young Azzuri. It has been a month since he died, and that time has gone so slow I hardly can bear it. One month since I met a first maid with a heavy accent of a long-dead city and a knife at my throat, and her noble Lady the Queen Leech. I told myself I would hear something from them. But now I've come to realize, slowly but surely, that Lady Hocquard won't be calling on me again. Because the Queen Leech was talking out of her no-bleblood arse. I see it now for what it was: a promise to keep me happy, while she took some information that could be of use for the cause. Sweet-talk the strange little maid, then send her back to her carpets. It seems that secret underground networks of maids work just the same as the Lords: saying whatever they want to get what they want. It doesn't matter which path I take. They all end up at the shitheap.

The worst part is, I haven't even braved using the forbidden section of the library yet. All that knowledge waiting for me. But the knowledge that the Leeches have their eyes on me, if what the Lady said was true, makes me wonder who else might. For the first time, I feel nerves. For the first time, I feel obstacles strewn across my path to freedom, just when I thought I finally had a clear run at it.

It's unbearable.

Sage

We turn the corner and there they are: the city walls of First Light a mere half mile ahead of us.

Since our tense encounter with the Grays in the southern Centerlands, we have not seen them again—not so much as a glimpse. With the freedom this gave us, we made good time. Just under a month, from our temple to the gates of First Light. Just in time for the funeral. That is a remarkably quick journey, probably helped by the fact that we rode all day and as much as we could at night without tiring the horses. Although we knew we somehow had a pass through hostile territory, we still weren't that anxious to rest too long in the eerie, abandoned world of the Centerlands. And what a strange world it is, or, as Jacob pithily put it one morning, "I miss the shading desert." We took the route diagonally northeast across the continent, but stayed westward far enough so that we were away from the ruins of Lightfall and indeed from the ruins of any of the other major towns that fell in its wake. Our choice of route no doubt added a couple of days to our journey, but we weren't keen on being haunted—or distracted—by the remains of a once-great land. Most of what we encountered, aside from empty winding roads, was the occasional deserted village—once occupied by sorcerers or wolves or vampires, now abandoned—and the closer to the northern mountain ranges we got, the more vampire-based it was.

We had an inkling of what to expect from the few reports over the last century of those who managed to survive the journey through the Centerlands—you can count them on the fingers of a wolf-mauled hand—but it was still a shock to see. There were no bones of the vanquished anywhere, no skeletal corpses. Vampires obviously leave no corpses anyway, but the bullets of the Grays leave nothing behind for any of the immortals; sorcerers dissipate in a burst of light as if consumed by their own magick, and wolves melt, as if drowning in wolfsbane. All that we saw, then, were the signs of the lives they had left so quickly or died attempting to leave. Farming implements rusting in the fields where they were dropped. Glass bloodvials abandoned on the road. An occasional cart tipped over, the rotting remains of the wood giving it the air of a carcass of a strange beast.

Villages aside, it was almost as if nothing had happened; wildlife was free, freer in fact with fewer wolves to chase them or vampires to bleed them. The farm animals were long gone, but the wilder beasts thrived.

Jacob and I spoke little; we were cowed by the discovery of our immunity and what it could mean for our kind, although I suspect Jacob was also suffering from not getting his eight hours every night and the whiskey spirits that saw him through it. I spent my time thinking about how the sudden loss of people in an environment can change it. How had the rivers changed in a hundred years? How had the forests? A sorcerer more inclined to these things could spend many happy investigations on this, and there was a large part of me that wanted to end my journey here and write my findings on a world without immortals.

Then there is the other great mystery of the Centerlands, the answers of which may be contained somewhere in its borders. This is the land where vampires, wolves, and sorcerers began, back before the Great Intelligence, when they were mindless beasts. The few still alive from that period cannot remember the transformation they underwent to self-consciousness; they just were, they claim. Suddenly sentient. Their memories are suspiciously hazy on this fact. I have tried inquiring of them as to whether they remember mortals being present. But it is no good. No, somewhere beneath the ground lies the answer.

But as long as there is a chance that it was Azzuri's investigations on our behalf that got him killed, and the ensuing mystery that would follow from this, then I have to keep going and ignore my scholarly calling; the twin perils of guilt and curiosity driving me forward into unknown territory.

Finally we reached the northeastern ridges of the Fang Tips, just beyond the valley where First Light lies, nestled below the start of the mountain ranges proper. When I last visited the first vampire city well over a century ago, the city wall had been nowhere near as impressive or well-built. It is not particularly high—certainly lower than I imagined—but then again there is no evidence that Grays can fly, and they have never shown any inclination to wheel around siege engines, so height is a little less important. Thickness, though, it certainly has that: great slabs of limestone two feet deep bound with mortar. It makes sense that the vampires would fear that an enemy with deadly weapons beyond reason might possess devices to blow through rock. I don't see any recent signs of building, though; perhaps the lack of any direct attacks on the wall since Grayfall have lulled the vampires into some false sense of security.

"Here we are, then," says Jacob behind me. "Can we run the last half mile? This biting little wind is pissing me off, frankly. I'm in strong need of a warm fire and a warmer companion."

"No," I reply. "We proceed slowly. With our hoods down. And we remain close to the torchline. If they mistake us for Grays, the wind shall be the least of your worries."

Jacob sighs. "You know you're the cause of all these worries, don't you?"

I groan. "Remind me why you've accompanied me again?"

"Because when you get going, you sound like you're reading from a thousand-year-old scrap of parchment, whereas I can talk to people in ways they can actually understand."

"I didn't realize it was that hard to communicate with coingirls and bartenders."

"Work on that joke, old friend, and in a few years you'll get some jest out of it."

As we near the gates, sticking to the long line of torches, we hear the faint sound of a bell ring out to mark our approach. Soon archers appear at nooks in the wall, and guards peer down at us from the top of it; soon after that, the wall is awash with torchlight and half-concealed figures. They look like tiny insects darting through a great hive, or ticks on a great animal, jumping about while the beast itself slumbers. I have a sudden urge to flee into the night, back to the forests and the Grays and the solitude. I resist it. I have, I believe, had quite enough of solitude.

"Why would it have mattered anyway if we had arrived by day?" Jacob asks. "Why don't vampires have a roof, like the one that covered half of Lightfall? Vampires have always been slow at innovation and shit like that, but I have to give them their due; that was impressive. But this place is a lot smaller. In the hundred years since Grayfall they could have covered the whole shading place."

"I don't know," I reply. "But if I had to guess, I would say it is fear."

"Fear?"

"They built a roof over half of their city. Barely a year after it's finished, the Grays came out of nowhere and destroyed said city. I believe the more religious of the vampires think that the Grays were punishment from the Blood Gods for having the audacity to walk so freely in the day."

"Light of Luce," says Jacob. "I'm missing home already."

We are almost at the wall now. They must have established we are not Grays, because slowly, inexorably, the stone gates are swinging open. The hidden levers behind their opening groan and shriek through the night. I turn to Jacob.

"Once we're in, we're in, old friend. Are you ready?"

Jacob shrugs, and the thoughtlessness in his eyes suggests to me that he is not as wary as I am of the place we're about to enter. "You're here to satisfy your curiosity," he says. "I'm here to sleep with vampires. What is there to think on?"

We walk on, and First Light swallows us.

First Lord Azzuri

I do not know what to make of these sorcerers. They are the first to have entered First Light since the Kinet bloodmages came with us in the desperate flight from the Grays a century past. This in itself is surprising enough. But shortly before they were ushered into my chambers, Redgrave told me who they were. Now I am *very* curious.

We are seated by the fire; I would not normally have it roaring like this, but we are fast approaching the official beginning of winter and the weather has taken a turn toward the wind-chilled mountain cold; I barely feel it on my blood, but the desert-based sorcerers will not be used to it. After the usual pleasantries, I give them a quick appraisal before we begin the conversation proper. The one introduced as Brother Bailey is tall, slim, brown-haired and stubbled, with the light brown skin of the desert mages closer to the Centerlands. However, his companion is short and muscular; he has the short, groomed beard I associate more with vampires than mages, and his skin is midnight black, like the mages in the deep desert south.

They wear identical robes, not surprising for sorcerers of the same sect, but it is the style of the robes I am drawn to. The lack of markings is unusual, at least if the trends of the mages left in First Light are anything to go by. The Kinets who work on the Blood Farms wear robes of red with orange stripes, with patterned wrist ribbons and robe ties denoting their sect. Meanwhile, the handful of Neuras in the city wear disconcertingly bright white robes, unpatterned on the front but with the ink drawings of a large pair of eyes on their back, with small gemstones set into the cloth in the middle of the pupils. The same ink and jeweled eyes pattern appears on their ribbons and robe ties.

The mages before me? Nothing, just plain green robes bereft of pattern or variation anywhere. Even the color I am not used to. I have not come across Quantas very often. It is not a mage type I am familiar with. This could be diverting.

"I have a number of questions," I begin as my valet plies them with the finest Lucemead I could get my hands on. It is not quite as good as the kind you get in the sorcerer south. But we can hardly send a cart down there to get the good stuff anymore.

"Of course, First Lord Azzuri." Brother Bailey nods. His colleague has, I notice, taken a great liking to the mead. His cup is almost empty already.

"Please, call me Vermillion. You speak for the Archmage while you are here, after all. Now I have to admit to being *extremely* curious to know how you both survived the journey here. I hardly need tell you that you are the first since Grayfall to do so. I understand you are both Quantas, are you not?"

"Yes, we are." Brother Bailey nods again. "As are all in our sect. And please, call me Sage, and my Second Brother here Jacob."

"Your sect is the Cult of Humanis?"

"Yes."

"I have heard of you, I must say. Many in Lightfall followed your studies with interest pre-Grayfall. You believe the mortals were real, not myth, am I correct? And that they ruled across all the continent, only to disappear and be replaced by immortals?"

"A very workable summary, yes," replies Sage.

"And have you found proof of this yet?"

"We have accumulated . . . suggestive artifacts. Certain carvings from underground sites that may pre-date the oldest immortal settlements and suggest materials or crafting superior to anything we have.

Nothing definitive as of yet that is worth boasting about. One day we hope to find solid proof."

"And what will you do then?"

"We will show our findings to the continent, of course. And strive to learn if anything can be learned from such a race of people. Perhaps about our own origins."

"And when do you think that will be?"

"Not before too great a time, I hope," he replies, and I see now that this is not the first, or perhaps maybe even not the hundredth, time he has had this conversation, and I am less likely to get definitive answers from him than I am to get a tan.

"I see," I say. "I am told by my first man that it is the fashion in some mage circles to believe that the Grays are such mortals, returned from wherever they have been to claim their lands back. Your reputation has been much improved based on this, I believe."

Sage nods politely. "Some people think this, yes. We have not been able to formulate an answer on this one way or the other. As for our reputation, I suggest you overstate its luster."

"Can I ask why you have not come to a definitive answer?"

"Because the Grays are quite hard to study, what with their habit of killing anyone in their vicinity."

I can't help but smile. I thought the sorcerers in their desperation to send anyone might have sent a loosetongue or someone shorn of any idea of how this game works. But while this Sage Bailey is clearly more at home with relics than people, I can see that he isn't a complete fool, either.

"But you must have an opinion on the matter, surely?"

He shrugs and inspects his mead before taking a long, slow slip, the sign of someone who is purposely taking his time over a well-prepared answer. He is taking well to this diplomacy game, but I have been doing it for centuries and I know all the signs.

"It is possible, though I have my doubts," he says eventually. "The strange weapons fit with some myths of the mortals, though nothing we know of them corresponds to how the Grays look or explains why they have spent the last century simply roaming the land as killers, restricting us to the outer reaches of the continent yet building no cities nor staking any physical claim to the land."

There is a strange sound from Jacob next to him, and I turn expectantly, only to see he is just finishing the last dregs of his mead loudly. "Well, that leads me to my next question," I say quickly. "How in the Bloodhalls did you make it here alive?"

"I wish I could give you a definitive answer," replies Sage, who for a man who wants to give answers is remarkably bad at doing so. "But I fear it may have been luck. I know the more subtle passages across from my years of traveling the land on the cult's behalf prior to Grayfall, searching for clues to the presence of mortals across this land. I can only assume that in taking such ways we happily avoided the path of the Grays."

"And yet," I reply, "you made it here remarkably quickly. Just in time for the funeral, in fact. These subtle passages appear to have corresponded surprisingly well with the quickest route to First Light."

"As I say, our knowledge of the land is great."

I pause a little, toying with the idea of pulling this argument apart. As if the Grays could be avoided by taking a slightly less traveled path. It is an answer borne of idiocy, and this sorcerer is clearly no idiot. But it would be undiplomatic to press the point—at least for now. I lean forward to pour some bear blood from the cut-glass decanter on my side table into my flute. Then I sniff it, dragging the moment out, using the time to plan my next move. The bear is not magicked. It does not pay to be too . . . energized in a careful game of cat and mouse like this. "So that brings us to the question of why. I am grateful, of course, that you are attending my son's ceremony. But why would you risk your lives, when so many in your kingdom decided not to?"

"Honestly, First Lord?" says Sage. "Your library. It is a veritable treasure trove of information, the biggest in the land, even bigger than that which remains in Luce. There are tomes in there that, I believe, would cast valuable light on the time before we immortals ruled the land. Potentially information on the mortals, maybe the kind we could use to prove their existence beyond doubt." Well. A man of his books, apparently. There are few left in my city like that.

"Hmm," I reply. "Well, I would not be surprised if there was, Brother Bailey. I could live for millennia more and not touch the sides of the collection in there. I once found a book, old and faded, about a village far in the northwest of the continent, far north even of the ruins of Shadowfall. In this village, the vampires worshiped cows as gods, can you believe that? Believed that they were the first animal to have blood, and that only cowblood was the true kind. If enough cows could be bred, then the gods would reward them with invulnerability to the sun. They conquered ten villages in the end, had themselves a miniature empire of sorts, but since cowblood doesn't stop aging, it didn't last long. But when I spoke to the oldest vampires I knew, even they had never heard tell of such a place. There are wonders in those tomes, I have no doubt."

The mage nods. "That is what I am hoping for." I see something shift in his eyes then, as if he has decided something. When he speaks, it is hesitant. "Do you know, Vermillion, why I devote my life to these myths?"

I am intrigued. I sense a real confession that goes beyond diplomacy is forthcoming. Such things happen about once a century. "Why, Sage?"

He turns to his fellow sorcerer, as if regretting his forthrightness, but Jacob simply shrugs. "If the mortals were real," Sage begins, "and I know I have no proof of this yet, but if they were . . . then we don't know where they went. And we don't know if they will come back."

"If they came back . . . would this be bad?"

"From what little we know or suspect?"

"Yes."

"It would be very bad."

I sit back and sip my blood thoughtfully. There is so much this sorcerer is not saying that lies behind what he is. I take back what I said about the bear blood. I wish my blood today had been more magicked and a better animal. I could have done with my mind being just a little more alert for this conversation. It is just like my father used to say: always choose the right blood for the right meeting.

"You keep making allusions to what you know of these mortals you devote your lives to researching," I begin, hoping I can keep up with myself. "You say you have no definitive proof of them, yet you seem to suggest you know a great deal more than you say. What exactly is it you have in your temple there? Is it just scraps of lies and indeterminate bits of rubble, like most think, or are you holding on to something more?"

"When we have things worth saying, I assure you, First Lord, that the streets will resound with the sound of our saying them."

"A bold statement for a pair of such devoted dreamers."

"First Lord?"

"It's in your motto, is it not? *There are worlds beyond mine and things I have dreamed to touch.* I do my research," I add, seeing their surprised faces. "Do you have any particular worlds in mind, or is it simply the realm of sleep you are referring to?"

"Like all dreams, ours are best kept to ourselves until we have fully ascertained their meaning."

"A very diplomatic answer. You are taking to your charge rather well, Sage Bailey. I also feel you are lucky few sorcerers respect or believe you, else you might have more visitors to your cult temple. And trapped in First Light, I have no power to satisfy my newfound curiosity. I wish I had visited you pre-Grayfall."

Sage's eyes narrow a little, and I fancy I see in their dark hazel depths a twinkle of joy in the game we are playing. "It would have been a pleasure to have you, but I suspect you would not have come away satisfied."

I stare at him. He stares back. He looks away. He is more adept than I took him for at this business, but he hasn't quite mastered the confrontational stare.

"Well," I say eventually, smiling to lighten the mood again. "Perhaps one day you will give me some answers that I need, and maybe you will play a role in the fights to come." I turn to his deputy, who is eyeing the bottle of Lucemead on the drinks cabinet. "And what of you, Jacob? Feel free to speak your mind. We are all allies here, in this strange era of the Grays."

The bearded sorcerer looks up from his mead cup, with a look of what I think might be lack of interest or boredom. It is difficult to tell. "I hope very much the mortals existed, First Lord," he notes, placing the cup down, having seemingly abandoned all hope of a refill. "Because otherwise I have spent fifteen decades on study when I could have spent them on women."

I see Sage raise his eyebrows and try and stare through his deputy's head.

"Pardon me," says Jacob. "I mean, I could have spent them on *more* women."

The three cups of blood are before me, and I try each one. I do not have to do this kind of thing today, of course. In one hourglass I will stand just south of here in Sunset Square before throngs of Lords and Midways, with thousands of Worns crowded in the smaller squares beyond, straining to get a view of me. I will read the rites of the Blood Gods over an urn containing my youngest son's ashes. Then the Gothia of the Bloodhalls will read the psalms of entry, preparing my son, still trapped in the ashes, for his journey there, and the urn will be carried out of the square and to the nearby suncrypt. There it will rest until lightfall the following day, when the sun will stream through the aperture in the roof of the crypt directly onto the ashes and take my son up into his afterlife.

It is not a common ceremony. Not recently anyway. There were many of them straight after Grayfall. But almost none for any of the nobility since. So I should really be practicing for my part—but the dry business of ruling does not go away simply because my son can now be held in my hand. I tell myself that, and it almost sounds true.

"These are the latest batches, are they?" I ask, turning to Redgrave before studying the cups of blood again. We are in a room on the cellar level of the West Wing to which only Redgrave and I have access. It is sparsely furnished: simply the basic gelmwood table in front of me and a leather-backed armchair Redgrave placed in here to make the place look more presentable, as if we would ever use this for anything other than the task at hand.

"They certainly are, First Lord. From the left, the latest magicked batches of stag, hawk, and whale."

I smile. "One from the earth, one from the air, and one from the sea. Very elegant." I sniff them. I am immediately impressed. There is less of the slight tang you usually get when magick has been applied to the brew. "Are they really as good as the Kinets say?" I ask my first man.

"The sorcerers claim that they have increased the maximum strength of the non-wolfblood varieties from an increase of four times a vampire's strength to five times, First Lord."

"Really. And how the bloods do they know that, then? Do they have rows of volunteers punching walls being monitored by scribers who observe the dents?"

Redgrave gives me his best neutral expression. "Actually, First Lord, I think that is *exactly* how they do it."

"Hmm. Well . . . good."

"I know some of the boasts from the Kinets make the eyebrows rise, First Lord," Redgrave continues. "But I do think they are making progress. Slowly but surely, the magick is making the blood more potent, I am sure of it. And so are the official tasters."

I study my first man. He is very hard to read, especially with that ridiculous moustache, but I think I see conviction on his face, not the usual subtle way of saying one thing when he wants me to sense something else. It was he, I recall, who convinced me to bring the blood-specialist Kinet mages to Lightfall shortly before Grayfall. He had heard of their exploits: how these days they were increasingly focusing not on moving large objects, like the Kinet sorcerers of old, but on the small, on the invisible. They began with alcohol and food, changing their properties. Then they claimed they could move the very makings of animal blood, permanently, in ways that make it stronger, more potent.

Redgrave convinced me their claims had merit and that it could change how we think of blood forever. I risked outrage giving sorcerers so much power over how we get our blood. I am not sure some of the older Lords have ever forgiven me. But the results were impressive, more so than I ever dreamed, and so when those of us who survived raced away from the Grays back to our ancestral home of First Light, I made sure the Kinet bloodmages were in tow. They may well be our future, after all. If we can ensure that the blood of animals that are easier and less diplomatically troublesome to source than the wolfkind has the same potency of wolfblood, then the countdown to our fight against the Grays may be reduced to years, not decades.

"But are they close yet, Redgrave?"

"Well, you can judge for yourself now, First Lord, but the truth is that they are not yet there. Or anywhere near it. But it will come in time. Of that I am sure."

"Really? You think sorcerers will give us that which our vast supplies of wolfblood once did? Will we fly on stag? Have the strength of fifty on fox? Maybe one day achieve near bloody invincibility on cowblood?"

"Anything is possible, First Lord," says Redgrave. "I have learned that, in my time."

"Oh, but drain it all, Redgrave, I wish they would. Then we could abrogate that ridiculous arrangement with the wolves. Everybody thought we had arranged the deal of five centuries when we signed that compact. Getting the wolves to agree to provide us with a continuous supply of wolfblood, all on the off chance that one day we will have stored enough up to do battle with the Grays? We couldn't believe our luck."

"I recall," says Redgrave, barely disguising his deadpannery. "I was there."

"Well then, you'll remember it was what kept us going in those bleak bloody months after Grayfall. Gave us a little hope. But the more time passes, the more I think the wolves never believed our plan would ever work or even that we are storing it. They probably think we are just getting high on their blood in secret. All they care about, I am sure, is that they have a dumping ground for the worst criminals of their kind. And every time they escape—and they always bloody escape, even if Raven Ansbach always bloody catches them—we get a firsthand glance at how blooddamn dangerous they really are. I just hope it's worth it. I hope we can store up enough so that we can fly across the whole bloody land ten times over, if we so choose. Let the Grays try and shoot us then. Let them try!"

I pause, a little flushed. Redgrave is looking at me politely with *that* look.

"Yes, thank you, Redgrave, I am aware I am talking too much and might possibly have switched over to ranting. I am, as ever, very aware of what I am doing with you standing there. But if you say something, then, old friend, we will have words."

"Yes, First Lord," he replies, wisely avoiding eye contact.

I turn to the flutes on the table in front of me. I begin with hawk. I tip it down me in one.

"It tastes good. It is drier and more subtle than I expected. This is good news. We must not lose the complexities of flavor in the attempt to make it stronger."

"Wisely put, First Lord," Redgrave says. "And the mood?"

I wait a minute or so. "Mildly euphoric . . . I get the energy but controlled. Still calm. Perhaps a hint of aggression underneath. Less so than the hawk I am used to. More like . . . stag."

"Yes, the sorcerers do seem to be using that as a template."

"Interesting. Stag is almost perfect in that respect. I'm not sure everyone would like it if all blood felt the same, though."

"Something to be wary of, for certain, First Lord. Finally, what of the strength?"

I turn around, searching for a spot on the stone cellar wall behind me. As my veins begin to throb, I feel the surge of power of the superior blood coursing through them. I pull back, and then my fist punches into the wall, making a satisfying crack, small chips of stone flying past me. The mark is deep, slightly deeper than the rest.

"An improvement," I note.

"Not for the decor, I fear, First Lord."

"Well, bring me the Gray that killed my son, and I'll leave a mark on them instead." It is a strange way to broach the subject, but today is a strange day.

My first man does not reply. He knows when to remain silent.

"It has been a month, Redgrave. *A month.* Yet still I have barely more information on why my younger son is a pile of ash than the average Worn. I am losing patience for Saxe's plan. He has not gained any useful information from those whom my eldest son spirited so obviously from their homes, has he?"

Redgrave looks at me and I look at him, and we both know, in the way you do with someone who has been by your side for at least as many decades as two pairs of hands can count, that he is about to try and give me false hope. "There were many Worns and Midways to be . . . interviewed, First Lord. Just a little more time is all he needs, I am sure of it."

"I want answers soon. Or I will take matters into my own hands."

I am silent for a while, then, leaving the implications of my threat hanging in the air, hopefully sounding more ominous than it felt. I feel the mix of blood settle a little in me, calm me somewhat.

"I haven't been to his room yet," I say, looking at the table and not at Redgrave. "I remember showing him there, after our desperate flight from Lightfall. He was only four decades old, then. To be chased out of his home couldn't have been pleasant. I showed him around his suite, and then I grabbed his shoulders and looked in his eyes. 'We will not be here forever, my son,' I said. 'But this is our new home for now. We will make it strong and good, and we will put Grayfall behind us, I promise you that.' It was meant to be encouraging, words to bond me with him, but he just looked at me with sad eyes, not the fiery ones like those of his older brother. I remember being annoyed that my speech had just washed over him, and I wanted to shake him, shake him hard, until his sadness sloughed off him like dead skin and he snapped out of it. 'Father,' he said, his soft voice barely audible, 'our *old* home was strong.

And our old home was set to last forever." I remember being affronted by his cowardice, and wondering how a son of mine could wallow in fear, and I remember that I did not speak to him again in those strange first few months of First Light, and from then, of course, our relationship only deteriorated. But now, as I visit this memory, all I want to do is go back and do it again: stay a little longer in his room and speak a little more to him."

Redgrave doesn't say anything to this, and I am glad, because I could do without the words.

10

Of Tragedy and Flames

*When Lightfall died, many had to adapt to a new and, depending on
your perspective, much less welcoming and egalitarian society. Thus,
many of the great characters of legend are found in humbler roles now:
pay attention to your barkeep, for they may have changed whole cities.*

Redfold Steelclasp,
What We Lost (An Outlawed Text)

Sage

I'm in the library when I'm interrupted. I don't want to be disturbed, not
by anyone, but certainly not by this person. Tonight is my first chance to
make a start on our investigation, as the last two nights were taken up
with the necessities of diplomacy—endless socializing with all the vampire nobles seeking to converse with the first new sorcerers in First Light
since Grayfall. All expressed surprise at us being here, though none with
the intelligent suspicions of the First Lord, I was relieved to confirm.

So while Jacob is finding some alternative disguises for us—even on
our most innocent sojourns to find evidence of mortals across the continent pre-Grayfall, we always found we needed to cover our identities
at some point—I am drawing up the foundations of our investigations;
getting back to first principles, if you will. Start at the basics before you
dive into an investigation, or you might find yourself diving into the
shallows.

So here I am, with some parchment and a quill, and a slim selection of
volumes to help me. The first point I noted is that we are not investigating
the young Azzuri's murder. We are investigating what *he* was investigating: what Saxe and the other Lords uncovered under the ground shortly
before Grayfall, where it is now, and what it is. If that is also what got
him killed, then in that sense, we can honor him, given our role in what
happened. But if it is not, we must still focus on it, since it is the only
known example I am aware of of someone other than the Cult of Humanis finding something that may have been of the mortals.

With that basic tenet sorted, I can finalize two lines of inquiry. The first must be the Blood Bank, that repository for all the most valuable types of blood the Lords own and, no doubt, other items that Lords want stored in its ultra-secure vaults, too. That is the only real clue we have to go on as we know from my original meeting with him that the young Azzuri believed whatever it was had been found had been secured in the bank. In that respect, the book currently in front of me is a slender volume detailing the inner workings of the Blood Bank. It was written a mere five decades ago post-Grayfall, so I hope its accuracy will be high. Somehow we may need to find what vault this great find was put into.

The second line of inquiry is vaguer. If we are to know what new information Azzuri found that may have led to his death, we must follow in his footsteps: know his associates, those he spent time with. That will be difficult. There may be little written down in the library about that. This may require getting acquainted with the locals. Jacob's forte, in other words.

I lean back, gazing at the great frescoed library dome above me, and allow myself to succumb to memories for a moment. I have not approached a task like this for a while, not since my inquirer days back in Luce, when I investigated rogue sorcerers—thieves and murderers. The sorcerer capital gave me many opportunities to fine-tune my skills in this regard, although I also had to go to some effort to avoid lightning-wielding killers and illusion-creating criminals while doing so. My last fifteen centuries of the cult have been less interrupted, but our attempts to travel the continent to find any evidence of the mortals required less investigative zeal and more archaeological capacities, and since Grayfall I have not had to use even these skills for anything, becoming more of a curator.

It is . . . refreshing. I wish it were not due to the murder of a good man, but still.

I return to my book, only to find the spymaster of First Light about to break my peace.

Lord Saxe walks up to my reading desk, a beaming smile on his face. He stops a few paces before me and looks up at the library beyond it: the endless rows of shelves filled with everything from mottled and ancient parchment to tied vellum bindings to elaborately carved and gemstone-inlaid volumes; the ladders that lead up on either side to the floors above; the desertmold sconces that permanently light them in that strange haze, all the way to the topmost floor; and above that, the domed ceiling, elaborately frescoed with scenes of vampire history.

Then he breathes in deep. The smell of these books attacks and flirts with the senses, offering strong aromas and pungent stenches. They have absorbed much over the decades and centuries. Some exude a damp, musty odor. Some seem to give off a bouquet of incense, reminding the reader they were made in places holier than this, certainly holier since the spymaster walked in. Although I have to give him credit. He knows his audience, and he is putting on a show here, wishing me to see his appreciation for the written form.

"Amazing, is it not?" he says eventually.

I leave that be, like most redundancies.

"I'm sorry, where are my manners?" he says after a longer-than-necessary pause. "I am Lord Saxe, spymaster of First Light and overseer of the Wolf Jails." I take him in: the tousled blond hair; the small eyes; the unexpectedly large grin; the thin frame, which combined with his all-black costume makes him appear as a walking shadow; and the ring on his finger with the key-over-the-owl sigil engraved on it, which told me who he was long before he introduced himself.

I stand up, resigned to a little more diplomacy and much more acting. "Sage Bailey, First Brother of the Cult of Humanis. A pleasure, Lord Saxe."

"No," he says, seating himself in a chair opposite. "The pleasure is mine. What a novel event it is, to see a sorcerer not already resident in First Light! Why, I fancy I would be less surprised if a Gray itself waltzed through the library doors right now!"

"I am glad to be a novelty."

"Ha, yes indeed. But let me be serious for a moment—and commend you. Such resourcefulness to avoid the Grays! I hear from my noble Lords on the First Councils you met with the other night that it was your knowledge of the lesser paths to First Light that ensured your life?"

"And luck, I suspect, Lord Saxe. And luck. And the smallness of my party."

"Yes, of course. We must never underestimate luck, should we?" Those tiny eyes appraise me for a second longer than is normal, but only a moment. He is good. Not as good as he thinks he is, but good.

"I must also," he continues, running a hand through his untamed locks, "commend your Archmage on the foresight of sending you in the first place. What a shrewd mage indeed he must be to know you would prove so capable at evasion. I'd almost call it magick, were you not a Quantas!"

I ignore the Quantas gibe, cleverly not dressed up as one, but a gibe nonetheless. "Well," I reply, "the Archmage knows of my extensive travels pre-Grayfall throughout the continent searching for mortal ruins. He had great faith in my ability to travel undetected as a result."

Saxe smiles far too widely. "Yes, I imagine as well." He gets up then, surprisingly quick, and turns away from me to survey the reading stacks.

"Speaking of extensive travels, did you know the young Azzuri spent some time in the Desertlands? Shortly before Grayfall, in fact."

"I did not," I reply, edging slowly around this new trap.

"Ah, no matter. I thought perhaps he might have paid you a visit. He went quite near to where your temple is located, I believe."

"You were with him on this journey?" I ask carefully.

"Ha! Good gods, no. But I would be a careless spymaster if I was not aware of the travels of the First Lord's progeny, would I not?"

"You would, yes."

Saxe waits a few seconds, extending the silence, massaging it. He is not the first spymaster I have known. He is not the first inquisitor of conversation. Their cheap parlor games to elicit information or nerves are no longer of interest to me, as I have studied all the finer arts of them. Still, although he's not effective, he still manages to be unnerving. It is important to maintain eye contact with such people, but with this one you risk falling into those eyes of his, eyes that have nothing within them, nothing at all.

"Anyway," he says eventually, "I have cruelly stolen enough of your valuable reading time. I imagine you are heartily sick of me and my kind and our blather, and I do not blame you! I shall leave you to your readings. You are an intelligent man, and such hours are valuable to you, I imagine. As they are to us all," he says, loading it with meaning that I am meant to parse if I could be bothered.

"You are very kind, Lord Saxe."

"Cinibar, please, Sage. Let's leave the titles for those who haven't earned them, shall we?"

And like that, he is gone, and I gratefully delve back into my words, thinking, not for the first time, how superior they are to people.

First Lord Azzuri

"What," I ask, staring at the urn, "were you doing?"

My son doesn't reply, because all that is in the urn is ashes, my son's spirit having left for the Bloodhalls for all eternity to feast on the finest bloodwine: even better than wolfblood, the scriptures say. I try to let this thought calm me, but the image feels wrong. My youngest had always stayed clear of the drunkenness on feast days, preferring to stick to his own company, or, if I am honest with myself, preferring the company of certain others throughout the city. He was not the kind of vampire you would expect in the Bloodhalls; not the blood-guzzling, womanizing, sun-mocking lord of darkness that most look forward to becoming if they have the bad luck to swap immortality for ashes. Either the Bloodhalls would have to adapt or my son would.

I examine the gold-coated urn, along the rim of which are two lines of scarlet red and sky blue; beneath these is painted a thin drop of blood, double outlined in the same colors—my family crest. It is strange seeing my sigil here. After all, my son had made it very clear in his early youth that he wanted nothing to do with the Azzuri line. He had calmed as he had aged, or at least had seemed calmer, but it seems now that maybe I knew nothing of what lay underneath. I will never know now because he is dead, and centuries of understanding him have slipped away in the blink of an eye and the impact of a bullet.

"What were you doing out there, my son?" I ask, and then repeat myself, louder, because I want the anger to come; I *need* the anger to come. "What were you doing?"

My questioning sounds hollow, though, and my rage dies in small echoes on the walls of the crypt. I look around. The crypt contains the ashes of my father, who died almost two hundred years previous in one of the Twin War's many battles, killed in the palace I live in now when he refused to abandon First Light to the wolves. It also contains the ashes of my grandfather, who died in one of the smaller wars three hundred years before that, when the city I rule now was the only one, and the small worlds of vampires and sorcerers and the wolfkind were beginning to collide. Of my line before that, I know not. There are few books or records detailing that far back, before the building of First Light, the first city, and the beginning of the recorded age. My father used to tell me of how the Azzuris were said to have played a part in the very first vampire town, not long after the Great Intelligence and the move from tribes to larger settlements. But there are no records to confirm this, and there are few vampires alive from then. For an immortal race, we are remarkably bad at surviving long ages, and those lucky ones from back then who have navigated and survived the many conflicts since have extraordinarily poor memories, it seems, or else a reluctance to disclose them.

So, compared to my ancestors, I have been lucky. I have survived great tumult, if you can call this life survival. It would drive a man mad, if madness had not been something he had come to terms with already. After all, how could you be in this city and not have arrived at a comfortable agreement to be both sane and insane? Inside the city I am Lord of all. But outside, I am the hunted, the soon to be dead—prey for the Grays. I speak of the coming war with pathetically scant evidence we can ever hope to fight it.

"Why did you do it?" I ask, and this time my anger hangs in the air before fading, and I find myself waiting for a response, waiting for the ashes to spill out of the urn and form the face of my son, mouthing the answers to my questions from the beyond.

Unsatisfied, I get up to leave. "Fine," I say to the empty air, "I'll do it myself."

Sage

"So," Jacob says behind me as I put the finishing touches to my ruminations, "what is our plan, then?"

"By the five magicks, Jacob, is it so hard to knock?" I reply, turning quickly in my chair to face my deputy. "I might have been . . . indisposed."

"If you mean naked, then I've seen you naked, which wasn't the greatest day of my life, I can tell you now," replies Jacob, depositing himself in an armchair in the corner of my chambers and resting his legs on an expensive quacian-wood side table definitely not meant for the purpose, "and if you mean indisposed with a woman, then that unprecedented sight would be worth the interruption."

I scowl at him, then walk to the window and peer out at the gardens stretching out across the palace grounds. My guest chambers face the southern gardens of the palace; the herb garden is directly below me, and I see laborers tending to it. I am surprised the Lords still bother with herb-mixing now they have magicked blood to get excited about, but there we are.

"Our plan," I begin, "is twofold for now. I will seek an audience with one of the Blood Bank's senior clerks, on the pretense of learning their processes to assist with sorcerer treasury practices. I will try and learn more of whether there is something in there that Azzuri could have been puzzling over."

"Boring conversation, very appropriate for you. And me?"

"You, Jacob, will go out and find his associates, and learn what, if anything, he told them of his own investigations."

"Debauchery and common folk, very appropriate for me."

"Needless to say, you will have to be careful. There is peril in everything we do here."

Jacob raises his eyebrow. "Peril? More peril than the time we went to Shadowfall to pick that relic up and accidentally came across a bloodvial heist?"

"That was high jinks at best. We are out of our natural habitat here, Jacob."

"We've never been in our natural habitat. We search for relics."

I riffle a hand through my hair. "And now we search for relics still, but also, incidentally, a murderer. It is a different order of things. Not something I've done since my inquirer days. When I didn't have you to worry about."

Jacob scowls and jumps out of his chair, only to search through my chest for any discarded flasks. "You've got it the wrong way round there, Sage, as usual. I'm the one who worries. Worries for the skin off my back after all your plans. I didn't want to come here, remember? But your guilt and your desire to know always win the day over my desire for a quiet life."

I laugh. A thousand miles away from home, but the conversations still end the same. "If you really wanted that, you would have stayed in that bar in Quintile when I met you. Now get ready. We need to find a lead. It's time to start looking."

"Well," says a new voice from behind me. I spin around and notice that the door Jacob left ajar is now opening farther to reveal a face I don't recognize. "You won't have to look very long."

11

These Eyes

The sorcerer met a vampire, but the vampire met a mage,
But the mage had met a wolfkind of considerably lower age.
It all got mixed up, so it did, and in the end they vowed
That four be better than a pair—who cares if it's allowed?

Jane Brown, unnamed song from
A Collection of Worn Favorites,
edited by Stephanie Manning

Sam

I don't think I've ever made an entrance that good. I doubt I ever will again. I walk into the room, riding the wave of whatever madness seized me, and I look the mage I know to be Sage Bailey in the face.

It had started with a hunch. Glum over my snub from the Leeches, I was pushing a mop sadly across the tiled hallway floor in the South Wing, adjacent to the bloodstores, when it had suddenly hit me. Azzuri's note had mentioned the mortals. And the sorcerers who arrived in First Light? The ones who caused such a stir by making it here alive? They, Beth had informed me earlier, were from the Cult of Humanis. I had never heard of such people.

My readings on sorcerers weren't as advanced as those on my own kind. I mean, I've had only ten years and it's a big library. I knew the basics. I knew that each sorcerer type, even the magickless Quantas ones, had their own city. The Kinets had Kintile; the Cloaks had Clostile, the Neuras Neurile, the Atmos Atmile, and the Quantas, Quintile. Very tidy. Very strange. Very sorcerer. Within these cities, the sorcerers were further divided into their own sects. The sorcerer capital city, Luce, was home to the sect headed by the Archmage, that oversaw the others. Then there were the cults, the gatherings of sorcerers who wanted nothing to do with the cities and went off to do their own thing in the Desertlands outside the populated areas. The Cult of Humanis were one of these, but that was all I could work out. That, and the promising name . . . for could it really be a coincidence that Azzuri had mentioned mortals, and the cult obsessed with their legend are the only ones brave (or foolhardy) enough to attempt such a dangerous journey to pay their respects?

Well, yes, it could, but I'm not going to engineer my freedom simply by putting everything to chance, I know that much.

Time to frequent the library, then. When I'd entered, that familiar aroma of parchment, vellum, fragrance, and musk enveloping me instantly, I headed straight to the sorcerer shelvings on the ground floor. But I could find nothing, only some general tomes on cults and some specific ones on others but nothing on the Cult of Humanis. Not even a brief mention. I spent two nights on this. Then on the third night, I had a thought. I retrieved my vial of wolfblood from the back of the wardrobe where I'd stashed it—dangerous, but where else was it going to go—and I returned to the third floor of the library and the bookshelf that hid the forbidden section.

I took out the vial of wolfblood, and then I froze. The sound of the great library doors swinging open reverberated across the library tiers. I could hear footsteps on the marble floor, stopping at one of the ground-floor bookcases, two levels directly below me. I held my breath. This wasn't just for effect—you never know how good the blood is that a vampire stranger's on and just how good their hearing will be. After what seemed like an eternity, the footsteps headed back to the main doors and these shut again. At least I hoped. Unless this was a ruse. I thought back to Lady Hocquard and the Leeches, and who knows else who could be watching me. For a second, I rethought my plan. But that moment was brief, and my need? My need was great.

I tipped a little blood in and the bookcase swung open, revealing blackness. Venturing into the corridor, I once again downed a little fox to improve my eyes. At the first shelf I came to, I quickly pulled out tomes haphazardly, not really knowing yet exactly what I was looking for, and realized something I hadn't before: unlike the rest of the library, these books weren't ordered by category or subject matter. They were randomly placed. Here was a volume on the effects of wolfsbane on the wolfkind. Here was a tired-looking collection of pamphlets recording the failed expeditions to the Ashlands seven centuries ago. These weren't meant to be easily found. They were simply stowed away; forbidden texts the light of which had to be dimmed. I should have guessed this, given the lack of seating areas and the random nature of the arrangement of the shelving. But it hit me at full force and I felt pure rage. Rage on behalf of the authors whose thoughts were deemed too poisonous to be given air. Rage at the idea of topics deemed secret by a ruling class. Rage for the opportunities lost to scholars. Secret knowledge; the paradox of a fallen society. For a second I wanted to burn them all, just like when I found my mother's ashes outside my door, just like when they took my father away, just like when my sister blew away at my feet.

Then my rage died and my ambition returned, and if I admit that the second always wins, then I won't apologize for the admittance. I remembered what I came here for. I searched anew. From the looks of the rows of shelves that stretched beyond into the gloom, there must have been a few thousand volumes in this forbidden section. I realized how long it was going to take.

It didn't.

The fiftieth book I came to was the one. Entitled *A Storied Overview of the Many Cults,* volume 1, and written by a sorcerer called Neuras Sondallion, it was modern by the standards of some of these books, written only ten years before Grayfall. Sapphires winked from the binding and the cover. Sondallion was clearly a respected writer. I sat there and absorbed what I could. Then I slipped from the library to the bed, with the decision made. One more act of bravery, Sammy. One more.

Sage

I stare at the maid with the intelligent eyes. Those eyes, a thinking person's if I ever I saw a pair, are narrowed now, and she has a fierce, determined look about her, but she can't hide the slight tremble in the little finger of her right hand or the erratic movement of her pupils. She is not used to this kind of thing. Quite used to it. But not fully.

"I see," I say, skipping the pointless steps. "You're a maid in the palace. You know something. About the young Azzuri. You've gambled that we're allies."

She stares at me, then past me at Jacob.

"I'd just go with it," Jacob says, shrugging. "He's like this."

"I've read about you," she says, fixing me with a stare. "You were an inquirer in Luce. Two hundred years ago. You hunted sorcerer killers. Solved mage murders. Then one day after the Twin War you went to an abandoned cult temple in the northeast desert, far from Luce or any of the sorcerer townships, and you founded the Cult of Humanis. You recruited members to look for relics of the mortals. There's stories of you digging into the earth or hunting down relics in Dawn Death, Shadowfall, and Lightfall, as well as the Desertlands. Most people believe you are chasers of myth. That you have found nothing but old immortal relics, mistaken for evidence of a kind that never existed.

"Some, though, believe you now that the Grays are here, those that wonder if they are the mortals returned. Mostly you're still mocked. But if the scrap of paper I found in the young Azzuri's room tells me anything, then it is that he believed you. And now you're here. The least likely candidates for diplomats ever. So here I am, putting my life in your hands."

I inspect her. "Where did you get this book? I wasn't aware so much information was on me."

"In the forbidden section of the library."

I smile. "That sounds like something that could get you killed."

"Yes." She nods. "I seem to be doing a lot of those kinds of things recently."

"Can I ask more of this note you just said you found?"

"Perhaps. Am I right? Can I trust you?"

"You knew you could trust us the moment you saw us."

"Maybe, but I'm not very used to trusting anyone, so my judgment might be suspect."

"Excuse me," says Jacob. "I hate to interrupt this clever conversation, especially as I'm sure you both had many more clever lines to use that would have been very witty and everything, but can I ask my good friend Sage here why we skipped the denial part and went straight to the 'yes, we are here under false pretenses' bit? I feel pretty strongly that this admission was perhaps something we could have discussed beforehand."

"Oh, what's the point of wasting time, Jacob?" I reply. "Our new friend here is clearly on the same side as we are." A slight caution comes into my voice. "Right?"

The maid looks at us for a while, deciding something. "Yes," she says eventually.

"Yes, what?" I ask.

"Yes, I've decided to trust you. It's either that or back to a life of rags and cleaning drunken Lords' piss stains from carpets, so it's not really that much of a choice, to be honest."

"I don't blame you," says Jacob. "You should see what I've done to my room."

I watch her carefully. Her demeanor is fascinating. She has the look of someone who has spent a life in a box and has just been let out. I can see her teaching herself to be the person she needs to be. I went through a similar process a long time ago, when my chance came. I feel myself desperately wanting to trust someone I have just met. I always jump to conclusions, but can I be blamed when the conclusions so often turn out to be right?

"You know us," I say, "so maybe we can start by finding out your name."

"Samantha. Ingle by blood. Call me Sam. And there's someone I think you should meet."

12

The Wolf of All Streets

Poverty and riches exist so close in a comparatively small city such as First Light that to travel from one area to another feels positively grotesque at times. I am glad vampires have expanded to more modern Centerlands locales such as Lightfall. The times when First Light was all vampires have to offer are gone, gone forever. The continent is better for it.

Quantas Quastan, in a letter to his wife,
Scarletia (dated one year before Grayfall)

Raven

I read his scent like I am reading a book. I'm with him on his journey, just not at the same time. He is a much harder hunt than Tawny Stubbe. He's not running scared. He's enjoying himself. He thinks he will evade me. Or if not, he will have a good time while he tries. He is much more dangerous than Tawny; what a privilege to have another hunt so soon, and one of this caliber. I feel a thrill race along my fur.

I sniff the ground again, and I put his journey together. Upon escaping the wolf jails that lie on the eastern tip of the city, escaped wolf prisoner Sunset Garnier—red-blond, insane, a genius and a serial murderer—ran west until he reached Southeastfall. He then raced through this part of Worntown, heading west. As I follow his path, I weave through the outer streets, where the homes are little more than hovels built of straw, not even the basic Worn houses you find deeper in. Even a wolf taking shelter on a hunt in a wolfshack would want better surroundings than these.

Most of the time Sunset ran on all fours, but sometimes there were obstacles best suited for a human, so he quickly changed, before changing back to wolf seconds later. It is an odd strategy, but perhaps it is better suited for a city. I wouldn't know. It has been a long time since I spent too much time in one.

It is night; a night hunt is much different from a day one. Especially when you are hunting in a city you are not really supposed to be in.

Everyone knows that wolf prisoners sometimes escape, but they rarely flee into the city. I am allowed to be here to catch him, but does everyone know that? I do not particularly care, but if I do not keep to the shadows sufficiently, they and their terror may come to do all the caring for me.

Soon I am deep into Southeastfall, and the straw hovels have become the basic Worn houses of wooden strips lined with mud, straw, and sand that you find in Worntown proper. The sun has only recently gone down, so the streets are still bare, allowing me to run at speed without causing chaos. I try and push away all the scents coming my way. There are the physical ones: the fumes of bloodwine from the night before, still pungent even as the new night begins; the aromas of flowers from boxes in the street-facing windows, part of the continuing quest on the Worns' part to combat the smell of stale spilled cowblood in the streets; the stench of bitter piss, where some at the end of the previous night didn't wait till their latrines—you know when vampire piss is around, this is for certain. Then there are the emotional ones: the lingering decay of lust (for wolves smell sweetness only on our lust or that of our lovers; everyone else's is decay); the scent of roselily, where the sad drunks stopped to weep on their way home the previous night; and the fresh crestwood scent of adrenaline and excitement I get, which tells me that some young urchins have got up before everyone else and are parading the streets, perhaps to play or perhaps to pickpocket. Who knows with these lawless vampires?

I surprise only one soul as I race through these lanes. A woman with no home, still stinking of the previous night's affairs, starved of blood, her woolen cap half off her head, stumbling along, rubbing her hand on her face like she's trying to raise herself out of her slumber. She takes one look at me stalking the shadows, and I know she won't tell a soul, because her eyes tell me that to her I am merely a figment of one of her vampire hells. I smile to show her that this vision will not eat her, not today, but I do not think it helps.

Eventually I leave Southeastfall, groaning inwardly as I realize that Sunset proceeded into Centerfall, the central hub from which all the chaos of this overripe city extends like spokes from a hub. Soon I am at the Centersquare, which houses all the buildings of business and pleasure for the nobles and the professional Midways. I have very little time before this place becomes so crowded that even my centuries of dancing through the shadows just outside of the sight of others will not help me. I feel a need to stop caring; to sow chaos as the Midnight Assassin dances her way through the halls of commerce and finance. But I do not wish a dressing-down from my spymaster Saxe, as such a conversation may end with my jaws around his face, and that would cause me tiresome diplomatic problems.

So I try and quicken the pace without losing Sunset's scent. It is stronger now, which is good, as it means I am slowly catching up with him. I glance to my left and note the squat form of the Blood Market building, three stories of limestone and marble in the Old Mage style. The frieze running atop the columns that support its entrance displays carvings of what looks like thin containers of blood crossed over each other like swords. Sometimes when I am forced to talk to the younger vampire Lords, they try and steer the conversation to what goes on in there. They patiently explain to me these new, or at least only fifteen decades old, concepts of the invisibles: the things you own in the market but cannot touch. They tell me how it is like buying a vial of blood, except you don't buy it, you buy the theory of it, the invisible vial. If the actual new batch of magicked blood is popular among the Midways or the Lords, then you make coin on your invisible as the cost of the blood itself rises, but if it is not, then you lose your money you placed to hold it.

They patiently explain all this, these youthful Lords of Tomorrow, and then I tell them that I have been around for five times their lifetimes, and I already know all they know, but I simply do not care. Then I tell them I did care for the original market in Lightfall, when there was actual blood to be had and Worns could have some of it.

This usually shuts them up.

Suddenly I catch a scent—strong, ripe—coming from one of the makeshift cloth tents behind the Blood Market, where the early reports of the new batches of blood are sent to be scoured over before the information is sent to the Blood Market itself. I go to inspect, knowing what it is before I get there. At the tent's opening, spread out before a table with scrolls laid out on it, is a Midway, dressed in simple cotton shirt and breeches, which are covered in his blood, now dried, which came from a large hole in his chest, the organs that once occupied it scattered all around him in a playfully random arrangement. Even wolfblood cannot bring him back from this. His eyes alight on mine and fix themselves on me, the life almost gone from them. He will turn to ash soon once it has gone for certain. I turn back to my quest. It is not appropriate for me to be there when he bursts into dust. More precisely, I do not have the time. I nod to acknowledge his death and wonder if the sight of a large black wolf from the realms of history will be the last thing imprinted on his irises.

I run quicker now. This will cause a lot of trouble. A serial killer wolf running around the city murdering Midways. I wonder if Saxe will get in trouble with the First Lord for this. For a second I wonder if I should perhaps leave Sunset to his fun and see what chaos it brings to these well-blooded nobles, but the ones below such people do not deserve to die for my amusement. Probably.

Sunset's scent takes me out of Centerfall, and to my great and endless fucking relief, it does not take me up to Northfall and the First Lord's palace, or northwest to the Blood Farms and the lodgings of the Kinets who magick the blood. The last thing I want is for his scent to be masked under vats of varied bloods or, even worse, for sorcerers to be involved in this. Instead, it seems to go to Westfall. Sunset's lust for kills happily accords with my desire for an easier environment in which to get lost in the shadows.

I hear the three bells ring out now as I approach Westfall; my tour of the city has taken a third of the night, and the city is teeming. I linger in the dark along the roads west from Centerfall, avoiding the main one. At this time, the only reason I am not seen by all is because on these paths are mostly Worns and poorer Midways, whose eyes cannot discern the pitch-black of lesser-lit paths from the raven black of my fur.

As I enter Westfall, that strange place in this city of strangeness where Worns and lower Midways perform and live together and do the arts and the plays and the painting and the crafting and all the things that wolves do not quite understand or have a care for, I sniff the ground again and see that no, he did not stop here, he turned south to Southwestfall, the other Worntown. I think of all the hovels there, and the Worns, now bustling around the place, easy prey for the fun Sunset will want to have. I growl to myself. Better a blood to die than a wolf, but I would not have the lowest of the low ripped apart by this madman. I have seen their pointless lives up close; they are nowhere near merry enough to justify such an ending.

I pick up the pace.

Urn Street is the most westerly point of Southwestfall, almost at the mountains. I have run the entire course of this rotting-scent city, and even on my legs, with centuries of untired feet at the end of them, I feel it a little. His scent is strong enough now for me to know my journey is almost over. Nearly as strong is the fierce metal taste in my mouth, which tells me fear is hanging over this street; that its residents have fled or are quaking in their hovels, having encountered a large insane blond-red wolf in their midst.

In support of this, I see a cart knocked over; glass vials lie smashed in the mud outside the trader's house it must belong to. Blood rats have scurried out from their hideaways to lick at it—a feast better than their usual cow, it seems. The street torch has gone out; vampire torches do not go out easily even in Worntown, so I sense the fun of Sunset here, no doubt inspiring terror in the locals.

There is another stall farther down the street, but this one is more intricate, perhaps the stall of a visiting trader more wealthy than the Worns he came to chance his luck with. Vials, jugs, and carafes and everything in between lie smashed across the street, as well as some night orchids and day flowers and rugs and pots and shawls and boots, some with nails in and some barely worth the name. I sniff hard and catch the sharp steel of the trader's fear still lingering, and I see a pool of blood, vampire blood, that tells me he did not escape from the remains of his stall completely unscathed.

Now that I know Sunset is not too far away, I briefly consider masking my own scent, giving myself an added advantage in these unusual surroundings. But that is not what wolves do. The hunted, whether wolf or otherwise, should always know that they are being sought. If they escape, so be it. I wouldn't know. It has been several centuries since I have lost my prey.

At the end of the street is a small hovel, half hidden behind the bend, where it curves around to a darkened alley that runs parallel, where it seems by his scent that Sunset stopped a short while. I switch to person form and step lightly, in case of disturbing its occupants. The door is open.

The ground floor consists of a single room, with a stove in one corner; the murky contents of a pot on it haven't cooled yet. Whoever lives here was warming blood a short while ago. I proceed up the stairs in two silent bounds. I know he is no longer here, but I am quiet anyway, out of habit.

It is a fairly large bedroom for such a hovel, the slightly rotting timber frames that support the thatch roof arched across its high ceiling and casting down thick rectangular shadows in the candlelight. I can smell immediately that it is the house of a coingirl. You get used to many odors as a wolf. The salty tang of semen is not among them. On one side is a bed, little more than a blanket on a straw base, with a thin fraying pillow. A dressing table stands next to it, adorned with makeup and jewelry. Opposite the bed is a large wardrobe, with faded gold panels—surprising excess for such a place. It must have looked nice once, but now it is splintered and lopsided on its hinges. I have no time for furniture myself.

The rest of the room is cluttered with clothes, and all the clothes are covered with blood. After a few seconds, I find what I am looking for, through smell rather than sight, as the body has been stuck behind the wardrobe. I am not sure why. There was no point in hiding it. Maybe he just thought it was funny. The body is badly torn up; he was short of time and took no care in it. Her face is unblemished, aside from a spot of blood. Beneath the neck, the internal organs have been rearranged and muscles ripped aside, all for the sake of covering his fur in as much of her blood as possible. The taking of an immortal life just to try and disguise his scent from me; such an empty act. I almost wish it had worked. At least she would have served a purpose. But instead I will just sniff out her blood, rather than his scent, so her death was entirely pointless. He must have lost his brain when he lost his freedom.

I stroke the blond hair of the dead coingirl stuck behind the wardrobe. It is soft and dry, in stark contrast to the liquid carnage of the rest of her. "I am sorry, strange girl," I say. "I will make sure he hurts."

It is no consolation. She doesn't feel better. I don't feel better. I switch back to wolf, and I am about to jump out the window to carry on the hunt when I get the scent. I stop for a second and sniff. There it is again. It was hidden beneath all the vampire blood.

In so short a span of time as to hardly be a moment, I realize that I was half-right. The blood was meant to be a disguise. But not for him—for his trap.

But then the full second arrives, and the blow to the back of my skull knocks me unconscious.

I hear him first as I come to.

"The great Raven Ansbach. Scourge of the vampire battalions in the Twin War. The Midnight Assassin. The Endless Hunter. The Black Death. Have I got all your names right? You seem to have a predilection for them."

My vision comes back, and surprisingly late, so does my nose. I wish it hadn't. The wolf in front of me is filthy, even aside from being covered head to toe in blood. He is in person form, with sun-blond hair, long and ragged, and an even more blond and ragged beard; the blond is tinged with a hint of red. You would never guess his true nature to look at him, aside from his eyes. We wolves have very expressive eyes. And this one does not disappoint. They are wide and blue and bright, and as completely insane as they are fiercely intelligent. I would try and rip them out, but the wolf behind the eyes currently has a blade to my throat.

"A blade," I note. "That is ambitious, Sunset."

Sunset Garnier shakes his head. "Not particularly. It would not cut your throat, not completely, but it would take an inconvenient amount of blood from you for a while. Perhaps you cannot be stopped, but you can, like all living things, be seriously . . ."—he licks his lips a little—"inconvenienced."

"So what is your plan, Sunset?" I ask.

"Who says I have a plan, Raven? Perhaps I simply wanted a respite from my captors, who are, to a man, dull, even by vampire standards. Perhaps I just wanted to run. Perhaps I just wanted to . . ."—he sniffs the air and smells some of the blood on the paw not holding the knife—"hunt."

"This is not hunting. This is pure slaughter."

He smiles, those large eyes taking me in. "Well, I don't really have much challenging prey here, do I? Sometimes you have to make do."

I sigh. I am annoyed with myself. I have gotten sloppy. A couple of centuries ago I would have still spotted his scent in the room lingering beneath that of the blood. That's what happens when you don't have a war or a feud to hone your skills. A century of hunting desperate criminals has taken my edge off. But only to a point.

"I mean, Sunset, what are you going to do now? I will heal a couple of hours after you slice my neck, assuming you have the strength to do it properly. Then I will hunt you again, two hours behind the pace. All it will achieve will be to add to the challenge, make it more satisfying for me."

Sunset sighs. "I don't think you understand, Raven. My hunt is over. You see, you don't have to chase to be the hunter. Sometimes you just have to run."

I growl. "This cryptic nature of yours is getting boring."

Sunset shakes his head. "I doubt that. I think your current life is boring, Raven. I think that, when you are not hunting escapees, who, let us be honest, hardly compare to your hunts of old, you are forced to stay near to First Light, prevented from returning deep to the Wolflands for any great time; forced to commune with the bloods. Well, I offer a chance for something a little new. It is why I escaped. I wanted to meet with you. To make you an offer. Of course I thought it best to do so on my terms, because you do not always converse when you catch your prey."

"I always offer last words," I point out.

"But I am in need of words that begin something," Sunset says, his eyes looking off in the distance for a moment, as if tracing the sanity lost to him. "Something very exciting indeed. I am in the business of chaos, and you will gift it to me."

"There you go again, Sunset, with the cryptic. But I can spin a riddle, too. Let me tell you a story."

His big blue eyes look at me, and I look at his hand holding the blade to my neck. Despite his insanity, he has a very still hand. "Why not," he says. "Tell me."

"Once there was a wolf," I begin, "who wanted to be better at being one. So they went to the best wolf they knew, and they asked him how they could become the perfect hunter. He told them to go to a fast-moving river and stand by the side, then prick themselves and let a couple of drops fall in. Then keep abreast of the drops until they hit the bend of the river, and then swallow them back into their body."

"I see," says Sunset. "A basic parable. Let me guess. You are the wolf, yes? And this is a story to tell me how powerful you are?"

"No," I reply. "Not powerful. *Fast*." As the word comes out of my mouth, I shoot my right hand up and grab the blade, even as he edges it into my throat. His reflexes are quicker than I thought but still not as quick as mine, and though it nicks my flesh and some blood flows, I have pulled his hand away before much damage has been done. With my right hand still holding his wrist, I use my left to chop his throat with my outstretched palm. He gasps and drops the blade, and before he can breathe again, I am standing, and now I focus on the arm of his I am holding. It is hard to break a wolf's arm. As well as strength, the act needs the right angle and a bit of luck. I have anger in me, helped by the spotless face of the coingirl staring at me, and so I quickly find both the strength and the luck and snap his arm, watching as the bone shoots out of its socket. Then because I have lost myself a bit to my nature, I carry on bending the arm and watch the bone stick out farther and farther, before suddenly bending it in the opposite direction so it breaks anew.

He screams and half gargles, and the sound is unlike anything I have ever heard. All screams are different, like fingerprints or irises. The variations I have heard in my time are endless.

But after the screaming has stopped, he begins to laugh, a little blood coming from his mouth. "Now I shall have to kill again, to speed this healing up," he says, face collected again, as much as that expression can ever be, "so all you have done is ensured more prey."

"And what makes you think this is anything but your end, Sunset? You killed the alpha of your own pack. The sentence is clear."

"He was rude and also a rapist."

"Is that meant to be a defense?"

"No. But merely to point out that the thing that got me imprisoned was perhaps the most understandable of all my crimes. We must all bathe in our hypocrisy a little sometimes, you just as well as me."

"Perhaps. Yet this is still your end, Sunset."

"No, it is not, Midnight Assassin. I will tell you something, and it will preserve my life."

I laugh and pull on his twice-broken arm for fun. To his credit, he does not scream again, but real pain makes his face sane for a second. "Remember who you are talking to," I tell him.

"This is something you will want to hear, Raven. What they do with the Grays. What they had *me* doing. There are secrets to tell that can make both our lives very interesting."

I am reluctant to pause in the pain I am bringing him, and I can smell his death in the air, so I hardly want to stop. But of all the things for him to come out with, I was not expecting that.

Still playing with his arm bones, I acquiesce.

"Tell me everything, Sunset Garnier."

He does.

13

True Allies

*The Cult of Humanis, depending on who you ask, are either a raving
bunch of mind-be-gones, a harmless group of outcasts who really believe that a strange stone here or some odd symbol there is evidence of
an entirely new race, or a dangerous outfit whose real aim is to rede-
velop old sorcerer crafting in the name of pastscribing. As with most
things, the answer is most likely a mixture of them all.*

Neuras Sondallion,
A Storied Overview of the Many Cults, volume 1

Sam

In a guest room somewhere on the second floor of the Queen Leech's
mansion, there's awkward silence, and I'm in no hurry to break it.

When I turned up at Lady Hocquard's unannounced, with two sorcerers in tow, the look on Alanna's face was something I won't soon forget. I explained everything in a slightly breathless fluster, as if someone
was in the act of pickpocketing my words. She didn't say anything, but
her mouth narrowed a bit, and this was more unnerving than anything
she could have said. Then she escorted us to the guest lounge, leaving us
there, still wordless.

Now we wait. I hope we don't have to wait long. All that balled-up
energy I was carrying when I first burst into the mage's room has drained
away. My newfound friends seem a lot less nervous. Sage is very closely
inspecting the portraits of Lady Hocquard's family and ancestors that
dominate one wall of the room. I see he's drawn to the older portraits.
The oldest is a roughly drawn canvas that depicts a startlingly tall vampire shrouded in fog and bearing his fangs, all feral and beast-like; it's
nothing like the newer portraits, all clean strokes, posh stitches, arranged
decor, and careful smiles. Times and styles change, I suppose.

Jacob, meanwhile, is very closely inspecting the drinks cabinet,
which sits next to the fireplace on the wall opposite. It's an impressive
three-shelved monster in varnished redoak. While the first two shelves

are full of freshly stocked blood carafes and flutes, small engravings denoting the animals, the lower shelf, which Jacob is inspecting, appears to hold the plain bottles and jugs, which I assume are mead, normal wine, and other mage spirits. Lady Hocquard hasn't had time to have these stocked especially for the mages. She must be a woman who prepares for all things.

As for me, I'm sitting nervously on a leather-upholstered Ceruli seat big enough for three people. My other options were a long green padded seat and two mahogany chairs, cushioned on the seat but not the back, in contrast to the luxury of the other seats. There's something not quite right about this arrangement; everything at the palace is carefully coordinated and carefully manicured, but here it's thrown together like someone who's trying to put up an extravagant front, but whose heart isn't really in it.

I turn from the seats to stare at the grand marble fireplace, above which is some fancy plasterwork that took someone a lot of time for a pile of coin. Under a plaster dome is an elaborate frieze, and if I squint, I can just about make out that it's a scene of foxes chasing hares. A lot more effort has gone into this than into the other decor. Maybe the Lady is telling us something. I suppose she couldn't exactly put leeches up; foxes had to do.

When the Lady herself finally comes in, at a pace brisker than a wolf on a hunt, I can tell she's wary, angry, and a little confused. Not that she's making it obvious, but her eyebrows are slightly raised and her lips are a little pursed, and when you've spent a decade trying to avoid upsetting or rousing nobles, you learn to tell the small signs of unhappiness. She's wearing a light yellow dress, and the blue scarf is still there from last time we met, but her necklace is gone and the curls of her hair seem a lot less carefully arranged under those elaborate braids, with fewer flowers woven in. I wonder if she's changed in a hurry from her Leech clothes. Behind her enter two maids, including Alanna, who fixes me with one of her manic stares. You've done it now, Sam.

"Sit down, please," Lady Hocquard begins, businesslike. Sage quickly takes a spot next to me on the Ceruli seat, and Jacob collapses on the long chair, thankfully not putting his feet up but instead awkwardly slouching against its back.

"My first maid tells me you are the mages who came for the funeral," Lady Hocquard continues. She pauses to pour herself bloodwine from a large carafe into a thin bloodflute, while the second maid pours us drinks before leaving the room. I (worse luck) get oxblood, while the mages get Lucemead. "The ones who evaded the Grays. A remarkable achievement, I have to say, gentlemen. Makes you wonder what the rest of us are doing trapped in this city, doesn't it?"

"Well, it seems you've heard of us, my lady," replies Sage, dodging the comment about the Grays, which sounds like a sensible decision to me, judging by the layer of ice it came in. "But for the sake of an introduction, I am Sage Bailey, the First Brother of the Cult of Humanis, and my associate and old friend here is my Second Brother, Jacob. The Cult of Humanis is—"

"The cult obsessed with the myths of the mortals, yes. I am not completely unaware of events outside my kingdom," says Lady Hocquard sharply, seating herself carefully on one of the mahogany chairs.

"Of course, my lady. Obsessed, if you don't mind my saying so, is perhaps a little strong. We merely believe that the mortals once existed, and we search for proof of this."

"And you believe they have returned as Grays, if I have the rumors right?"

Sage shakes his head, and I see he is completely unperturbed by Lady Hocquard's forthright inquisition. "There are some who think that, my lady, but our cult are not among them. We have no strict opinion on this. There is not enough . . . evidence to confirm it either way. Now, if you don't mind, I will explain why we are here."

Lady Hocquard waves one hand a little too gracefully in front of her. "The floor is yours, sorcerer."

"I will be completely open," Sage begins. "We are not just here for diplomatic niceties. And thanks to Sam here working this out and putting her trust in us . . ." At this point Lady Hocquard turns to stare at me, and I can't even begin to guess what her knowing expression means, except to hope she's not planning to set Alanna on me. "Well, it seems that we might have a common cause. The story I'm about to tell you would put me and my cult in danger if it became common knowledge."

Alanna, who has remained standing a few yards behind Lady Hocquard, snorts loudly; I assume at the obviousness of his statement, though you can never tell with her.

"For the last few decades," Sage continues, "ever since shortly before Grayfall, we have had an understanding with the young and recently deceased Azzuri." Sage pauses then, to note our expressions. Alanna and Lady Hocquard don't look surprised, but then, why would they? Hearing men's secrets is their firstblood, lunchblood, and dineblood. I give him a shocked look, just to be kind.

"I first met him about five years before Grayfall. He came to our temple—the first vampire to do that in a long time. He wanted to know about the mortals. Said he was interested in the history of this land and the myths that might be real. Strictly speaking, we keep ourselves to ourselves, but I was gratified by his interest—it seemed genuine, not part of some vampire or sorcerer politicking. He was a thoughtful, intelligent young man. I liked him."

Sage looks sad, like someone's only just told him Azzuri the Younger was now a pile of gray ashes. "A true mindsplitter, too," he added.

"A who now?" asks Lady Hocquard.

"A, uh, a mindsplitter. Someone who devotes different parts of their brain to different skills. A man of many talents, I suppose you might say."

"Don't worry about it, my lady," says Jacob quietly behind him, slouching even further on his long chair. "He just makes up words sometimes."

"Anyway," Sage continues, "he told me of a burial find under Lightfall. Lightfall is—was—a big city, built on older, smaller towns, and I no doubt missed out on much information of strange finds by not living there."

"And excitement and women and spirits and fun and . . ." Jacob mutters helpfully.

"Azzuri mentioned that what was found in the ground was put into the Blood Bank, under the orders of your spymaster, Saxe," continues Sage, ignoring his companion.

"Ah, bloods, not that little prick," growls Alanna.

"Was this evidence of your mortals?" I ask. It's the first time I've spoken since the start, as I'd assumed it wasn't my place anymore, but no one seems to mind me interrupting.

"He didn't know. He couldn't find out what it was. Only that it had been given over to Lord Saxe and placed in the Blood Bank. After our meeting, I heard nothing from the young Azzuri. Nothing at all for decades. I wrote to him and never received a reply. I assumed that whatever trauma Grayfall had inflicted on the survivors in First Light, it had affected him, and our arrangement was over. It was immensely frustrating not to be able to go to the city myself. Thanks to Grayfall, I have spent near enough the last hundred years pondering over this find. Then last month I received a letter. A letter from Azzuri." He reaches into his pocket and pulls out a piece of parchment. I can see the writing on it; it has the same emotion-filled loops and curls as the piece I found in the chest. It is from the First Lord's youngest son, all right.

"It is a short note. But it conveys a lot . . ."

Dear Sage,
I am sorry for not responding to your letters. It has been a poor century in this cursed city, and I do not trust anyone, or that such a letter will not be intercepted. But I must take the risk now, because I think I have happened onto something. I also think I may know how to find out if I have. I daresay I might even have put some of your inquirer principles you told me about into practice. I dare not put it into writing until I check for sure. It is part of something big, something bigger than we ever suspected. But if something happens to me, know that it is worth the risk of Grays to come and find out. This might be everything.
                                                                Yours, Red

Sage puts the parchment back into his pocket. I smile to myself. It's the first time I've heard someone say Azzuri the Younger's nickname since he died. It gives him a realness denied by his birthright.

"Well, at least he wasn't vague," says Lady Hocquard icily.

"I'm sure he intended to tell me more when he could. His death intervened," replies Sage, trying to match the lady for temperature but falling several icicles short.

"So allow me to summarize," continues Lady Hocquard. "Something is found under Lightfall. Over a hundred years later, the young Azzuri discovers something more about this. Shortly after, he is dead. You decide to come to First Light, under the guise of diplomacy, to investigate this further. Have I summed this up correctly?"

"Admirably so, Lady Hocquard," says Sage, and I see Jacob roll his eyes. "Of course, we don't know that his death is connected to whatever he thought he had found."

Alanna snorts quietly in the corner. "True," says Lady Hocquard, studiously ignoring her, "but it is a little bit suspicious, you would have to agree."

"For now, it would be fair to say there is a chance the two are connected," replies Sage.

"Well," says Lady Hocquard, "so now we come to the question of what to do next."

Sage fixes her with a stare, and for a second it feels like two stags in the room, antlers at the ready. "I think that part is clear, is it not, my lady?"

Lady Hocquard leans forward on her chair toward Sage, so close I reckon he can taste the blood on her breath. She stares at him for a few seconds, and we all watch, as if a fight has begun that no one noticed.

"Tell me, Brother Bailey of the Cult of Humanis. Tell me why I should put my faith in men who put their faith in myths."

"The mortals existed," says Sage. "Trust me."

"I've just met you."

"Then believe."

"Believe in myths?"

"Nothing stranger than what you've seen," says Sage, pointing past Lady Hocquard at Alanna. "What you saw in the last days of Last Light."

Alanna's face remains blank.

Lady Hocquard leans back in her chair and sips her blood. Then she turns to me. "Do you trust them, Sam?"

I try humility. "Perhaps you should ask your first maid, m'lady," I reply. "You've known her for longer."

"I have, Sam. And I trust her more than anyone. But she is not so trusting of others. She does not come from a trusting place."

Alanna nods. "M'lady is right. If it was up to me, I would probably knife these mages just to be sure and then part ways."

"You can't kill sorcerers with a knife wound," retorts Jacob.

"Yes, but you wouldn't be forgetting me in a hurry, would you now?"

Jacob looks alarmed. "She's jesting, isn't she?"

"To you, Jacob, probably not," says Sage.

I think on it a little more. "I do trust them. It's why I went to them in the first place, once I realized who they were. But I didn't just do it from instinct. I did it because of my reading. The members of the Cult of Humanis aren't tricksters or politicians or rogues. They're on the edge of sorcerer society, mistrusted at best, mocked at worst, trying to put together a picture no one else cares about. They've almost been killed for it, and I've not read of them doing any killing back, at least in anything other than self-defense, and you know by now that I've done a lot of reading. In fact, though there's a lot of shade thrown about them in the tomes, I haven't found anything that I think casts a bad light on them. There are a lot of snakes in this city, m'lady, but I don't think these two are among them." When I finish talking, I turn to see Sage and Jacob staring at me, mouths open. I might have got a bit carried away. I do that sometimes.

"Well," says Lady Hocquard, doing her worst to suppress a smile, "I think, gentlemen, that you have at least one admirer in the room. Hmm. So there it is. May I suggest that we work together, rather than apart? Until such time I find out Sam has been wrong about you, when of course I will set my first maid on you."

"Is that an offer or a threat?" asks Sage. "It's hard to tell."

"Oh, lighten up, sorcerers, good gracious," she replies, picking up her blood flute, "and join me in a toast."

"To what?" asks Jacob.

"To a fledging new alliance. May it not turn to ashes like everything else in this godsforsaken city."

We clink glasses. Jacob and Alanna down theirs in one. Sage and Lady Hocquard take a small sip, and their eyes meet cautiously. I can't see much trust. But it's a good start. I think.

"Well," says Lady Hocquard, "I suppose we should begin by asking what our next move is. I assume Sam told you about the two names on Azzuri's note."

"She did," says Sage.

"The first name was Commander Tenfold."

"I'm not familiar with that name, my lady," says Sage.

"But everyone native to First Light is. He is someone of great importance in the city. He is the commander of the Scout Guard, those brave souls who venture outside the city walls."

Jacob blows his cheeks out. "The ones who go out to check for Grays? They sound like a bunch of mean bastards."

"I rather think you are right, Jacob," replies Lady Hocquard. "They are indeed a collection of unusual men. The bravest, or wildest, of the Blood

Guard, if you will. Commander Tenfold is almost nobility. About as highly regarded a Midway as you can be without being called a Lord. He is not as fierce as the men under him, though. More the silent type, who saves his violence for when he needs it, at least according to the Leech word."

"I see." Sage nods. "Any idea of what the young Azzuri's connection with him was?"

Lady Hocquard glances at Alanna. "We don't know of any link between them, do we? We've never received any word about any rumors, not to mention any truth. They could always have been lovers, but I am sure we would have heard of something of that nature, unless Azzuri kept it much more secret than the rest of his, ah, male company. Commander Tenfold seems to be clean as they come."

"So how do we approach him?" asks Sage.

"I'm not sure we should be approaching him. He is a dangerous man surrounded by more dangerous men."

"That doesn't sound like the stories we know of the Leeches," says Jacob. "You can get to anyone, I heard. You can be very . . . persuasive."

"Well, it's flattering you fall for the legend, dear, but we are not all-powerful. The commander keeps no maids, despite his status, and he is not the coingirl type, so that limits our influence. Even if we could get to him, he is hardly of the blackmailable variety, as I've said."

"I see," says Sage. "Maybe then we should turn to the final name on the list."

"There's always the Rushes," says Alanna quietly. "He practically be livin' there, I'll be reckonin'."

Lady Hocquard's face blanches. "I'm not sending one of our girls in there. I'd rather have them go to a Blood Bank orgy."

Alanna shrugs. "We may not be having much of the choices about it, m'lady."

"I can go," I say, a little louder than I intended. "I can act as one of their cleaning maids, if they have them."

Lady Hocquard ignores this. Whether she's still angry at me or because it's a ridiculous suggestion, I can't tell.

"I'm sorry?" asks Jacob. "The Rushes? You mean the gentlemen's club the Rushes? Famous den of iniquity?" He grins. "Well, why didn't you say so earlier?"

"No," says Sage, glaring at Jacob. "Absolutely not. Do not even begin to contemplate that plan."

"Well, who else?" says Jacob. "First Lord Azzuri is hardly going to think it normal if you go, is he? He may have known you for only a short time, but I reckon that's enough to realize you're no more the gambling, drinking, and whoring type than I am the careful go-to-bed-early type."

"Whereas you are, I assume?" asks Alanna.

"At your service, m'ladies," says Jacob, bowing. He looks around the room and, seeing everyone's unimpressed faces, continues unabashed. "No one will find it strange if I attend the club. I think I've more or less announced my character fairly well over the last two weeks to the palace. Unless the rest of you have suggestions as to how to get to Tenfold?"

Sage hangs his head. "I can't believe I'm saying this, but he's right."

"Is most typical of men," says Alanna in the loudest whisper I've ever heard. Sage looks at her, confused.

"I think what my first maid is referring to," Lady Hocquard says with a thin smile, "is that it is typical how quickly a plan of action initiated by me has been commandeered to a course of action that can only be completed by a man. A man whom I'm beginning to think may be more like the Lords of this city than I am comfortable with."

"My lady," said Sage, "please let me make one thing clear. Although my associate here may . . . share some of the characteristics of the nobility in this city, at least in the amount he drinks and probably the state of his rooms, I would not have had him by my side in the cult for so many years if he shared their darker temperament or looser grasp of basic morals. And we are certainly not trying to commandeer anything. If you study our history, you will see we have had no time for the power games of the sorcerers, much like I imagine you have tired of the machinations of the Lords. Or, to put it simply," he finishes, pointing at Jacob, "he's harmless."

Lady Hocquard considers this at length. "A thoughtful speech. I can see you earning your name already." She sighs. "Very well. I agree. Let us do this."

"Thank you," Sage says. "Then may I suggest that Jacob goes to the Rushes tomorrow night?"

"Ah, my head could do with a day of rest tomorrow, Sage," says Jacob, "to recover from my previous intoxications and be ready for the ones to come." He pauses as everyone stares at him. "Tomorrow it is."

"And what of your plan to find out what this Tenfold knows?" says Alanna. "You bringin' any threats or wiles to this party?"

"Rest assured," says Sage, "Jacob has a wide set of people skills that have served us well over the years, a set of skills finely honed by—"

"I'll get him drunk."

"Well," says Lady Hocquard after an awkward pause, "I am so glad we have a plan. I do not see any more reason to keep this risky little meeting going any longer now that we are all settled on our next move. Let us convene here again shortly after sunset the night after tomorrow to find out what your man's strategy has uncovered there. I will think of some convincing reason to invite you over once again."

A few polite words of farewell, and then it's our time to leave. I can barely believe it. A short conversation in a room, and now our lives could be changed forever. Is this how this works? A conversation here, a conversation there, and our futures go down a different path forever.

As the sorcerers walk for the coach, and I begin to follow, Lady Hocquard taps me on the shoulder. "Sam, my dear, where are you off to?"

I turn back to face her. We're standing in her porch, enclosed by her bloodred columns. The air is warmer; we've talked for longer than I thought. Half the night is gone. Out here in the relative dark, the plans made inside seem far-off fancies.

"I assumed I was returning to the palace, m'lady."

She smiles. "I rather thought Alanna could show you a little of how we work tomorrow."

I try not to grin, hope blooming in me. "Will the palace be all right with that?"

"I am well acquainted enough with the residents of the palace to know they will not mind me taking a maid for a night. It is not uncommon."

I pause, trying to get my words right. "I was a little afraid you would be angry at me for taking the risk of bringing the mages here."

Lady Hocquard studies her gloves for a few moments. "Do you know why it is fashion for us ladies to wear these stupid things, Sam? Because our hands are soft and pale from the near-perfect blood we drink, so we cannot bear to get them rough from handling things. We protect our beauty by hiding it away for most of the night." She clears her throat then, and her words come quickly now. "I can't tell if what you did was stupid or clever. Bringing the sorcerers into our little pact, that is. It could be the end for all of us, if Saxe was really involved in the young Azzuri's death and thinks we are working with the mages. But I suspect that you judged both them and the situation right. I think you have taken to the little games we play, me and Alanna and others . . . I think you have taken to them well. I suspect maybe you have been waiting for the chance to play them for a very long time. So though part of me fears what could come of knowing you, there is another part of me that is cheering you on and welcoming the chaos you might bring. You remind me so much of . . ." She stops, catching herself. "But for now, I remain cautious, for what else can I be in this ugly little city of ours? So I will watch you carefully, my dear. Watch you until I know for sure."

As I fall asleep that night in a foreign bed, I think on those parting words, wondering whether they were a warning or a promise.

14

Animal Spirits

Key dates to the beste of our knowledge:
−400 AL*: The Great Intelligence
0 AL: Founding of the first Everlands city, First Light
50 AL: Founding of Luce
200 AL: Founding of Lightfall
250 AL: Founding of Last Light
420 AL: The Twin War begins
440 AL: The Twin War ends
450 AL: Last Light falls
500 AL: Grayfall
*AL = After Light

Quantas Quastan, *A Timeline of Our Ages*

Sam

I awake in a new bed for the first time in ten years. Silk sheets, down pillow, scent of roselily everywhere. For a second I'm confused. And then I remember. I remember arriving at the mansion a second time last night, this time without a dagger at my back. Conversing with two sorcerers from a temple a thousand miles away and one of the most respected noble Ladies, not to mention a woman from Last Light.

And now I lie in the finest surroundings I've ever slept in. Because the Lady's maids sleep like Ladies themselves, or at least like Ladies in very small rooms apportioned for bedrooms. The room I slept in is three times the size of the quarters Beth and I share. It has proper sun-curtains, so I can see the stars upon waking. There's a massive light brown lacquered quacian wardrobe, most likely more valuable than all the furniture in the palace servants' quarters put together.

I should be in awe. But my cheer is only at half flag. For my dreams, still lingering in my skull, are the same as always. Or should I say my nighthaunts. Half-awake, I linger on the memory of it. The memory of the first time I really understood what First Light was about.

I was nine years old. It began with a knock on my door. My mother opened it, and there was a Lord standing there. A real vampire Lord. I'd never seen one this close up. None of our family had. We Ingles weren't anybody of import. The Ingle name was known on our street, and that's about it. I didn't recognize this particular Lord then, of course, but I've seen him many times since.

It was shocking to see him in our doorway. We lived deep in the Worntown lanes of Southeastfall. Not quite as dangerous as Southwestfall, but not the kind of place you get nobility wandering around. Not that Lords have much to fear, with superior blood literally running through their veins, but this one seemed to be on his own, which was a little too cocky even for them. And they certainly didn't normally call in on the likes of us. I'd seen Lords pass through the main thoroughfares a few times, normally in carriages, and I'd even seen some of the First Guard, the ones allowed to take wolfblood, *fly* over us once.

But they never normally visited Worns. There must have been a special reason, and when I studied his face, I saw what it was. Even at that age I could tell the look of desire on a man, as well as the look of a man who had never had any call to control such desire. Had he spied my mother in the market earlier? Or working down by the gardens? Who knows. But he strode into our home with only one thing on his mind, and I'm sure he would've gotten it if it hadn't been for my father, who came from the hearth to see who had called so close to lightfall and then stood like a post between this Lord and my mother.

The Lord just smiled at this, and I knew then—for I'd learned a lot by that age, I'd already started my reading with whatever slim pickings Worns could get their hands on—that depending on what blood he'd downed most recently, he could put a fist through my father if he wanted. But he stared at the grim look on my father's face, and then he turned and looked through the open door at the houses opposite us, where our neighbors stood, each come out into the street to stare at him, more and more until there was a line of them. When he saw this, the smug expression on that well-bred face faded a little, and what drunken nerves had brought him here washed away.

Nowadays, with Grayfall almost a century behind us, Worns are fully cowed by the Lords, and I don't think our neighbors would've stepped up to our defense today. Maybe I'm wrong, but I don't think I am. But when I was a child, the Lords had not yet sapped the will from the common folk.

The old emotions of Lightfall still remained, just about: memories of a time when the titled classes could be said to have ruled the city only in the sense that a lion tamer can be said to rule their beast.

So, for that reason or maybe another, the Lord turned right round and walked straight out of our house, and I did a little dance up and down the stairs and told my sister what had happened and how we'd kicked his fancy rags right out of Worntown.

My father just told me to shut up about it, though, and my mother was white as a sheet, and the next day I realized why, for the Blood Guard came and whisked my father from us mere minutes after sunset and I never saw him again.

The night after that, the Lord came back. He must have been confident that he would have his lust out on our mother this time. But my sister and I stood in front of her and wouldn't move. I remember my sister's eyes, much more certain than mine. I sometimes think that's why she felt fine about signing up to be a palace maid years later, because she'd faced down a Lord as a child and reckoned she could back down any others now she was an adult. If the sun hadn't scattered her to ashes, I wonder if she would've been proved right.

At first I thought the Lord would simply brush us out of the way without a second thought, but his eyes locked onto ours, and we didn't turn away, and something in his expression changed again. Except it wasn't calculation or doubt, like the other night, but something else. I couldn't put my finger on it. Maybe he simply couldn't be bothered with the hassle anymore; the children had taken the fine edge off his lust. But it wasn't that.

So he turned and walked out of our house for a second time, and we celebrated another small victory.

Of course, like the last one, it soon turned sour, for a year later my mother was gone, too.

I get out of bed on that thought, wishing I could start the night a different way for once and tiring of the wish even as I make it.

A glass later, while somewhere in Eastfall Jacob begins to ready himself to brave the Rushes, looking for Commander Tenfold and whatever secrets he hides, I'm not doing much at all. In fact, Hallsday aside, you might call it my first rest day for ten years. It appears I really am at Lady Hocquard's beck and call for the moment. I started the night still worried that someone might get suspicious, but she reassured me once again before leaving for some society function that it's fine and common for a Lord or Lady to keep requesting the same maids from the palace for a time. They tend to take a shine to us, she said; we are, after all, the best in the city.

Not that I'm simply lying about today. I'm being shown around by Alanna, who is explaining in her own unique manner how the citywide cloak of lies and secrets that the Leeches wrap around their unsuspecting prey really works. First, she shows me around some of the secret palace rooms. A dress room for costumes and outfits for everything from a Lady to a maid to a coingirl to a street rogue to a bloodvatter. A weapons room.

Then I start to learn the really interesting things. I learn, for example, that the Leeches pay children to run past Lords who venture into any part of Worntown. These children carry buckets of blood and feign accident to spill it on the Lords' expensive clothes. Knowing that time is of the essence with bloodstains, the Lords immediately go to the nearest stain-house, which of course is always the one with a Leech stationed in it, all the better to poke through any scraps of parchment or other hidden things you always find stashed away in a Lord's finery.

Then there's the sinstone you find in all the major prayhalls. The idea here is simple: a vampire speaks into this stone, normally located behind the statue of the blood made flesh, telling it all their sins. Then when they reach the Bloodhalls, the sins are announced during the bloodfeasting, and the vampire is born anew in the afterlife. The part where they atone for their sins seems to have been lost in the theology here, but it is great for the Leeches, because any Leechmaid who cleans the prayhalls knows there are catacombs underneath almost every one of them, or at least secret niches, where a maid can hear the sins of any Lords being spoken. The slight catch is that the worst of the Lords are not the ones who tend to adhere closely to the concept of sin confession, or as Alanna put it "we hear more 'armless bedroom stories than we ever do of dark deeds."

My favorite Leech scheme, though, is what Alanna calls the *intercession of the letters,* which seems to me a fancy way of saying letter thievery. For when Leeches suspect a Lord of something worth a blackmail, but they need more evidence, the best way to get it is to take the letters that Lord sends to others about his schemes. Ideally, you don't want the Lord to ever know that the letter was taken or read. So what a Leechmaid does in this situation is wait until a new letter is placed in the post-basket awaiting the postrunner, then thieve it. Depending on when the letter was placed, the Leechmaid may only have a small amount of time to return it, so it's become a tightly run operation. The letter's taken to someone who can steam off a Lord's seal and replace it, allowing it to be read without the receiver ever knowing something was amiss. Given the elaborate seals the Lords place on their letters, I wondered who this someone could be—surely not a Worn—but Alanna just smiled wickedly and said, "You get all our secrets now, there'll be none left to amuse you with down the road," and that was that.

There are a thousand schemes like these, and the way Alanna speaks of them, it's clear they're mostly her idea. This makes me wonder who she really was in Last Light.

After a few hours of such revelations, grateful though I am, my brain's no longer able to deal with the twisting avenues of made-up language that is every sentence Alanna speaks, so I almost cry out with joy when Lady Hocquard herself returns from some dineblood party and asks me to take some eel tea with her in the parlor. Eel tea is a strange concoction drunk only by the nobility: eel blood from off the northern mountain shore, which for some reason has a refined taste to it, combined with tea leaves, the leaves soaked in the blood for hours beforehand to give it the strongest taste. For some reason it seems to work only with eel blood; anything else, and the bitterness overrides everything. Not that I'm an expert—it's godsdamn expensive and certainly not drunk by Worns, and I try not to like it because I don't know when I'll ever be having it again.

We sit there, on chairs worth more than all the clothing I've ever worn put together, and sip at our tea, like two nobles passing the gossip. *Strange* doesn't even begin to describe it. I realize now that Lady Hocquard is keenly aware of the divide between us, and like many of her self-aware kind, she's almost too desperate to tear it down. But it's sweet of her to try, if you like that kind of thing.

"How was your insight into our world of secrets today, dear?" she begins, taking off her gloves and stretching her hands out in front of the fire. It isn't that cold today—a little chilly for Greendeath, maybe, but not that bad. She seems to get cold easily.

"I learned a lot, m'lady." I stop at that. I'm still finding my way into this conversation.

"Yes, I'm sure you did. Alanna has created many rules and strategies for our little enterprise. All taken from Last Light. The intricacy of her doings in that city, the care, the attention! I confess when I first met her, I took her for a wild one—unplanned, anarchic. But there's more planning in that head of hers at any one time than most of us do in a year." There's a long pause then. She seems anxious. She has good reason to be, to be fair. We all do. Any moment now Spymaster Saxe could burst in and take our lives in a completely different and interesting direction.

"Do you think Jacob is doing well at the Rushes?" I ask, wondering how conversation ever flows freely in such staged surroundings.

She laughs, tilting her head back and having a full go at it. "I have no bloody idea, Sam. He's a curious one. There must be something about him or the mage Bailey would hardly have had him as his deputy all this time, but I can't help but worry that we've just sent a liquorfiend in there to have some fun while we twiddle our thumbs here hoping for the best." She grins at me. "I do not like leaving serious work to men, you may have noticed."

I smile. "I think I have, m'lady. It's a refreshing change."

"Do not get me wrong," she says, on a roll now. "There are some good men in this city, even some we work with. You might meet them one day. But there is so much pressure to conform. I have known good men to gain a whiff of advancement, and the very next day they are doing things that make me want to set Alanna on them and damn everything we have built to the twin hells."

"You're playing the long game, m'lady. And you'll be all the fiercer for it."

"Ha! Do you know, Sam, you sound just like my daughter sometimes."

I try not to look surprised at this, but I am. This is the first time she's mentioned a daughter.

"What is she like, if you don't mind me asking?"

"She's dead, darling. It's okay," she adds quickly, holding her hands out to preempt my apology, "you did not know. But oh, you would have liked her, Sam. She was clever like you, book learned, but brave as well. She wasn't afraid of anyone. She would tell Lords what she really thought of them to their face. But she had this wisdom in her, too. She used to say that it wasn't that all the Lords were bad—or for that matter, the Ladies who stood idly by or helped them in their sinning. It wasn't that they were *born* like that. It's that they came to learn it as a habit. She used to say it was in the bones of the city, like a miasma; a disease in the bricks of the city that laid waste to them and made them monsters. I asked her what in the Everlands she could mean, how that was possible. But she would just give me this look so much older than her years, and she'd say, *It was a metaphor, Mother,* and then smile to make me feel less stupid, because she was kind, too."

"It must have been hard, losing her to Grayfall," I say, instantly regretting my words. I had a choice at that point. I could have poured some calming oil on the sadness so strong in her eyes, but I chose to seek information. To make a bet that her daughter had died in Grayfall, and if not, that I'd be corrected and find out the true cause. Maybe such tactics will make me a great Leech. But right now they make me a shit of a person.

Lady Hocquard stares at me, and her coldness comes off her in waves.

"It was a long time ago, Sam. Or at least it feels like it. Maybe it is not so long in the course of our lifetimes. But it does no good to talk on it too much."

"I understand, m'lady," I add, thinking that I had already offended her, so I might as well as carry on. "I would just like to know what motivates you. If I can understand, I can serve you better."

This does not go down well, either. She drains her tea and stands up. "I am not the First Lord, Sam. You do not need to serve me. We all serve the city. And if I may say so, darling, just because I have discussed a little of my past with you does not mean you should presume to know me. That," she adds in an ice-cold tone, fixing me with a thin-lipped stare I have not seen before, "is a very dangerous road."

I bow my head. "I overstepped, m'lady. I am sorry."

My apology lingers in the air for a while, waiting to see if it's taken. "No matter," she says eventually, her jovial manner returned. "Well, I must converse with Alanna on Leech business now. I trust you will amuse yourself, Sam, for the remainder of the night. Let us hope tomorrow brings us good fortune from that den of iniquity and the mage who is enjoying it so."

She quickly leaves the parlor then before I can reply, and I sit there in silence and sip slowly on the last dregs of my tea.

Then I hear commotion in the hall. I think nothing of it. Some Leech visitor. But it's not. It's Sage Bailey.

I watch the scene in front of me, Sage by my side, having requested my company here. Half a glass earlier I was in the quiet confines of the Lady's mansion. Where we are now? Well, it's not so peaceful for a start.

"Stag Five has sixty percent approval!" booms the voice of the blood-trader across the square. In response, there's a mild panic as the throng of well-dressed vampires milling about the square whisper feverishly to one another.

The vampire standing nearest to me, dressed in a smart ermine-lined jacket and wearing a carefully sculptured moustache that does nothing for his dull face, turns to his colleague next to him and grunts in surprise.

"We have to sell right now," he says.

"Yes, but sixty percent isn't too bad and it's only the first responders," replies his colleague, who's wearing similarly fine clothes but is taller and clean-shaven—fairly good-looking if you like that sort of moneyed Midway look.

"Oh, come on!" replies Moustache in frustration. "It was predicted around a seventy-five—that's a poor return!"

"Yes, but even if the price drops a little, if we wait it out, there's a chance that the follow-ups will come back higher. I mean, it was always a risky proposition—stag blood can sometimes take badly with magick. But I had a source at the tasting, and he said it was genuinely good stuff. It might just take a while to get used to. I bet the second responders will be closer to the prediction."

"Tell that to our friends," Moustache replies, pointing at a crowd flocking to a building at the farther end of the square, waving bits of parchment in their hand. "Everyone wants to sell. There's no recovering after that."

They both look at each other then and the taller one sighs. "Fuck it. Let's limit our losses." Then he stares up at the early evening sky and grimaces. "I see the Blood Gods weren't smiling on our trades today."

Moustache laughs. "They've not smiled on me since trading season started. Ornery little bastards." He laughs, then adds quickly to the skies, "No offense intended."

After the two vampires have followed the crowd into the building, I turn to Sage, who is sitting next to me on a bench at the edge of the square, taking it all in. "And why are we here again?" I ask him. "Has this got something to do with the young Azzuri?"

Sage shakes his head. "Not directly, Sam, no."

"So we came here because . . ."

"Because I've never seen the Blood Market in the flesh before. So to speak."

"I see. So we're sightseeing. A murder to solve, and we're on a tour of the city, that it?"

Sage turns to me and frowns. "Hmm. Well, when you put it like that . . ." He frowns and stands straight, as if to leave.

I smile. "I am jesting with you, Brother Bailey."

"Sage, please." He grins. "And you would think I'd be used to that with Jacob."

"Are you worried about him?"

"He can handle himself. There is a lot more to him than he shows."

"I assumed so, otherwise you wouldn't have made him your deputy. You must both have conviction to live out there on the edges of the Desertlands. Why do you do it?"

Sage shrugs. "You're an avid reader. I assume you know the histories. You know the gaps. What came before. Someone has to fill them."

"And you're certain they can be filled with the mortals? Vampires believe the Blood Gods made us in their image, put us on this earth, and there was nothing before."

He stares at me, trying to work out if I'm serious. It gives me time to study his face properly. I'd taken him for a little too on the thin side and a little too fierce in the visage. But when he's not furrowing his brow in thought, he has a good profile, I'll admit.

"I don't think you believe that," he says eventually.

I grin. "Are you saying I'm not a devout believer?"

A tiny smile appears at the corner of his mouth. "We're not here to talk about me, though, Sam. I want to see how the Blood Markets work."

I raise my left eyebrow. "I know you know how this works."

Sage nods. "Yes, but I want to hear it from someone who lives here. Sometimes you learn something new that way."

"My knowledge of the Blood Markets is from my reading, too. I don't get much free time to dally around here."

"Nonetheless."

"Okay. Well . . ." I look around the square, wondering where to start. "There . . ." I begin, pointing at a large red tent pitched on the Eastfall side. Through the opening, I can see a series of parchments arranged on a long table; the vampires who had not raced to the building at the far end of the square are scrutinizing them.

"That's where the blood traders go to find out new information about the new blood that's made available from the Blood Farms. The traders read what animal it's from, as well as other details like the magick the sorcerers have used to strengthen it and purify it and any extras that have been added, and then they compare the new blood on the market to similar ones in the past. Finally they put their money in the invisibles."

I point to the building at the Southfall end of the square, an imposing four-story limestone and marble affair in Old Mage style: Cynthian-style columns topped with plain flat designs. The frieze running atop the columns all around the building contains carvings depicting thin containers of blood crossed over each other like swords.

"The invisibles?" asks Sage slowly, doing a poor job of feigning ignorance.

"Yes," I reply. "The invisibles are what you own when you put your money up. It's like you're buying a vial of the new blood, except you don't actually buy one. You buy it in theory—an invisible vial. That way, you tie your money to the success of the blood without actually buying it. Whether you make more money for your invisible ownership depends on how popular the new blood will be. How much will be bought by the Midways and the Lords, and the percentage of them who consider it good enough for a repeat purchase."

"How does that work?"

"Well," I reply, trying to conjure up all my library sessions. I wish I'd read more about blood trading now. My hazy memories of Quantas Quistile's *Of Currencie and Blood* will have to do. "Let's say the experts in the Invisibles House decide that from the sounds of the new blood that has been created, it will be as popular as a type of existing blood that sells for five bloodcrowns per vial. So now a trader gives five bloodcrowns for the equivalent of one vial of blood—an invisible vial. If it turns out that this new blood is *more* popular than the price it's been given originally, then your invisible vial of blood is now worth more than the five crowns you gave for it. You can keep your ownership of the invisible vial in case the blood gets even more popular, or you can sell it and take a tidy profit. Of course if it turns out to be less popular, then you will lose some or all of your five bloodcrowns you started with."

"How do they know how popular it has been?"

I turn to the Westfall side of the square to point at another large tent, where the announcer who caused the stir moments earlier still stands. This tent has many openings, through which vampires with rough dull jackets are racing through and whispering to others within.

"Those are Worns who act as messengers, collecting the opinions of the merchants after the delivery of the blood. They race back here and inform the announcer, who has a group of clerics who work out over-all how popular the blood is on any given day. Then he announces the popularity of it and the traders buy or sell their invisibles accordingly."

Sage smiles, satisfied, and stands up. "You continue to impress, Samantha Ingle. I don't think I've ever met a Worn like you."

"Have you met many Worns?"

Sage squints at me, and for a moment I think I've offended him, but then he laughs softly. "Point taken. Faulty logic. I see I still have a lot to learn."

"As have I," I reply. "I want to know about the mortals. The myths. What evidence you've found."

"Do you now."

"Yes. You've not written a book about it. So that's my normal route to covering up the gaps in my knowledge gone. So I've got no choice but to get the information from you." I almost gasp at my own boldness. I'm not used to talking like this. My main conversation partner almost exclusively for a decade has been Beth. I'm at home in books, not con-versations. But after holding my own with the Queen Leech, I now seem to be sparring with a sorcerer. I wonder if whatever rush of blood that's taken me this far will carry on, and for a darker second, I wonder what will happen if it fades.

Sage smiles. "Well, help me solve this mystery of ours and maybe we can talk at length about it."

I roll my eyes. "A convenient stalling tactic."

Before he can reply, we both turn at the noise of a crowd; the traders are emerging from the Invisibles House to hear some more announce-ments. A few moments later the announcer at the tent cries out. "*Bear Seven, Re-Magicked*: ninety percent approval!" he roars, and the traders descend into the typical frenzy of market gamblers throughout time: animal spirits unleashed.

"You know it's funny," Sage says, "a lot of sorcerers assume that in First Light post-Grayfall, Lords banned Worns from taking the good blood. That this was the only way the system would remain like it is now. I think they would be surprised to learn that it is the market that bans them, not any diktat from above."

I nod. "I bet the Lords would liked to have forced us to have low blood only, cow and suchlike, after Grayfall. They certainly didn't like the way things were going near the end of Lightfall. But I think there would have been an uprising. There's more Worns than Lords. Many more."

"But they don't need to use force."

"Exactly. As long as the blood stays expensive and we stay poor, there's no chance of us ever getting the good stuff."

Sage thinks this through, rubbing the one-day stubble on his chin that seems to be a permanent feature. "But surely you could band together. Save up. Have some noble blood distributed throughout the Worns."

"That was tried. It was part of what led to the bloodvatter rebellion, before I was born, a few decades after Grayfall. But the Lords don't play fair. Never have. They took Worns on good blood to be a sign of rebellion, twisted the narrative to suit themselves. They came down so hard there's not been an attempt since."

Sage nods. "The gloved hand of the market, the solid fist of power."

I shrug. "Or in other words, life is shit."

He doesn't reply to that.

15

There's Always a Better Room

O the Green is for the gaming,
And the Red is for blood drinking.
The Yellow is but a mystery,
*But the Blue is full of sweet ^^^^^*

"Ode to the Rushes" by Anonymous, in
A Collection of Ditties, 100 AL–300 AL,
edited by Redquill Fasttide (corrected for language)

Jacob

I look up at the entrance to the Rushes and get a weird feeling in the pit of my stomach. It might be the nerves or the three tankards of spiced Lucewine I downed before I came here, who can say? Never turn up to a new location sober. You don't know how long it might be till your next drink. That said, I'm not completely wasted. Merely tipsy. People think of me as the frivolous drunk. Perhaps I overplay my role, but it has its uses. To be underestimated can be good, too. It's just about finding the balance. One day I'll get it right.

The Rushes is an impressive building, I'll give them that. Sage would know what style it's in, so I'll settle for prewar at the very least. How much older? Who knows? It's grand, anyway. Grosshunt arches, spires here there and everywhere, a big painted-glass window above the door showing a bunch of Lords standing around with drinks, presumably having a great time. The Rushes is big enough to be one of the midsize prayhalls, and that's not even including the underground bits I'd wager they have. They can build, can the vampires. Or at least they used to back when the great cities still stood. I doubt they've built much in the last century. Time seems to have slowed down in First Light—almost as bad as our temple back in the Desertlands.

It must be strange to be trapped in one city. We sorcerers have the entire desert to wander in, untouched by Grays. Not that there's much in it except temples and other sorcerers, so I can see why the Grays don't bother with it. They have taste, at least.

I pause before the entrance, where two heavyset vampires guard the doors, wearing black jackets that would fit them properly if they lost thirty pounds. They stare at me as if they've never seen a sorcerer before. Depending on their age, maybe they haven't. From the sounds of it, the Kinets of First Light don't get out much. The Rushes, then, won't be used to having a mage in their privileged club. I think it's time I corrected that. To do so, to give off the right impression, I'll have to lean into a side of myself I lean into often. But that's why Sage sent me here, after all. Tonight I need not to worry about how much I believe my own performances. I just have to act. The plan is simple: Find Commander Tenfold. Somehow ascertain how he knows Azzuri the Younger; why his name ended up on a piece of paper that is the only clue so far to his death. As for how I do all this, I am currently . . . awaiting inspiration.

I go to open the heavy stone door, but one of the doormen does it for me.

"Thank you, good sir," I say. "Any advice?" I wink at him. "It's my first time." His face doesn't change and he doesn't say anything, but as I walk in, I hear him grunt, "Stay alive." Well, with wit like that, they won't be stuck on the doors forever, that's for sure.

Before me is a long dim corridor, with torches hung on the walls and nothing else. I see a brighter light at the end, and I walk toward it, wondering again how I get myself into these situations. As if I have to ask. The posh but fiery lady and the scary beauty from Last Light clearly had a first impression of me as a drunk jester who has somehow tied himself to Sage. My fault, of course. A new city, so many people. It's easy to slip into the old character. I overdid it, as I always do. And of course, the way I've chosen to prove them wrong is to go to a club known for drinking, coingirls, and mage knows what else. A plan for the ages, this one . . .

The brightly lit room at the end of the corridor is more in keeping with what I thought this place would be. It has long benches piled high with silk cushions and long tables with carafes of blood and, I hope, drink without blood in it. At the far end are four doors painted green, blue, red, and yellow. Unlike the others, the yellow one is a heavy locked door of stone, not wood. There are a couple of dolled-up frock-coated vampires sitting on the couches, one getting involved in choosing his blood, the other one staring at the doors, deep in thought.

I walk over to the doors and remember what I was told. Blue for women, green for larks, red for blood (I think I might give that one a miss), and yellow for . . . well, even the Leeches don't know what's behind that one. A best-kept secret, apparently.

I walk toward the green door. Larks it is.

The room beyond is dark, attuned to vampire eyes, and at first I can hardly see anything, but then my pupils adjust and I see that the room is actually an adjunct to a larger hall, which is (slightly) better lit by torches on the walls. I hope I don't have to play any cards here. It won't be easy to cheat in this light.

The hall contains about ten card or board tables that I can see, most of which are fairly full. I can see the main games being played: Redeye and Tascuza for the cards, Empirefall and Lords for the board games. A few card games at the back are too hard to see. By the look of the pissed state of some of the players at the back of the hall, I'm not sure they even have a clue what the rules are. More vampires congregate at the bar on the right side of the hall, and others are seated in velvet chairs at the far end. There's a low murmur of conversation, punctuated by sharp cries of anguish or triumph at the tables. Unlike the waiting area, there's no painted wood paneling here, just stone walls with various tapestries hung on them as an afterthought. Whoever decorated this room must have thought that everyone would be too focused on the games or else simply too tankarsed to care what their surroundings were like. Very wise, that person.

I survey all this wearily and murmur to myself: "Where do I begin?"

I begin at the bar.

"I'll have a glass of Lucewine," I say to the bartender, a tall willowy vampire who looks liked he wafted into the club when someone left the door open. I try and slur my words a little. Let the performance begin.

"Any particular vintage, brother mage?"

I'm impressed. I wonder if they got the wine especially for me or if they just have a particularly well-stocked cellar. On the one hand, I don't think the First Lord thinks that much of me to put on such a show, but then again he's exactly the kind of careful, politicking little shit who'd err on the side of caution.

"I didn't realize the options would be so wide," I say. "In that case, forget the wine. You don't have the five-spirits, do you?"

The barman looks at me blankly. I sigh. No one ever has the shading five-spirits.

"Just give me a vintage that'll knock me sideways." The barman shrugs and pours me a glass from a nearby bottle that looks suspiciously like the one he was going to give me anyway.

I'm halfway through draining the glass when one of the vampires not on the tables but congregated at the bar sidles over to me. He has large sad eyes, carefully combed black hair, and a black beard, which is too large to be in the Lord's style. I take from this that he must be a Midway. You don't spend the best part of two centuries working with Sage Bailey and not pick up a few habits of observation.

"We don't get many sorcerers in here," says my new friend, and the way he slurs the s on sorcerer makes me think that he's a few glasses ahead of me. The burning in the eyes confirms this. With vampires, it's so easy to tell what state they're in, at least when they're on blooddrinks.

"Really," I say, hoping this isn't a sign of the quality of conversation to come. "Well, what kind do you get in here?"

"All kinds really. The well-to-do, the wish-they-were-to-do, and the simply well drunk. Any Midway, even one such as myself, is allowed in, as long as we're not the kind that's barely different from a Worn. The slightest hint of a connection and you're in. Lords and Midways mix freer in here than the outside, certainly freer than some of the Lords-only clubs. The class lines are a little more blurred—we have a common bond that stretches beyond our social circles. It's why I like it."

"Oh. I thought it might be the coingirls, liquor, and gambling."

"Ha! The sorcerer has wit. I like it." He rubs his beard and signals to the barman to refill his glass. "My name's Redflute Silverside. I'm on the Blood Bank Council."

"The Blood Bank Council? You must be one of the more connected Midways, then, for that position."

Redflute nods, impressed. "You must have some knowledge of the city, to say that."

"Not really," I say. "I just spend a lot of time with a man who does. Things rub off, no matter how much you try to ignore him."

"You've not said your name," says Redflute, giving me the curious drunkard's smile that looks good to the wearer but comes across less well to the receiver.

"How do I play a game?" I say, ignoring the question. The fewer people I tell my identity to, the better. The cult's reputation sometimes has a strange effect on people. It's why I have to be so disarmingly charming all the time, just to counteract it.

"Wait until a game's finished, then join the table," he replies, pointing behind him at the games. "We don't stand on much ceremony here. It's all very informal."

"Excellent. Well, enjoy your drink, Red." I begin to walk away. Then I stop and turn back to Redflute and, in the most offhand tone I can muster, almost as an afterthought, I ask, "Oh, by the way, I hear Commander Tenfold is an ace at the card game I prefer, Take the Light. You haven't seen him, have you? I'd love to test my wits against him." I don't know why I went to such careful lengths. I'm fairly sure I'm not going to raise the suspicions of the pissblood in front of me.

"Oh," slurs Redflute, steadying himself against the bar in a failed attempt to look all-knowing, "you've asked the right man. You'll want the rouge room. Down the end of the hall. Not that they'll let you in, I'm afraid. You have to be a real somebody to get in there. A Lord only, or a Midway as well-known as Tenfold. Better drink, better company, all that."

"What happened to the *common bond that stretches beyond our social circle*?" I ask.

Redflute looks confused. "It's okay," I add, "don't mind my cynicism. I get it. There's always a better room. Good rule for life, that." Then I nod my thanks and leave Redflute to his drinking.

The rouge room that my new bar friend referred to is indeed down the hall. Unfortunately it is guarded by a wide, tall slab of a vampire. He has an otherwise average face with one unusual feature: a lock of gray hair. For a Worn to start to go gray, you must be a century at the very least, and the rest of your face would be showing your age as well. Quite why he should be youthful but with a smidge of gray is beyond me. I make a mental note to ask someone when I've not got a murder to help solve.

"Evening." I nod to him, with the casual look of someone who expects him to step aside.

He doesn't even bother to meet my eye. He just shakes his head.

I sigh. "Believe it or not, that's worked in the past."

Back at the main bar, I look around. Normally, if I need to get somewhere in a drinking den, I resort to the oldest of tricks: start a fight. Preferably one where, despite your key involvement in starting it, you don't actually have to participate. But these vampires don't look like the rowdy sort. If I threw some of their blood over their shirt, they'd simply signal for a new one while that mouthless slab at the door picked me up and gave me a diplomatic exit.

I do, however, have a plan B.

"Redflute," I begin, returning to the bar. He is still slumped over it, staring into his wine. I'm not sure he's moved since our last conversation.

"Redflute, my new drinking partner," I say, putting my arm around him, "seeing as you seem to be the only fellow who's deigned to speak to me so far, would you share with me in my favorite tipple?"

Before he can answer, I nod to the barman. "Two pints of Lucemead, please."

The barman gives me an odd look. "Pints? You mean—"

"I know what I said," I reply sharply before he can finish the sentence. I realize, with a sense of the inevitable, that I am warming into my act. The showboating drunkard role slips onto me and hugs me tight like a desert robe a size too small.

The barman shrugs, and with an "As you wish," pours them.

I turn to Redflute, who has lifted himself into a proper sitting position, still not ready to admit how pissed he really is, and I hand him a tankard.

"Have you ever drunk Lucemead, Redflute?"

"I'm afraid I haven't had the pleasure, my mysterious sorcerer acquaintance."

"Oh well, you are missing out, I'll tell you that right now. There's none of the red stuff in it, I'm afraid, but it more than makes up for that by its taste, its warmth, and its kick. Back in Luce, they've started to use Kinets to age it quickly, which ruins the taste if you ask me, but seeing as the stuff you've got here must have been sitting around since Grayfall, this must be the proper aged stuff. And let me tell you, Redflute," I say, leaning in closer, "Lucemead has inspired some of the great sorcerers of old to do some really magical feats. The literal mountain movers, remember them? All off their tits on the stuff, if you pardon my Worntongue."

Redflute has been listening to me wide-eyed, and now he nods enthusiastically. "I love those stories."

"Well then," I say, beaming at him, "this is the drink for you. Atmos Reclantis first learned to conjure ball lightning from the clouds with this liquid inspiration in him. Not only that, they say that when the Kinets first fought your kind on the site of First Light itself, Kinet Lorillion, absolutely tankarsed on the stuff, was moved to move an entire cliff edge onto you. No hard feelings, of course," I add hastily. "You still won that one after all. And then there was the Battle of Swamptide, when the Cloaks of Kascantion banded together and created the greatest illusion of them all, the cliff within the swamp, and all their enemies in Dawn Death feared it so much they went around the cliff, around it to their doom. What do you think gave them that idea?"

"Well," says Redflute, eyes so wide now they stretch around his head, "given all that, mage, then it would be rude of me not to have a little taste, would it not? I daresay a bloodless drink will be an intriguing little change anyway." He raises his tankard, but I stop him.

"Ah, not so fast, Redflute, my friend. You don't want to be taking a first sip. To really get the full sorcerer experience, you want to do as we do back in Luce."

"And what's that?"

"Drink the whole lot in one go." He starts to protest, but I cut him off. "Don't worry. It tastes like heaven, but it's hardly much stronger than the fine bloodwine you've got here. We sorcerers can't handle it too strong," I add, very much hoping that he was one of those vampires that kept to their own races pre-Grayfall.

Redflute shrugs. "Well then, sorcerer . . . to Luce, and the mead it produces!"

And to my endless shading delight, he swigs the whole lot.

The whole process takes about ten seconds. First his eyes water, then his face pales, and then he tries to stand but falls to the floor. His body makes a satisfying *thunk,* and many of the vampires look up from their games to see what's happened. I turn to the barman. "I think he might have had more than he could handle."

"Really," he says, more deadpan than I would have given him credit for. "What a shock." Then he signals to my slab of a doorman, who, despite being at the far end of the hall, has come over to see what everyone is looking at. "Someone needs their carriage home," the barman says. The slab nods, pleasingly still wordless, and picks up my new, and soon to be old, friend in one swift move and takes him out of the bar.

Sometimes it really is that easy.

I take my chance. I quickly stride down the hall and open the door that was barred to me. I don't know what I was expecting—what new shade of luxury or indecency I thought would be behind the door—but what I see is little better than the last room. The wood paneling is back, the rugs are a little thicker and more expensive looking, and the side tables are quacian rather than crestwood, but other than that, I see it for what it is: simply another level to make yourself feel more exclusive. There are several games being played, but most of the vampires in here are just in their armchairs sipping on their blood, looking like they were born in their chair. I sigh. I've been dealing with pricks like this all my life one way or another. I know what to say.

"Commander Tenfold," I announce loudly. There's no point in beating about the bush, I've always felt.

Everyone turns to look at me, and then, in the spirit of a true gentlemen's club, everyone immediately turns away back to their private vices. Everyone except one of the biggest vampires I've ever seen. He is clean-shaven and has a shock of red hair. Red hair is rare on a vampire; between that and his seven-foot height, he's the kind of person who'd still stand out in a midnight orgy. His actual face is fairly bland and gormless, as if it's trying to make up for how memorable the rest of him is; a chin cut from rock, but nothing much to the eyes. I can see him giving orders, but I can't see him thinking them through much. Let's see if I'm right.

"Commander Tenfold," I say again, trying to summon up something better to say than his shading name. Part of me didn't expect to get this far. I perhaps should've planned this conversation out. Sage would probably have weighed up all the options carefully: go in strong versus gain his confidence slowly; show your cards immediately versus play them close to your chest. I'll just go with what comes to me naturally. Sage has his skill set; I have mine.

I open with: "The young Azzuri told me all about you, so I thought to myself, I must have a drink with the man who made such an impression on the First Lord's son."

I see anger flash across his face, but I also see a flicker of panic. That's good. That means I already have something on him. Or maybe I've just sipped a little too much of the same drink that did in Redflute and I'm seeing things. One of the two.

"Sit the fuck down," he begins, "and tell me why you're here."

It's not the best invitation I've ever received, but it's not the worst, either. I sit down in the one of the comfiest chairs I've ever seen and inspect the room a little more. There's a drinks cabinet in each corner, high and many shelved and filled with everything you could need to see out a good few nights with no memory to show for them. Even more noticeably, there's a wolf's head—wolfkind, that is—fixed to the wall, its glassy eyes staring at me over its fanged smile, still managing to look more welcoming than the man sitting opposite me. I can see why this is an invitation-only room. I'm not sure the wolf-head look goes well with the last couple of centuries of peace and diplomacy.

"I'm assuming you're one of the two sorcerers that came for the funeral," begins Tenfold, drawing me away from my wolf gazing. "The mad bastards who made it past the Grays. That's why you're sat opposite me now instead of eating your teeth, after that entrance. But your diplomatic status gets you only so far. Either you've come to threaten me or you're just plain raving. I can't bloody wait to hear which one it is."

"Neither," I say. "Well, maybe a little bit of the second one. But only on my sober days. The truth is, I was a friend of the young Azzuri, too. Met him a couple of decades before Grayfall, when he went wandering the land. He used to write to me, tell me about what was happening in Lightfall. After Grayfall, when we were cut off, he did the same about First Light. We grew quite close, you could say. He used to mention you in his letters. Said you were a decent character. So I thought since I can't pay a visit to my only friend here anymore, I'd see if I couldn't meet one of his. Toast the soppy old bastard with you."

It's a risky bluff I make, the idea that Tenfold would crop up in his letters—not even the kind I make on my worst card-playing days—but I can see him go with it. Maybe he thinks I was his lover. Or perhaps it's just vanity and he wants to hear what was said about him.

"I see," he says, staring at me closely over his tankard. "Well, given the kind of people he hung around with, your story does make sense."

I don't think that's a compliment. But it's progress.

"First thing you should understand, though," he continues, "is that we weren't friends. But we did talk some. I respected him, more than others did anyway. He was more than people thought. So I'm sorry he's dead, and I'm sorry for you, too, if he was your friend. I can't tell you much more. So now you've met me, you won't mind if I carry on my drinking alone." At that he gives me a look, the kind that doesn't need words behind it, since there's already a considerable amount of muscle there instead.

I think quickly. I've already bluffed once, and I played a shading blinder. To bluff twice would make me the fool of the table. But a fool can win a few pots before the wise men take over.

I stare at his drink for inspiration. Simple bloodale. It's always a tragedy when a good drink gets ruined by blood. I'm trapped in a city full of the slaughter of good liquor.

"Drinking," I say, giving the commander my widest smile.

"I'm sorry?" he says, his fuck-off stare replaced by confusion.

"Drinking. It's my specialty. I know all the Lucemeads and all the Desertlands wines, and the ones from Lightfall, when vampires still made the bloodless kind. I can tell my Wolfsbane whiskey from my Shadowfall spirits, and I've got the lost days—and sometimes lost weeks—to prove it. Of course I don't know the blooddrinks. But I assume they follow the same rules. They're still just drinks, even though they've been spoilt by the red stuff, no offense."

"I'll probably take offense, to be honest."

"But my *point being* is that with my knowledge of drinks comes my knowledge of drunks. I know all the types. The weary traveler, pleased to be drinking anything now he's off the road. The cautious drunk, testing his limits as if it's the first time he's ever got tankarsed. The barfly, drinking for no reason, because that's his life and why not? And then there's your type. The type you've been for a few weeks now, I reckon." I nod toward his drink. "The clenched fist on the glass. The haunted eyes. The endless drinking without really getting drunk. Sound familiar? You are the guilty drunk, Commander. I reckon a good friend of yours has died, and you suspect pretty damn highly that you had a hand in it, though you didn't mean to. So why not unburden yourself to a fellow drunk? At best, it might undo the harm. At worst, it might help you sleep a little lighter."

"I sleep fine," the commander replies, looking away from me.

"But do you drink fine?"

Tenfold pauses. There's no conviction in his face anymore. I did a speech. Sage would be so proud.

"But why in the Bloodhalls should I trust you?" he says eventually, staring into the fire.

"Because," I reply, "if someone sought to hurt you, they wouldn't send a drunk mage arse like me, would they?"

The commander smiles for the first time. "Ha! I can't bloody argue with that." Then he looks at me, studies me hard, like a man who wants badly to accept a gift he's only just realized he needed. There's a moment when I think I have him, but then the mistrust sets in his face again, and I see I'm losing him—for shade's sake, I'm losing him—and then he downs the rest of his ale in one, and the acting Jacob, now indistinguishable from the real, cheers his liquid bravery. A friend in need is a drunk indeed.

"Okay," he says eventually. "I'll tell you what I know. Blood knows what your fucking agenda is. But to twin hells with it, I owe him. I warn you, though." His face suddenly sobers up and he points at me with a jabbing finger and that steel jaw of his. "If it comes back to me in any way—in *any* way—I'll round up my lads and we'll find you and send you back to your Archmage in pieces, neatly wrapped in that poncy robe of yours. Do you understand?"

"Pretty vividly, yes."

He pours himself another drink, and notices for the first time I don't have one. He nods at the cabinet. "There's some bloodless spirits in there. We've got quite the collection." I go to the cabinet and reach out and touch the smooth-paneled sides. I see my red-faced reflection in the glass: the current me, not the real me, but also, I realize, like the old me. Like the me who spent his youth, his first few decades, wandering from inn to inn in Quantile. Quantile, the home of Quantas, the sad city full of magickless mages, many of whom concluded that if the Light had created them without magick, then they would fill that hole with drink. I was one. There are so many ways you can be made to feel lesser in life by others, but to have a head start on that emptiness by your body itself? Well, that's something few can bear sober. It was after being consumed by some of the spirits in front of me that Sage found me. And now? Now I re-create the worst part of my life, to continue a role I feel I need to play.

I should probably think on that some more, sometime. But not this time. Seeing that they still don't have the five-spirits, I pick out a bottle of spiced Luce ginberry, cactus fuzz lurking in the bottom of the bottle, and take it back to my seat.

"I've known the young Azzuri for a while. He tried to join us, did you know that? About fifty years ago. Just turned up to one of the Blood Guard training sessions once, said his father had given it the nod. It actually worked for a couple of days, until the First Lord himself got wind of it. I was impressed with his balls, I have to say. He clearly wasn't guard material, or any kind of soldier—but he had a determination to him I admired. He was a good sort."

"So you became his . . . drinking companion?" I ask as carefully as I can, which is not very carefully.

Commander Tenfold grimaces at me and rewards my comment by pouring himself yet another drink.

"I know what you're getting at. No, I wasn't his lover. Oh, don't look shocked, it's an open secret. The Grays are deadly, and Azzuri the Younger likes what he likes. The only two facts you can depend on in First Light. Could depend on," he adds, looking away for a second. "No, I was just his friend. Not that I judged that. When you're outside of those walls, you stop giving a fuck what hole anyone sticks it in."

"Beautifully put," I say.

"Anyway, we'd talk, you know. Nothing unusual. He hated his dad, big surprise there. He hated his older brother—again, no secret. But every now and again he would say a strange thing."

"Like what?"

"Like whether I knew of anything strange that had been found in or around Lightfall—before Grayfall. Any, you know, relics or things. Anything hidden. He never explained why. He could be a mysterious little shit when he wanted to be."

"Sounds like it," I say. I'm enjoying this conversation. I don't have to do much except make my way through the spiced gin, feeling its cooling warmth spread across my limbs.

"Anyway, I never had anything to tell him when he asked those strange questions. Except one day when I did. I only noticed it six months ago. But for all I know it's been going on for years. Since Grayfall, perhaps."

"Noticed what?" Now you're talking.

Tenfold takes a long pause and stares into his Atmos fire-grain (no blood in his, I note approvingly). I can't tell if he's regretting telling me all this or if it's just that the Atmos special is burning his throat. "When we do the patrols outside the walls," he says eventually, "we always send two scouts ahead to the ridge overlooking the valley south of First Light. You get a good view of everything from there. Of course, it's fucking dangerous, because you can get very isolated. Cut off from the rest of the patrol. So it takes a particular kind of scout. A tough piece of work, the kind that's ready to die every time they get up in the morning and can't wait to go down swinging. And there's one that's been doing that role for the first patrol ever since Grayfall. A man by the name of Rickard Deckard. A Worn. A sergeant. Balls like night brass."

Rickard Deckard. What a name. "What came first," I ask, "the name or the balls?"

"What?"

"Nothing. Sorry, carry on."

"Anyway, one day he and his partner go off on their route. Only some fucking runner from the city comes up with an urgent message for us just after they'd left. Some poncy Lord wants them to look across the ridge, check the shitting weather or something out that way for their records. As if they couldn't just risk it themselves, get permission to down some wolfblood and fly out there. Risk a Gray bullet instead of us doing it for once. Anyway," he continues, his brief moment of anger thankfully pissing off. Last thing I want is a big drunk slab of muscle like that getting the rages. "I ran after them. Commander's responsibility. Not having one of my men risk themselves for such a pointless bloody task."

I study the commander carefully as he speaks, and I notice his suddenly bleary eyes and slightly sweaty forehead. I don't have Sage's gift for the body signs or whatever he calls them, but I'm wondering if maybe my horseshit earlier about him drinking because he feels guilty is more on the mark than I realized. It can't be usual for the commander of one of the most important regiments in the entire city to be mouthing off against his betters like that, at least not to a mage he's only just met. I feel a bit of a prick for thinking this, but his pain can be of use to me, if it makes him this willing to talk.

"So I catch up to them both. His partner's up at the ridge, but Rickard's been crouching down next to some bloody tree. At first I think he's pissing, but then I see he's putting something there. A package. In a metal box, by the looks of it. Like a small chest. Not that small, but small enough for him to conceal in his armor. He didn't know I'd seen him."

"Did you go back later to check what was in the box?"

"No, did I buggery. Wasn't worth a Gray bullet for what was probably some Lord's business. But I told the young Azzuri about it. Not because I really thought it had anything to do with his strange questions, but I thought it might shut him up. Of course, that just made him more curious. What did the box look like? How big it was? I couldn't tell him much more. Except that old Rickard was doing it a lot."

"How do you know?"

"Because I checked on them every night for the next week. I didn't let them see me though. Every patrol, he did the same."

"Why? Why take the risk for, as you say, some Lord's business?"

"I wasn't going to stir up a hornet's nest by asking Rickard what was in it or who had told him to put it there. But I did want to get as much information as I could. Make sure it's nothing that's going to fuck up my men. That's the only way I sleep at night in this crazy fucking city, with the Grays out there—knowing I've done everything I can to make it less likely they're going to die."

"And is that all you found out?"

"Yes. And one month after I told young Azzuri this, he was dead." His rheumy eyes suddenly clear for a second, and he has the look of a man who knows he's said too much. He goes to speak, but I cut in instead. "I know, I know. You'll send me back in pieces if I say anything. I haven't forgotten the mental image."

"Good."

"Well," I announce, suddenly very tired, "it's been a pleasure, Commander. I think I'll leave you to your drink." I get up and look at Tenfold, who has turned away and stared into the fire. Only the clenched knuckles on his tankard give anything away.

I'm about to leave him to it, but I turn back one more time.

"One more thing. Why . . . why did you tell Azzuri? He didn't need to know. Weren't you worried what he would do?"

Tenfold turns from the fire and his eyes seem fine now. The flames have taken whatever regret he was holding on to for a second. A useful trick, that.

"I told you, I just wanted to stop him asking his questions."

I shake my head. I feel sober all of a sudden. I have something, and I won't let it go. "But a lie would have done that."

For a second, I think Tenfold is going to ignore me and return to the fire, but then he barks out his words quickly, almost like they're an afterthought.

"My daughter died in Grayfall. Was shot as we fled. Gray bullet to the heart. She died in my arms. Turned to ashes and blew across my face. She had the prettiest smile and her mother's eyes. Every time I'd think of those I'd killed in wars or those I'd lost in them, she would laugh and bring me back to the world. Nothing else could do that. Only her. I'd started to forget what she ever looked like when I met young Azzuri. So he drew me a picture from my description of her. He didn't tell me. He just gave it to me one day. It was perfect. I don't know how he did it, but it was her. When I look at it, I can hear her laugh again. If it wasn't for that picture, I think I would have run outside the city and let the Grays have me long ago. If you're doing what I think you're doing, then do it well. And do it for him."

I don't know what to say to that, so I just leave him be.

As I leave the Rushes, having had a couple more glasses to wash away the heat of that heavy encounter with Tenfold, I tell myself I'm not drunk. I have to tell myself that a few times, because the weaving side to side I'm doing as I walk is making me doubt my own story. At this point it's hard to tell where my act begins and the reality of how much I have drunk ends. I stumble on into the courtyard. Hold on. Why is my carriage not there? And where are the guards assigned to me for my protection (or for the First Lord to keep an eye on me, one of the two)? I look around, feeling my drunkenness slip away as my body comes alive with a creeping sense of the not-quite-right. Or in this case the sense of "oh, bugger me, I might have made a mistake here, Jacob, you silly prick." The courtyard is eerily empty. I feel like I'm being watched. That sounds like something people just say, but now I really feel it. Like a soft vibration in the air. I don't know what the Light I'm talking about, and I *really* don't like this.

"A quick exit, I think," I say to myself, fairly confident that I'm not slurring anymore. But as I make to leave the courtyard, I see a figure standing in the entrance, blocking my way. He's mostly in the shadows, but from what little I can make of him from the flickering torchlight, it's obvious he's a sorcerer; the robe gives that away. But it isn't a robe of any of the five kinds. It's black. So the sorcerer's in disguise. And a veil covers his face. I don't like where this is going.

I check behind me for a second, and then when I turn back, the figure is gone. I turn round again, and he is there right behind me. No one moves that fast. Well, *almost* no one moves that fast.

Your thoughts are very easy to read when you're a few tankards down, Jacob.

"Light of Luce," I say, more a statement than an exclamation. "Light of shading Luce," I say again, because I suppose the first time didn't seem dramatic enough. "You're a Neuras."

You can do better than that, Quantas.

"You're speaking into my mind. You're one of *those* Neuras."

It does appear that way.

"I thought all of you were dead."

Did you? You should be careful what you think around me.

"You could start a war simply by being in Lightfall," I say, not fully understanding what's happening but hoping I can muddle through somehow.

And yet here I am, thinks the sorcerer.

"Is it possible that someone slipped something into my mead?" I ask, more to myself than the sorcerer. That would make more sense than what my eyes and the voice in my head are telling me. The sorcerer before me is a Shade. Shades were all killed after the Twin War, executed by the vampires. There was a good reason for that, because they're not your average mind-reading Neuras sorcerer. They're something else entirely, and at the end of the war when the wolves and vampires had made a reluctant peace, the Shades almost came in and destroyed the tired remnants of their armies with their mind-reading combat. There's a reason it's called the Twin War, not the Great War, and that reason is standing in front of me now.

He walks closer to me, this ghost of yesterday. I don't see much point in moving. I know what he can do. Perhaps it's the warm hold of the liquor inside me, but I feel strangely calm.

He stops in front of me and lifts up his veil. I see his eyes, and in that instant there's only one answer. "I know I'm actually back in the Rushes facedown on the tiles now, and this is a spirit dream," I say matter-of-factly. "I know this because I'm looking at the face of Neuras Sinassion."

Sinassion looks away briefly, and it looks like two suns have changed position. It's impossible to focus on his features.

"Hold on," I say, slowly putting something together, "why are you talking to me at all . . . oh. Oh. Oh, I see."

I won't gloat, Jacob, and I don't offer any apology. You know too much and now I have to kill you. I take no pleasure in killing another sorcerer.

"Well, in that case you've not had a life full of much pleasure, then . . . What are you involved in here, Sinassion? Are you with the vampires? Have you done a deal with the Grays? You mad bastard, what are you doing?" I stare at the mage a little, as much as I can. I never thought I'd meet the leader of the Shades. The man who almost won an entire continent. The man who taught his followers to speak into minds, not just read them. The man who taught a combat so advanced that it seemed to those they fought that they were invisible. The man who is as robe-wettingly scary in the flesh now as he is in the stories.

I breathe out and feel my head go dizzy from inhaling my own spirit fumes. "You know what? I don't know and I don't care. I just wish I'd had more time to sleep with more women and try new liquor."

We both know that's your act, talking. Your bravado. You don't need to pretend with me. I knew you the moment you gave me your mind. And I say that you give up very quickly, Jacob. I think there is more to you than that.

"Confidence tips from my killer. What an excellent night this is turning into. Is there anything I can do to help myself?"

In no way whatsoever.

"Then my fault is realism, is it not? I can think of worse character flaws. Go on then, Sinassion. Do what you will."

You are saving your friend's life by dying, most likely, he thinks. *If your search ends here, he can go back to his temple. He can be safe.*

"I didn't know you were this considerate. You're meant to be a monster."

I do monstrous things on occasion. He draws a blade with a glowing green light out from his robe. *That is most likely enough for the term, I suppose.*

Sinassion raises the blade before my chest, and I stare into the two glowing suns and wait to find out my afterlife.

But the blow doesn't come. There's a rush of wind, though—a rush of wind in front of my face. I open my eyes and for a second all I can see is black.

"I should have died years ago," I note. "That was almost . . . painless." And then I realize—and how many spirits must I have drunk for this realization to come so slowly—that the black is fur, and it belongs to the large but lithe and muscular frame of a raven-haired wolf, who has Sinassion pinned to the ground.

The sorcerer isn't pinned for long, though. With his free arm he directs a quick jab to the underbelly of the wolf; it doesn't pull back much but enough to allow him to break free and leap, in one swift backward roll, into a standing position once again. The wolf goes for his throat, spittle flying from its mouth, but he steps aside as its jaw glances by him and connects a one-two punch to the wolf's chest; the beast is not hurt but growls in frustration. I should probably leave now, but I can't look away.

They circle each other, the wolf crouched low, waiting for the moment to pounce; Sinassion maintaining a distance from it, seeming to glide rather than walk. I'm feeling hypnotized just watching him. The sorcerer lashes out first, a direct kick to the wolf's face, but this time it's the creature that dodges the blow, pouncing backward somehow from their crouching position. I've never seen a wolf do that before. Sinassion lands from his attack perfectly and is ready for the outstretched lunge of the wolf, ducking it with perfect timing. By the five magicks, this could go on all shading night. At least it's one way to sober up.

The wolf growls even louder then and launches at the sorcerer with both jaw and claws, all timing gone and instead a whir of black kinetic fur. Sinassion is nimble enough to avoid it for a few seconds, but his quick timing cannot survive for long against the random frenzy, and suddenly the wolf barrels into him and he is knocked to the floor, and I see him struggling to recover. Once again, though, before the next blow hits, he is back on his feet, though a little slower this time. Then the wolf descends on him again, jaws wide open and ready to enclose his head, but Sinassion finds his speed and pirouettes on his feet to the right, just avoiding the wolf's jaws. Now facing it side on, he chops at the neck muscle with his left hand and at its haunches with his right, then repeats the one-two. The wolf roars in pain and backs off.

Then the air shimmers, and for a moment the shadows of the night are filled with all the colors of a rainbow, and a hole seems to grow out of the air, and in that hole I see bones and flesh mutating, changing. Then it all dies down and opposite Sinassion stands a naked woman, tanned brown, all lean muscle. Long dark hair covers her face, and her eyes are set in shadows behind it. I've never seen her before, but I'm a gambling man and I'd lay all the Lord cards and my remaining Midways on knowing who it is.

Sinassion's eyes glow fiercer. *I didn't expect to meet you here, Raven, on this night and in this city.*

Raven. Wonderful. Just what I needed. The most feared wolf either side of the Borderlands. There are no ends to the pleasures of this night.

I'm here more than you, Sinassion. Or at least that used to be true. Why are you with Saxe?

I'm not as wise as Sage, but I've seen a few things, and I've learnt to make the quick judgments he has, and that's how I realize that Sinassion is talking into Raven's head, like he did to me, and Raven is replying, using her thoughts instead of her voice. They know each other, then, or at least they've fought each other. I can hear their thoughts because Sinassion is near me and he was recently in my head and . . . granted, that last thought is just guesswork. Sage can stuff his shading inferences.

You want to know my plans? I could tell you, Raven. But you never had much patience with me, did you?

Raven shrugs. *I know some things.*

We all know some things, my dear Midnight Assassin. It helps to know it all. I missed you, you know. The problem with exile is that you never get to fight.

Raven growls, human sounding but still part wolf. *Fighting with you is not a real fight. Not when your opponent reads your mind to anticipate you. Wolves play fair. You do not know the meaning of the word.*

Well, I cannot turn into a giant wolf, Raven, can I, so we all have to use our tricks, do we not?

I'm glad you said that, Sinassion. I've learned some tricks of my own since we last fought. I have had many years to think of it. Think on the wolf mind, and how it is different from the person mind.

I just fought the wolf and I was doing perfectly fine.

No. You fought me in control of the wolf. Now you should meet the wolf itself.

The air shimmers again, and the illusion of color, cartilage, and chaos returns. Raven is a wolf again, but her eyes look wilder, like all the thought has gone out of them, and she lunges at Sinassion in one bound. The sorcerer steps away nimbly, but as he does, she sticks out a paw even as she lands on the other three, and she smacks him in the chest with it. He falls back to the ground but recovers his stance and backflips away a moment before she can pounce on him again but only just, and as he goes to step away with that smooth footwork of his, Raven is on him again, relentless. She pins him to the ground, her jaw drooling, saliva splashing on his face, eyes still bereft of anything but the kill. She rakes a paw down his chest, slashing open his robe and some of his skin, and then she opens her jaw wide for the killing blow.

Suddenly there's a loud noise from the entrance of the Rushes. A group of vampires are leaving, and their drunken cries quickly reach us. They sound even more tankarsed than I was a few moments ago. Raven turns her head at the sound, and the movement lifts one of her paws off Sinassion. The sorcerer takes the opportunity and punches her snout with his flat upturned hand. Then as she lifts her other paw to keep her balance, he rolls away and dashes into the night, with a speed that would make no sense even if I was as clearheaded as a meadless mage. I don't see him go; he is simply there, and when I next look, he isn't. The wolf stays there for a moment, panting slightly, and then its small yellow eyes turn to me and it bares its teeth. For a second I think I'm back to square one, only this time with a different shading killer, but then it, too, leaps into the shadows by the alley and is gone in a bound.

When my heart has stopped trying to hammer its way out of my chest, I walk up to the raucous vampires who unknowingly broke up one of the fiercest fights I've ever seen. I need a lift back, and more important, whether still in my role or not, I need another drink.

16

All Your Stories End in Death

It is quite possible and indeed likely that after the battle of Extinction Valley, the wolfkind, their numbers reduced by a third after that massacre, would have accepted defeat, but they would surely never have eagerly worked with the vampires and their sorcerer allies on the same side were it not for the subsequent threat hot on the heels of the bloody vampire and wolf battles: Neuras Sinassion and his Shades.

Atmos Regardis, *A Historie of the Twin War*

Lady Hocquard

I pace up and down one of the southern balconies, hands playing with my scarf, fangs pulling at my lip. Back when my husband was alive, we would take our firstblood here, enjoying the early night air. Not everything was perfect, but he was far from the worst of the Lords, and I have fond memories of these precious moments with him. They haunted me a little after he was killed in Grayfall. But now they bring me calm. But try as I might, there is no calm to be found here.

"I know you be worryin', m'lady, but other Leech business is still to be heard. The maid who sweeps the vestry of West Gods is one of ours, and she's been hearin' some right awful whispers about the priests there, and I got news of a scrubber in the Blood Farms who be thinking she has information on the Midway in charge there. Some coin-meddling he got into way back when behind the Blood Bank's nose. It would be good to have a hold over someone like that. Not to mention the—"

"I'm not sure we're ready, Alanna," I say, interrupting. "We have put our faith in Sam, so early, and now these sorcerers, who we know nothing about. I will be sundamned if she isn't ready at all."

"We had little choice about it, m'lady. We have some of the best information we've had for a while, and we 'ave to move fast. If you stop making moves yourself, then things move against you, I learnt that in Last Light."

Alanna reaches for where she keeps her dagger as she says this. I don't think she realizes she does it, but she does it whenever she speaks of her home city. She has never really explained who she was, but from the pieces of information I get, she must have been a spy of some sort, or an assassin. I have wondered on it often. I hope one day we will be close enough for her to tell me. I hope that one day comes sooner rather than later, but the decades do have a habit of flying by before you know.

"I don't know, Alanna. If Saxe suspects the sorcerers, then chances are he knows about us. All he would have needed to do was have them followed here. Lord Saxe is not a man to be trifled with. I am worried we might be in it up to our jugulars here, Alanna."

"Just because sorcerers are comin' here doesn't mean they suspect you, m'lady. They are still a little too short-thinking about women to be leapin' to those kinds of conclusions. And they're not watchin' the house and there's no creeps askin' around about you, m'lady."

"Oh, he won't make it obvious, Alanna. He'll be very subtle about it. That is his art after all, subtlety and secrets."

Alanna moves closer to me until there is barely a couple of inches between us. She is shorter than me, so she looks up at me with that strange face full of secrets. It would take but a second to close the space between us farther.

"Do not be a-fearing, m'lady," she says after that long second is over. "I've got plenty of Leeches on it. If he is onto us, then he is quieter than a billbird in its nest."

I pause. Give myself some Alanna time. "Alanna, what in all the Bloodhalls is a billbird?"

"They flew over Last Light, m'lady, all the time, back in the day. Peculiar to the Ashlands. Fur as well as feather. Makes nests out of its own fur. Funny little things."

"I've no doubt." I move away from her, breaking the tension, and sit down on the low quacian bench that spans half the balcony.

"Is this what you did, Alanna?" I ask. "I know you don't like to talk of those times. But you've told me enough. It was all like this, wasn't it? Big secrets, spanning the city. Things that change everything, not just individuals. Not like we Leeches do day to day. Deeper secrets. The ones the men spin until it collapses down around them."

There is a long pause while Alanna considers this. Far away an owl hoots, one, twice, and then no more, and I chastise myself for all my worrying when I should be absorbing the night, which out here in Northeastfall is so calming.

"It is true I found out some big things in Last Light, m'lady, yes," she says eventually. "Things that could tear cities down and ruin new ones forever. So many of them in that place, that sometimes they canceled each other out. It got a bit tirin' in the end, if you wants some truths. If the city hadn't fallen, I'm not sure I could have seen my way through any more of that frenzy, if you want my honesty."

"And what about now?" I ask. "Will you be tiring of this one?"

Alanna grins. "I've not used up but a quart full of frenzy yet in this place, m'lady. I'm just warmin' to it, I thinks."

I can't help but return the smile at that.

"Besides," she adds, "I hardly have anywhere else to go. Not many places for a vampire like me worth my skills. Even if I could get around the Grays, I could hardly tolerate the mages and their wandering hands. And could you imagine me with the wolves? I would cause more trouble than I stopped."

"Yes, I saw how you looked at Raven Ansbach at that Diplomacy Ball a few years back."

"I am not sure what you could mean, m'lady."

We are silent for a little. I like our silences. They are the kind where there is no expectation of words, which I rather think is a sign of how you feel.

"Would you like to hear a little story from the days of Last Light, m'lady?" Alanna says, when enough time in our own spaces has passed. "Might put things into some better light, if you pardon the punning."

I nod. Such stories are rare, and I drink them in.

"They were four families doing most of the things in Last Light," she begins. "No one ruled it, you understand, m'lady, it being a free city, but these four, they spun its wheels and meddled in its cellars, if you get my meaning."

"Rarely," I say, trying not to smile, "but do go on."

"One of these families, the Cosvinti, there were rumors round the city about them makin' a flying machine."

"A flying machine?"

"That's right, m'lady, a machine to take you into the air. To solve the problem of Last Light. As you know, m'lady, you could not travel through the Ashlands beyond the city to find out what was hidden there because of the banshees, among other things, so you had to fly over them. But a flight that long, the amount of wolfblood a vampire would need . . . it ain't possible. But this thing—a machine based on the wings of vampires, like a giant vampire that you sit on, if you take the meaning well—it would fly you right over the dangers themselves all the way to whatever mysteries are beyond them. Which of course was why vampires came to found Last Light. To explore. Before we got . . . distracted."

"I can see how everyone would get excited about a machine like that."

"Excited? M'lady, they were up in arms about such a thing, such a shriekin' and a hollerin' you never did see. And the other families, well, they knew that this would give all the riches to the Cosvinti, so they wanted a juicy parcel of whatever contraption this was. The eldest son of the Cidemi was the one who first heard where this thing was being built. So he snook down there to take a look, with some of his best men. Snook all the way down to the harbor, where they found a secret warehouse." She pauses then. Always a fan of a dramatic pause, is my Alanna.

"And?" I ask, not bothering to hide my impatience. "Did they find it?"

"They did not, m'lady. All they found was an empty storehouse and some dry tinder, which, covered in oil, soon took a quick spark to it, and shortly thereafter they found out what it feels like to burn to death for a vampire, long and slow and painful, till all that was left was ashes. They tried to escape, but the doors were barred, and if you imagine how long it takes a vampire to die, then you can imagine their sufferin'."

"Bloods . . . so it was a trap?"

"The very sneakiest and the very most patient, m'lady. There never was such a flying machine. But the desire for it and the sounds of it drew their enemies closer, all the way to their death."

I take a moment to think on this tale. "All your stories from Last Light end in death, have you ever noticed that, Alanna?"

"It was not the best place for a restorative, m'lady, this is true. Probably best there is nought of it left anymore."

"And why are you telling me this now? Because we might be chasing our own flying machine? Are we falling into a trap of our own, and set to burn, is that what you're saying?"

"Oh no," Alanna says, sitting next to me on the bench, bringing us close again, so the soft scent of sandalwood stands out. Alanna has denied using scents before, claiming she is too practical for them, but you cannot fool the nose on the kind of blood I drink, and I wonder why she bothers. Well, I do not wonder it. I hope I know.

"What I'm sayin' is that if we think far enough ahead, then our enemies will burn, too."

Alanna stares at me, and I see the wild in my eyes, always there but so fervently strong now, and for a second, I recoil from it. But then I let it take me, and I think of fire, and all the ways it burns.

Sam

"So let me see if I have this correct," says Lady Hocquard, giving Jacob a look that would make most men cower, if most men weren't too steeped in liquor to notice it. "One of the most dangerous sorcerers in the history of this land attempted to kill you but was stopped by one of the most dangerous wolves, who proceeded to engage him in combat in front of you."

"That's about the size of it, yes," says Jacob. "You can imagine my surprise."

"Not as much as you can imagine mine," she replies, glancing sideways at Alanna, whose eyes are narrowed at Jacob in an expression that makes me worry for his safety. We're meeting again in Lady Hocquard's mansion, two nights after the last meeting and a night after Jacob's narrow escape. We're in a different room, though; a long dining hall in the East Wing, with large windows framed by thick velvet curtains. We're in armchairs by the fireplace on one end; the other end is bathed in shadow and a tiny dapple of moonlight.

The hall couldn't be more different from the rest of the Lady's mansion. Stone and more stone instead of marble and plaster; above the fireplace there's no elaborate friezing but instead two swords crossed over a goblet, the sigil of the Hocquard line—the male line, at least. The high-vaulted ceilings of the hall and the arched windows contrast with the rest of the mansion. Alanna told me when I first stayed over that it was kept in this style when the rest of the mansion was rebuilt in the Old Mage fashion after the Twin War as a nod to the history of the house and the Hocquards. That was her husband's choice; I wonder now that he's gone if the reason why it remains the same is so Lady Hocquard has one spot above cellar level where she doesn't feel she's playing a role.

Speaking of playing a role, I'm still struggling to juggle both of mine:

every time I return to the palace, I have to spin Beth a web of deceit that is great practice for being a Leech but terrible practice for being a friend. I think I might have to tell her the truth soon; I can't take looking into her friendly face and spitting a pack of untruths into it.

"It is certainly unexpected," says Sage, bringing me out of my thoughts. "I mean, the appearance of Raven Ansbach is not a surprise—she has free rein of First Light, given her role as hunter of escaped wolf criminals, but Neuras Sinassion? Remarkable."

"Is it remarkable? I feel like as a sorcerer yourself you maybe know more of this than you are willing to admit," asks Lady Hocquard, her voice rapidly dropping in temperature.

Sage smiles at this. I eye them both. It's like watching two swamp tigers circle each other. Both are used to being the dominant one in the room, clearly.

"I can assure you I am as alarmed as you at this appearance, and the fact he is alive. All I know is that he clearly believes we know too much and saw his chance to scare us away by killing Jacob."

"Or so says whiskey-breath over 'ere," says Alanna.

"I do not have whiskey breath," replies Jacob.

"I can smell your fumes from over here, mage."

"They're not mine," says Jacob, smelling the inside of his robe and wrinkling his nose in disgust. "*That*, on the other hand, is definitely mine."

"I see," says Lady Hocquard, ignoring them both. "Well, before we go any further, I think it best if I receive a little education in this man. We all know his role in the Twin War, but I think we could do with a little more than that at this rate, don't you?"

Sage nods and goes to speak, but the Lady raises her hand and stops him. "Not from you, dear. I am still in the suspicious stage with you, I am afraid. I wish instead to see what a girl who has spent more time in libraries than most of my Leeches put together can tell me instead." I do my best to suppress a smile and I almost succeed. I assumed I'd be an onlooker once again while the key players take their turns. But not all my speaking parts have been scrubbed from the travel yarn, it seems.

"Well, m'lady, much of Sinassion's life remains a mystery," I begin, trying to work out if the thin smile on Sage's face is one of annoyance, admiration, or amusement. "No one knows when he came into this world. There are written records of a strange sorcerer with glowing eyes. I've read some of them, contained in some of the older tomes. He appears all over the land. Some scribes say he could be one of the first sorcerers, though others disagree. What we do know is that about a century before the Twin War, he begins getting followers. Soldiers, I suppose you might say, given what came later, but maybe . . . *adherents* or *disciples* are better terms for how it began. He took them into the southernmost reaches of the Desertlands and he trained them to be as powerful as him, or nearly so. They became known as Shades."

"Explained like a pastscribe yourself, Sam dear," says Lady Hocquard, as I try to get used to the sight of a whole room hanging on my words. "And what exactly are his powers? From the general stories I know, he seems capable of doing everything except turning night into day."

"No one knows the extent of them, m'lady. We can work it out only based on what we've seen him do, he and his followers. Maybe I should let Brother Bailey take over now? This is quite complicated sorcerer business."

"And yet you are handling such business with aplomb, so please do not stop now," replies Lady Hocquard, who, I'm beginning to realize, is a master at making an ice-cold order sound like a polite request.

"Well. . . . I'll begin with what a normal Neuras can do, and forgive me if I'm stating the obvious here. A Neuras can read someone's mind only by touching them; even then, a well-trained person can guard against their reading, at least for a time, and perhaps forever with deeply held secrets. Without contact, however, they can sense only the most basic of thoughts and emotions, and within around fifty feet, this fades to just the presence of someone's mind in the area. Useful, but hardly mind-reading. Even this fades within about half a mile, for most Neuras.

"But of course, Sinassion is not a normal Neuras. What we know for sure—and if I take anything away from the books I read, m'lady, it's that what we know wouldn't fill a bloodvial, so to speak—is that he can read what is in someone's mind without touching them simply by being near them, at least what's at the forefront of it. And while this can be prevented by someone with intensive training, once he has his hands on you, there's nothing that can be kept from him. Sinassion taught a weaker version of this to all his followers, along with the ability to speak into someone's mind."

"Yes, I know about that," says Lady Hocquard. "I am glad I have never experienced it. It sounds . . . unnerving."

"You can say that again. It's about as pleasant as some ice in the undergarments," adds Jacob, who, I've noticed, has been taking a lot of enjoyment from seeing me upstage his friend and superior. At least I assume that's what the smirking's about.

"But what made him and his Shades particularly dangerous was another of his powers," I continue. "Essentially, he developed a form of combat that involves reading the enemy's mind. Not properly, just their most basic thoughts—where they intend to strike next, what they're looking at, that sort of thing. To the person watching a Neuras with this kind of training, it can appear that they're untouchable, that they know every move the other is making before they do. The war histories say it was something to behold. Like a dance. They didn't have the strength of wolves or vampires, and they didn't have teeth or claws, but it didn't matter. There was only one outcome when you danced with a Shade. And, of course, these powers were used for things other than combat. According to the war histories, Sinassion and his Shades held their ground for so long in the war simply by disappearing and appearing somewhere no one expected."

"But they didn't actually disappear?" asks Lady Hocquard.

"To put it simply," cuts in Sage, who has obviously decided it's safe for him to make a contribution, "if you know where someone is looking all the time and can react accordingly and with enough speed, then your movements essentially become invisible."

Lady Hocquard shakes her head. "I am trying to understand that statement, but it's slightly hurting my head."

"Welcome to my life," notes Jacob.

"These followers, these Shades, they were his army in the war, yes?" she continues. "I know the basics of the Twin War, but I was born thirty years after it, so my knowledge is somewhat rusty."

"They were." Sage nods. "And we all know how deadly they were and what it almost came to."

"Yes, even my rudimentary grasp of history covers that. The great war of blood and wolf, ended only by the threat of Sinassion that united them both, and most of the sorcerers, too, in the need to stop him. Although I'm unclear what his goal was. Apart from slaughter, obviously."

"I don't know any more than you do," says Sage. "Why was he motivated to take part in the Twin War to such devastating effect? People say power. Others say he lost his mind long ago and simply wanted to rack up a body count."

Lady Hocquard turns to me. I shrug. "The tomes are pretty undecided on the topic, m'lady, unfortunately."

"We called him the Silent Death in Last Light," says Alanna, her contribution as cheery as ever. "Tales of his battle slaughter came across the Southern Sea to us. The Twin War didn't touch us, but his count of death still left a large mark."

"And yet such evil doesn't fit with the man," Sage says. "Not the man I met anyway."

Lady Hocquard raises her carefully penciled eyebrows in shock at this. "I'm sorry?" Lady Hocquard says. "You met him?"

"Only once. Before the war, when he was drawing followers to him. Back before he and his Shades massacred thousands," Sage adds. I lean forward, excited. This isn't in the books. When you've read as much as I have, new anecdotes are something to be prized.

"I was just starting my travels to look for evidence of the mortals," continues Sage. "It was just me then. I had no cult. I came across a small stone construction in the desert. There were four people kneeling there, and one was Sinassion. He knew what I was doing there already, of course, and I said I had heard of him, which to my alarm he had also picked up without touching me. But he was friendly, in his slightly quiet, unnerving way, at least as friendly as someone can be when you can't really see his face. All you can focus on is those glowing eyes. Huge orbs of light, drawing you in. Very . . . disconcerting."

"What did you talk about?"

"Very little. He wished me well on my travels to seek out the mortals. Said he would be interested to learn what I found, and that I should return some time."

"And did you?"

"No. I was too busy setting up the Cult of Humanis, and then the Twin War came, and the next time I saw him was from a mile away, as he painted such scenes as sometimes haunt my dreams. He was a very different man that day."

"That was then," says Lady Hocquard. "What about now? Why is he in First Light?"

"I don't know. He fled to the very south of the Desertlands after the war, when he escaped his execution. Alone. All his other Shades were killed, executed by the vampires. So he's been hidden there alone for two centuries, without any allies. What plans he's been making—what drives him now—is just as much a mystery as it ever was."

"So let me see if I have this correct," says Lady Hocquard, "because this is quickly developing into something even more alarming than the normal machinations of Lords that I am used to."

"You're telling me, m'lady," says Alanna. "I am fondly eyeing me memories of Lords stealin' blood and fuckin' the wrong people, pardon me Wolftongue."

"Oh, come on now," says Jacob, "I'm sure you saw more plotting in a day in Last Light than I have in a century."

Alanna grimaces. "That could mean you had a boring century much more than me havin' an interesting day, couldn't it, mage-breath?"

Lady Hocquard quickly cuts in. "So, Brother Bailey, here is how I have it so far, assuming I am abreast of this increasingly layered web. According to Azzuri's letter to you shortly before his death, he had discovered a strange connection between the Grays and what was found under Lightfall and transported here to the Blood Bank by Saxe. In the course of investigating this, he is killed. Thanks to Jacob's discovery from the Rushes, we know that someone has been ordering a member of the Scout Guard to leave packages outside the city walls. Oh, and one of the most dangerous sorcerers in history has come out of hiding. Have I covered it so far?"

"Very admirably," says Sage. "And I suspect it will get even more complicated from here on in."

"Oh, good," says Lady Hocquard. "At this rate I fear I shall have to start taking notes."

"It's funny you should say that," begins Sage.

"Don't even think about it," cuts in Jacob. "Please, m'lady, if he ever gets his paperbook out, then you have my permission to bleed him dry. He even makes notes about the weather."

"One day the weather will be of great use in helping solve a problem like this," says Sage.

"Has it ever been?"

"Not as such."

"Anyway . . ." interrupts Lady Hocquard, "we still have many unanswered questions. For example, what is in the package? Who is it meant for?"

"Well, unless they be anyone going on their walkabouts outside the walls for larks, surely it must be the Grays, m'lady," says Alanna.

"What about Sinassion?" asks Jacob.

Sage nods. "Maybe. But for so long? Surviving out there? He's good, but I don't know if he's good enough to risk a Gray bullet. And if he can come into the city, then why bother risking himself out there?"

"But what would they have to say to the Grays?" asks Lady Hocquard. "Messages asking them nicely to stop killing anyone they see and return to wherever they came from? Bribes to make them go away? Or perhaps they have opened a secret communication line? Negotiating a truce, maybe?"

"I don't know that anyone's ever heard the Grays speak, never mind be capable of making a truce," says Jacob.

"We do not have enough information yet," says Sage, "although we can say one thing with some confidence."

"And what is that?" asks Lady Hocquard.

"That Azzuri was most likely out there on the night of his death to try and get the package for himself. And he was killed for it."

Lady Hocquard blanches. "So someone knew he was trying to get the package? But he was shot with Gray bullets!"

Sage shrugs. "So we were told. Perhaps that is the story we were meant to hear. Or it could be true, and he was indeed shot by a Gray, perhaps one that was simply passing, and it was simply very bad luck. Unfortunately, there's too many possibilities for my liking. Like I say, we need more information."

"Hmm," says Lady Hocquard. "We do. But at least we know that whatever is in those packages is worth dying for."

"Maybe we also know someone who can help us more," I say quietly, staring at the far corner of the hall, where the shadows by the curtains are long and drawn, and in one place much longer than they should be.

Everyone turns to me and then swivels to see where I am looking. "Raven Ansbach," I continue. "We've not yet discussed why she was there to save Jacob's life. What has the Midnight Assassin got to do with all this?"

"Oh," says a voice right then from the shadows I've been watching; a deep, thick accent floating out of the dark. "I thought you'd never ask."

17

The Scent of a Woman

If you're not a wolf, put it this way: imagine you have a second pair
of eyes, and they do what the nose does but then they help you to see,
in a way. Makes sense? No, of course it doesn't, because you're not a
fucking wolf.

Mahogany Stubbe, *The Law of the Wolf*

Raven

I smell the change in them as they see me in the shadows and slowly realize who I must be. It is not them I smell, but their fear itself. Fear has a metallic odor, but underlying its general scent are deeper smells, depending on the individual. For Jacob, it is a deep, pungent scent, like a ripe cheese; he is barely over his near death, and the sight of me is taking him back to that moment. It is this and his general fear of me that are responsible for the overpowering odor. For his fellow mage Sage, it is a slight tang, almost like sea air. He is afraid, but he is also curious, and the emotions mix intriguingly. I could taste him all day. Sam is stronger, somewhere between Sage and Jacob, but it is muted. In fact I think this whole experience is muted for her; she is still walking in a dream. All her emotions smell drained. I wonder how she will taste when she wakes up.

That leaves the one they call Lady Hocquard and her first maid. The lady is slightly sweet in her fear—not too much, but what is there is heightened, like the first taste of summer fruit. She puts on a brave face. But wolves can see past that sort of thing. The one she calls Alanna . . . now there is a scent. Or rather, *not* a scent. No fear comes from her. Why should it? She is from Last Light. She has seen much, much worse than me.

"The Lady Raven," says Lady Hocquard, her fear scent fading even as she speaks. "I see you have found your way into my home. I suppose you are most welcome." I smile at this. She is almost as impressive as her first maid, I think.

"Forgive me, Lady Hocquard," I reply. "I do not sneak into homes regularly." I think on this. "Anymore, anyway. But I wanted to get the measure of you all before I met you."

"Classic wolves. They lurk before they talk," says Alanna, her eyes on me. I'm not sure she's blinked since she's seen me. She should have been a wolf.

"So says the spy from Last Light," I say back to her.

"Alanna, please, let our guest speak," cuts in Lady Hocquard, and I feel her aroma strengthen a little. I wonder if she ever feels fully in control of her so-called first maid.

"Thank you, my lady," I reply. I turn to Jacob, whose fear stench refuses to wash away. I suppose I should reassure him. I could do with a clean nose. "Don't worry, Jacob. If I had come for you, you would be dead already."

"Oh. Very, ah, reassuring, Lady Ansbach," he replies, turning paler. "You don't mind if I carry on having heart failure, though, do you?"

"Be my guest," I reply. Then I turn to his fellow mage brother. "Brother Bailey of the Cult of Humanis, the one they call Sage. Are you as clever as I have heard?"

"Almost certainly not," he says, but his odor tells me he doesn't believe his own words.

I step down from my perch on the window ledge behind the curtain and properly appraise them. It occurs to me that not all of Jacob's stench is just fear. I remember I am naked. I sigh. It is hard to be around non-wolves.

"Would you like something to wear, Lady Ansbach?" asks Lady Hocquard.

"I bloody well hope not," says Alanna, not so quiet that I cannot hear her.

"No, thank you. And it is just Raven." I continue studying them. "I am very interested in this little gathering, but I am also not in the mood for long conversation. I hope you understand. I will get to the point. You know that I attacked Sinassion and prevented him from murdering Jacob here."

"Thanks again." Jacob nods. He has found a whiskey vial in his pocket. Its fumes mask his scent of desire a little, thank the moonshine.

"What you don't know is why I was there. Two days ago, I hunted down an escaped wolf from the wolf jail. He told me two very interesting things after some . . . persuasion. One concerns the packages left outside the walls. You already know about these from Commander Tenfold. The second is that the packages are being left under the orders of Lord Saxe."

There is silence in the room. I had hoped that this information would be enough and we could move on to what must be done, but I can smell that there will be questions. When creatures other than wolves are in the room, there must always be questions. I sigh. Wolves can wait for days for their prey, but they find it hard to last through a long conversation. Whoever invented discourse wasn't using their nose properly.

"That is . . . that is quite something, Lady Raven," says Lady Hocquard.

Enough of this lady shit. "Raven," I say forcefully. "Only Raven. Wolves do not have titles." Though no matter how many times we tell the rest of you, you never seem to fucking listen.

"Er, yes, Raven. Do you mind if I ask . . ." She frowns. I wish I were in wolf form so I could wag my tail impatiently. "Er—"

"How did the escaped wolf know this?" cuts in Sage.

I shrug. "He was the one asked to deliver the packages by Saxe. At least at first. In return for more privileges within his prison. When he started trying to use this to bargain for his freedom, this was stopped. They decided to use a guard that could be bribed instead."

"Why would Saxe entrust a wolf with this?" asks Sage.

"Who are they going to tell?"

"Do they not have . . . visitors?"

"Visitors?" I reply, trying not to laugh. "When wolves cross the line and murder innocents, we stop caring about them. We do not share the sensibilities of the rest of the immortals. We would rather you weren't draining the blood of other wolves, even those who have committed such crimes as cannot be forgiven, but such is the reality we came to accept after Grayfall." I leave out the fact that, actually, many wolves are not happy about this reality back home, because throwing in wolf politics would make this conversation last until the next fucking moon rises.

"What is Saxe's aim in all this? Why is he working with Sinassion? And what is in the packages he is leaving?" asks Lady Hocquard.

I see she is now firing her questions at me in packs. Slightly quicker, at least. "I have absolutely no idea," I reply.

"Then how did you come across Jacob at the Rushes?"

"After learning of Saxe's involvement from the wolf fugitive, I followed your spymaster. Followed him to his house, on the edge of the city, past the wolf jail. I was about to follow him in to see who he was meeting. It is very good that I didn't, because that's when Sinassion appeared, entering through the back of house. I almost missed him. He's a shadow at the best of times, even with my eyes. Few others would have noticed him. At that point I could no longer approach to hear what they were saying."

"Why?" asks Jacob.

I stare at him. Sometimes a look is better than trying to explain the obvious to someone.

"I imagine," says Sage, stepping in to save his friend, "that Raven was unable to get close to Sinassion, because he would have sensed the presence of her mind and known she was there."

"Ah," said Jacob. "I knew that. I was just testing. A little test for you there."

"Yes," I continue, "I have training as good as any wolf, but not enough to shield my mind from the most talented Neuras I have ever come across. So I could not hear what they talked about. But I could follow him to where he went next. At a decent distance, of course, working on the remains of his scent. He has the odor of a dark cellar, not dirty but just old, if anyone is wondering."

I look around. I do not think anyone is wondering.

"His trail led to the Rushes," I add. "And a sorcerer quietly shitting himself as he faces his own death."

Jacob's face lights up. "Ah! I know this one. That was me. I wasn't that quiet about it, though," he adds helpfully.

"Then, as you know, we were interrupted and Sinassion fled. I waited until Jacob left the palace this evening and followed his trail here."

"And what do you want?" asks Lady Hocquard, refreshingly direct.

I shrug. "I normally do things on my own. But I am not quite so arrogant to think that I can handle Sinassion and Saxe and whoever else is involved. If you are committed to this, then I would like to join you. No more, no less."

"But why?" asks Sage. "Just because Saxe is leaving packages?"

"Oh, mage," I say, smiling and showing him some teeth, "do you think you and Azzuri are the only ones who noticed when Saxe found whatever was in the ground beneath Lightfall and then mysteriously disappeared it? We may not be muddied in your politics, but wolves smell all. Well, I do. Saxe has been up to something. I have not lingered near First Light, working with the bloodkind, simply to chase my own kind down when they escape. I am watching for the wolves. Because if there is one thing we learn from our history, it is that the secretive schemes of the bloods know no bounds."

"I am standing right here, you know, darling," says Lady Hocquard. A pause. "But you also have a point."

There is a little silence. No one wants to seem too eager to make the next move.

"I think I speak for us all when I say we could do with the help, Raven," says Lady Hocquard eventually. "Especially if you are all your stories say." I smile. I am glad she sealed it. She has the most intriguing scent.

"I saw her in the Twin War," says Sage. "I can attest to the fact she is."

"Then it is decided," says Lady Hocquard.

"It is," I reply.

"Well," says Sage, "unless anyone has any other ideas, I say we assess what we have so far."

I sense a long explanation coming. Sorcerers do tend to the verbose.

"We have separate pieces that are starting to come together," Sage begins. "We know that Azzuri believed that a great find was buried in the earth and discovered before Grayfall, and it was then placed in the Blood Bank by Saxe. We now know that Saxe is leaving packages outside the walls, possibly for the Grays. We know, or at least we have strong evidence, for the fact that Azzuri left the safety of the walls to find one of those packages. It seems therefore that there is now equally strong evidence that what Azzuri was pursuing for me, which lies in that vault, might be related to whatever Saxe is doing with those packages, and is certainly related to his murder."

"So the packages may come from the very same vault?"

"Exactly," says Sage. "Still supposition at this point, but logical."

"Which is why the second name on the note that Sam found in Azzuri's room is so apt," says Lady Hocquard.

"And who is that, mage?" I ask.

"Redscar Keepsake," replies Sage.

"And who is that?" I ask again, my knowledge of vampire society having hit a blank.

"He's a Midway. A bank clerk at the Blood Bank," Lady Hocquard says. "Clerks are responsible for overseeing the administration of certain sections of the bank, certain vaults. Most of them are dull fellows. He's certainly never been a person of interest for the Leeches."

I smell Sam's realization and the heat of her blood as her heart beats quicker. "Do you mean . . ."

"Possibly," adds Sage.

"Care to inform the rest of us?" says Jacob.

Sage shrugs. "What if this bank clerk has knowledge of the vault? What if Azzuri went to this bank clerk to find out what was in it?"

"It obviously wasn't very successful if he felt the need to go out of the city to check the packages himself," Sam points out.

"But we may be more successful," I reply, smiling at the thought of what may be in this clerk's future and how many of my teeth will be needed for it.

"Yes," says Lady Hocquard, "it does rather seem he's the last piece of the puzzle."

"Ah, excuse me a moment, sorry to interrupt here," Jacob interjects. "I hate to question the plan of, ah, carrying on with what we're doing, but it seems we're overlooking something."

The lady of the house stares at him. You don't have to have the best nose in the land to smell the disdain for him falling off her in waves.

"And that is?" she asks.

"The city's spymaster and the most dangerous sorcerer alive are working together and killing people to cover something up," Jacob continues. "They know I'm involved, so they may well know we're *all* involved, which means we're all in incredible danger. We should probably go into hiding, you know . . . immediately."

Jacob scans everyone's faces. Sage and Lady Hocquard look unconcerned. Alanna has an active look of scorn on her face. I stare at Jacob with the smile you might give to a small animal you've just found in the bush.

"I note that no one has gone into hiding yet," says Jacob eventually.

"He be a perceptive one, don't he?" replies Alanna.

"So . . . we have to approach this bank clerk?" asks Sam.

"Or break into his office in the Blood Bank." I smile. "Unlike wolves, you vampires like keeping records of things."

"Hmm, well I like that idea more than approaching him directly," says Lady Hocquard. "Especially if Saxe and Sinassion suspect the sorcerers, which means it won't be long until he finds out that I have been in communication with them."

"It is settled, then. I will scout out the bank tomorrow, work out the best—"

"Hold on there, Raven," says Lady Hocquard. "One of the most, ah . . . notorious wolves in the land breaking into one of the most well-protected buildings in the city is a little risky, don't you think? Certainly not the most subtle approach."

"I was subtle enough to go unnoticed by you all until I wanted to be."

"Yes, but if you are found, then if the stories are true, your subtlety would quickly go out of the window and be replaced by rather a lot of blood."

I smile. My respect for Lady Hocquard has increased by measures. I'm not used to the tone of disapproval.

"I cannot argue with that," I say.

"So a more careful approach is needed," the Lady continues. "Someone who would go unnoticed in the Blood Bank, even if seen." She turns to Sam, who, since her history lesson, has been silent. I can smell her frustration; it is strong and metallic, like the forging of a weapon yet to be yielded. She desperately wants to be more than she is in this crowd. She will have to find a little more bite if she is to do so, however.

"Ah, why is everyone looking at me?" Sam asks.

I smile. It will be refreshing for someone else to do the sneaking for a change.

First Lord Azzuri

My remaining son is torturing someone. I know this because I hear the screams as I enter the catacombs. I would say that it is his way of dealing with his grief over his dead brother. But honestly, I suspect that Rufous just likes to torture people. I do not particularly approve of torture, at least when there are other options available. It rarely gets the information you want, only the information the tortured one thinks you want. But I gave up trying to change Rufous's excesses long ago, and now I simply try and rein them in as best as I can.

The catacombs under the palace were first dug in the early days of the Twin War, the idea being that if First Light was ever overrun, vampires could hide and flee via a secret entrance. As it was, they came in extremely useful; when the wolves finally broke through the lines and invaded the city and the last of the vampires were held up, it allowed my family and many others to escape. My father was killed in the palace, however; he said he would never abandon his family home and, when it came to it, he kept his word.

Since then, the catacombs have been converted into a series of prison cells where my surviving son has his way with the Worn population for any little grievance he can think of. Today he is playing with a particularly shriveled-looking specimen; he does not have the muscles to be a blood farmer or a blood hunter, and he is not quite emaciated enough to be simply a blood beggar or a complete recalcitrant. In fact, his face has a carefully manicured look about it, or at least it did until Rufous began his work, which makes me think that my eldest is still fixed on his latest obsession.

"Not again, son," I begin as I walk up to the cell. Rufous is currently taking a break from whatever agony he was currently inflicting on the Worn, who I see is missing a couple of teeth. His ears have the ragged, bloody look of having been properly seen to, and one of his nipples is gone. Nothing that will not heal—my son has not begun on the strange methods of torture that a vampire cannot recover from yet.

"Rufous," I say again, as his back is still turned to me. I wonder if he is in one of his frenzies. He gets like that sometimes.

"Yes, Father? I am afraid I am a little busy at the moment." His voice is impatient and clipped. Rude to his father, as always.

"Who is it this time, Rufous?"

"It is another . . . of these sots that seem to plague the city. This one claims not to have known my brother, but I fear otherwise from Lord Saxe's spies, and I am soon to get the truth out of him. A second nipple may do it, I feel. Or if not, some more permanent injuries. Introduce a little light into his life, so to speak!"

"Rufous," I begin, but I see the Worn is still awake, and I have no wish to speak over his cries. "Walk with me, Son."

"But, Father—"

"He is hardly going anywhere, is he? I won't ask again."

My son turns, pushing his long blond locks out of his face. He has some of the Worn's blood on his cheek, but he does not seem concerned about this. He never does with others' blood.

"All right, Father. Let us walk."

We exit the other side of the cells into the catacombs. The walls are occasionally lit by torches, but it is mostly dark. This does not concern us, of course. We hardly need torchlight given the fine blood we drink. It is more for the benefit of any Worns that may have to come down here. There is a dank smell. I do not come down here often; I always mean to have it renovated, though Rufous does not seem to mind. No surprises there.

The catacombs lead into the gardens; what was once a secret passage is now a useful shortcut to the Rose Garden, if you don't mind what you have to walk past to get there. We stand before the garden now, the even lines of roses before us in red and blue, with herbaceous plants in between, docklily and tangania and russelwart. This garden was my wife's idea, of course. I secretly brought in the Kinets when it was planted to turn the roses blue; their art of bloommagick is nascent, of course, but in this garden it has perhaps seen its zenith. My wife was pleased. My youngest liked it, too, the short time he was here. I was slightly put off by his love of the flowers. I do not know why. When I stand here now, I feel at peace.

"I was thinking, Rufous, of putting a statue of your brother in the Rose Garden here."

"Yes, Father, of course."

"But I want it to reflect . . . how he was. Perhaps holding something or doing something of importance to him. I . . . have not been as close to him since Grayfall."

"Since Grayfall?" asks Rufous, arching his eyebrow. I ignore the implication.

"I mean, I did not keep track of his interests in the city."

"Well, I did. That's why some of them are in the catacombs."

"That's enough!" I shout at my son, louder than I intended. My voice carries across the Rose Garden, which thankfully is empty aside from us. Rufous has the grace to look a little ashamed for a second, but then that arrogant grin returns, the one so opposite to the permanent nervous smile my younger son wore.

"Father, I don't know what he got up to. I am avenging him now, though, which I think is enough."

You are not avenging him, I think to myself. *You are giving in to your worst instincts as usual, under the thin veil of a cause.* But I can hardly stand in judgment.

"We really don't know what he got up to, do we?" I ask.

Rufous shrugs. "He tried to join the Blood Guard a few decades ago. Can you imagine!"

"It's not that ridiculous. You used to battle him when he was a child, taught him a little how to fight. Showed him how to use his claws when fully blooded."

Rufous grins. "I attempted to. He was hardly a natural. He was scared of cutting himself with his own claws."

"But he tried."

"Yes. Yes, I suppose he did."

I try to remain in that brief moment of remembrance between us, but an awkward silence falls, and the moment is gone.

"I should get back to my prisoner, now, Father."

"Yes. Yes, you should. I will stay here and walk a little in the garden."

"Yes, Father," says Rufous, and he is gone before I can turn back around, leaving me to think of statues and the shadows they cast.

18

Westfall and Down

Once upon a time, the currency of vampires was blood alone. Which makes sense. It is their gold, though they have use of gold too. But now they have coin. But they still have blood. And which they ultimately prefer when it really comes down to it, for all the progress of modernity, can be ascertained from a simple fact: there are three times the number of guards in the Blood Bank than there are in the Crown Bank.

Quantas Quistile, *Of Currencie and Blood*

Sam

I've only ever seen the Blood Bank this close up once, and it was almost fifteen years ago now, so I can hardly remember it. It's not quite in the exact middle of Centerfall, the four square miles of land from which all the other parts of First Light come off like spokes on a wheel. That honor goes to First Gods, or the First Earthly Hall of the Blood Gods, to give it its full, ridiculous name, the biggest prayhall in all of First Light. The Blood Bank sits behind it. They could not be more different. First Gods is peak Grosshunt style; now that almost all the castles and old manors are gone, it's maybe the best example of it still standing.

The Blood Bank, on the other hand, six hundred years old and dating back to the building of First Light, is Old Mage; before the postwar craze of new Old Mage buildings set in, it was the only example of its kind in the city. According to my reading, it was built on the orders of First Lord Cyania, whose wife had spent some time in Luce and developed a love for classic sorcerer buildscaping. Columns run right around the entire building, designed in the Distoric style: slender, fluted, and topped with elaborate leaf designs. The roof is flat, and there are no windows. Not as elaborate as the palace, it is beautiful in its symmetrical simplicity. Above the entrance side, there's a great relief, a series of bloodvials of different shapes and varieties, in case anyone wasn't sure what's stored in it.

I watch the people walking past me. Only in Centerfall can you get so many Midways and Lords in such a small area, and so few of my kind.

The only Worns you see are the ones hurrying to their jobs cleaning or serving the Lords in the buildings about, and they have the hurried and stressed look of those who know they're not in their natural place, of people expecting any moment to be picked out as an impostor and carted off back to Worntown. I don't blame them. They're surrounded by things they will never experience and can never enjoy. If I walk to the west, I reach the Sunsphere, where the Lords and Midways watch past events that half of the audience can still remember being told onstage in verse. Tickets are too expensive for Worns; they must make do with the Westfall stagehouse. If I go to the east, I reach the council buildings, where most of the city councils meet to discuss the administration of the city—how to keep the blood flowing and the Worns quiet, if you want it in shorthand. If I turn around, I can see across the vast centersquare to the strange, squat form of the Blood Market, the building in which people do not so much buy blood as bet on the success of new bloods, tying their bloodcrowns to the things that can't be touched. Part of me wishes I was back there now, talking again with Sage of the invisibles and gamblers and betting.

I'm dawdling. I'm reluctant to go in. Because once I'm in, I'm in, and if it goes wrong, then not only have I just put myself in danger, but I've failed my first real task, and aside from all the kindness and gentle encouragement I've got from Lady Hocquard, I know there's steel in there, too, and if I can't do what the other Leeches so often do, then I know there will be no place for me there, no matter my role in starting this whole thing. This is when I find out which blood I'm suited for.

At the entrance to the bank are the thickest stone doors I've ever seen. It would take a lot of wolfblood to smash through those, which I suppose is the point. Luckily they're currently open. There's a tall, broad-shouldered vampire standing before them who looks like he could punch through the columns in front of him just by stretching. He's clean-shaven with short hair and nothing else happening on his face, but his eyes have the slight red mist about them that suggest he's on more than decent blood. I'm guessing he could do a lot of harm to many things if he wanted, so I give him a smile to know that I'm not one of them. He doesn't stare at me but at a fixed point past me, and I wonder to myself if there was ever a doorman in the history of buildings who wasn't auditioning to be a massive prickard.

"Letter," he says. For a second, I wonder how he knows what I'm here for, but then I remember who I am and what I look like. I'm hardly here to put a deposit in. I hand him the letter from Lady Hocquard.

"Cleaning quarters are straight ahead to your right. Don't deviate," he says, then adds, "Don't wander off," because we Wornmaids don't understand words, clearly.

Inside it's exactly what I read about, but bigger and more vivid than I ever imagined. In front of me lies a massive square. You could fit an entire row of Worn houses from Southeastfall in here. On each side of the square are a series of doors with small brass plaques fitted to them, and on each corner of the square is a corridor that leads to more of the same doors.

The floor of the square is a giant mosaic: bright blue, white, and red tiles in concentric circles growing outward, forming the shapes of all the noble blood animals: hawk, eagle, stag, whale, snaptail, bear, greatshark, mountain cat, and of course, the wolfkind.

My eyes are drawn to the middle of the square. Rising up in the center is a spiral staircase, which must be a hundred feet high, its stone steps leading up to the great bank vaults above, the huge stone doors of which can just about be seen from down below.

Hoping I look like the overawed Worngirl I actually am, I turn to my right and follow the doorman's directions down some stairs in the southeastern corner of the square, arriving at a sad, worn wooden door. Servants' quarters are the same everywhere. I walk in and see a sea of sullen faces before me. I've seen them before, every day for the last ten years. Sometimes I see them in the mirror. I sit down. I have to wait till eight bells till the bank clerks leave and the cleaning begins.

I wish I had a book.

First Lord Azzuri

I look out my carriage window at the two bloodguardsmen flying above us, keeping pace with my transport. They are my personal bloodguards, so of course they are part of the few who have access to the wolfblood that gives them wings, but I wish they would not use it for a simple journey like this one. I do not need eyes in the sky for a trip to Worntown. But whenever I try and stop them, Redgrave gives me that look and patiently explains how the First Lord has traditionally always been accompanied by wings wherever he goes in the city. Yes, I point out, fair enough, but when this tradition was first begun, things were different. Before the Twin War and the truce with the wolfkind, we used wolf-blood all the time, depending on how many wolves we caught in the forest, and back then we hardly had to save the precious substance for some future war with a superpowered army of blood-knows-what who keep us trapped in our city like rats in a cage. Given this, this practice seems wasteful. Not to mention that the show of force it is meant to provide might have been of use to us once upon a time in Lightfall when the Worns were a boiling underclass of rage and ambition, but now that they are simply a mud-stained horde of weakened peasants, it seems like overkill and, frankly, a little bit arrogant.

I explain all this to Redgrave every now and again, and he nods and says *hmmm,* and then I end up doing what he advises anyway. Pick your battles, as my father used to say, though he was never that good at winning the bloody things.

I stare at the guards and their wings a little longer—I never fly myself or take wolfblood these days, so I always take the chance to stare at the long bony wraps of flesh covered with thin layers of hair, hair that used to be dyed a multitude of colors back when wings were a more common sight. Then I retreat back into my carriage, where Redgrave's stare awaits me.

"I hope you don't mind, First Lord, if I say again that I do not think this to be the wisest of ideas." He strokes his moustache, which is slightly wiry today and not as waxed as usual. He has been a little stressed of late, though I cannot imagine why; it is not as if the so-called investigation into my son is bearing any fruit. In fact, this is the first time we have had a chance to venture out on our own investigation, under the pretense of a grieving father visiting his dead son's past haunts.

"I do not mind your pointing it out at all, Redgrave, as long as you do not mind my ignoring you, as I have the last five times." A little curt, but given the circumstances I am sure he will handle it.

"It's just," he continues, gamely not giving up, "until we know more about why he died, going to one of his . . . hideaways . . . could potentially present a danger to you. If Saxe becomes suspicious."

Hideaways. That is an interesting way to put it. I was wondering what moniker he would go for. More polite than *den of iniquity.* Less honest than *sot-house.* Innocent, almost. Like my son had made a treehouse at the back of the palace gardens.

"Saxe has no reason to suspect that we suspect him. To him, I am simply a grieving father. And I have waited long enough for us to seek out the truth ourselves. I agreed to wait a little longer after the funeral, like you said. But now I will have my answers. Even if whatever my son was looking into had nothing to do with Saxe, I will uncover the answers, and I have had my fill of sitting around, no matter what you say."

Redgrave just smiles at this. When I reach this level of grumpiness with him, his Midway servant instincts kick in.

"I am sorry, Redgrave," I add quickly. "I am being a little short with you. You are right to be concerned. But I cannot wait any longer. I can sense the outline of a scheme developing, and I am done being the impotent Lord who cannot see what his men are doing around him."

Redgrave nods but does not reply. Like all good first men, he can sense when I am not myself and bend around it accordingly. Suddenly the carriage comes to a halt. I hear the thump as both my guards land. At least they no longer hover in the sky for the duration of my palace visits. A small token of wolfblood austerity at the very least.

The street I step out onto is in most ways like a Worntown street, but with the occasional touches of a Midway avenue. Westfall is not really Worntown, but an in-between place, a not quite anything. If Southwestfall and Southeastfall are Worntown proper, and Eastfall is mainly home to the Midways, while Northfall and Northeastfall are the playground of the Lords, then Westfall is . . . its own place. Yes, many Worns live here, but they are the ones with good trades, not attached to Lords but not surviving off scraps or passing trade, either. There are a few Midways here, though they do not bother themselves with the more elegant and respected arts. Instead they create stagetales, talecasts, musiscenes, and paintsprawls, all of which my late son wrapped himself up in when he was not busy with . . . whatever he was busy with. It is a mix, this place.

I can see this mix before me in the modest buildscaping of the road. At the end of the street I am on, there are several houses of brick with slate roofs, standing out among the rest. A stagehall owner, perhaps, or industry men. The rest of the homes, more modest buildings of thatched roof and timber frames, are much higher than Worntown; lacking the space to grow outward, they have instead added stories over the years to accommodate the various goings-on. This is a sign of ambition for which I have a little admiration; in Worntown proper, you do not get beyond two stories, for the minds of the populace there are far too concerned with thieving and worse to ever think about expansion. Worns, as we Lords know, do not dream like us; but in Westfall, when they live among Midways, they catch a little of the dreaming, it is true. If only they did not catch a little of the sordidness with it.

"My lord, we should go in, rather than be outside," Redgrave says, rousing me out of my thoughts. He points to one of the tallest houses, a strange rambling edifice that leans to the right the higher it goes. There are no candles lit on any of the floors except the top; compared to the rest of the street, it looks eerily abandoned.

"I see you have asked everybody to leave for my visit," I note. I walk up to its door, but before I go in, I turn to the street. There are no Worn faces watching me, at least that I can see. The whole place has been emptied of life. As if I would really be in danger from those who drink cowblood. Everywhere I go, I realize, I empty streets, turn busy thoroughfares into empty mock-ups. This is ruling; this is inevitable. But it never becomes normal.

Inside, a small rotting staircase runs before me, with doors on either side. I turn to Redgrave. "What is this place again?"

"It's where a number of the . . . artisans of Westfall live. Some actors of the stagetales, some musicians, an artist or two."

"And did they know my son? Or did he keep to himself here?"

"We have interviewed them . . ."

I look at him.

"Not like that, First Lord," he says hurriedly. "That was reserved for the coinboys."

"And anyone Rufous thought it would be fun to have his way with."

Redgrave is wise to let that go. "What we have found, my lord, is that they did not know who he was. They knew him as Olly Roche, a painter and lyre player from Southwestfall come to make some money in this more forgiving district."

"By the Blood Gods, Redgrave, you mean to tell me my son had a false identity?"

"Well, he could hardly have lived here peacefully otherwise, my lord."

I look at him.

"Would be one observation I might make," he says, giving me his most diplomatic expression.

We walk up the stairs, right to the top, and I resist the urge to open the doors on the way and see where the humble artisans of Westfall sleep. I do not want to stay any longer than I need to. I will see what answers may be found here, and then I will fly away (sadly not literally) from this street of ghosts.

At the final door at the top of the staircase, I pause and turn to my first man. "I assume that Saxe will have already been here?"

"Yes, First Lord, as part of our . . . that is to say, his, investigation, he cleared out everything here."

I scowl. "I did not realize this. This may make it harder to look for clues, Redgrave, if there is nothing here."

"I'm sorry, First Lord, there was nothing we could do without—"

"Yes, yes, I understand." I think about my son, memories of his youth. What little I knew of him before he grew up and became even more unknowable. "This still may not be a wasted journey, though."

We reach the door at the top, and I open it gingerly, the handle rough to my soft hands like everything in this place.

His room lies before me. I do not know what I was expecting, given that I knew there would be no personal possessions left of my son's, but I am nevertheless taken aback by the emptiness of the room. There is a thick pile of woolen blankets against the far wall, which I take to be whatever passes for a bed in these parts, and there is a lopsided three-legged gelmwood cabinet to my right, the wood warped and faded. A large mirror hangs to my left; there is a crack in the top right corner, but the rest looks in good condition—a perfect piece ruined by a tiny fracture. The roof beams are low here, and I have to duck as I walk to the middle of the room. I turn to face a chimney, not the main chimney of the building but a smaller one, and I can see no fires have been made. I look beyond these bits of furniture for signs of my son—signs of what he was doing, thinking, feeling—and I get nothing. Just motes of dust on the splintered wooden floorboards and cobwebs hanging idly from the beams, the commotion having scared their creators into the recesses of the ceiling for now.

I do not know what I was thinking coming here. Did I think to see something that Saxe and his minions would have missed? Did I think some father's instinct would kick in and a great clue would reveal itself? I would have to have known my son better for that. As it is, I cannot even begin to guess at why in the twin hells he chose to be there. Was it rebellion, sleeping on dusty blankets with the eccentric denizens of Westfall, sticking his middle finger up at his father in the palaces? Was it desire or drunkenness, losing himself where no one would know or recognize him? Or was it something more, some part of his hatred for everything his family stood for?

I suddenly notice some smudges on the floor, rubbed into the boards. Red, blue, yellow, an array of colors. "This is odd, Redgrave," I say, pointing to them.

He comes over and inspects the marks. "I would surmise, First Lord, that these would be paint marks from his paintings."

I take a moment to contemplate this. "Paintings? Redgrave, you didn't tell me had paintings."

My first man has the grace to look awkward. "It is not . . . pertinent to what we are looking for, so I didn't think, First Lord, I'm sorry. I assumed . . . I assumed you were already aware of his inclinations in this area."

"Where in the Halls did he get them from?"

"Get them from? I . . . ah, I see. I apologize; I did not make myself clear. He did not purchase them. He painted them himself."

Now it is my turn to look embarrassed. "My son was a painter?"

"Yes, First Lord. A prodigious one, it seems."

"Who was he, Redgrave?" I ask, and my first man has the good sense to spot the rhetorical nature of that question.

I turn away from him and inspect the wall behind me, unwanted memories seeping in, suddenly wishing I was alone.

I never saw my youngest son draw when he was young, in those precious few years before he looked different; before he grew into the form he would take for endless centuries. I saw him run, though. He loved to run, and he loved to hide. Before he grew into a sullen adult, cryptic lines of disapproval laid at me from behind his long, dank hair, he would put such joy into hiding—and I would put equal joy into the finding. Sometimes I would find him and pretend to grab him as he squirmed out of my grasp and ran to the new hiding place. Other times he would remain unfound, and I would give up and go and sit in the gardens of the palace in Lightfall and wait for him to unearth himself, triumphant, covered in the debris of wherever he had been: weeds, dust, cobwebs, gravel. Such short years of joy, fallen apart for reasons I cannot even remember properly.

I look at the wall ahead of me some more. He didn't just used to hide things. He used to hide *things*.

"Redgrave," I say, "can you see anything strange about this wall?" I point to the section before me.

My first man walks over and touches it, then leans close toward it. "The timber here is a slightly different shade, and newer."

"Yes it is," I say, knowing nothing would get past him.

I flex my knuckles. "You know, Saxe may be the spymaster. But we have been doing this for many centuries, have we not?"

Redgrave allows himself a low chuckle. "You could say that, First Lord."

Then I throw my fist back and punch through the wall. I may not be on wolfblood anymore, but the bear still in me from half a glass ago is quite up to the job of taking on some basic timber.

The wood explodes before me, and I see there is a small hollow in the timber frame, and in that hollow is a stack of parchments, tied together with string.

For the first time in a while I smile, and I mean it.

19

Keep It Secret, Keep It Safe

I myself am fascinated by the question of lockboxes. To purchase a lock-box in a vampire city, you must not simply ask yourself how valuable are the contents but what blood can you expect the thief to be on. A Worn? Poor quality metal will do. One on Midway blood? Or un-magicked weak noble blood? Make it stronger. Magicked noble blood? Thick, thick metal and bars, my friend. Wolfblood? Keep your contents on your person, is my advice.

Carmine Ceruli,
Amusing Observations on Vampire Societie

Sam

I stop before a long row of offices that stretch out before me, all identical thin wooden doors with small brass nameplates on them just like the ones off the main square. These are the ones I will be cleaning, merci-fully close to Keepsake's office. I've spent the last two glasses sitting in the scullery of the bank, watching dead-eyed maid after dead-eyed maid wander in, then out again, no one so much as glancing in my direction or speaking a word to me. This place feels more on edge even than the palace. I assume this is true because of the valuables it contains. Even more opportunities for maids to be blamed for damaging or stealing valuable documents about the contents of the blood vaults, with the sunburst punishment I reckon would follow. Not to mention that aside from the emergency wolfblood stores for the Blood Guard and the reg-ular stores for the Flight Guard and First Guard, this is the only place where wolfblood is kept, and in the largest quantities; quantities that will one day be used against the Grays. The knowledge of that seems to have added a strain in the place. You can feel the tension in the air, taste it on your tongue.

So I'm slow in my walk back to the offices. I'm here to snoop. I don't want to walk in on Keepsake leaving. I don't want to know if he's one of the ones that likes to blame maids for anything going missing.

But when I arrive at the offices in my section again, they've all left; I see the last retreating figure of a bank clerk fast-walking off in the opposite direction toward the central square and the entrance. The night is a little shorter than the day at this time of year after all; no one wants to spend the last hours of night in a bank office. No one except old Sammy here.

I'm patient, even though it's hard. Lady Hocquard made me promise to clean all the offices on my rota. I can't be caught slacking by anyone. It's how none of their Leeches have ever been caught, she said. Caution before all. It's lack of caution that allows the men to be suckered out of their information by Leeches in the first place, after all.

Finally I've done all my cleaning. From the doorway of the last office of the row, I look down at room 85, also known as the office of bank clerk Keepsake, also known as the room where I find out if I'm really Leech material. All the oil lights are out in the main square and the offices are lit only by candles left burning, most likely because their occupants were too lazy to put them out rather than anyone thinking of keeping them lit for their maids. The effect is strange, like a row of empty houses on a street, all still lit even though the people inside them have fled. I feel very alone now, but somehow not alone as well, as if a crowd of people are waiting around the corner to come flooding back to their abandoned candlelight.

No time like the present. I walk slowly to room 85, making each step more silent than the last in case its occupant has found his way back while I've been cleaning other rooms. But no one's there. Just a long wooden desk with an old bloodstain across part of it, a tall-backed chair, a sideboard covered in papers, and some neat but dust-covered shelves; everything in light, faded crestwood, nothing expensive, nothing cheap, nothing noticeable.

Except for one thing in the corner.

A lockbox.

This is the only room I've seen so far with a lockbox in it. Of course it is. Why wouldn't it be? Why would it be as simple as ruffling through a few papers, finding out Keepsake's secrets, and getting the twin hells out of here? That would be easy. And nothing, as I am beginning to understand about this life I've half leaped, half stumbled into, is ever easy.

I check the papers scattered all around the room, hoping maybe they're what I need, not what lies in the lockbox. But if they are, then they're keeping it very quiet. They are, I think, lists of bloods against the lists of vaults they're in. But nothing about any mysterious withdrawals destined to be left outside the city walls. That seems like exactly the kind of information you'd keep in a lockbox.

So I walk up to the thorn in my arse, the end of my mission, and I size it up. It's a rectangular metal chest, which must be a foot long by a foot wide by two feet deep. It looks like it's made out of iron, painted a dull red. There's a central key lock on its front side and three iron bands wrapped around it, each with their own lock. The walls of the chest itself must be at least an inch thick. It is, in short, a lockbox not to be taken by a fool, unless the fool has the strength of wolfblood.

I try and think like Sage for a second (a voice in my head that sounds a lot like me asks if he's already a role model of mine, and I tell it where to go), and I conclude that the only reason for Keepsake to have a lock-box like this in his office, given that the whole bank is filled with even more secure vaults, is if whatever is in there is not something he wants anyone else to see, or at least to see him storing.

That's about the only information I'm getting from this trip, of course, because I'm not getting into the lockbox. I wonder that no one saw this coming. No one thought to give me any instructions on how to pick a lock or give me any firepowder to blow through it. Here ends my story. Mission failed. I wonder what Alanna would do, all instinct and skills and experience, bundled up in a barely contained coil of fury—but I'm about as similar to her as a rabbit is to a lion, so what's the point?

That's when I hear the footsteps. Loud against the stone mosaic of the bank, coming this way. *Thank the Halls I shut the door,* I think, but I'm not relieved for long, because there's no hiding place in this room unless I duck behind the desk, which works only if they're not intending to use it. I do this anyway, and I wait and pray for those feet to move right along past this office, carry on walking straight out of my life. But the Blood Gods aren't listening today, because I hear a key in the lock and the door opens, and from the world's worst hiding place I can just about see a figure enter the office.

It's a man, and it must be a bank clerk, because he's dressed in the tight-fitting gray tunic they wear, with a long-sleeved white shirt underneath that has the ensign of the bank on the collar: a key dripping with blood. His long hair is tied back in a ponytail (which is the fashion among the Midways in their first century) and he's clean-shaven. Most important, he's not looking my way, because he's standing in front of the lockbox fumbling around in his tunic pocket for a set of keys, and he hasn't so much as glanced over at where I'm hiding.

I wait as he unlocks all three metal bands and then the main lock, the lockbox swinging open with a dawdling creak. I can't see what's in it from my perch behind the desk, but I can see him rummaging around in it, looking for something. Finally he takes out a piece of paper and starts to read it, and to my great surprise, as much as I have room for surprise with all the other nerves holding me hostage, he starts to cry.

In a few seconds my opening will be gone; he will have closed up the lockbox and, at best, assuming he doesn't see me, I'll be back at square one. So while the clerk I assume to be Keepsake is busy with his tears, I stick my hands in the pocket of my smock and I take out one object in particular: my backup plan. I am, I realize, about to put my life in the hands of a man I've barely known for a week, and I try and recall the words we spoke the previous night.

Sage

THE PREVIOUS NIGHT

Sam is looking at me strangely. "I'm sorry, Sage, I don't really . . . What is this again?" she asks, staring at a small object in her hand. It is a metal cube, smooth and light, the size of a die. The metal is indeterminable; not steel or brass or iron, certainly. It has no markings and no etchings on it.

"This," I say, pointing to the cube, "is to be used only if you have to. If you get caught in the bank by someone and you need to get away. Shake it very hard—as hard as you can—and then throw it at them. Make sure you are not in the immediate vicinity when it goes off."

"Goes off?"

"Ah, yes. I hope you don't have to see what I mean. It won't hurt the person, I should add. It will just . . . incapacitate them for a good amount of time."

"You've tried this, have you?"

I smile, impressed. She's progressed quickly past the part where she expresses shock at my possession of powerful objects with strange effects—shock in this moment would be pointless, illogical, and a waste of time—and has gone straight to the point. If everyone thought like this, half my conversations wouldn't be wasted on a daily basis.

"I . . . ah, have a couple more. I have tried them, yes. With volunteers, of course."

"How much did you tell the volunteers?" she asks.

"I may have withheld some pertinent information that might have affected their willingness to assist me."

Sam smiles. "I bet you did."

"There's another quality it possesses, without which you would not really be advised to use it."

"I'm on tenterhooks."

"It robs the person it incapacitates of the ability to remember a short while previous. It relieves them of their immediate memories. Approximately the last hourglass, although I am very unsure on this point, I'm sad to say. But the key point is that they won't remember why they were knocked unconscious."

"I see," says Sam. "So I could make my escape, but then not have to fear the consequences of it."

"Exactly."

Sam pauses. I hear the question coming. I would be disappointed if she didn't ask.

"Where are these from, Sage? I'm sorry, I can't not ask."

"No, I'm glad you did." I lose my thoughts for a second. She has a very direct stare. "Where do you think they are from?"

"I don't think they're sorcerer magick. Not any kind I've ever heard of."

"And why do you think this?"

"Because sorcerer magick can't be put *into* things and then remain in those things forever. It's one of the most important mage rules, isn't it? Sorcerers can use magick to affect things—an Atmos can change the weather, a Cloak can create a temporary illusion, and so on. But they can't keep that magick in something permanently, making it into something else. At least that's how I understand it."

"What about the Kinets and how they change the blood?"

"The magick changes the properties of the blood to make it more potent, it doesn't stay in the blood. Most people don't realize that, but that's right, isn't it?"

"Indubitably."

Sam inspects the cube a little more, stroking its strange edges. "But this . . . this would have to have it . . . stored in it. So that leaves a big question I probably shouldn't ask, because I know you don't want to answer."

"But if you were tempted?"

"Then I would ask whether, in the collection of items you keep in that temple of yours that you say are of mortal origin, you have a lot more than bits of ruin and strange carvings."

I sigh. "I wish that were true, Sam. More than anything, believe me. The truth is that these are . . . I am fairly sure, anyway . . . of sorcerer origin."

Sam's left eyebrow shoots up at this. "Sorcerers did this?"

"Yes." I nod. "Jacob and I found these two items in the ruins of Kinesthes, an old Kinet outpost of Kintile that died out around the time Lightfall was built. I can't speak of how they crafted this strange metal . . . Kinets have many strange material building skills, some lost to time, but the incapacitating and memory-stealing qualities are fully explicable. For the former, a small burst of firepowder is contained within, and when released, it is enough to cause a concussive blast within a small radius. For the latter—and this is rather ingenious—the cube releases a small liquid spray form of a plant commonly found in the Swamplands, just above the Southern Sea, known as takepast moss, which, as the name suggests, robs you of your recent memories when inhaled or ingested."

"Oh," says Sam, disappointed.

"I'm sorry, Sam. You were hoping for a little more than that, weren't you?"

She grins. "No, it's okay. I should still be impressed at the artifice of the sorcerers. More than I ever realized possible. I shouldn't get too greedy."

"Nothing wrong with a little lust for revelation, Sam. It's literally my life, after all."

"It is, isn't it," she says, and I hope there's approval in there, but I can't quite tell.

I make a move to go. But she stops me, her hand on my sleeve, lightly brushing against my hand. "Why are you giving me these things? They sound valuable, even if they're only of sorcerer origin. Why me?"

Because you're interested. Because you keep up. Because I don't have to simplify what I say to you. Because living in a temple in a desert, I don't get to talk to many women, and I would quite like to keep on talking to you. All these are answers. But they're not the one I give.

"We need to know where those packages come from, Sam. And I have the feeling you're going to need all the help you can get."

Sam

I look up from my hiding position at the bank clerk I assume to be Keepsake, who is still reading the parchment, the lockbox open. Then I throw the metal cube at him. It hits him in the chest and then falls to the floor in front of him. Nothing happens.

We look at each other, his look of confusion growing wider. I begin to wonder how sensible I was to put my faith in a sorcerer with long words and bold claims. I might be tits up in a vat of blood here.

Then as Keepsake goes to mouth something, there's a bright flash, and for a second his whole body is lit up, as if blue waves of flame are lapping around him. Then he falls to the floor. I have to act even faster now. Someone might be waiting for him, or someone could walk past and check why the candle is lit. I walk over, still wary in case any of the flames of light are still going. I've never seen firepowder have that effect, and I don't trust it an inch. I look down at the cube, now lying next to the prone body of the clerk. He's still breathing. Good. I didn't think Sage was the kind of person to turn me into a killer without warning me, but you never know.

I pick the cube up, expecting it to feel warm to the touch, but it feels and looks no different than before. I pocket it, hoping to the twin hells that it's done its job of robbing him of his memory as well, and then turn to the lockbox. I reach inside and pull out the only thing in it: a collection of yellowed papers tied together with string. There must be at least fifty pages. I carefully flick through them without breaking the string and see that the pages are covered with small writing. If every page is like this, I don't know how I'm going to find what we need. I can't take them with me; not because I'm worried they'll be found on me— I've already crossed that bridge—but because there can't be any evidence I was here. But then, when I start to examine the pages properly, I see that the Blood Gods have decided to shine on me tonight. Because you don't have to be a ponytailed bank clerk to understand what the writing is. It's a record of withdrawals, all from the same vault. Every entry is the same: date, time, number of chests taken from the vault, the number given to each chest . . . and the same vault number. Vault 1015.

The dates go back. *Right* back. I scroll to the bottom of the pile. The first date is soon after Grayfall. Blood Gods. That would track with what Sage said . . . that Azzuri was looking for the vault that contained whatever Saxe had dug up shortly before *Grayfall*. I'd wager my life that these chests are the same ones that Azzuri ventured out to his death to try and open. So whatever was found . . . has been left outside the city all this time?

What the twin hells is in that vault?

I quickly commit the vault number to memory, then place the papers back in the manner I found them and close the lockbox. I bend down to prise the keys gently from the clerk's hand, fearing any twitch of the fingers as I do so. I lock the vault and then the iron bars around it. I return the keys to his hand and see the crumpled letter he was reading in the other, the one that drew tears from him. I prize that from his hand and I read it. When I've finished, yet more pieces have fallen into place; I know how Azzuri began his journey now, the one that ended with his body full of Gray bullets. The letter makes me a little sad, but I don't have time to be right now.

I go to leave then, hands shaking from the thrill of it all, sweating slightly, but at the door I stop. One last touch. I've created something here, a work of art. But there's one more detail to be added. I go to the desk and open the bottom drawer, hoping to see what I've seen so far in every office. A small vial of blood. A spare one for an occasion. I'm sure it's good stuff; the bank pays well. Maybe even magicked. I drop it on the floor next to the unconscious clerk, the blood spreading out its tendrils around his tunic. It's dangerous. I might get blamed for not cleaning it up. But if the clerk's memory really is fuddled, then he'll hopefully assume when he wakes that he poured himself a drink upon reading the sad contents of that letter, only to drop it, slip on the contents, and knock himself out as he fell.

I take one look back at the scene as I leave the room, trying to remember it in case there's a time when I'm not sure it happened at all, and then I'm gone.

20

A Friend in Need

They don't see us as people. The worst ones anyway. We are cattle to
the Lords, little better than the animal that provides us with our blood.
How does someone get like that? I can barely begin to understand it.

Caroline Finlay,
in a final letter to her mother

Sam

When I finally return to my bedchamber in the palace, there's an hour-glass left to sunfall. All the way in the carriage from the Blood Bank to the palace I'd felt lightheaded, as if I'd just downed a Lord's bloodstash. But it's not the blood. It's the living. It's the living after years of death. Even after the last few mad days, of stealing a dead Lord's secrets, joining a secret spy ring, and taking my life in my hands by trusting a pair of sorcerers, I haven't quite felt like this. I feel like there's a drummer behind me, pounding a rhythm. I feel like I'm a child again, running through Worntown, my parents making token attempts to slow me down as I try and take in every sight I can, making stories with my eyes as I take in everything and anything that's new to my world. I feel . . .

"Beth?"

She's sitting on the bed by the window, her back to me. I hadn't noticed her in the gloom. Her long blond hair falls down her back, hairnet to the side.

"Do you remember when you first came to the palace?" she asks, not turning around. Her voice is quiet and emotionless, and there's hardly any of her memorable Southwestfall twang in it. She doesn't sound like Beth, like *my* Beth. Although I've been so busy at Lady Hocquard's in the last week or so that I've almost forgotten what my Beth sounds like.

"How could I forget?" I reply, suspecting the worst.

"You were so quiet those first few days, Sam," Beth continues. "When I met the girl I would share my chambers with, I thought, *Crikes, I can see I'm the big talker here.* I'd seen what 'appened to your sister. Seen her burn in the sun like she was nothing, just before the roof fell down on her and you, runnin' in to save her. It were horrible, and I felt for you so much, Sammy, I really did. You just stared at me and hardly said a word. I thought you'd be done for—thought the Lords would be rid of you, like all the girls who go funny and don't speak no more. But you survived it, just. You made it through.

"I babbled and babbled at you. I don't know why. I thought maybe I could talk the sadness out of you, I suppose. And you came round eventually. And since then, you've gone from strength to strength. You've got ambition. The ambition to leave this place. And you're right. Who would want to stay here? Only a coward like me."

"That's not even close to true, Beth," I reply. "Don't ever say that." The drumming is louder now. *Droom, droom, droom.*

"They came and asked me about you. Asked if you'd found anything in Azzuri's room. Something about a secret chest being empty. Asked if you'd mentioned the Leeches."

"Oh, gods," I say. "What did you tell them? Did they hurt you?"

There's a silence. I realize the order of those questions. I see Beth realize it, too.

"It was Saxe," she continues. "He didn't say anything. Just smiled. Smiled in the worst way you've ever seen, all friendly but nothing behind the eyes. Asked me if I knew where you were, when you'd return, why you were there. I said I didn't know. He said it didn't matter. Then he left."

"When?" I ask.

"An hourglass ago." She turns to me now, and I see she's been crying. She looks hauntingly beautiful with a tearstained face. Her rose cheeks are even redder. I've never seen her cry before. Even in this life. Her cheer is indestructible. Or so I thought. I've managed to break her.

"I don't want to be a coward anymore, Sammy. I want to run. Before they come for you. Come for us both."

I go to argue, but I can't. She's not wrong.

"I'm sorry I didn't tell you about the Leeches. It's a long . . ."

She cuts across me. "Sam, normally it's you telling me to stop talking, but this time, you need to shut up. You can tell me when we're safe with your new Leech friends. We can go to them, right?"

"Yes," I say, confident. "Yes, we can."

We run then, Beth sort of galloping along in a daze, me sprinting ahead, checking around the corners. I'm alert to every sight and sound. But not as much as I need to be. I'm on the wrong blood for that.

"This isn't the way to the back gate," says Beth quietly behind me, her breath heaving in her chest.

"I need to go somewhere first," I reply as I turn right up a staircase that leads up to the East Wing, where the First Lord's guests stay. At the top I stop and signal to Beth to stay behind me. I hear footsteps, but I know they'll turn away down another corridor before they reach the staircase, because these footsteps belong to the palace guard. I know because I go this way to get to the library, and I've learned the palace guards' routines by heart. When you risk your life every night by sneaking around outside your hours just to read a book, then doing what I'm about to doesn't seem all that crazy.

Once the guard has gone, we dart away in the opposite direction. I hear Beth's footsteps behind me, too loud for my liking. I'll just have to hope the guards' senses are a little dulled today from the Westfall bloodale they like to swig of an evening.

I stop at the end of the next corridor, in front of a door on which hangs a small brass plate with the initials LS engraved on it. Behind this door is a suite of rooms used on occasion by Lord Sapphiri, who chairs the Bloodshares Council, not the highest council but not that far off, since the only thing Lords love as much as drinking fine blood is betting on the sales of it. Many a Lord has lost all their money from the Blood Market, and Sapphiri is meant to stop the whole thing from getting out of control. In reality, he accepts bribes from people to look the other way when the blood prices get manipulated. I used to suspect that. But now I'm a Leech, I know it for certain. He receives his bribes in the finest blood, not just coin.

I know this last part is true because I used to clean this wing until three years ago, and I saw a tiny vial of what I think was wolfblood under his bed, presumably not locked in his lockbox because he'd been too pissed the night before to do it. I knew it was wolfblood because it had the red and blue thread wrapped around it that all the wolfblood vials have that are given to the Flight Guard, the few members of the Blood Guard who are allowed to fly. And I got that from *Wolfblood Across the*

Ages, a long but detailed account from a Midway pastscribe who was clearly longing for the stuff himself.

Now, standing before his door, I'm betting my life and Beth's on three things.

I push the door. It swings open easily. Number one.

I glance around at the rooms before me. He's not here. Number two.

I look around properly while Beth stares at me dumbfounded from the door. I don't have time to explain. She can keep her stare. I check under the bed, hoping this will be easy. No vials of any kind. What a time to keep a tidy bedchamber.

I search the drawers in his cabinet, then, and underneath some sheets of parchment in the bottom one there's a vial of blood. They do like to stash their vials. It won't be wolfblood, but if it's hidden, it will be something good. I down it. I wait. I don't have to wait long. The tingling begins in my arms and legs, and a warm, powerful feeling flows though my body, like I'm hovering off the ground. I've not sneaked enough Lord's blood in my time to know for sure, but it feels like hawk, definitely magicked, and magicked hard: no wonder he's hiding it. I've not done this for a while. It's hard to keep a clear head. The new blood is pulsing through me potently, and my hands and fingers have gone temporarily numb.

I'll have to think quick now. There wasn't much in the vial, so my newfound alertness won't last long. Hawk is good for thinking, though. I know he'll have the wolfblood somewhere here.

I run into his dining quarters and I see a table I don't think was there last time. There's room to store something underneath, a little alcove beneath its rim if you look carefully. He's been a little more subtle, but not much. I race over to the table and stick my hand in the alcove, and I take out one vial, smaller than the last one but completely full of the deepest red blood you will ever see.

Number three. Wolfblood.

"We'll leave by the servants' entrance," I whisper as we run down the stairs, stopping every now and again to peer around a corner.

"Slow down, Sammy, I can barely keep up with you," replies Beth. Then: "What did you take?"

I turn to her, and she sees my blazing eyes. "Oh my god, Sammy, what have you done?"

"I had to take wolfblood, Beth. We have a wall to jump over." We might face resistance, too, that would require the blood that makes you fifty times stronger, but I decide not to add that. We fly down the stairs into the servants' basement, avoiding the corridor to the kitchens. We don't pass anyone on the way. It's a blooddamn miracle.

"I . . . can't believe my Sammy is on wolfblood!" says Beth, but then nothing more, as she's run out of breath to ask questions. I see her staring at my face when I turn back to her, looking at me like I might sprout fur anytime. Come to think of it, I might. Not all the effects of wolfblood have been documented.

The cellar is dank and dark, though I don't need even the smallest torchlight anymore. I'm in a post-light world. A couple of rats scurry from our footsteps. The palace rats are normally tame (unlike those that live in Worntown, they have no fear of being drained for blood), but perhaps they've sensed I'm something different now. We run to the door at the far end of the cellar, old decaying wood; I can taste its rot on my tongue, and that's how I know that the wolfblood has really hit my senses. Up the steps beyond there's a small courtyard with a gate that leads on to grass. Here on the east side of the palace there are no rose gardens or gardens at all, just muddy earth and small allotments where the gardeners grow the herbs to season certain blood types. The allotments stop at the palace wall, twenty feet high and spiked at the top. Are they to keep servants in or to keep the Worns out? If you have to ask, you've not been paying attention.

I start to walk toward the allotments, and then my nose, a whole new level of sense on even this small amount of wolfblood, tells me that we're not alone. But my body is slower than my nose and we don't stop in time, and that is how we end up face-to-face with two guards and Henry, a junior valet who has never liked me, judging by the sneers I've been greeted with for ten years.

As my nose promised, Henry is sweating profusely, and I can see why; he holds an empty vial of what I can see is magicked boar blood. It's a good Midway blood made even more potent with the magick, and he's sharing it with the guards. They will normally be on boar, but it won't be magicked, not unless they need it, so this will be Henry's way of gaining favor with them.

Henry turns his cabbage head my way, and the smile almost splits his head apart. "*Samantha!* Well, girl, I must thank you for making my job easier. I was meant to be finding you, and here you are. What a night this is turning out to be. One to remember!" He nods at the two guards, who, eyes still soft red from the magicked boar, saunter toward Beth and me, looking excited at the thought of escorting us to the cellars and maybe other places besides.

I don't move, but I stare at Henry, really stare at him, and as we lock eyes, I wait for him to realize, because he's clever, Henry, cunning—let no one ever say he isn't—and I know it won't take him long to see. See the deepness of the red in my eyes and how it contrasts to his.

The guards are almost upon us when he sees it.

"Wait!" he says. "I think she's on—" But it's too late for waiting, and it's too late for them. There's a voice in my head now: it's my own, but it's also older and wiser, the voice of the wolfblood, and it's telling me how nice it is if I extend my nails into fifteen-inch talons. So I do so, and I stick these talons in the lower chest of the first guard and pull them out. He collapses to the floor, hands over his belly, moaning softly and bubbling a little at the lips with speckles of blood, which quickly turn into pools. My own voice cuts in *I've hurt him* and then the wolfblood reminds me that he'll be fine in a few hours, and by the way, do you remember the palace guards are the same ones who escort maids to be sunburst when they're falsely accused of pilfering rooms?

I nod at that, and I duck the punch of the second guard, who to his credit has recovered quickly at the shock of his comrade on the floor, but is no doubt wishing he had his own talons, because a moment later he finds mine in his thigh, deep and fierce, hitting where the artery is (the wolfblood told me that). He goes down quickly, too, and soon he is passed out like the first.

Then, still in a daze of energy and power and more in tune to the wolfblood than myself, I slowly saunter over to Henry, much like the guards sauntered over to me and Beth, and I place one taloned finger where his groin is, noticing how wet his britches are with his own piss, and I stroke it up to his face. Then I lean forward and whisper in his ear.

"I want you to remember, Henry, that not all who look meek are meant to be. I want you to remember that for a long time." I retract my talons and pull my right fist back, and the sound it makes as it breaks his nose I know will make me smile in the darker days to come.

Then with three unconscious men round me and an even faster pouring hourglass over my head, I turn to Beth—to shocked, openmouthed Beth—and before she can speak, I pick her up, throw her easily onto my back, and with one swift leap clear the palace wall, diving into the bushes beyond it before the guards a hundred yards away at the gate can get any sight of us.

"So . . . that just happened," says Beth. "This new Sammy is summat, I'll tell you."

"I didn't know I could do that," I reply, the wolfblood really beginning to work now, speeding up my heart until it feels like a dozen stallions are running for their lives. "I mean, I did, but obviously I've never done that. I saw it play out in my head and I thought . . . maybe I could. I didn't know if I'd taken enough wolfblood, though, so I . . ." I stop and look at Beth, who's staring at me with a worried expression on her pale, shocked face. "Sorry, Beth. It's the blood. My thoughts are coming at me a thousand miles an hour. Blood Gods, how do Lords do this?"

Beth turns back to the palace, looking out for more guards, her blond hair still free and now plastered across her face. "Where do we go now?"

I take a breath. This might be a bit awkward. "We'll go to Lady Hocquard's."

"Why would *she* take us in?" asks Beth.

"Because . . . she's the Queen Leech. I gave her the list of Azzuri's names and I've been working for her ever since she first summoned me."

Beth's face does a number of things. She can't hide her emotions on her face, so I see it all play out. First comes the surprise. Then the anger of the extent of my lies. Then some disappointment. Then acceptance that this is not the time. After that, all she can really say is "Oh."

"I'm sorry I didn't tell you, Beth. It was a lot to take in at first."

"I think it's a good job you didn't tell me, all things considered, ain't it?" she says. "If Saxe had decided to apply some of his tricks, I don't know how long I could have lasted. Probably right not to trust me, Sammy."

I've never hated myself more than in that moment. "Beth, I—"

"Sammy, we need to go," she says firmly, and I suddenly remember we're running for our life. It seems getting distracted is another thing that's easy on wolfblood.

I peer through the bushes. If we can creep around until the road that rings the palace turns into woodland, then we can skip across the river north and follow it through the trees around to Northeastfall and Lady

Hocquard's. It will take an hour of running to get there from here. More if Beth tires easily, and she will.

"Wait, Sam," says Beth. "You can fly, can't you? You can get wings if you think on it. You're on wolfblood. You should go. Leave me."

I don't have time to turn back to her and I also don't have time for her misplaced heroism, as harsh as I know it sounds, so I speak as I run, cold and quick. "It wouldn't help. They'd probably see me in an instant, and I've never flown before, so I wouldn't exactly be fast. On the amount I've taken, I doubt the wings would last for long anyway. Maybe never even come at all. Our only chance is that it takes them a while to get our tracks. The river will help with that, even if the guards that follow us also take some wolfblood." *Also*, I think, *I'm not leaving you*. I don't know why I don't say it out loud.

The bushes run out, and we're forced into crossing the road that cuts across the north side of the palace, heading east. We dart across and continue into the woods beyond. Then I turn to Beth, who is panting now, trying to keep up with my rapid pace.

"Climb on my back."

"What?"

"I can run fast now. You can't. I will barely feel you." Something in my face—possibly the rictus of my jaw thanks to the wolfblood—makes Beth not argue with this, and she jumps on my back. I start running, legs like pistons, feeling none of it. My eyes are wild, my throat is tight, my muscles are on fire, and my body is more alive than it has ever been. I wonder how much time we have before they come for us.

Not enough.

It takes us less than an hourglass, though bloods knows how. I could've gone on for another glass more at this speed on this wolfblood. I haven't come close to testing its limits, thinking of Beth on my back. Her breath is a harsh wheeze in her throat and tears stream down her face, whether at the terrifying speed or what I've become, one of the two. Maybe I should have given her a little of the wolf as well—did I think it more important that I took it all, or did I not trust her on it? Best not to think on that.

We come out of the woods finally, onto the wide-open lanes of North-eastfall, each leading to a different Lord's estate. This is so far from the narrow, built-up streets of Worntown that it might as well be a different city. There's no light at all here save the moon, which is mostly cloud-hidden tonight; I see fine, but to Beth it must be a struggle. Eyes at their peak thanks to wolfblood, I peer through the gloom and see the domes and columns of the Lords' mansions far off in the distance. Some are awash with dozens of oil lamps, some with great torches burning out-side their pillared entrances; others are darker. Some are in pitch-black, simply shapes in a field. The homes of the nobility, scattered across these green stretches like great tiles of stone and marble spilled across the earth by a careless, unoriginal god.

From here it is only a quart glass to Lady Hocquard's. I start to make the final run.

"Wait!" Beth calls out, behind me.

I turn to her. "We need to move, Beth. We'll be safe once we're there."

"What if they've followed us here? Will this Lady protect us then?"

I don't know the answer to that. But I'm not nervous, and I feel no doubt. Just the pulsing, steady beat of the blood within my veins playing the same tune over and over again: *It's not an issue. All will be fine.* I'm beginning to understand how the Lords always have such confidence in everything they do. They get it from more than their status; they get it from their blood. And for the time being, so do I. I might even enjoy it a little . . .

"Sammy, I'm sorry," says Beth, shaking me from my blood haze, her voice cracking, half wheezing from the run. "In case I don't get a chance to say it again. I'm so sorry for trying to get you to stay at the palace. Something like this was always going to happen. I should have been helping you more. I was scared of losing you. I was a weight on you, I see that now."

"Beth, we need to get—"

"No, Sammy, I need to say it now. In case I don't get the chance. I need to say it while I still have a breath in me. I need you to know how much I admire you. You never give up. You want more. Me? I'm content. Content with me gossip, and content with you as my friend. And the more I see of this world, the more I realize that's the worst thing you can be. I could have had your spirit, Sammy. I really could've. But I chose not to." She breathes in. "If we get out of this alive, you're going to see who I can really be, Sammy. That I promise."

I look at my friend, more or less my only friend for ten years, apologizing to me, eyes a mess from the tears she's been crying even as she's been running. And something in me clicks. Maybe it's the wolf-blood opening up new paths in my head, helping me see things I'd been blocked from seeing before, or maybe I'm just thinking straight for the first time. Whatever it is, I see now the true cost of my tunnel vision. I see now what Beth might have done or become had she had someone invest in her, and not someone who was there like a fair-weather friend, eye on the prize, dreaming of a better future, like a self-absorbed little brat. I see this funny, spirited, whip-smart girl apologizing, apologizing to *me,* and I finally know what I have to say.

"Beth, I—"

Whoosh.

I stop. "Did you hear that?" Beth shakes her head. Of course she didn't. My hearing is ten times hers at the moment.

"Don't move, Beth," I say, and I see the fear leap into her eyes, because now she's thinking what I'm thinking.

I look up at the sky, but I can't see anything.

Whoosh.

A shadow passes overhead, over Beth's head, but whatever it was is out of sight again. There had been no mistaking the sound, though. No mistaking the sound of wings.

"Beth," I shout, the blood throbbing in my veins even louder. "Run."

As I start to sprint, I turn to make sure Beth isn't too far behind, and I see with relief that she's only a few steps away. But suddenly the sky goes dark and then Beth isn't there anymore. I stare at the night sky, but I can't see anything, even on my blood. I'd never imagined they could be so quick.

Crack.

The sound of something being dropped onto the road behind me makes me spin around, and for a second, I can't really understand what it is I'm seeing, because it doesn't immediately make sense. The angles are all wrong. After a couple of seconds of dawning realization that I know will dictate my dreams for years to come if I survive, I begin to understand that it's Beth, her arms and legs broken, distorted into macabre shapes, bleeding from a hundred cuts, eyes glazed with shock. Then the thing from the sky comes down and picks her back up, slower this time so I can get a good look at it, and then it shoots up into the sky again, its leathery wings wrapped around Beth's body like a cocoon.

"Beth," I cry out, though it's more a whisper than a cry, because I'm not capable of anything more. All I can do now is watch; the voice of the blood has gone quiet. A few seconds go by, and I try to use what little moonlight there is to scour the skies for them, but it is hopeless, even on my blood, even with my newly sharp eyes.

Crack.

The noise is behind me this time. I run over to the broken body, and I see that this time most of her bones are shattered, including the ones in her face, and Beth does not look like Beth anymore, but a discarded heap of fabric and bone and blood. She's still alive, though. And she's still calling out. Faint, but still there. *Sam,* she whispers, as I stand there, a haunted statue. *Sam.*

Then the winged vampire descends from the blackness of the skies for a final time and scoops her up, even as I reach out to her to take her hand, or what is left of her hand, to hold her one last time. Up she goes instead, with what is left of one eye staring unblinkingly at me until she is lost in the blackness. The next few seconds are a strange form of misery, longer than any seconds should be. But eventually it's over, and a final crack behind me again signals the end. What is on the ground now isn't really my friend. Beth is gone, and just a heap of bones and flesh remains, already slowly turning to ash. I turn away, throwing up as I do so.

A few moments later the wings in the sky land, and I see who he is.

"Samantha, isn't it?" says Rufous Azzuri, putting his wings back in, before shaking some of Beth's blood off his red and gold tabard and then stretching out a hand to me.

I stare numbly at him, the taste of my own vomit strong in my mouth, overpowering even the tang of wolfblood.

Rufous looks down at his unmet hand. "Fair enough. I thought I'd just shake your hand because I've never seen a Worn have the balls to do what you have. You're clearly on wolfblood, which is how you got this far and got over the gate. Stole it from one of the guest suites, I imagine. I wish those lazy fuckbloods would store it better if they do insist on stealing some."

I stare numbly at the First Lord's last surviving son. Some of Rufous's blond fringe has fallen over his forehead, and he spits in his hand and slicks it back. There is a clump of something in his hair, and I wonder if it is Beth's blood, or her skin or her bone.

"I had to come for you myself," continues Rufous. "I insisted. Not technically First Guard business, chasing a couple of maids, but it is not every day one does what you have. One for the memoirs, this!"

I continue to stare at him blankly, trying not to think about the fact that Beth's mangled corpse is only a few feet behind me. Rufous grins at me, and I see fascination in his eyes, like I'm a new species of animal he's admiring. I wonder, or at least the part of my brain that isn't numb with shock wonders, how he could do that to Beth and then just talk to me normally like this. It is not a sane transition.

"I assume you're one of those Leeches we keep hearing about?" asks Rufous. "Sounds like Saxe thinks you stole something from Azzuri's room when cleaning it, that you might be involved in his death. Sounds a little farfetched to me. I reckon you're just a little Leech spy after any information you get to blackmail. Sound about right?"

"Why did you kill her?" I ask quietly, ignoring his question. "She helped you. And she didn't have anything to do with it."

"Which is why she was running away with you, yes?"

"I knew you would kill her, too, if she stayed, just for being my roommate. I know you."

"Yes, probably," agrees Rufous. "Although now she is dead anyway, so how did that plan work for you?"

"You didn't have to kill her like that."

"No, I didn't. But you didn't have to go taking things that aren't yours, did you? So there we go. We all make our choices."

"What will you tell her family?" I ask, having given up on getting any firm grasp of the conversation and deciding to float through it instead, like a dream you know you'll wake from soon.

Rufous smiles, and I notice that his incisors are much longer than normal, turning his handsome face slightly feral when he grins. "Why in all the Bloodhalls would we bother to tell them anything?"

"If you tell them that she ran away, that she is hiding somewhere safe in some imagined sanctuary, then I will come with you quietly, and I won't resist," I say, a little more steel in my voice.

Rufous walks up close to me, so close that I can still smell the wolf-blood on his breath, stronger than mine because he's taken it more recently, and no doubt taken much more than I have, enough to give him flight. I can smell the fur on his wings, too; smell the sandalwood oil that he's rubbed on them, as if going out to a ball. He puts his face in front of mine, and I inspect it closely, expecting some form of madness, but all I can see are bright green eyes and a chiseled jawline. *He thinks this is normal,* I realize in horror.

"You don't have a knife on you, do you, Sam?" says Rufous, grinning, face now just an inch from mine. "I think it's sweet that you want her family to think she's still alive. How nice to give them hope. But I won't tell them that, because it would make us sound weak, and because as much as you have surprised me and impressed me today, you're still a fucking Worn girl who stole from a Lord, and you will burn in a few hours, so I'm essentially talking to a heap of ashes." I see anger in his face now for the first time. "And I won't take orders or threats from a pile of ashes, although to be honest, it is not much of a threat, because you are barely the same species to me." His face is almost touching mine now; his spittle rains down on me. "Today you feign to be me, flying so close to the sun and burning your pathetic little wings. It's why I can even talk to you. But all your other days you have been so much lesser, in what you drink and how you think and everything you do. You could be happy like that, but no, you choose to fly. And people like me will always be there to fucking shoot you down."

I show no emotion at this. It's important I don't for this next part. To say the things I need to this Lord of all the Lords. It's time he knew, time he knew the extent of my hate for him.

"You killed my father. And my mother," I begin.

He cups his chin in mock thought. "Hmm. Did I now. Should I remember this?"

"They didn't die by your hand. But you had the main part in both of them. You tried to *have* my mother, came to my house to do it. My father stopped you, and the street. Then my father was taken and sunburst. A year later, my mother killed herself in her anguish."

I can see him thinking on this. "Oh, that sad story you told me in your room . . . that was *my* doing? Oh, girl, what composure you have! If you are expecting me to have any inkling of this, though . . ."

"You won't remember. It was nothing to you, I expect. Maybe you remember the humiliation of being stopped, first by the street and then by me and my sister."

I see recognition in his eyes then, and a slow smile that grows into a full-glare beam.

"Oh yes, I do remember now. The children, standing defiantly in front of their mother. Interesting that you thought it was fear that held me back."

"Well, what else are you made of, if not cowardice?"

He grins a snaptail grin. "Many things, Samantha. That day I saw in your eyes a strength, and I respected that. It is rare to see such fire in a Worn. Rare to see anything. I gave you a small victory that day, and I was happy to do it."

I see the gratitude he thinks I should feel, and it makes me throw up in my mouth a little bit. There is a powerful beat in my chest—a little bit wolfblood, a little bit loathing. I raise my fists. Rufous smiles. I'm sure he wants this. And I'm nowhere near ready. Not yet. But right now, I want it, too.

I pull back a fist and aim it at his rib cage. It's a powerful blow, but he isn't standing there; he has leaped back several yards in anticipation of it and he lands, perfectly balanced. I jump in the air, five meters high, and I direct my second punch downward. It's a move I saw a bloodguard do to a Worn many years ago, and the wolfblood has made my memories real, I suppose. Once again Rufous leaps out of the way, sideways this time.

"Experience," he murmurs. I howl in frustration, and as I do so, I extend my nails, the wolfblood turning them into talons. I go to lunge at Rufous, but at the last second I dive to the floor, rolling with his punch and kicking my legs outward at his chest. He'd readied for the punch but not the kick, but his arms come together at the last moment and hold my legs in place, before flipping them upward and sending me crashing into and halfway through a tree trunk. Rufous unties his robes then, and his wings shoot out from his back; he slices one spiked leather winglet through the air in a circular motion, slicing me across the chest as I struggle to free myself from the trunk. I collapse into the undergrowth and roll down a short embankment.

"Nobility," says Rufous softly at the top, gliding down toward me on his wings.

I'm still shocked from the chest wound (although I can feel it already heal, stitching itself back together), but I roll aside in time to avoid the second downward slice of the wing, roll through his legs and jump up behind him, my now-extended canines at his neck. I go for the bite, but an inch from contact, Rufous jolts his head back and connects with my forehead with a dull smack, and before I can recover, he draws a fist back, and then it connects with my face.

"Victory," he adds as I fall to the ground.

PART III

The
Great Illusion

21

Dawn of the Dead

It is a hard bargain to be given eternal life, as far as we know, yet be cast from the sun. If you ever doubt me, do two things. First, watch the simple joy of a wolf or mage on a sunny day. Next, look into the eyes of one to be sunburst. For a moment, just a moment, I swear you will see relief.

Redlight Lutehold,
Meanderings of a Reasonmind

First Lord Azzuri

I'm on my way to see the Wornmaid Rufous is about to torture when Redgrave informs me my spymaster is in the portrait room.

"Cinabar, my friend," I begin, "it is always a pleasure." Saxe is sitting at the table when I walk in, but he jumps up with a sudden burst of energy upon my entrance. He is not wearing his usual black ensemble; he rarely does when he comes to the palace to see me. Instead he is dressed in an extravagant cream jacket with gleaming silver buttons and a red silk shirt underneath, with a blue cravat completing the look. I sometimes wonder if he dresses up like this to mock my own tastes. I wouldn't put it past him.

"The pleasure is very much mine, First Lord, as always," he replies, clasping my hands in his and giving me his biggest, most amiable grin, the one I do not trust for a second, the one that is meant to go with the slapdash hair and genial manner and lure you into complacency. "I'm dreadfully sorry to drag you over this side of the palace, but better safe than sorry and all that!"

I want to ask him who he thinks is listening, but I refrain. He is, after all, one of only two men in the city that even I am careful of angering. "No problem at all." I point to the decanter in the center of the table. "Please help yourself to some bear. Magicked, of course."

He shakes his head. "No thank you, First Lord. I like to save the very best stuff for Hallsday. Gives me a little motivation during the week."

Well, of course he does. Our spymaster is famous for his self-control. *Notorious* would be a better word in this city of Lordly excess. No one knows what he really gets up to though, bachelor that he is. He lives alone with no children or other family in a small, modest manor house not far north of the wolf jails, where the woods meet Eastfall proper. Even his servant staff is small; I hear he has only five Worns in that empty heap of his.

"Actually, I was studying your portraits, as always when we meet," he continues. "Your last relative to die, I see, before the tragic death of your youngest, of course, was your uncle." He points to a portrait in the middle of the wall opposite the door that shows a man with a long thick beard with a highly unusual tinge of gray in it, a blemish that gave him the imaginative nickname of Azzuri the Gray. Given the subsequent fate of that particular word, it's perhaps better he didn't survive what came next.

"Your only loss in Grayfall, I believe?" He doesn't give me a chance to reply. "That was a loss I carried hard, I must say. Your uncle was of great help when I took up my role as spymaster of Lightfall, in those chaotic years after the Twin War. I have to admit, First Lord, that I was floundering a little then. Struggling to come to terms with the sprawl of the city. Of the behemoth it was becoming. I suppose I was a little overawed by it all. I even—and please keep this to yourself, for I have a reputation to maintain—I even considered trying to implement a less strict regime, to try and let some of the things that were happening . . . follow their own course, if you see what I mean."

If I could be bothered for this story, I might see what he meant. But I cannot, so I do not.

"But your uncle put me back on the right path," he continues. "He showed me that when you give any of the Worns an inch, when you let the smallest transgression go unpunished, when you give the beast at the door a little food, then it will never stop coming. The masses need only a small chance to tip the whole bloodcart over, and it is we ruling Lords that must keep it steady at all times. Your uncle knew how we vampires ruled best. Knew the value of order, the value of boundaries; the place we Lords play in the whole system of the city. The noble position in which we keep ourselves. That position was hard to do in Lightfall. Things began to change, even with my efforts. But here in First Light, boundaries remain."

I stare carefully at Saxe. I sense a point coming. He could hardly have flagged it up more clearly.

"And it's of boundaries I come to speak of to you today, First Lord."

Ah, here we go.

"You see," he continues, "I am afraid I have learned of some troubling information concerning someone . . . in a high position. Someone we both know well, I fear."

"Oh yes?" I ask, not trying particularly hard to hide my disappointment. "I had rather hoped you had come with news of what happened to my son."

Saxe clears his throat and prepares his most oleaginous smile. "Let me reassure you, First Lord, that that is on the upmost of my mind, and I am leaving no stone unturned in my quest to get more information on that matter."

"There must be a lot of stones in your way, then," I say, finally letting my anger get the best of me, not for the first time this past month.

"I'm sorry, First Lord?" asks Saxe, his mouth smiling but his eyes unmoved.

"Never mind. What of your matter? Who is this person in a high position you so ominously speak of?"

"It's ah . . . it's Lady Hocquard, First Lord."

"I'm sorry?"

"Lady Hocquard. We . . . that is to say, my whisperers have uncovered disturbing information about her."

I try and contain my anger. It is vital that I do not rage at him. But the contents of those parchments I found in my son's old Westfall abode scream at me. For justice. But I must bide my time. The last First Lord to fall out badly with his spymaster was assassinated three hundred years ago, and that began a civil war, one that ended with the ascent of the Azzuris and my father becoming ruler of Lightfall.

"Cinabar, my old friend," I begin, hoping that the use of *friend* will not sound too insincere, "what could you possibly have found out about her?"

"Well, you see, First Lord, the Lady was seen by several of my whisperers conversing with your son the day before his death. Disguised as a Worn. Strange, I'm sure you would agree. We have long suspected that she might be conspiring with certain rebellious elements in the city, and so at the very least, I believe it warrants some investigation of the Lady herself and her property."

I look carefully at Saxe's open, jowly features, and those small, curious eyes of his. He really is serious.

"Cinibar, are you actually suggesting that because someone saw a Worn that resembles her, we should now suspect her in my son's death?"

"Not resembles, First Lord. *Was* her. My whisperers were very certain of this."

I try and trample down the anger rising up once again within me. I was distracted from my bigger issues and dragged halfway across the palace for *this*. I summon every ounce of calm I have and try and fortify it with every pound of patience, hoping the entire odious concoction won't bubble over into rage and leave me foaming at the mouth.

"My dear Cinibar, forgive me, but the only certain thing is that Lady Hocquard—Daphnée, as she is to me—is a good friend who I have known for well over a century. Since the death of her husband in Grayfall, and especially since the tragedy that followed on its heels for her, she has wholeheartedly committed herself to good works across the city, charitable works, for both the city and its Worn population. As a result, she is respected by her peers and loved by many Worns, which is not something we can say of many of the Lords and Ladies."

"First Lord, I—"

"But you, Cinibar, would have her taken to your . . . interrogation chambers and have your men ransack her house on the word of your whisperers, who, lest we forget, are Midways at best, and all because they thought they saw her dressed up in *Worn garments*?"

Saxe grins that harmless snaptail grin of his again and holds his hands up. "I can see that perhaps I was a little hasty, First Lord. I did not take into account the repute of the Lady, nor the evidence required to accuse a noble."

"You did not, Cinibar."

"Well," he says, rubbing his hands together, "if I may be excused, First Lord, I should get back to more pressing matters, as you say."

"It would be most appreciated."

He walks over to the door, and I am about to pour myself another flute of magicked bear to calm myself when he turns back to me.

"But perhaps you will grant me, First Lord, that if I find more compelling evidence of Lady Hocquard's involvement, then you will reconsider?"

I nod, sensing a chance to be more emollient to my spymaster. "No Lord or Lady is immune from your reach, Saxe, you know that, but only as long as the evidence is there. They are not Worns, after all. They are *us*."

"Indeed, First Lord, they are not. Which is why any disturbances of the careful balance we seek must be so thoroughly disapproved of, don't you agree?"

I stare at him and, not for the first time, see something behind those small eyes.

"Indubitably, Cinibar. I look forward to our next conversation."

Then he is gone, and my health and my heart are all the better for it.

Sam

I'm awake. I'm alive. It's a start. Then I remember Beth, and what she looked like in the end, and all my relief rushes out of me and the tears come, except I'm too tired to cry. There's a dull ache in the back of my skull. I can't tell if it's from where Rufous hit me or the aftereffects of the wolfblood. Probably both.

I look around. I'm in a room of stone, with an equally stone door and not much else save a hard bed that makes my chamber's sleeping arrangements seem like lodgings in the Bloodhalls. There's a stench of dried blood in the air; even with my once-again-normal senses I can tell it's vampire, not animal. I try and get up, and that's when I realize that one of my legs is manacled to the bed in thick steel; ludicrously thick. They must be unsure if any of the wolfblood is still in me. I wish it was. I can remember what it felt like.

I hear footsteps walking to the door. It doesn't take a genius like Sage Bailey to work out where I am and what is about to be done to me. I hope they make it quick before I'm sunburst. Probably not.

The door opens and Rufous Azzuri walks in. My living nightmare, dragging on and on. He is a different sight to how we last met. His long locks are tied back in a ponytail, and he wears nothing but an ankle-length basic gray tunic with a red apron over it. He looks like he's tending bar at one of the worst Serftown dives. I would spit at him, but my mouth is too dry. He has the same awful grin that he wore when he killed Beth. His hair is no longer stained with her blood, though. I'll take what I can get.

"Ah, it's the maid who fought," Rufous begins, standing over me, adjusting his apron a little in readiness for the blood that even a moron could tell you was about to be spilled. "I'll be telling stories about you for decades. What spirit!"

"Let me out of these chains and I'll show you some more of that spirit, you evil highblood fuck." I meant it to come out strong, but my voice breaks as I say it. Whatever grit I had is slipping out of me. I'm not a heroine who goes around saving the day. I'm a palace maid with a book obsession and an uncurable ambition. The wolfblood took me over for a while. The person who's left now it's gone is having an identity crisis. It's a harsh comedown.

"Ah, the time for fun is gone now, I'm afraid," he says. "Well, fun for you anyway. The fun for me is just getting started, I am happy to report."

Rufous reaches into his apron pocket and takes out a thin stick of silver metal. It's not quite the torture tool I was expecting.

"I have a secret to tell you, ah, what was your name again?"

"Sam," I said. "And the woman you killed was Beth."

"Ah, well. Now you've named her, it seems like I've grown a conscience. Excuse me while I go cry in a corner." He holds his pointed chin in thought for a second. "Ah. Hold on a moment. No, no, I still don't give a shit. Now, Sam. About that secret. I'd ask if you can keep one, but since I'm the last person you're going to ever speak to, I'm fairly confident that you can. So let me tell you about my stick."

I look at Rufous, really look at him. There is a tiny little twitch in his left eye. I wonder if he is mad or just cruel. It doesn't really matter now.

"I found this stick under Lightfall two hundred years ago. In some temple ruin. Maybe that sorcerer cult is right about the mortals of the old stories being real. Because it isn't just a stick. It's much more than that. Would you like to see?"

"Fuck your cousin."

"That's good enough for me." And he points the stick at the ceiling of my prison, then taps a small dent on the end. A thin beam of light shoots out of it, like the sun itself, and the beam dances on the ceiling. I don't like where this is heading. He puts the stick back in his apron pocket.

"I shall return to my stick in a second. But first I want to know why you stole a piece of parchment from my dead brother's quarters. What was written on it? Who told you to do it? Who did you give it to? Very simple questions, Sam. A learned book reader like yourself, I'm sure you can handle them."

What was written on it. Beth really didn't mention the names to them, then. Good for you, Beth. If I can take an ounce of your bravery, I might get out of this with some of my body left. I turn away from Rufous and stay silent. I know how this will go. And I won't give him the satisfaction. At least I think I won't. I've shown I'm brave in the last week or so; I think I've earned that trait. But I'm nowhere near brave enough to handle the kind of things I hear about that take place down here. I'll keep up my newfound courage as long as I need to. You never know: maybe the dull, deep ache I feel now after Beth's death, the one that stops me caring whether I live or die, will carry me through the rest.

"No answer, eh? Ah well. Back to the stick, I suppose." He takes it out of his robes again and shines it on the ceiling, as if I've forgotten what it does already. "I never know where to start," he begins. "Torture is such a funny thing."

"Spare me the prepared speech, you overblooded cunt, and hurt me," I spit, almost accidentally. There it is, still. The rage. Beth's crumpled bones and misshapen face, all in a pile, at the front of my brain. Keeping me sharp. Thanks, Beth.

Rufous's eyes twitch slightly, and I see my lack of fear is ruining his melodrama. Life is a play for him, I suspect. If I can mess with the staging a little, then at least I'll have a little satisfaction before he kills me.

"As you wish, little girl. Let's see how far that bravery carries. I wager you wear it like an undergarment that comes off too easy." Then he shines the stick briefly on my little finger, and I watch in silent horror as it turns from orange to brown to black, and then slowly into ash. I told myself I wouldn't scream, but you can't prepare for physical pain; a Wornmaid who'd been beaten senseless by a Lord for knocking a bloodflute over told me that. You can prepare for the mental kind (I've had some practice now, I reckon, not as much as some, but more than many), but not the physical.

I scream, I grunt, and then briefly the pain is so bad I can't make a proper noise but can only gasp a little. Then it dulls to a mere burning sensation, as I stare at the softly glowing, ashy black stump where my little finger used to be.

"If you're wondering if it will grow back," says Rufous, leaning into my face, "then you can be sure from me that it won't, no matter how much fine blood you steal and drink. It's as good as the sun, my stick."

I raise my head and look up at him and summon everything I have to shelve the pain for a second. Then I smile and say, "You should've started on my face. Now I know you're a coward."

Bloods. I didn't even realize I was going to say that. Beth's hanging eyeball and stuck-out tongue and odd-angled limbs are still pinwheeling through my brain, still stirring me into the mouth of madness.

"Ah," he says, staring at me in a way I don't like the look of at all. "Well, perhaps I should restore my reputation." He holds the stick in front of my face. "Where you're going, you won't need eyes."

"Rufous!" The shout comes from the door. There is a key in the lock; it turns and none other than First Lord Azzuri himself walks in. Ten years in the palace, and I've never been so close. He's all dressed up in his finest; I feel concern for his washermaid if he stays around here too long. He takes a quick look at me, glancing at the strange new space where my finger used to be, and then turns back to Rufous. "Can we at least talk to her first while she has some body parts left? We're after information this time, not your brand of punishment."

"Father, now is not the time, please," says Rufous, a mixture of panic and annoyance in his voice that is a song to my ears. "I have this under control."

"Rufous, this is your brother! I'm not going to risk losing any information about his death to your . . . habits. Look at her, she can hardly stay awake, how are we going to get anything out of her that way?"

He points to me, and I'm indeed looking like I'm about to pass out. But not from the finger, though that's still a pain beyond words. From a decision I made when he walked in. A decision made in a split moment, based on a simple question—what would a Leech do? I've nothing to lose, and so I close my eyes and I start shaking and dribbling too for good measure. I'm giving them the stagetale of their lives.

"Father," says Rufous, "if she's in the palm of someone, someone like the Leeches, then only pain will get us what we want."

"Really. I believe you may have mistaken those maids, if they do exist, for hardened soldiers. Unless the art of blackmail also requires combat training as well."

"Father—"

"Now!"

Rufous sounds furious and defeated, and I try not to smile. I hear him sweep past his father out of the cell, leaving me with the First Lord of First Light, the man whose house I have lived in for two decades but who has never given me so much as a second glance, so close I can smell the tang of fresh, magicked bloodwine on his tongue and, when I finally open my eyes, see the slight remains of the bloodshot in his eyes from his last vial.

"Can you talk?" he asks, not kindly, but at least carefully.

"Yes, F-First Lord," I say back to him, trying my best to make my words as weak as possible, which isn't that hard given my newfound stub of a finger. I wonder if what he said was true about it not growing back. I wonder what things in life use the little finger.

"I am not going to lie to you," he continues. "I will show you the respect that you have failed to show me with your discourtesy. As if taking something of my late son's was not bad enough, you stole and ingested wolfblood. At lightfall tomorrow, you will be sunburst. I make no apologies for this. But if you tell me the truth now, I will see to it you are untouched until then and given a respectful death. You have my word as First Lord of this city. Lie to me—and I will know if you do—and my son will return, and I am afraid to say his appetites for hurting those in his care are growing by the day, and I have no doubt he will unleash the full brunt of them on you with their full and horrific consequences. Do you understand all that I am saying?"

I look at his long aquiline nose and his small, dainty ears; his wide, completely uncreased eyes and skin softer than ninety percent of the population of First Light, and I think—I know—that there was an error in his speech, one he doesn't even realize. He *won't* know if I'm lying. He would have to know me and my kind for that, and that's one skill he's never bothered to learn.

I lie in my cell, having convinced the First Lord that I was a Worn thief, nothing more, no Leech at all. My performance is good, and my reward is the rest of the night undisturbed while I wait for them to come and tie me to a stake at dawn. My thoughts turn to my sister, to her end—not for the first time, but likely for the last.

I remember jostling in a crowd, trying to get a better view of her.

My sister, poised to go from being just your run-of-the-mill Worn to an actual maid of the palace. I came even though I told her I wouldn't be attending the ceremony, that I didn't think she should be joining the palace. That the Sun Ceremony is not a source of pride but nothing less than a branding, the branding of an animal you wanted to mark as your own. The fact that no one sees it that way is exactly part of the problem, I told her, but she just laughed, and said that if I didn't want to come, then I didn't have to. She never got angry at my feelings about our lives or the city. She just laughed patiently. She was tired of the streets, and I could see on her face that she'd given up. Her anger had died while mine had simply grown. I hated her and loved her for it.

Then that Lord spied us in Second Gods, assuming we were praying when we were really playing the charity game, spinning lies for some coin, and he took a shine to her, and before we knew it, she was being summoned to be a maid at the palace. They can't all be bad, she said. She'd make friends with some and find me a position, she said. There's no other way for us, she said.

So I went in the end. I attended the Sun Ceremony. It didn't take place in the palace of course; the idea of the First Lord letting all the families of the maids into his home was about as likely as cowblood giving you wings. Instead it took place in the First Lord's own private prayhall, separate from the palace. Joined to the prayhall is a smaller building. The Sun Trap, they call it. It works like this. The crowds gather in the chapel, and each maid goes into the Sun Trap one by one. They stand before a small aperture in the wall through which the first rays of the dawn sun filter through, tiny enough so that only a small amount of light hits the spot where they put out their arm, burning a mark on them for eternity. A sun scar is the only kind that doesn't heal for a vampire. They call it getting sunkissed, which as names go is about as misleading as calling a fist in the face a hand hug. Once you're sunkissed, you belong to the palace. Body and soul.

All the maids do this, and then the crowds disperse, except of course now the sun is up, so the families have to sleep in the catacombs of the chapel for the day. Not that they mind. It's all part of the ritual. See your beloved children get the best Worn job in town . . . then spend one last, teary night with them before they move on to bigger and better things.

Our only family there that night was my uncle and his wife; they were kind but not much else. That was the last time I saw them, as they moved to Southwestfall after the ceremony and didn't tell me where, so I suppose they weren't that kind after all. Not that we ever needed them. It was my sister and me against the world—her with her grin and her beauty and a habit of walking through life pretending it was the only one anyone could possibly want, and me with my smarts and my hate and my truth. Together, we could do anything. It was a foolproof plan.

Except it ended on that morning, as I watched, and the first rays of light shone through the gap and burned the maids in turn. Because when the time came for my sister to be sunkissed, a beam in the centuries-old wood of the Sun Trap snapped, and half the roof began to cave in. The crowds watched in horror and backed away as the sun shone in, covering my sister and the master of ceremonia in bright, hot death. I ran in then—of course I did, what else could I do? I pushed and shoved through the crowds and half jumped, half collapsed inside, trying to dodge the beams of sun covering the room and the wood falling around me, and for a cruel moment I thought I could grasp my sister, my screaming, burning, disintegrating sister, but then something hit me and I don't remember any more.

When I came to, it was night again, and I was being pulled from beneath the rubble of the Sun Trap, nothing wrong with me except a bruise on my head and a couple of cuts, which healed in an instant with one bloodvial. I was led to the palace, still in shock, and they told me how lucky I was that the beam had protected me from the sun, and that I was to take my sister's place; that something about my bravery impressed the watching First Lord and his sons and so I'm a palace girl now. They put me up in my rooms and told me what I'd be doing and where I'd be scrubbing and cleaning, and I remained in shock, just nodding at everything everyone said to me, until I found myself alone three days later and cried for the first time since her death. I cried and cried and cried, weeping more than I ever have.

Whether I was crying for my sister or for the death of my old life, I really couldn't tell you.

They come eventually to drag me out of prison and into a carriage and from there to a courtyard a half mile from the palace, where a wooden cross awaits me. There's eight bloodguard in total, which seems unnecessary for a Wornmaid, but that's the rule. You never know what blood someone might still be on, after all. I could have some secret wolf lingering in me and be biding my time. If I do, then I am biding it very sundamn close.

The men are dressed in the standard plain red tabards of the blood-guards, over which is a thick blue robe covering their arms and legs. I smell the tang of magicked blood on the breath of the one who strings me up on the cross, and I wonder that they will have the strength to punch through walls for a good couple of glasses, all for the sake of a maid who can't even escape some ropes.

Once they're satisfied that I can't move, head tilted back and fixed in place so I can stare at my fiery reaper, the bloodguards don blue hoods so their faces are covered, aside from tiny eyeholes. If what I know of sunburst executions are right, those are only precautions, in case some-thing should go wrong and they find themselves spending any time in the faint but still deadly predawn glow. In reality, they'll wait until shortly before lightfall, when it's too late for me to escape to the safety of cover even if I did somehow manage to free myself, and then they'll run the short distance to the guards' barracks behind the sky tower, where they'll spend the day.

I stare at them. Lined up in a row, they look absurd, and I cough out a strange short laugh that echoes pathetically in the silence of the courtyard.

The sky lightens a bit, and we wait. When it seems to lighten even more (or is it my imagination?), one of the guards steps forward (*careful you don't trip, you can hardly see, ha-ha*) and speaks, the words lacking any passion, sounding exactly like those of someone whose job it is to say the same thing at the same time every day.

"Samantha Ingle, servant of the palace. You have been sentenced to sunburst. May the Blood Gods take pity on you and give you safe passage to the Bloodhalls, where you may be forgiven for your life here and serve the blood of old to the Lords of Forever."

Then, with as much import as that leaden speech deserved, he steps back to stand next to the others.

There's a stillness in the air now. I can't hear anything. Not even any dawnbirds. The world has hushed for my end; nothing is outside this courtyard. Just my eight hooded watchers and me. We are the world now. I turn my thoughts to my mother, her face cutting across my thoughts of death just like she used to cut across my reading with her booming voice, telling me to quit eating up all those words and down some blood instead. She was never quiet, my mother, never whispering, always carrying life with her, letting everyone know that we weren't dead. I can see her now, in her best days, not the sad ones when my father was taken but before, cradling me in her arms when I was young, singing to me of the old days of Lightfall, when there were no mountains in sight and you could run through the fields, run all the way to the southern shore if you wanted to. Singing to me of Last Light and all the fictional girl heroines who got up to no good there.

I see my sister now, too. Not the days when we grew apart and she took up that crazed dream to work at the palace, but the days when we would run free through the city streets, not caring about the dangers but laughing at how close we came to them. My sister, singing, her voice just like my mother's, so similar it would give me chills.

And finally my father, ruffling his hands through my hair, telling me the world is mine and he would always be there, then seconds later pausing to roar at his neighbor John, saying *Get off my bloody wheelbarrow, you thieving prickard, or by the twin hells I'll nut you something good.*

All those faces, somewhere in my head.

It's almost time now. I won't, of course, see the sun. As an end, it's not nearly as dramatic as it's made out to be. I'll be turned to ash long before the sun itself makes an appearance proper; my bringer of death will be its first shafts strobing out from beneath the horizon, tentacles come to whisk me away to the afterlife. I stare hard at the horizon, willing it to happen, so hard in fact that at first I don't notice the figure walking through the archway of the courtyard, straight toward me.

They're dressed in a robe and veil, just like the guards, but theirs are red; and I wonder for a moment if only I can see them, if this is my death come for me. But then the guards stop and turn in disbelief. One runs back and tries to grab this strange new apparition. But the figure reaches their own arm behind them lightning-fast before the guard can even grab their shoulder, and twists the guard's arm all the way around, still with their back turned. The guard roars in pain, and then he stops roaring because there are now two blades in him, one in each eye. Two others have caught up to him now, and they spend a moment in shock looking at their fallen comrade before they spend the next moment looking in more shock at the blades in each of their groins, the arms of the figure moving impossibly fast. They fall back, making a gurgling sound, grabbing at their impaled cocks, and then the figure calmly carries on walking toward the rest, but now I see they are . . . skipping? *She* is skipping. I think it's a she.

She skips round the five guards still standing, who have bunched themselves into a protective circle, still numb at the way their predawn is going. From somewhere inside her robe, she takes out two more daggers and backs away from the circle, waiting for the next guard to advance. But they don't, which is clever or maybe cowardly or maybe both. So she throws one of the daggers in the air, and there is a long pause that drags on as we all watch it, until its fall is broken by her outstretched punch that launches the blade through the air and straight into the nose of one of the guards, splitting it in two, lodging itself in its face as blood pours either side of it, the guard's wails arcing through the predawn air.

I wonder at the strength you would need to ruin a magick-blooded vampire's face like that with such a small dagger, but I don't wonder for long, because at that moment all the twin hells break loose. The remaining four charge at her, plan seemingly forgotten. They have no weapons, but they're on good blood and I still like their chances if they attack her all at once. But she is not where they have charged; instead, in one smooth motion she has jumped from a standing start over them and then landed behind them, slowly backing away by gliding her feet back, like some kind of dance. Another dagger appears in her left hand to join the one still in the right, and now it's her turn to charge, except it's not really a charge, it's like she's skating on ice, skimming across the ground. As she nears the guards, who are ready to attack, she slides down at the last moment, the stone pacing of the courtyard her personal ice pond, and she arcs her right hand up as she skims underneath them, the dagger it holds sticking deep into the upper thigh of the nearest guard, and the blade in her left hand doing the same to the thigh of the man on her left. They both buckle to their knees, and that's when she comes to a quick halt and lifts herself up from her slide into a small jump, her fists landing on the necks of the fallen, making them collapse to the ground, whimpering as they do so.

The two left are still stunned by this, but one reacts quickly and punches her, a good fist on magicked blood, and she falls fast to the ground. The two guards exchange glances, unable to believe their luck, and they descend upon her with blooded talons and fangs outstretched ready to rip her to shreds. But the newly fallen figure lurches back up, as if a puppet on taut strings. Somehow she has, in the split moment of her fall, managed to resupply the blades in her hands, and they both stick into the throats of the guards looming over her, choking them as blood gushes from their gullets. With her outstretched palms she hammers the blades deeper into their throats, nails them in, until fountain jets of blood are gushing out from them, before their bodies finally slump to the ground to join their comrades.

Then she turns around and sees that the first guard, the one with blades in his eyes, has managed to remove them both; his eyeballs are pulp and blood still pours from them but he stumbles forward toward her regardless, presumably acting on scent now. Much good does it do him, though, because Alanna does a quick two-step to him, more waltz-ing than anything else, and then with one quick movement thrusts two more daggers into his weeping eyeholes to replace the others.

With a final look, the figure surveys the bodies on the floor, some guards out cold, some struggling and moaning with their wounds. All survivable, all curable, all painful.

Then my savior skips toward me and I try and form words, but the oncoming dawn has sapped all my strength. I can feel the light coming, and all I can say is a question.

"Raven?" I ask.

"You be a cheeky bitch now, ain't ya?" says Alanna, and I try and laugh at the mistake, but everything fades and my laugh dies on my lips.

22

The Fearful and the Furious

Stick your courage, be so bold,
And tell them that you love them;
For you never know what shall pass
And for how long you will haunt them.

Sinopia and Carminia, act 3, scene 4,
playwright unknown

Sam

The first thing I see is Lady Hocquard sitting at the end of my bed, her pretty, calm face looking as stressed as I've ever seen it in our short time together. She's trying her best to hide it, but every now and again her eyes or mouth gives it away, like a stone being skimmed across an otherwise still lake. She's wearing no makeup and a plain yellow dress, and her hair is tied back and covered in a blue linen cap. Straight from Leech business, I assume. I can still smell her roselily fragrance on her, though. Whatever her dress, it's always a constant.

"You're awake," she begins, and I don't know what to do with that, so I let her carry on.

"I was worried when Alanna brought you in. Your hand looked in bad shape. Your finger has grown back already, though, I see."

I stare at my hand. She's right, there's almost no sign left of the fun Rufous had. Must be the last of the wolfblood fixing me up. So much for that stick having the power of the sun.

Lady Hocquard must have noticed the concern flash across my face, because she quickly adds, "I do not care a bloodcrown that you took wolfblood, Sammy darling, although I would love to know where you found it. We are always looking for some. I am just glad you made it out of there alive."

"Do you know?" I ask carefully.

"What happened? Yes, most of it we have been able to work out. You were . . . raving . . . a little when Alanna rescued you, which filled a lot of the blanks in, I must say, and through our other Leechmaid in the palace, a picture was painted. A very clear picture, indeed."

I imagine ice in that last comment, but I'm not sure. I could be on steady ground here, or I could be about to fall on my arse. You can never tell with Lady Hocquard, as I'm slowly learning.

"I didn't tell Beth about us, m'lady. About you, I mean. The Leeches, that is." *Pull it together, Sam. You're off the stake, don't tie yourself to another one.* "All she knew is that I'd found the note in young Azzuri's room. And I told her that before I even knew you actually existed."

"I know, dear. That is why we remain unarrested and you remain unburned."

There is a long, still pause and as I ponder the double meaning of that sentence, I stare into those wide blue eyes and wonder, not for the first time, what is really behind them. At least Alanna wears her madness on the outside. I'm not sure where Lady Hocquard keeps hers.

"Sam," she says, clasping my hand suddenly. It's the first time she's ever touched me. Suddenly her face is all concern and sympathy, and I wonder if I've been harsh these last few minutes, or if this is a part of her, too. "I am so sorry about Beth. I know it's not the first person close to you that you have seen this city and its rulers kill. But even so, I cannot imagine how you must feel, to see your closest friend die like that."

"Thank you, m'lady," I say, trying to keep my voice steady, trying not to let myself go and trying with every sinew to keep the last image of Beth at bay. I think Lady Hocquard would probably prefer me to collapse into a pool of tears. But I don't know if I'd like it. "I think that maybe you could imagine it, though," I continue, treading carefully, keeping the tears away with a little questioning of my own. She seems taken aback by the question, and her eyebrow arches up as if hit by the force of it.

"Always thinking." She nods approvingly. "Always alert. There's the steel I saw in you from the start." She stands up then and turns half away from me, staring at a portrait on the wall. "Yes, I suppose that was rather a pathetic little platitude of mine, wasn't it?" she continues. "I think we both know that I would not be living a life like mine if I had not served my time in the darkness. Which is why I know you will get out of yours."

I suddenly realize what's missing from the conversation. "You've not asked me about the vault, m'lady. The reason I went to the bank. I know which one it is. I know—"

"Yes, dear," she replies, neatly cutting across me, still wrapped in her portrait study. "You have already told us everything. As I said, you were raving somewhat after your ordeal, and you told us all that you had found. Several times, actually." Perhaps sensing the edginess of her jest, she adds, "I cannot tell you how impressed I am at you getting it all."

"Thank you, m'lady. Did I tell you about the letter? The . . . relationship Keepsake was having with Azzuri?"

"You did. And Sage, with that whetstone sharp mind of his, has pieced it all together now and believes he has the outline of what happened."

"And do you believe him?" I say, hoping she'll bother to actually tell me of this outline.

"Yes, I do. It all seems very convincing. He contends that the young Azzuri, who had long known that whatever had been found under Lightfall had been secreted in a vault by Lord Saxe, had found out that Keepsake was in charge of this vault and was keeping records of the regular withdrawals from it. When later—or perhaps before, we shall never know for sure—Azzuri found out from Commander Tenfold that someone was leaving packages in the form of Blood Bank chests outside the city walls, he surmised that these were from the vault. What more he surmised we do not know, but it was enough to take him over the walls to find out."

"Wait . . . so could Keepsake have—"

"Betrayed his lover to Lord Saxe? It certainly makes sense. In that letter you described to us, you said Azzuri was warning Keepsake of the danger his charge of the vault posed, what he could be unintentionally wrapped up in. It is perhaps not too much a leap to suggest that those tears you saw him shed as he read it back were not just those of grief but of guilt as well."

"I see. That's a little sad. He took the young Azzuri's kindness and made a noose for him out of it."

"Fear overrode his feelings. It often does, I find."

I nod. "So now all that's left is to find out what's in that vault."

"Indeed, dear."

"But I imagine, m'lady, that because of what happened with me we need to, ah, lay low for a while?"

She smiles thinly. She sees straight through that line. "Speak your mind, Sam dear, you're among friends now."

I hope that's still true, but I don't know much of anything at the moment. "Because of me my closest friend is dead," I say. "I don't want any more people to die."

Lady Hocquard doesn't reply straight away to this but instead nods toward the portrait she's been staring at all this while. It's of a woman in a bright red dress; she has long, brown hair and sharp, graceful features like Lady Hocquard, but with a firmer smile and smaller, more forceful eyes. She looks like she's tired of sitting down and wants to get off her arse and on with life. I can relate to her already.

"That's my grandmother," she says finally. "She was killed in the Twin War, in one of the first wolf raids on First Light. She died in this very house. The things I hear about her! She lived at a time when vampire society was even less respectful to women than it is now. To noble ladies, I mean. To keep her house following her husband's death in a wolf skirmish, she had to undress in front of his brother. He ogled her, like the commonest coingirl. He was then found dead a year later in his own bed. His blood had been poisoned with ashcap. One of the many unsolved mysteries of the time."

I stare at the portrait, trying to imagine another Lady Hocquard, but the one in front of me is so striking in herself that all I can picture is her face in a distant past.

"Then there was the time her valet was attacked by one of Lord Beryl's valets," she continued. "She didn't hesitate. She went straight to Beryl's castle and demanded compensation and acknowledgment and atonement. He laughed at her, of course. He didn't even try and be polite. Worse still, the offending valet in question taunted her, taunted her in front of Beryl, but the Lord did nothing and continued to find the whole thing amusing."

"I'm wagering your grandmother did not find the whole thing amusing," I say.

Lady Hocquard gives me a grin of the pure night. "No. No, she did not. The next night, she invited the valet to her own parlor to make amends. He came, no doubt to gloat some more. She drugged his eel tea with slackweed, a strong but little-known brew that can knock even a highblooded vampire out for a short while. Then she dragged his slumbering body to her garden and tied him to a stake, tied him tight, so that even if he woke up in time, he would not pull loose, unless he was on much more than cowblood at Beryl's, which, given the tight-cheeked nature of the Lord, was unlikely. Then she watched from her window as the sun rose. Saw his screams as the first rays of sun touched him and woke him; then, moments later, saw him turn to scattered ash in the dawn's glow.

"Then she waited until night again, and what little of him she could round up that was still on the soil she gathered and put into an urn. She took the urn to Lord Beryl's castle, right to where he and his wife were feasting, and poured the ashes over them and their meal. Sputtering, with the last remains of his first valet on his tongue, Lord Beryl made threats and promises of vengeance, and Lady Hocquard, my grandmother, looked him straight in the eye, and with a voice as calm as the morning, she said, *Lord Beryl, if I would perform such an act when I was mildly annoyed, then what, pray tell, would I do when I was furious?*

"Then she walked out of there, knowing that Lord Beryl, a coward if ever there was one, would do nothing and pose no threat to her at all. So you see, Sam, if she could have lived then and suffered the indignities of that time and yet still fought like a lioness, I rather think, regardless of the danger, that we have to carry on and do our part now, don't you, Sammy dear?"

I smile. "I do."

Lady Hocquard stands up then and moves to leave.

"What happens now?" I ask.

"Now we take your information and see what we can do with it. Discuss the next stages with the rest of our curious little brigade."

"How I can help?"

"You can rest, Sammy. You are not the only Leech, you know. You have played your role well, but there are more parts to come and other people to play them. I will see you when it is done." She says this so abruptly that for a moment I don't know how to reply.

"But, my lady," I start to say.

"No, Sam, I have made my mind up. This next part is without you." She turns away from me then, to leave.

"That's not fair."

She whips back around, and I see rage in those oval eyes, for the first time directed against me.

"Of course it's not fair, Sam. None of it is. But you almost died, and the price of that is that you need to take a bow. We have sorcerers, an assassin, and Alanna. I don't worry about them. But I worry about you. I can't worry about you for this next part. I need to be clear. This is my city, Sam. My city. I will not apologize for doing what I have to. I won't ever do that. This is not about you and your ambition. It is about *my city* and the things I will do for it. Do you understand?"

"Yes," I say, quiet and shocked, battling down the tears like my life depended on it.

"Good. Then do what I say and rest."

And then she strides out, leaving me feeling more useless than I've ever been.

Sage

"Is she all right?" I ask, staring down into my Atmos fire-grain. For once, I am imbibing as well as Jacob. It has been one of those days.

"She will be soon," replies Lady Hocquard. She is sitting on the long seat in the same guest room where we first met, hair in plaits. Jacob sits opposite her; I am standing by the fireplace, too full of plans to sit. Raven is standing, too, but in the corner, where the lamplight barely hits, her naked form bathed in shadow, the light catching her canines. Alanna is elsewhere, presumably recovering from her remarkable rescue.

"She barely caught the first beginnings of rays before Alanna pulled her into the carriage," the Lady continues. "Mostly it's shock, blood dehydration, a little pain from being on the stake."

I nod, relieved, then quickly reduce the amount of relief on my face, as Jacob is watching me closely.

"And what, then, did she find?" I ask.

"The vault number of the packages being left outside the city. The bank clerk had records of all the withdrawals from the vault, weekly ones that correspond to the time Tenfold said the boxes were being put outside. We can't be sure, but it does seem like this is the same vault. The letter between him and Keepsake was there, too, suggesting they were in a relationship."

Well, I think. It is clearer now. I see the lines intersecting. Not enough facts to make anything a certainty, but enough to make the assumptions strong enough. Enough for the final piece. I down my drink, and I look at my conspirators one by one.

"Here is how I have it, then," I say. "The Young Azzuri, after decades of looking out for such information, finally finds the vault containing the find in the ground that he first apprised me of. Perhaps this was luck, having come into contact with the clerk Keepsake. Perhaps the clerk Keepsake was approached by Azzuri, who suspected he would know of the vault. His attempts to discern its contents—which Keepsake did not know of, or at least remained unwilling to divulge—are then helped enormously by the lucky stroke of Commander Tenfold, who informs Azzuri of the packages being left outside of the city. He most likely suspects a connection between that and whatever is in the vault, and his connection is most likely confirmed by Keepsake. Seeing as how venturing out of the city is easier—at least logically, if not infinitely more dangerous—than gaining access to the vault, he decides to do just that."

Lady Hocquard smiles at me. "There are a lot of *perhaps*es and *most likely*s in there, sorcerer."

"Indeed, my lady. Normally this would be too many for my satisfaction. But we have a lucky advantage. We do not need to be certain of everything. We need do only one thing."

A quiet wolf accent comes from the shadows. "Look inside that vault."

"Oh, is that all?" asks Jacob, pouring himself a second glass of Lucewine. I notice he has gone off the fire-grain since his meeting with Tenfold. "And what are you going to do after that, sleep in the First Lord's bed and steal all the wolfblood?"

"He has a point, Brother Bailey," says Lady Hocquard. "Now that Lightfall is gone, the Blood Bank is the most closely guarded building in the entire Everlands."

"I think the sorcerers at the birthing temple in Luce might have something to say about that," I reply, "but regardless, we have an expert in such matters, don't we, Raven?"

The wolf nods. "I can get into the Blood Bank easily."

"Oh, can you now?" asks Jacob.

"I have given much thought on how to get into it. Vampires are not hunters, so they never give enough consideration to such secret ways. Security is pitiful."

"Yes, Raven," says Lady Hocquard, rearranging a pin in her head, "but there is getting into the bank and there is getting into the vault. There will be many guards between you and any vault. Especially one, I suspect, of this importance."

"Thirty on each floor," I add. "If the book records I read were correct. That is not taking account of any extra guards who will be near the vault, given its significance."

"I can handle them," says Raven. "Blood Bank guards are not on wolfblood. They will be on a Midway kind, with noble blood nearby if they require it."

Lady Hocquard frowns. "I have no doubt you could massacre your way through them like, well, like you do through vampires, my dear. But what then of vampire/wolf relations? Would you start a war to solve a murder?"

"Depending on what Saxe is really up to, there may be worse things coming down the track than a little slaughter," replies Raven, "but . . . it would cause some problems. I agree."

"There might be a way to make your task a little less obtrusive," I say.

I see Raven smile in the gloom, white teeth flashing. "Do tell, mage."

"There is someone else in the city who can help—a sorcerer. I have . . . already questioned him on this. He would be willing to assist. Cause a distraction that would make your path easier."

"Oh, you didn't!" says Jacob, almost spilling his wine. "And when were you planning on telling me this?"

I glare at my deputy, attempting to convey with my eyes the lengths to which this is neither the time nor the place.

"One of the Kinets?" asks Raven. "I'm not sure those blood-fiddlers can move large things anymore if that's what you were thinking."

"No. Not the Kinets," I reply. "Someone . . . someone else."

"Do you mean the Neuras that the First Lord employs to send messages? I don't need to know what the guards are thinking."

"No," I say firmly, "someone else."

"That sounds deliciously vague," replies Lady Hocquard.

"You just have to trust me," I say. "I can't compromise their identity. But they can give us a distraction that will help Raven get to that vault."

Lady Hocquard turns to Raven, eyebrow raised. "Do we trust the sorcerers?"

Raven shrugs. "I do not see we have much choice. If they fail, they know I will be displeasured with them."

Jacob scowls. "*Them?* I have nothing to do with this. Eat him, not me."

"So when do we do this?" asks Raven, ignoring him. "I am impatient to put an end to these schemes of Saxe's. I have smelled him. He has many things coming to him."

"We must act quickly. He is not stupid. He will know the Leeches freed Sam. I have escaped his attention only because it will not yet have crossed his mind that I, so high up in noble society, can be connected to Sam. But that will not last. He will get there eventually."

"So tomorrow then," says Raven.

Lady Hocquard turns to me. "Can your . . . distraction be arranged by then?"

"Yes. He has already agreed to help."

"I'm sorry?"

I shrug. "It was inevitable that it would come to this. The vault. I prepared as soon as Sam went to the bank."

Jacob splutters some of his wine into his glass as Lady Hocquard narrows her black-lined eyes at me. "I'm not sure if you are well prepared or presumptuous, Sage Bailey," she says.

"Let's settle for both for now," I reply, standing my ground in her wilting glare.

"Well," she concludes, relaxing her face and giving me her widest smile yet, "let us plan our conclusion to this little alliance."

I return the grin. "Yes. Let's rob a bank."

Lady Hocquard

Alanna finds me in the portrait room. I thought I could hide here, bathing in my self-loathing for what I had to do for Sam, but I should have known she would hunt me down. I sit beneath a portrait of my grandfather, a stern-looking joyless man whom I never knew but who left a lasting and unpleasant impression on my mother. He died in the Twin War, and his children left the ancestral home here for Lightfall, like most, after the damage caused to First Light in the war. When I fled back here after Grayfall, the grief of my husband's loss stuck in my throat, I thought to burn these. Start all over. But I am glad I did not. Your history can be painful, but it is not always bad to bleed.

"A bloodcrown or a dozen for those thoughts of yours, m'lady, if I may be so bold," Alanna begins.

"Oh, Alanna," I say. "We may be in it up to our necks here."

"And when have we never been?" she replies.

"True, Alanna. But this time . . . this time, I fear, has a different quality to it. There is simply nothing you can say that will make me believe that Saxe does not suspect me. There are too many threads now that lead back to me. The sorcerers, Sam . . ."

"I was not followed when I brought Sam here. I made blooddamn sure of that, m'lady."

A dark cloud passes over Alanna's features, and I see a little hurt there. She likes to give off the impression that nothing stings her, but she is more sensitive than she lets on. It is a part of her personality I have enjoyed discovering. It is a sign our friendship is deepening.

"Oh, I didn't mean that, Alanna. I doubt very much there is anyone who could track you, even in a carriage, even with an unconscious girl to look after. I just mean that we have left so many large footsteps, no longer the dainty steps of the Leeches, that somewhere there will be a trace that will lead Saxe straight to my door."

She shrugs. "So let him come a-callin' and let him see what happens." She nods to the blade in her petticoats, always present. Then she reaches into them and grasps it and shows me the tip of the blade, and her gaze follows me there and lingers. My reply takes time to get to me, and both our eyes stay on the blade even as my words come out.

"I have no doubt you would, if I asked. You would tear through the city if you had to, would you not? Maybe I should have asked you to from the start. No, I never doubt you. You . . . are the one reliable thing in my life." Our eyes meet again now. Holding them, fixed. I should not be speaking with her so soon after Sam. I do not have the strength to keep myself from passing thoughts.

"But once we go there, Alanna," I try again, my mouth dry, "once we are in the open, our advantage of the years, of the decades, falls apart, like so much theater." Her left hand is closer to mine now. Blade to the left, palm to the right. The two things she offers me most.

"You see this, don't you, Alanna?"

She nods and secrets the blade away once again. "I see it, m'lady. I see it for a long time, more's the pity. My old days of chaos are behind me, I understand that now."

"Oh, I don't know," I reply. "You've caused a pretty whirl in my orbit on occasion, I daresay." Neither of us speak for a moment. It lingers. I am in no hurry to stop it.

"Wait." Alanna turns, listening. Her ears are better than mine, even though we are on the same blood, and my blood frequently better. Then

I hear it. The sound of hooves coming down the mansion drive. We exchange looks. The carriage nears. We quickly slip through to the parlor room down the second-floor corridor, and peer through the curtains to see the moonlit drive beyond.

When we see who gets out of the carriage, Alanna turns to me. "When I said let him come a-callin' . . . I didn't mean actually, my lady."

I don't reply. I just keep staring. Staring at Lord Saxe, right at my door.

23

Lords and Ladies

One day you have decades, and then the next you have days. The Light laughs at plans in that way.

Atmos Reclantis,
Ruminations of an Assassin

Lady Hocquard

I sit in in the ground-floor receiving room, opposite the spymaster of First Light, who is sitting on the divan while I attempt to perch comfortably on a quacian wood chair with a red embroidered padded seat. I sent Alanna away—the last thing I want is for the spymaster to see me associating with someone so obviously from Last Light, a city that practically invented spying. But knowing her, and I do know her, from head to toe, I am in no doubt that she will be eavesdropping on us, most likely from several rooms and maybe an entire floor away, having imbibed some magicked hawk we keep for such occasions, the blood most suitable for improving the hearing. At least I will have an ally should Saxe seek to attempt something. But he is too canny for that. I think.

"Is the blood to your taste, Cinibar?" I begin, attempting to apply some form of charm.

"I'll say it is. It has been a while since I've tasted whale this good. Magicked and decade aged. You do spoil me, my lady." I examine that insincere face, wondering how much he means it. I wonder if this man has ever meant anything.

"Oh, please, Cinibar, we have met enough for you to call me Daphnée, have we not?"

"I daresay we have, Daphnée, I daresay we have indeed."

"But as much as I am intrigued by this unexpected visit of yours, I imagine it is more than a social call, is it not? I normally have advance warning of such visits."

"Ah yes, indeed." Saxe places his bloodflute on the table adjacent to the divan and rubs his hands. This makes me look at his hands; long spindly things you could easily imagine around your neck, even as that permanent insincere grin remains fixed on his face.

"It appears you are as perceptive as you are generous," he continues. "I do apologize for the lack of warning. In my profession I get so used to sneaking about that sometimes I forget the formalities. Perils of the job, you see. And as you say, I do not come for mere socializing but with my spymaster tricorn on—not that I would wear a hat, for it would scarce help my fondness for anonymity!"

I give him a thin smile but no laugh, and let his attempt at wit drown in the shallows where it belongs.

"You see, Daphnée, I come about a maid at the palace, by the name of Samantha Ingle."

Another pause. His eyes stare patiently at me, no doubt looking for any flicker of recognition at the name. But I have had many years of lying to men and others besides, and it is a long time since I have ever let my face betray me.

"Ah, I am sorry," he continues after I give him the nothing he deserves, "I should not expect you to remember such Worn names as if they are your kin. I would hardly remember mine! Allow me to expand. This would have been a maid you requested on leave from the palace this last week—for three nights total, I believe, until she returned to the palace one night previous to this."

"Ah yes, of course," I reply, allowing my face a flicker of pretend recognition. "A most hardworking girl. I didn't request her personally; rather, I requested that they send someone with a bit of nous about them to help me with the arrangements for the Greendeath ball as well as general cleaning duties, and they sent me her. She was up to the task, I may say, although I am very curious what brings you here to talk about her, Cinibar."

"Well, there's the rub, Daphnée, there's the rub. You see, last night this Samantha was meant to be sunburst, for stealing from a Lord's room."

"By the gods! I am shocked."

"Well, prepare yourself, dear lady, as it gets even stickier from here on in. For she was not, in the end, sunburst, because she was rescued by an assailant, who in the process of rescuing her injured eight of the bloodguard in . . . rather unpleasant ways."

"My dear Cinibar, this is beyond the pale!" I put on my most shocked face at this, and I try and remember that I am not meant to be enjoying this performance, and that a little too much of it and my life could begin to unravel much sooner than I have planned.

"Quite, Lady, quite. We are keeping this under wraps as best we can, so I appreciate it if you would do so, too."

"Of course."

"You can imagine, therefore, how much I want to find this Samantha and her dangerous helper, and try to conjure some kind of sense out of this bizarre turn of events."

"Why of course, Cinibar. Although I am not sure how much help I can offer. I am afraid I never actually spoke to her myself. I left that to my first and second maids. And if there was anything to report, then I can assure you they would have kept me abreast of it. I fear I can offer you little in the way of assistance here, much as I would like."

"Ah," says Saxe, taking a moment to sip his blood, his thin lips grasping the rim of the glass like a dying fish. "I thought as much. In truth, I expected it. But you can appreciate how I must follow up all loose ends, no matter how frayed."

"Of course, Cinibar."

"So you won't mind if I speak to your first maid, briefly, in case she knows more?"

"I do not see why not. Alas, you may have to call back tomorrow, as she is away in Eastfall until shortly before lightfall, securing some goods for me for the ball."

"Ah, a pity. But, as you say, I shall return on the morrow if that suits?"

"Why yes, of course. I am sure I can muster up some whale again, if you fancy?"

"Oh, I fancy, Daphnée. I really do . . ." I am unsure if this is meant to be salubrious or mere banal conversation, but I feel the beginnings of bile in my throat nonetheless.

"Shall I see you out?" I ask, pushing back the nausea.

"Ah no, I arrived unannounced, so it is only fair I leave so. I will see myself out." He stands up quickly, a spider jumping from its web, and then pauses.

"Oh, just one more thing. Forgive me if I sound a little fanciful, but you are so connected in the social fabric of First Light that I could do with your knowledge on this."

"Why, ask away, Cinibar."

"One of the guards swears that the assailant was a woman. A woman's figure, at least. She was wrapped up well, it being almost dawn, but he is certain. And that set off some trains of thought in my mind. A woman rescuing a woman. Hardly usual for First Light."

"Not in my experience, no."

"And yet I hear . . . rumors. On occasion. Of women who defy the nobility. Whispers of the *Leeches*. And I wonder if there are connections to be made here to something more." His voice slows at the end of this sentence, like a jawtooth circling from below.

"Yes," I begin, watching the surface of the water carefully, "I have heard of such rumors, but I assumed it was more of jest than any truth. I rather suspect that for all my social gatherings, I am talking to other Ladies and not the Worns you seem to be interested in."

"Though you give money to them?"

"Darling, just because I give them kindcoin doesn't mean I have to talk to them. Have you ever tried talking to Worns? They are hardly a path to an enriching conversation, my dear."

"Ha! Indeed. I cannot fault you there. Ah well. I expect one day I shall have my answer one way or the other. Sometimes I find that the truth appears when you least expect it."

"Indeed, Cinibar," I reply coolly, "I have found that also in my time."

After Saxe has left, I speak to the empty air. "You can come out now." Alanna appears instantly behind me. I manage to avoid gasping. It is not like I am unused to her sudden appearances.

"I assume you heard it all?"

"I did, m'lady. I wish I didn't, but I did."

"He knows, Alanna. No question of it."

"Yes, m'lady. It does seem that way, especially given what he was twirpin' on about at the end there."

"All our efforts. All our years. Over. Because of *that man*." I grip my bloodflute tight in my hand, and for a moment I want to smash it on the marble floor. But I won't give him that little victory, even in his absence. Then I feel Alanna's hand on my shoulder. She doesn't squeeze. She just rests it there. I close my eyes, and my heart slows down.

"Not over, m'lady," she says. "Not over yet. We just have to make *him* over first. Which I believe is our plan anyway, m'lady, is it not?"

"Two nights hence it is."

"So let us make it tomorrow instead, then. Before he can so much as sweat some more."

I turn to her, her hand still on my shoulder, and I allow myself a smile.

"Well, Alanna of Last Light. Time for that fire, wouldn't you say?"

24

Dream to Touch

*It must be painful to be thinking of the bigger questions when all oth-
ers are concerned with smaller matters at home. You come across such
people sometimes, and you can see the pain in their eyes. They would
rather not be here. They wish to be in other worlds instead, seeking
answers and fashioning new lives. They can never go home; they have
none and they will die unsatisfied.*

Reddust Lostchance, *On Ways of Being and Existing*

Sam

I feel exhausted after Lady Hocquard's conversation, so I fall into a deep
sleep—the best kind; there's no dreams of sorcerers with glowing eyes
or sisters being turned to ashes as I look helplessly on. I'm awoken by a
sound at the door, and I open my eyes to see Sage Bailey standing there,
watching me.

"Do you always creep up on sleeping girls?" I ask, blinking the sleep
out of my eyes.

"Ahh . . ." begins the sorcerer, floundering, "I was informed you'd be
awake. Shall I come back another time?"

"No," I say, smiling. "That's an example of me and my great wit. Please
stay."

Sage walks over to the chair beside my bed and sits down, his ner-
vousness coming off him in waves. Whether it's because of what he wants
to ask me or the fact I'm wearing nought but my daydress, it's hard to say.
I notice with interest that his cheeks are freshly shaved from the week's
worth of stubble he had. His robes seem freshly washed, too.

"I'm glad you're okay, Sam," he begins. A pause. "Are you hurt? They
said you might have been exposed to some early dawn light. I'm not
fully versed in such things, although I know even the faintest suggestion
of light can sometimes cause great injury, and the process is fairly . . .
unpredictable."

"It is all right," I say, deciding to put him out of his misery. "I won't be offended if you ask me what you really want to know. You took a risk helping me, after all."

"I'm sorry," he says, relieved, "it's just—"

"I know. Really I do. You want to know if I used your strange sorcerer artifact when I was at the bank, and if it's now in the hands of the Lords. Well, I did, but it's not. I used the . . . cube thing?"

"Good enough." Sage smiles.

". . . on the bank clerk, Keepsake, who interrupted me. He will have woken up thinking he slipped over some spilled blood, assuming it really does what you claim it does."

"Impressive. And did you . . . That is to say, have you—"

"Told Lady Hocquard or her terrier from Last Light about it? No, I haven't."

Sage switches from relieved to confused in a moment. "Why?"

"They might not be as trusting as me," I say carefully. "They might not believe your story, for example, about it being a sorcerer artifact alone. They might start to ask you questions you don't want to answer."

I stare at him, giving nothing away, and if I'm smiling ever so slightly, then it's not so he would notice.

"Thank you," says Sage, a little color in his cheeks. I realize I'm enjoying making him feel awkward. It's not often I get the chance. "And how did you—"

"Get rid of it? I buried it deep in the woods as I was fleeing the palace, so they wouldn't find it on me."

"Excellent," says Sage. "You were thinking carefully, even as you were fleeing for your life."

"Well, the blood in my veins at that moment was pretty helpful in that sense."

"Even so. I wish you'd been a sorcerer. I could have done with someone like you at the cult these last few decades."

"A woman?"

"A quickmind!"

"I know," I say, grinning, "I was just teasing. You tease pretty easily, you know. I would've thought you'd be used to that after all those years with Jacob."

Sage laughs. He has a good laugh. More carefree than his usual self, like he's letting go for a moment. "Oh, you never get used to Jacob, trust me."

"How did you two meet?" I ask, sensing that he's comfortable enough now for me to pry some.

"It was a few years after I'd first founded the cult. It had suffered from a . . . rocky start, and I was trying again, making a renewed effort to find some people with enough lunacy about them to go across the land looking for relics of a race no one really believes in. I was in the town of Quintile, looking for my own kind, for Quantas like me, having decided that they were the only ones who should be in the cult. And that's when Jacob robbed me."

"Sorry . . . what?"

"I was in an inn. Well, a den of liquidity, as we mages call them. That's a good place to start in Quintile if you're looking for those who want a new start in life. Jacob, after I'd raised him from his liquor daze with some nonalcoholic fire-grain, sounded interested. It was only after he claimed to have been going to the lavvy that I realized my coinsleeve was missing."

"I'm amazed he managed that. You're pretty observant."

"Yes, well, I was . . . not fully at my sharpest."

"You were tankarsed, you mean."

"Ha! I suppose I was. I was completely taken off guard by his demeanor. And, ah, he convinced me to have some Atmos fire-shots with him. Lulled me in. It's an unusual skill, but showed a cunning I was in need of. So I tracked him down . . ."

"You followed his footprints?"

"Well, actually, he was slumped unconscious not far from the den. I said he was good at skills, but he didn't always have the ability to walk in a straight line that you need to fully carry them out. When I'd sobered him up, we talked through the night about what I was trying to do and about sorcerer life in general. He phrased it differently, but we saw the world in much the same way. In that sense, I felt I could trust him. I'm a good judge of character. So he became the Second Brother of the Cult that day, my deputy, and he has been ever since."

"You weren't concerned he was going to rob you again?"

"Jacob had lived a hard life up until then. Much harder than most. Most Quantas do in sorcerer society. I wasn't going to begrudge him what he was doing to survive. We don't begin our lives equally, so it's not equitable to judge people on how they act just to get through the chaos we call self-consciousness. Some people say you should judge a man by how he acts when he's desperate. I disagree. I judge a man on how he fares when the odds are rebalanced in his favor. When he finally has the freedom to choose how he wants to be remembered."

There's a little silence then. How could there not be, after that speech.

"It's my turn now," says Sage eventually. "To ask about you."

"I'm sure you've already asked Lady Hocquard about me."

"I have." His eyes stare into the distance. "You were born on Ashfall Lane in East Southeastfall. Your mother taught Midway children to read, which is how you learned, and your father worked for a tanner. You were not the poorest of Worns but not the best-off, either. Your father was sunburst by the Lords when you were nine for protecting your mother from one of their advances. Your mother sunburst herself a year later in grief, leaving you and your sister alone. You roamed the streets, stole, took what charity you could. Became hardened against the world. Then you grew up, and your sister tired of the life and went to join the enemy—be a maid at the palace. There was an accident in the joining ceremony, and she burned to ashes. You tried to save her, almost killing yourself in the process. The Lords found this amusing; they put you in her place. So there you were in the heart of everything you hated; waiting, using the library to arm yourself with knowledge that would one day set you free."

"Well," I say, suddenly wanting badly to be in a den of liquidity myself, "there's nothing like hearing your entire life summed up in a few breaths. Thank you for that."

Sage shrugs, undeterred by my sarcasm. "Your biography is not what interests me. It's what drives you I want. But I'd like to hear it from you."

"You're the one who's meant to be good at reading people. You tell me."

He grins. I can tell he was hoping I'd ask. "Okay. Let us see." He fixes me with his eyes. Hazel eyes, not bad if you like that kind of thing. "You always knew there was something else. Something more than Lords and Worns and blood and this city and this land. There's something more, and you want to be a part of it. You want to be ready for what comes next. You imagine worlds that were and could be, and you never give up hope of living there permanently one day."

I smile. "That sounds like your cult motto. What is it again? *There are worlds beyond mine and things I have only dreamt to touch.*"

"Yes, it does. And that's no coincidence. We're the same. There's people like me and you everywhere. We're not happy. I don't mean not happy with the standard tasks of life. I mean unhappy with the meaning behind it all. And why shouldn't we be? Most of this world makes no sense. No one is questioning it, no one is probing."

My ears prick up. "Probing what?"

"Everything. For example, why did we go from beasts to civilization in the blink of an eye, timewise? The Great Intelligence, they call it, as if that helps explain it. Why can't we explore the Ashlands, that strange continent that lies beyond the Southern Sea, and why does no one care? We hear tales of how impassable it is, of the banshees and the fall of Last Light, and we just accept it. Where's that curiosity to explore? Where's the need to know more? Where are the vessels to take us to new continents across unknown seas? Come to think of it, why are sorcerers simply born as adults from a chamber the contents of which are known only by a couple of sorcerers who guard their secrets? We simply say that it's the Light of Luce, and we accept that, like children. No one presses the matter; the sacredness of the process alone cannot explain it."

I study him. "I can see it frustrates you."

Sage rubs his temples. "You have no idea."

"Maybe you can't know everything."

"Perhaps. But we've gone too far the other way. We don't want to know *anything*. It's like everyone is in a waking dream, walking around perusing the small things; even the wars seem pointless. Only a few of us are truly awake."

"I see." I nod, forcing my sleep-addled brain to think and beginning to wish I had some stronger blood for a conversation like this. "And you want to wake us all up. Shed some light on it all. Yes, that sounds right," I say, pleased with myself. "You want to bring about a kind of enlightenment."

Sage smiles. "I'm not sure you vampires would call it that. Light has a habit of turning you to ash. But something along those lines."

I smile back. "That sense of needing something more. It's addictive."

"It's what keeps us all going. But people squander it with religion or their cities."

"There's nothing wrong with cities. This one's fine, it just has some questionable rulers."

"You're right." He sighs and turns away from me. "But they're not enough, Sam. I want worlds." He holds my hand then, still turned, avoiding my eyes. It's only for a moment, and I think he's going to do more, but he releases the grip just as suddenly. "It means a lot to be able to talk like this, Sam." Then, as abrupt as his hand-holding, he stands and makes for the door.

"Sage, wait," I call out to him. "I appreciate the dramatic exit, but it would be nice if someone told me what was happening next. Lady Hocquard's casting me aside me for this next stage. I know that Raven's breaking into the Blood Bank. But what is your distraction?"

Sage narrows his eyes. "I know you know that I haven't even told Lady Hocquard this."

"You think you're so clever, don't you?"

Sage gives me an eyebrow raise. "Takes one to know one, Sam."

"A vague hint?"

Sage smiles. "I'm getting a little help from another sorcerer. One resident in First Light."

"One of the Kinets? The blood mages?"

Sage shakes his head.

"One of the Neuras, then? The messenger ones?"

"Neither. Let's just say there are more mages in Lightfall than is generally known. In hiding. One in particular I have a prior friendship with. Neither a Neuras nor a Kinet. He was very effective in the Twin War. A little too effective. He's been hiding here ever since. He's going to put on a distraction that will go down in history, I suspect."

"And that is? And he is?"

"I'm not going to say any more until it's over, Sam. He's risking his cover by helping me, so I must remain discreet."

"Of course. Aside from all the information you've just given me, of course."

"Exactly." Sage nods. "I'm glad you understand."

"You just love being mysterious, don't you?"

"I couldn't possibly comment." Sage winks at me as he leaves, and almost hits the door on the way out doing so.

"Yes," I mutter darkly, lying back on my bed. "I can see why I'm not needed at all."

Lady Hocquard

It is time. My carriage awaits to take us to First Gods, the planned meeting place, where we will sit up high on the roof—getting there will be easy, if Sage's ambitious plan works—and wait for the mages and then wait for a wolf. Then we shall go to the First Lord and show him what we have found, and then reveal it to the city itself, and then it will be over. It all sounds far too neat to my ears, and a chill passes through my veins, so I turn to Alanna and try and replace it with the flame I feel for her. But it is no good.

"I got a bad feelin', m'lady."

"You always have a bad feeling, Alanna," I reply. "Not everything is a trap, you know. This is not Last Light."

"It isn't a walk in the meadow, either, m'lady."

"Ha! It most certainly is not. I will defer to you on that."

Alanna holds my gaze. "Maybe we take a walk when all this is over, though." The threat of a smile appears. "Maybe we should have some words. Of m'lady and me, and what we could be."

She continues looking at me for a while, does my Alanna, locking her narrow mischievous eyes with mine, and then a devil of a grin goes wide around her face and my heart races off without me.

"Yes, Alanna. I think I would like that."

25

Ravenfall

Extinction Valley. The worst battle of the Twin War, at least if you're a wolf. When the vampires (and some sorcerers also) went too far. When they almost wiped us out with their hinterhältig tricks. The wolfkind learned a valuable lesson that day. There is no ruse, no roguish method the vampires will not stoop to in order to have their way. We can only hope we never have to learn that lesson again.

Ashen Ansbach, *Memoirs of the Alpha*

Raven

I wait in the shadows. I have my entrance point, I have my time, I have my plan, and I have my goal. I need nothing else. Here in the black and the blood where one shadow meets another, I lie, and if you stared, really stared into the darkness, then perhaps you would see a hint of me, and if you were a wolf, you would certainly smell me. But these are vampires, and soon they will have greater things to worry about than a wolf in their midst.

It is time to rob a bank.

Private Ruddock

I awake a half of the hourglass after lightfall. I've slept in a little. Good; I was tired from the five pints of oxwine last night, the result of bumping into the Walsh twins, Jonny and Claire, and the havoc they bring down around 'em. Got some grief from it from the wife, but bloods knows, I needed a night like that. I have my sergeant at the barracks breathin' down me neck about me duties, and I wanted to spill a few drops, so to speak.

It means I have to rush through me washin' and me dressin', and I have to run to Southfall, where my bloodguard barracks are, making the most of my morning vial. At least I live near enough that I can do that. I'm a Westfall man now, but just on the southeastern edge, so it's not that far. I was freed from the slums of Southwestfall by marriage to a Midway. She's barely one herself, her father having part ownership of a stone quarry at the northern mountain line, hence why we're in Westfall, not Eastfall—but a Midway she is and a-movin' up the social ladder did I go. Our home is small and cramped, but it has a slate roof and a proper chimney and glass windows, and it's nothin' like the timber-and-straw huts you get in the proper depths of Worntown where I started. And like I say, it's near to the barracks.

When I get there, I settle down to a night of light duties, because what else is there? The city wall's where the real action is at, the heroes of the Scout Guard who risk their lives every night on patrol. Us normal bloodguards? Unless we're putting down some serf trouble—and there hasn't been much of that since the one and only uprising soon after Grayfall—then all we do is round up the odd pickpocket, or else we're tasked with doing the dirty work of the Lords, and there's no end of that. As for our barracks, we're in a no-man's-land. Half a mile south is the wall itself; between that and us there's nothing except the Blood Road, which cuts through us and carries on another mile to Centerfall. If the Grays get past the wall, then we're the next defense. But if they've got past the hard bastards you get on the wall, then we're bloodfucked anyway, good and proper. Best not to think about that if you ever want to get a wink of sleep.

Once I get to the barracks, I get to the first task, cleaning the crossbows. As if we'd ever need them. It's all part of the plan, though. If Grays invade. Stage one. The Flight Guard get wolfblood, fly above the fuckers, and see what they can do. Stage two, the rest of us stay the twin hells back and fire crossbows like our eternal lives depend on it. The barracks themselves aren't much of a defense, little more than wood and thatch and a few sturdier brick buildings scattered in between, but there's a long wall across the Blood Road, connecting both ends of the two Worntowns across the city. It's built with blocks of limestone, like the main wall, with arrow slits evenly spaced throughout where we can hide behind and fire through. They call it the inner wall officially, but the lads just call it the bugger wall, because if we ever have to hunker down there and aim our crossbows at Grays, who move like we can't see them anyway, then we may as well be buggered.

So that's the start to my day. Cleaning the crossbows. Waxing the strings and lubing the rails. I'm a warrior and no mistake. I'm ruminating on my position in life when I hear a yell. Captain Gulam it is doing the yellin', all fast and furious. They call him Broken Josh behind his back, because his name's Joshua and he keeps on breaking bones that don't matter. He plays a fine lute, though. A man of talents is the captain. But in that yell I hear fear, naked fear. And then the bell rings, and I near shit meself and almost drop the crossbow I'm holdin', because the last time I heard that bell it was the Worn riots. I'm old enough to remember those. It was hardly Grayfall, but it weren't exactly a walk in the park, either.

I run to the East Courtyard where we're meant to gather, but as I get there, I see no red flag flying for rebels. There's another flag instead. One I ain't never seen before. For a second I don't even know what I'm seeing. Then me brain pipes up, me helpful old brain, and I understand. Gray. It's the color gray.

Raven

I wait and I listen. I am having to use my ears more than I would like because of the stench of blood. This is partly my fault, because I am crouched in a sewage pipe that carries the wasted blood from the Blood Bank out into the tunnels below. My nose is full of discarded whale and eagle and hawk and fox and hillcat and snaptail and stag and dozens of others besides, and even with my centuries of experience, I am struggling to keep a balanced nose in all of this.

But this is the only way in, at least according to the Leech reports I was fed by the Lady and her guard dog. It is a moontide miracle that I can even fit in here, but the vampires design their wastepipes wide to cope with the torrents of blood that must pass through them. Such waste shocks me, as the only thing a wolf leaves of their meal is the teeth and a few marrow-sucked bones, but there we are. Some of this blood comes from that left over at the end of the day by the clerks in their offices or the servants in their quarters, but most of it is made up of the large vats of wasted blood from the bank vaults, which is why it's carted, not carried. A lot of blood spoils in the vaults, even the magicked kind, and so the Lords who store their wealth in there have to cut their losses and discard it. I wonder how much wolfblood was wasted back when it flowed more freely. I use that wonder to give me a little bit of rage for the task ahead.

The room beyond, at least according to the Leech diagrams, is a small antechamber with little way in besides the sewage grate. If my nose was working better, I could try and gauge its size myself, but I can at least tell it is unoccupied. The only person likely to enter this chaos of blood is the Worn cleaner who wheels the carts with the pots of blood in here and pours it down the drain. That hasn't happened yet, and I am fucking relieved of this fact.

Instead, I await the bells. They are my cue.

Private Ruddock

We man the wall, the bugger wall, although no one's calling it that now, surprise surprise. There's wings in the air, all twenty of the Flight Guard, a lot of wolfblood to waste, but it's Grays, right?

No one's seen nothing yet, though. Some are starting to doubt the captain, who was on the road near the barracks when he saw it. Because how would Grays get past the main city walls? And if they had, how would we still not know about it? We send one wing to the wall, to warn them or at least ask them what the fuck's going on. While we wait for a reply, we stare into the dark of the Blood Road. We scour the torches and we wait. We're all blooded now. No wolfblood for the rest of us on the ground, but we have bear, non-magicked, in good supply for situations like this. Though I'm not sure what good it would do against the Grays. A bit of strength, a bit of speed, some better senses . . . and how exactly will that top their bullets? Apparently we get the wolf only if it's a full-scale invasion, but even then I don't believe it. All that wolfblood? I know where it's going. It's going to the Lords so they can fly themselves out of here if that happens. That's one truth you can take to the Blood Bank.

I stare through the slits in my wall, and I wait. There's a silence everywhere now, a stillness in the air. The bells have stopped. No one's seen a thing. The air is cold, and the wind bites, but on bear, I hardly feel it. Ahead I can see far, even beyond the nearest torchlight—down the Blood Road and the trees that line it. I see shapes in the dark swim in and out of focus as I adjust to my last vial. No Grays move that I can see. My heart does a funny flutter, either shiftin' a little to the recent bear in me or letting me know I might be fucked, one of the two. I turn to my right and see me guard brothers all lined up, peering out into the gloom. I wonder how their hearts are doin'.

And then like a spirit from the beyond, like a shape from my day-haunts, a Gray appears right in front of me, just beyond the wall. There's a veil on his face and a small smooth weapon in his hand pointed at me, and before I even know it, my crossbow is loosed, but I know in my heart that it's too late.

Raven

Ring ring go the bells, all through the city, all through the bank. Sage's distraction will be causing mayhem throughout First Light. And what a distraction. For a man of such seeming order, he seems to enjoy weaving chaos into his plans. A funny kind, sorcerers.

I coil my body into as narrow a shape as possible and spring back on my haunches. Then I leap like a blood-soaked arrow through the sluice gate, knocking it out into the room, and land noiselessly onto the raised drain plinth beyond it. The room is indeed small, and there is nothing of note in it. I do my best to keep my nose in check; here the stench of blood is, if anything, even more overpowering than in the drain. I can sense all the qualities of the blood that the vampires take, too, but twisted into the scents that a wolf can taste: the strength of stag comes out as roasted tea leaves; the serenity of magicked whale is hillside grass after a rainstorm. For a moment I am helpless to the barrage of my senses, to the sonata of the blood. But then I shake my muzzle and I change, glad to be in person form again with the slightly reduced sense of smell it entails.

I hear now the commotion of the bank guards, running through the corridors and crashing past the sewage room. I hear the metal and clang of armor, which they put on only for one thing and one thing alone: a Gray invasion. A part of me wants to rush out and challenge them; I love a good fight in armor. It is like the wrapping of a meal. But I hold back, hearing them troop out through the great stone doors at the entrance. The noise goes on for a while, and it's almost as deafening as the bells. Then it stops, and though I can hear the great calls and clashing of steel outside the bank, growing quieter, inside, all is now still.

I open the door to the corridor and I sniff, and then I look. There is little else to see here. Marble pavings, stone walls. No torches, because there is no point, I imagine: the Midways and guards who work in the bank are all on good enough blood for pure night eyes, and the Worn servants will know these back corridors by heart anyway. This suits me fine. A wolf needs no quality blood to see in the dark.

I quietly creep along. I can smell the remaining guards, almost all those left in the bank. Sage thought that every single one would leave in response to the bells, that this was an overriding command. But no one is that stupid. This corridor, Sage informed me, runs all the way to the main center square. My nose tells me that three guards are there, one posted on each corner. In the middle is the staircase to the vault. One vault in particular, 1015, high on the tenth floor. I think about turning into wolf, but repeated changes so soon can dull the senses temporarily, and besides, the only threat to me in this bank was sheer numbers, and that is now long gone. All I have to concern me, in fact, is the promise I foolishly made not to kill the guards. Because if I am not to kill them, but to merely maim them without their knowing who I am, then I will have to be quick. It will be quite a challenge. I grin. It is a while since I have had to think like this. Like an assassin, not a hunter.

I move forward. Beyond the next turn of the corridor is the square. I smell the guard nearest to me on the corner post. I sniff his age, roughly forty, barely into adulthood. A stale, mildly fetid, light iron anxiety washes over him at what the bells portend. He is worrying about the wrong thing, poor boy. I have hatched my plan for these four remaining guards, left on their own to face a wolf having fun.

First, I whistle. A long, drawn-out whistle. I will have to rethink this part very quickly if one of his three other comrades joins him to investigate. But I can tell they have not left the experienced ones in the bank, because I hear his footsteps come around the bend, and as he turns into me, I hit his head against the wall before he can get a sight of me. It makes a satisfying but quiet sound, and he drops. He will have a headache and not much more, although that *not much more* comprises a few more wounds I must make in him if the next part of the plan is to work.

I whistle again. I hear the remaining three guards express their concern over this, and they call out the name of the body before me. They will all come together now, because they must have some brains in their outfit, and sure enough, I hear the footsteps of all three. One gives off mild chalk, confused about what is happening; the other has the ripened steel about him, sharp and pungent—he is not coping with anything well today. The third one is bland. He is a fighter and one who thinks little of it. Good. I shall save him for last.

They all come around the corner at once and see the slumped body of their friend, and they hesitate before reacting because they know something is not right. It is just a small hesitation, but long enough to realize that there is a shape—another body, perhaps—lying underneath their friend. This new body is hard to see, what with all the blood seeping out of the many different scratch marks over their friend's torso.

I give them a second more to puzzle on this. Then I spring up from my position underneath the boy's body and, using his frame to shield me from their sight—his cloak and all the blood aiding me greatly—I stagger toward them, like a marionette I saw in the sorcerer capital Luce once. The guards finally react then and draw their claws, readying for their attack, but within half a moment I have reached the one closest to me, mild chalk boy, and reached out a hand, my claws extended, from behind my body shield and swiped them across his throat. If they are on normal bank guard blood, his skin will be strong, so I made my claws extra long to compensate. It works, because he gurgles in shock as his fine arterial spray jets out, covering the face of my puppet in even greater volumes of crimson.

As he falls before his remaining two friends, I crouch down for a second, ready to drop my shield. Then I leap from a standing start up and over the two guards, the blood which now covers me head to toe flying off me and drenching them as I launch over them. As I land behind them, before they have even had a chance to think about turning, I shove my fist through the back of the second, with it coming out through the torso of the first, so the two are stuck on my arm like a meatstick. Then I pull out and inspect the hole in both; straight through their livers, nice and neat. Just in case they have the will to turn and catch sight of me before they pass out, I press my hand against the back of the second and they both topple forward, landing facedown on their friend with the new hole in his throat.

I survey the three guards before me. They have had . . . some severe injuries, it is true. But you should not guard a bank if you are not willing to get disemboweled once every so often. With some slightly better blood than they are used to, they will recover completely from all their injuries. Well, almost all. It takes a lot to kill their kind.

Often, it takes me.

Private Ruddock

My crossbow bolt misses, at least it must have missed, because I could swear it was point-blank but the bolt carries on behind, lost into the night. *That's it*, I think. *Simon, me old mate, you've done it now.* I see the Gray raise its weapon, slow but sure, and time slows for me, slows to a right old trickle. I think on Trissy, my Trissy, and how I'll never see her again, at least not in this life: how I'll never wake up in bed and feel her next to me, sweet-smelling as the night before even as I stink of the day, her arms grabbing mine and putting them around her so I hold her tight, like nothing in the world can ever hurt us, we won't age and we don't ever die and me and my Trissy will just be here in this bed, my lips resting against her neck while the world carries on around us.

I think on that and I close my eyes, and I wait for me death, all cold and metal and straight into my heart.

But when I open them, I feel no cold and my heart beats fine, and the Gray that was meant to spell my end is nowhere to be bloody seen.

I wait, peering through the gap, and when it doesn't return, I breathe, hard and fast, like I've never breathed before.

And then I reload my newly cleaned crossbow and start all over.

Raven

I stand before vault 1015 and I lick my lips.

Since my minor massacre on ground level, nothing of much note has happened. I climbed the central staircase, seeing no guards on the stair-side entrances to the floors as I did so. This skeleton crew is even thinner than I had thought. When I reached the top floor, another long corridor stretched out, weakly lit by oil braziers, tapestries hanging on the walls. The tapestries showed scenes from vampire history that I could have studied to see if I was there, if I cared, which I did not. At the end of the corridor, it branched right, and the one guard pacing it was dispatched with a running leap before he could turn, part of his neck still caught between one of my teeth. He will also be fine, but he will need several vials of good blood to fill the hole where his throat should be.

Then it was just one more left turn to the vault I wanted; the final guard here, taking in the sight of me and the bloody mess I am now, chose to turn tail and run toward the vault, which showed how much he was thinking. I bit his foot off because I was getting a little bit bored. It landed just before the vault, so I suppose his foot was a bit better than the rest of him at running away.

Vault 1015 is twenty feet tall by thirty wide, a huge door of steel-covered concrete, with hinges and pulleys and forest knows what behind it. Three red-painted iron bars go across its length, in addition to the central lock itself. It is built not to be broken into, even by a vampire who's just drained a full wolf. Most vaults, at least the big ones I have seen in my time, have fancy engravings all across them, either the sigils of those who own their contents or some standard bank patterns. This one has nothing. I take this to be a bad sign.

It is lucky, then, that I have the key. For the thing is, the Blood Bank is very, very secure unless you have a key, in which case it is not so. But the key is designed to be almost impossible to steal, as it is in the possession of the clerk who has been assigned to a particular vault, and that is a secret well guarded; moreover, the clerk must have it on him at all times, even at home. Except, thanks to Sam, we know that Keepsake had the key, and so while all of First Light slept, I paid him a little day visit to his home, and I took the key from him, followed in quick succession by his life. No one asked me to kill him, but I thought a little on how he betrayed the young Azzuri and how the First Lord's son, by all reports so far, appears to have been unlike the other nobles. So I gave Keepsake the justice of the wolf as I saw fit, which is, of course, never really justice but always the violence of nature. At least we are honest.

All of which is a long way of saying I shoved my claws down his throat and pulled out his organs through his mouth as his eyes watched me, full of the question why, a question I never answered.

I place the key in the locks one by one; the bars snap back, and then I hear the main lock turn, and all the little bits inside it twist and click. There is a great groaning noise as they connect to everything else and the door swings wide open. I cannot describe this as well as I want to, as I am a beast of nature, not engineering, but I will allow that it is impressive.

The vault revealed to me, I scan its contents. "Great Wolfsbane," I whisper. And then I say it again, because it warrants it. The vault, the entire vault, must be a hundred feet long and almost the same wide. And it's full of chests. Wooden chests. Or at least I think they are wood. They are the same color and pattern, but they look stronger, like maybe they are metal painted to look like wood. Their odor is hard to fathom given all the mix of guard blood still on me, but it smells strange, earthy, a little salty—an odor I cannot place to any metal I have ever smelled. And these chests are small. You can pick them up in your hands. There must be hundreds of them, maybe thousands, all piled high and stacked on top of each other. I venture inside and grab one; it clicks open to a small amount of pressure, with no discernible lock. I peer inside and survey its contents.

There is a long pause as I take in what I am seeing. Then I speak to myself, my voice bouncing softly off the walls of the vault. "It all makes sense now. The cunning little bastards. I'm going to slit their throats and wear their flesh." My nails grow and shorten, grow and shorten, and I smell the fury boiling off me like steam, the scent of a lemon orchard on flames.

Then I sigh and hold my head in my hands. "Sometimes I think I will get tired of these schemes, and they cannot shock me anymore," I speak aloud. "But each century brings new delights."

My voice sounds hollow and stupid in the vault, a centuries-old assassin talking to herself because she has no one else. Even my rage begins to die already. A new outrage for a new century, but the sheer pointlessness of it all already upon me.

I look around. I pick a box at random. I cannot carry more than one feasibly, not if I want to be able to switch to wolf if I need to.

But I need only one. One says as much as anything that has ever been spoken.

I leave the vault slowly on two legs, then as I round the corner, I shift to four, the prize in my jaws but the victory tasting sour in my mouth.

Fucking vampires. They have gone too far this time.

I am going to hurt quite a lot of them.

PART IV

Home Truths

26

In a Lightfall Minute

*For allegedly the holiest site in the city, First Gods has seen many
a bloody battle fought in its environs, especially in the early days of
First Light, when the Blood Gods had their fair share of competitors.
But then this should not surprise anyone vaguely familiar with the
religions of this continent; for where there is worship, there is often
blood, too, and not just of the voluntary kind.*

Kinet Lastassion,
On the Prayhalls of First Light

First Lord Azzuri

I'm on to my way to the Dome Room, where the First Council has assembled, when Redgrave suddenly appears.

"If I could have a brief word, First Lord," he says, motioning to an
empty room.

"This is hardly the time, Redgrave. The city's in an uproar and the
First Council are waiting."

"Which is why it is exactly the time, Vermillion," he replies, and I do
not know if it is the expression on his face or the fact he has used my
choicename for the first time in almost two centuries, but I have a rather
bad feeling about this.

Sam

I awake to the sound of bells. Not the hour bells, the alarm bells. Just
as it all started a month ago, before my life sped up like a wolf closing a
hunt. I look across the room. Four hourglasses have tipped over in the
timepass sitting on a dresser at the end of the room, so it must be just
after four sun. Four hours of the night already gone. Suns, I didn't mean
to sleep this long. At this point in the Greendeath season, that means I
have only seven hours left before lightfall.

The bells can mean only one thing. Sage's distraction has begun.

Raven will be robbing the bank. The rest will be meeting at First Gods. I know that last piece thanks to a little eavesdropping. So there is really only one question left to answer. The one I posed to myself as soon as I heard Lady Hocquard's refusal.

What am I going to do about it?

Sage

The plan was meant to be so very simple. Meet Raven at First Gods and have her reveal the mystery contents of the vault. Go to First Lord Azzuri with the evidence, perhaps solving the mystery of the Grays in the process or at the very least avenging his son, that quiet, introspective man, so very different from the other Lords who died on a journey I myself set him on.

But like all plans with so many unknown variables—plans in which I'm not the sole controller of all said variables and must work with others to control them—it has gotten away from us.

Now one of our group is dying, if not dead, one has abandoned us, and the rest of us are trapped on the roof of First Gods, with only a flimsy wooden door between us and our own death.

It had started so well just one hourglass ago.

ONE HOURGLASS AGO

"She's not coming. She's been caught. So will we be if we stand here much longer."

Lady Hocquard eyes Jacob with barely contained annoyance. "I did hear you the first few times you said that," she replies. "Are you really so fraught, or are your nerves simply frayed because I wouldn't let you bring any liquor with us?"

My deputy considers this. "Can it be both?"

Jacob might be overwrought, but it doesn't mean I'm not worried. I can see the concern etched in Lady Hocquard's face, too. Alanna looks normal for her, although I'm not sure what it would take to make her shift from her perpetual expression of half amusement, half barely concealed rage.

We are standing on the roof of First Gods, the oldest prayhall on the continent. More specifically, we're standing on a small flat patch of roof that sits between two short spires that themselves are placed behind the two towers of the southern facade. Thirty-foot-high pinnacles rise up from either of the towers, ending in tiny points.

When we first entered the church, the sight of the southern doors made an impression on me, with their elaborate carvings depicting the Blood Gods, the holy vials, and the rivers of blood. Above the doors are ten-foot statues of the Lords and Martyrs of the First Blood. Above them is a great arch shaped like an upside-down drop of blood, the tracery in front of the great window within an intricate network of wooden veins. The glass itself, part obscured by the tracery, is twenty shades of red.

Up here on the roof, though, there is nothing as impressive. But we didn't pick this spot for its buildscaping. It is a good place to meet, far away from the action below and beyond any suspicious eyes. From up here we can look south across all of First Light; I can see Centerfall beneath us, and beyond to Southfall and the city wall itself, and if I look farther east or west, I can see Westfall and Eastfall, which eventually give way to the respective sprawls of both Worntowns, Southwestfall and Southeastfall, dense clusters of tiny streets and buildings that look from here like great piles of flame-lit debris tossed from the sky by a careless deity.

What has my attention, though, is the area just south of Centerfall, where Southfall begins. There isn't much to Southfall; it's more or less a clear march along the Blood Road from the center to the city wall itself. Aside from the guard barracks and various armories, it is wide open and rarely crowded. Right now, however, it's a very busy scene indeed, because almost every bloodguardsman of First Light is currently lined up in a defensive formation, all the way along the border between Southfall and Centerfall, facing the Blood Road and the wall. At first sight, in the dark and with a sorcerer's comparatively poor eyes, I can't detect anything beyond this defensive line; it is as if they are a phalanx against the wind, a formation against nothing. I just see empty expanse from their line to the city gate.

But if I squint, if I really strain my eyes, then I can see things in the shadows beyond the army. Slight figures, flitting in and out of the torchlight that lines the Blood Road. They are not together; they are not in formation. They are demons in the evening gloom, shadows come to life, tormenting their watchers. They are Grays.

But I'm not afraid. Because all this is my doing.

"Illusions," says Lady Hocquard behind me, who is sitting down against one of the spires, her legs splayed out on the dirty wooden roof. She's dressed in Worn rags, plain and brown, with a red wig of dirty matted horsehair and no makeup on her. You'd never guess from her careless sprawl that she's one of the most well-known women in the city. "Illusions of Grays. In the actual city. Yes, I can see why you kept the nature of your distraction close to your chest. It is insane, darling."

"Only a Gray invasion would force all the guards from the bank to man the defenses."

"And the sorcerer doing this?"

"Cloak Kastannion."

"The sorcerer who helped win the war against the Shades? There's friends in high places, dear, and then there is that! He's actually in First Light?"

"Yes," I reply. "Sometimes the rumors are true. He lives with the Kinet bloodmages in Northwestfall, hiding his identity, concealing himself among those who strengthen your blood with magick. A fact I would request stays with you, because he is a man whose life would be much for the worse were he to be found. Cloaks that powerful do not get to just live an unmolested life, as he discovered in the Twin War."

"But . . ." says Lady Hocquard, struggling to articulate her thoughts, "I know Cloaks can make figures move in illusions, but I don't understand how they can make them . . . so lifelike, and the illusion so wide and lasting for so long. You have the whole of the Blood Guard in uproar, really believing."

I shrug. "The stories from the Twin War are true. His illusions take on a life of their own, and he can do as he pleases with them."

"Can you at least tell us how long the illusion will last? Surely the guards will notice at some point that the invader is but smoke and mirrors, and never attacks."

"Eventually, yes," I reply, "but he will have ceased them by then. By which time we will have already informed the First Lord and his council of the conspiracy around them, and thwarted Saxe's chicanery."

"Unless, of course, the Lords say thank you very much for the information. Now let us reward you with a painful and drawn-out death," notes Jacob.

"Here comes the spineless man," says Alanna, grimacing at my deputy.

"Have some fire in you, man," says Lady Hocquard. "They are hardly going to risk starting a war on two fronts by harming Raven Ansbach, sister of the alpha wolf himself, or two emissaries of the Archmage. And I am connected enough that sufficient numbers of Lords will listen. Assuming we have something to make them listen," she says, looking around hopefully as if that would magick the wolf we are waiting for from the shadows.

"Perhaps you've not been around as many desperate men as I have," replies Jacob.

"On the contrary," replies Lady Hocquard, "I've lived among a whole city of them for fifteen decades."

"Wait," I cry out. "Can you hear something?" There is a scrabbling sound. "Can you . . . can you hear that?"

"Is it coming from the stairs?" asks Jacob, staring at the door to the roof.

"I don't reckon they're usin' stairs. I reckon they're usin' walls," says Alanna, and before I can comprehend what she means, a black shape rises up from the crenelated parapet at the rear of the roof, leaping into the air. Amid the black, a blacker shade even than the shadows it has sprung from, I see a glint of yellow, and for a second I see Sinassion, the phantom himself, come to finish what he started with Jacob.

But the shape is too large, and it is not . . . humanoid.

Then it lands in front of us and growls, and I behold the huge bulk of Raven Ansbach in wolf form: jet-black fur, thin rows of pearly white fangs glinting in the moonlight, small, piercing eyes and a huge frame, yet somehow lithe, too, like she could trample you in a moment yet squeeze through the smallest of gaps.

She is carrying something in her formidable jaws, and she drops it before us as we watch her cautiously. Then the air shimmers and suddenly we are watching a show: a shadow puppet show, but with color and reds and whites and strange, impossible tones, like the very fabric of the air is being rendered while jerky shapes play before our vision. Somewhere in the shadow play is a paw stretching out to a hand, and somewhere a jaw is shortening, and somewhere else flesh is turning inside out, but it is hard to tell what order these things are in. It is not fur turning to flesh, that much is clear. It is a strange unspooling of time where at some point a woman comes from a wolf.

If you have never seen a wolf transform, then you have never been truly speechless.

Then Raven stands before us, naked, covered in what looks like dried blood. She points to the box that her wolf jaws dropped before us seconds earlier.

"I would open this if I were you," she begins by way of greeting. "It is quite something."

I look at Lady Hocquard, who looks at Alanna, who looks back at her, then looks back at me. Finally I look at Jacob, who groans. "Fine. If it's a deadly trap, though, I am coming back to haunt all of you."

He bends down and picks the small chest up. It certainly does not look like anything of vampire or wolf or sorcerer design. There is a smoothness to the painted wood that suggests metal underneath, but it has a . . . foreign quality to it. Foreign to us all, I suspect.

"The key?" asks Jacob. "Wait . . . if you were carrying it in your jaws, and you're naked, then . . . Oh no, I think maybe someone else should open it."

Raven growls. "There is no key, fool of a mage. Just press down on it."

Jacob does as she says, cautiously, tentatively, like the thing might explode on him. The lid pops up, and we all crowd in to see its contents, all except Raven, who is watching our faces carefully, her eyes even more narrow than usual. "There are hundreds of these boxes in the vault," she says. "Thousands, perhaps."

There is a long silence, a silence in which everyone is trying to form some kind of coherent explanation for what their eyes are telling them to be true. Inside the box are a series of small cylindrical objects, about an inch long and a quarter-inch wide, made out of some indiscernible material. The outer shell of these cylinders is translucent; you can see something inside them, but only the color of it—a slight glow of yellow in some, in others red or blue. All the cylindrical objects are stacked neatly in the box; there must be at least a hundred of them.

I knew what they were as soon as I saw them, and I can see that Raven knows, too, and Alanna—all those of us who have seen such death up close. Jacob and Lady Hocquard still have quizzical frowns on their face.

"Can someone explain this to me?" begins Lady Hocquard. "They look like . . ." She goes silent, and I can see the word slowly eating its way into her brain. "Bullets?"

I realize it all then, at least most of it. I can't believe it wasn't revealed to me before. Like a landscape watercolor hiding in plain sight among a sea of portraits, I see it now for what it really was. I look at Raven, and I spy now what I hadn't noticed in the shadows of the church's spire before: the anger in her face; the fury in her eyes. She understands it all, too, and I see her struggling to control her feral rage at it all.

"Yes, my lady," I reply. "They are indeed bullets. Gray bullets." I watch as Alanna's knife hand slowly uncloses and closes, and I see it dawning on her, too. Welcome to the club. Leave your morals at the door, the drinks are free in here.

"Does someone want to tell me why the fuck there are Gray bullets in a bank vault?" says Jacob. "These are the boxes that they've been leaving outside the walls for the Grays for decades, right?"

"Yes," I say. "Since Grayfall itself, according to the records Sam saw."

"So why in all that is shade and fucking light are they giving them their bullets back?"

"They're not giving them *back*," I say pointedly.

"For all the Blood Gods," begins Lady Hocquard, now a club member, too, and she sits down abruptly. "Never in my most lucid dreams . . . I . . . Lords. I need some bloodwine right now, in great quantities."

"I will knife them all," says Alanna. "One by one, with a great slowness."

"Okay," begins Jacob. "This shock party is all well and good, but my brains for puzzle-solving have been slightly addled by endless decades of mostly unidentifiable spirits, so will someone for the love of the five shading magicks please tell me what is going on."

Give them a while longer, Jacob. It is quite something to get your head around.

Jacob shoots up from his sitting position like someone has shoved fire powder up his cloak and backs away from us all, ending with his back to the spire, looking around in all directions.

"I heard it, too," I say, and I see from the looks on their faces that so did everyone else. "I wasn't aware you could do that, Sinassion. More than one person at once."

If I explained to you the things I can do that people are not aware of, Sage Bailey, we would be here all night and I fear you would get bored very quickly.

"Where is he?" asks Alanna, who has whipped out her dagger.

"He's somewhere below us," says Raven, sniffing the breeze, the air beginning to shimmer around her tellingly as she starts to transform.

"Don't change," I say quickly. "Wait. Hear him out. Please." Raven gives me a quizzical look and turns to Lady Hocquard.

"Let's listen," she replies, her face a noticeable shade of pale.

Thank you. I will not take long. I can see that most of you know the outlines of it. Do not worry, I cannot read your deepest thoughts from here. But the surfaces are clear. You all know.

"I don't bloody know," says Jacob quietly.

Almost all of you know, says Sinassion, and if a voice can chuckle without actual laughter, then that is what this sounds like.

Tell him, Brother Bailey.

I turn to Jacob, and I say what I should have guessed; what I was blinded by my obsession into missing. "The Lords—Saxe and whoever he's working with—they've been arming the Grays."

"Right," says Jacob. "And why would they do that?"

"Oh, isn't it obvious?" I reply, my exasperation getting the best of me. "The Grays are working for the vampires. They have been this entire time. Their personal army."

"Oh. So who in the Light of Luce are the Grays, then?"

That's where I come in, Jacob. They're my army, I'm afraid. My army of Shades, with lighter-colored outfits and stranger weapons, but still my old brothers.

Well, of course. All this time tantalizing myself with the concept that the Grays could be the mortals, my mortals, vaulted from my relics and the myths of time back into reality, when really all I had to do was look two centuries back, not ten. No wonder they couldn't be killed at Grayfall. Deadly weapons paired with mind-reading.

"But they died," I say. "They were executed after the Twin War. Only you escaped."

Did you see them die?

"No. But . . . I heard of it."

"As did I," says Raven, viscous anger still dripping from her voice. "There were wolves watching it, too."

You don't have to be a Cloak to pull off an illusion. You don't have to use magick to fool someone. Vampires can be . . . tricky like that. Raven knows this.

"I'm growing tired of this, frankly," says Lady Hocquard coolly. "How like a man to astound with his amazing plan rather than attack us and get it over with."

"M'lady is right," says Alanna. "I am in favor of stabbin' you in the darkness and skipping the discourse."

A fair point. Or at least it would be if I was the villain in this little drama.

"Oh, come on," says Jacob. "You're always the villain of the piece. You have the hood, the eyes, the creepy way of communicating. You really have the part nailed down."

Not this time, I'm afraid.

"Oh, I cannot wait for this," says Raven.

It is true, Midnight Assassin. I had nothing to do with it. You may not believe me, but know that I do not care what you think of me, and you cannot hurt me, so there is no reason for me to lie. You see, when I escaped after the war, my Shades were, following the faking of their deaths, taken by Saxe and his associates to Lightfall, to the cellars and catacombs beneath it. I cannot say much to what happened there, but I do know that they were tortured. You can do many things to a Neuras to put him in pain, real pain, not the laughable physical kind, if you know the right levels to pull. Almost a hundred years later, when Grayfall was put into action, they were no longer the men I commanded. I rather think they are broken now, tools to be used as Lord Saxe pleases.

"An explanation," says Lady Hocquard, "that very much fails to explain why you are in First Light now, working in tandem with Saxe. Trying to kill my companions."

I took no pleasure in my attempt on Jacob's life, if that is what you are referring to. But then, I took no pleasure in massacring whole armies in the war, yet I did so anyway. This is neither the time nor the place for a morality debate, as diverting as that would be. All you need to know is that I came to First Light with aims of freeing my Shade brothers from their effective imprisonment. My arrival, by one of those coincidences that seem so curious the more you think on them, happened to coincide with the younger Azzuri's attempts to uncover Saxe's plot. Rather than attempt to kill me, Saxe made the wise move of offering me a deal. Help his actions remain secret, and he would let me have my Grays back in not so long a time frame.

Again, I do not come here to justify my actions to you. But you should know that I have not come to do deals with the man. That was but a ruse, to placate someone who thinks himself more cunning than he really is. I come to free them all in my time frame, not his. In fact, it is you who are my best hope. With the secret out, all our aims are furthered. We are, in fact, allies.

"Allies? I do not think that means what you think it means," says Raven.

On a temporary basis, of course. I would never want to end our rivalry, Midnight Assassin. It is one of life's great pleasures.

"Can we all just remember for a second that he tried to kill me?" says Jacob. "With allies like that, who needs enemies?"

You were collateral, I am afraid, Jacob the Quantas. I had to kill you to keep Saxe on side. It was nothing personal. I judged your loss would not be too detrimental to all our causes. It might have even motivated Sage to work even harder.

"Excellent," says Jacob. "Real morale-boosting talk, this. Let's do it again sometime."

As for the fight with Raven, I never turn down an opportunity to spar. Our fights are always interrupted, are they not? One day, perhaps, we will see it through to the end.

"There's no perhaps about it," replies Raven.

Well. There we are. Now you know the truth of it, I will leave you to your own devices. I hope your plan works. I would hurry, though; I suspect for obvious reasons that Saxe will see through your diversion quickly and I fear what he might do. Goodbye for now.

"Wait! You can't go," I say. "On the treacherous assumption you speak the truth, we very much need you."

No. You have no need of me. Not for this final part. In Raven, you have an army in the form of a woman; and I suspect the spy from Last Light has a graveyard of poor souls to her name.

"You are one to talk, are you ever," growls Alanna.

"Well, at least tell us why, before you abandon us," I continue. "Why would a group of Lords conspire to murder a third of the vampire population and keep themselves prisoner in one city for a hundred years?"

Money? Greed. Power? Does it matter? In the end, such things are boring, cyclical notions that repeat themselves pointlessly. Over the arc of time, they cease to matter, except to remind us of the futility of life itself. I have a wider arc to contend with. Wider goals than such matters.

Lady Hocquard sighs. "That's wonderful, darling. But we're going to need more than that."

I'm sure you are, dear lady. So ask them yourself.

And then he is gone, his absence marked by a slight throbbing in the head.

We all look at one another. Raven pinches the bridge of her nose. "One day I would really like to kill that man."

"So to summarize," says Jacob, "the Grays are Shades, Grayfall was a vampire plot, and Sinassion isn't actually the bad guy. Meanwhile in other news, black is fucking white, and the five-spirits make you sober as an Archmage."

"It seems you were right, Sage Bailey," says Raven. "The great find beneath the earth you spoke of, that the vampires found under Lightfall, shortly before Grayfall. The one the young Azzuri was always on the lookout for, inspired by you. This must have been the weapon cache they used to arm the Grays."

"Yes, I imagine it was," I reply, wondering if *inspired by you* had any venom behind it, any implication that Azzuri died playing out my wishes. You can never tell with Raven. "I expect this was a fortunate find, something unexpected to give real teeth to whatever uses they had been planning for the Shades since the end of the Twin War."

"So the Grays are not your mortals," says Lady Hocquard, "but these bullets . . . buried in the earth . . . is this proof of them?" I see the way she is looking at me. It's not hard to guess her thoughts. How odd it is that I have found only indeterminate relics, while some vampires stumbled upon real proof. But now is not the time for such accusations, and the words thankfully go unspoken.

"Perhaps it is," I say. "Or perhaps this is sorcerer crafting. Something to think on after all this is over," I say, avoiding Jacob's eye.

"Enough of this wordin'," says Alanna. "We have some Lords to kill."

"Alanna," says Lady Hocquard, "we are going to tell them of the plot within their ranks, not kill them."

"That's what I mean, of course," says Alanna, disappointed.

"Great," says Jacob. "Let's get off this shading roof, then."

"I couldn't agree more," says Lady Hocquard, walking across to the door down to the belfry. Everything that happens then takes on a slow, curious quality, as so often happens when things take a turn for the worse. I see Lady Hocquard open the door. Then I see a puzzled look across her face. I see her turn to me, and I hear her ask:

"Sage, your illusions of Grays. Would any be here?"

"Absolutely not," I say. "The whole point was to have them well away from Centerfall so all the guards would leave the bank. Why do you ask?"

"Oh," says Lady Hocquard quietly. "Damn." Then she falls back away from the doorway and onto the floor, blood spilling from her chest near her heart. Alanna is at the door first with her dagger, impossibly quick, and she darts onto the stairwell, then darts back. "It's gone," she says, and she shuts the door. Then, as if the thought has only just hit her, she turns to Lady Hocquard and sees the true extent of it.

There is a moment of complete silence then. Alanna stares at the Lady, who has passed out, her arms splayed either side of her. Already her face seems to be glowing. There is no sign yet of the purple veins that appear closer to death—in the case of vampires hit by Gray bullets, the death being ashburst. For a moment it occurs to me that this cataloguing of symptoms could be an important moment, but then a coldness at the thought of my own cynicism takes over and I remember what a remarkable, spirited character the Lady is and the thought of her dying replaces my excitement with a chill.

Finally, the extended silence is broken by Alanna, who rushes over to her. "Daffers," she cries, all pretense at formality gone. She holds her in her arms and cradles her. "My Daffers," she says again, stroking her face. I look away, and I see Raven has already turned from them, having more grace than me to leave them to the death. I turn to the parapet and watch the evening sky, and I try and put from my mind the soon-to-be ashes of the woman who helped get us this far. I did not see Grayfall. But a little bit of the shock of it has appeared on this small piece of rooftop with us.

I hear movement behind me, and for a second I think it is Alanna, getting up with a pile of ashes at her feet. But then the woman from Last Light appears before me, with the Lady in her arms. Small shades of purple have begun around what is revealed of her neck. She is still unconscious. I can feel her heat from here.

"Alanna," I ask, "what are you doing?"

She ignores me and stares ahead, then looks down over the parapet, as if judging something. I move closer and see what she is looking at. There is a line of Grays guarding the eastern entrance far below. Five that I can see. Standing stock-still, like when Jacob and I encountered them in the Centerlands. From up here my eyes can't tell for sure, but I know they are not illusions.

Raven joins me and sighs. "If they are there, they will be at all the other entrances, too." She turns to me, giving me the full glare of her dark pupils. "What has that bloodfuck Saxe done?"

Then she turns to Alanna and looks at me, confusion in her eyes now, too. Alanna has still not said a word.

I'm about to say something when Alanna beings to sing, soft and halting. Her eyes are eyes closed but lips moving.

> *My love was once a darlin' flower*
> *Standing tall upon the hour*
> *And I be fixed within her gaze*
> *And smelling sweet for all my days*

I edge slowly away from her, sensing something. Raven stays still, a small smile playing on her lips.

> *But now my love has bloomed and gone*
> *And all that's left is stalk and none*
> *And I be fixed for nevermore*
> *Awaitin' death to save me*

And then, before any of us can say anything, Alanna climbs onto the parapet, standing with her feet wedged between two pinnacles. She looks down, as if confirming something, and then nods and jumps off the roof, her Lady in her arms.

27

Awaitin' Death to Save Me

Little is known of the combat practiced in Last Light. We do know that it quickly turned from training against the horrors of the Ashlands to fighting among themselves. We also know that those survivors of Last Light, on the few occasions these cautious souls have been caught showing off their skills, seem to be, when on the fighting stage, a curious mix of dancer, athlete, assassin, and something else entirely.

Neuras Satastion, *The City of Secrets*

Sage

I watch, a small sigh escaping my mouth, as Alanna falls. She falls straight down from the edge, so her fall is blocked from me. By the time I've climbed over the parapet to peer at the ground two hundred feet directly below, I'm expecting bodies. Instead, what I get is Alanna, seemingly unharmed, carefully placing the unconscious, dying body of Lady Hocquard on the ground before walking calmly toward the five Grays standing outside the eastern entrance.

"What in all of Shade and Light?" Jacob says, having joined me at the edge. He turns to me. "Shouldn't we do something?"

I recall her face, singing that song. "Yes, Jacob. I think we should probably root for her."

We look in helpless awe at the scene far below us as the Grays turn to face Alanna, with their weapons raised and pointed at her heart. But when the bullets fire, she is not there, because she's performed a forward roll toward them, and when she comes out of it, she knocks the gun out of the first Gray's hand. The three other Grays aim their weapons at her, but as they go to fire, she cartwheels toward them, whipping her legs across their outstretched gun hands one by one until the weapons are scattered across the floor. Then she comes out of her cartwheels and kicks the guns farther out of the Grays' reach.

"Well," says Raven next to me, "I wish someone had thought of that in Grayfall. Just disarm the bastards."

"I'm not sure it's as easy as that," I reply. "They were, are . . . Shades, remember. Sinassion's army. They can fight as well."

Sure enough, the Grays shift into a Shade fight stance, their right foot in front of them, their left and right arms raised and half crossed. Then the one closest to Alanna steps forward and strikes with a flat palm at where her neck should be if she hadn't nimbly sprung back in time. No sooner has Alanna backed off than she springs forward again, using the momentum of her back heel to power her front, but the Gray has anticipated this and kicks out with its left leg, tripping her up. Another Gray steps forward then and chops at her neck as she goes down. She gets up quickly, but even from up here you can tell she is riled from that first attack.

"Shades, Sage," says Jacob, reminding me how it became a cursing word in the first place, "she won't stand a chance, even with her skills. They can read her mind, the creepy shits. They know her every move."

This time it's Jacob's words that play out, as blow after blow come at Alanna from all sides. Even with her whip speed movement, she can barely soften the force of the palm hits that are always where she is. She rallies at one point, pirouetting around them and lashing out with her green-tinged daggers, and then leaping from a standing start over two of them and attempting to pierce them in the back with both blades.

But it is no good. Wherever her blades are, the Grays have just moved; wherever she is, the Grays have predicted it, and even though she handles each blow carefully and cradles and lessens the force of it with her own movement, I can see it is wearing her down.

"Aren't you going to help?" asks Jacob, turning to Raven.

Raven shakes her head. "By the time I get down the normal way, it will be too late, and if I jump off like her, I will survive but will not be much help for several minutes. She is better than me in that way, whoever that strange creature from Last Light is. Besides, she has not lost yet, and I would not insult her by interceding. She chose to fight, not run. She is defending her Lady's honor. I respect all these things." Raven squints, then turns to me. "Her lips are moving," she says, showing just how much better her wolf eyes are than mine.

"What?" But then I hear it. Faintly. She must be singing loudly for it to come up here. The same tune as she sang above. And as she sings, I see a wondrous sight, if such violence can ever hold wonder. I see her blades begin to connect, and she slides in behind one of the Grays, sticking him in the back with one blade; as he falls, she throws the other blade into the face of the one nearest him. Two left now.

"Ah! That . . . that is clever," I say.

"Care to elaborate, you endlessly smug prickard?" says Jacob.

"That singing. I would wager it is clouding her thoughts. Making them harder to anticipate."

"And the fact she's barely sane at the best of times probably helps as well," adds Jacob.

"Yes," I agree. "Probably why a good old sing-along didn't stop them in the Twin War."

Raven whistles. "I wish I'd known what a warrior we had in our midst. I might have talked to her a little more." She pauses. "I might have talked to her at all."

We watch the final act of this dramatic turnaround slaughter: Alanna, both blades now crimson with sorcerer blood, bright against the green of their gems, now faces the other two Grays, who, shorn of their surety of her movements, warily return to combat stance and both attack at once. Time seems to slow in that Alanna fashion, and still singing, her voice clear through the night, she sidesteps them both at the last moment, plunging one blade into the side of the head of the one nearest, then whipping it free, small geysers of blood jetting out in its wake. With a quick two-step she twists her body around so she is now behind the final Gray, whose back feels the force of her second blade: twisted in, twisted out.

"By the Five!" Jacob cries, but his relief is cut short as we hear the soft whine from below of a bullet. It misses Alanna and we hear the thunk of its impact in the eastern door just out of sight.

"Alanna!" I say as we watch ten more Grays coming from the direction of the north entrance, weapons raised.

"Don't do it," I hear Raven growl. "You've proved your honor. Run like the forest fucking wind."

For a second, as we watch from our high station while Alanna faces the Grays and their metal death, I see time stream out before me: all the possibilities, all the paths. I see a future where she stays and is cut down, another death to follow the imminent one of her Lady's. I see the courage and the pointlessness of it, and I see time carry on until all she represented is washed away in its eddies and no one remembers anything she ever stood for. And then the moment ends, the paths to different futures collide once again, and Alanna of Last Light turns on her heels, picks up her dying mistress, and runs away.

Raven

I can smell them all around. They have the tang of cinnamon about them, which I have smelled before, first in Grayfall, then on the few times I have ventured into the Centerlands and tried to get near as possible to them. Cinnamon backed with reeves bush, perhaps. It is the same thing the other wolves report. All those times we made no heed of it. But now I am surrounded by them, closer than I have ever been and in greater numbers, I see that their scent is not natural but worn, so wolves would not smell them for what they were: sorcerers. You can't fool a wolf's nose, but sometimes you can lead it a little astray at a distance.

I sniff strong and hard. There is one still on the staircase, no doubt waiting to try and attack the door, which is flimsy and will give way easily. I imagine they will be cautious to do so, however, as even they are at a disadvantage at a single pressure point. I sense at least five more lower in the church itself, and many more—perhaps as many as twenty—gathered outside it, not including the five dispatched by whatever Alanna is. A small army indeed. I do not know if Sinassion's old soldiers can climb sheer walls. I imagine they will attempt it. They did not follow Alanna when she ran, so they must want those of us who remain here very badly. And here I am, with just myself and two powerless sorcerers. I have not had a challenge like this since the war.

"Okay," says Sage. "We need a plan. First we need to establish why the Grays are here."

Jacob clears his throat. "Um, can we just check that Alanna is not returning? To, you know, kill them all?"

I shake my head. "She is with her dying one now. She chose to take her away from all of this for her death."

"A bit selfish," says Jacob.

"You did not see the way she looked at her, then, sorcerer," I reply. "She is all she cares for now. I wish them well in their final moments together." I turn to Sage. "And as for why the Grays are here, I assume that is obvious. That shifty bloodfuck Saxe has worked out the diversion, has realized we now know the truth, and has decided to risk his secret and send some of his Grays or Shades, or whatever we are meant to call them now, to kill us once and for all. And as the Grays didn't chase Alanna, I assume that you and I are the ones who cannot be allowed to escape, cannot be allowed to take our truth back to our homelands."

I can tell by Sage's face and his slight change in scent that he is a little disappointed.

"Oh, I'm sorry, sorcerer," I say. "You were hoping I would confess my ignorance and you would tell me, were you not?"

Sage has the grace to blush a little, and I have no grace, so I stare at him deadpan and let his embarrassment linger a little.

"In fact," I add, "your diversion has meant there are no guards or in fact anyone here, so it is the perfect scenario for us to be attacked and killed."

"I didn't think of that," says Sage. "I underestimated Saxe's desperation and the pace of events." The sorcerer turns away from me, and I smell the strong overripe lilac of his fury with himself.

"That last comment was a statement," I add. "It was not meant to be a criticism." It is a lie, but sometimes I do not know my own fucking harshness, so I will give him some balm. "You got me into the bank, and for that I owe you a debt, Sage Bailey."

"Thank you, Raven. I fear we might not live long enough for you to repay it, though," he says, peering cautiously again over the roof parapet.

"I wouldn't do that if I were you," I say carefully. "Or you might end up like the noble Lady. They have very good aim."

"Well, what about you, Raven?" asks Jacob. "Now that Alanna's gone, now would be a good time for you to do some of that Midnight Assassin stuff you're famed for." I stare at him. "That is," he continues, "if you don't mind." I stare a little longer. "I won't speak for a while," he concludes.

"Well," I begin after my uncomfortably long silence has done its work, "the Grays are not moving yet. We need not rush ourselves into a poorly thought-out fight. We have some time to play with. They are not overly happy at there being only one way of entry, I imagine."

"But why don't they just rush the door? We might kill a couple of them, but we'll quickly be outnumbered."

"Perhaps, Jacob, they are being cautious because they know that plan might end up in one or more of us dying," says Sage.

"Isn't that the point? We know his secret now. He needs us dead."

"Yes," continues Sage, "but you need a fairly good explanation for why one of the best-known wolves in the land and the diplomatic representatives of the Archmage have both been killed. Last thing Saxe wants is a new war to distract him from his scheme. I imagine our creative spymaster is trying to put that little ruse together—hence the delay—and then once he's assured of that, we'll be swamped by Grays."

"Oh, excellent. More good shading news." Jacob thinks some more, and I smell a peppermint whiff of realization on him. "Hold on!" He turns to Sage. "The Grays won't touch us, remember? That's how we got here in the first place! We can just walk out of here!"

I look at him.

"That is something we may have been keeping to ourselves," Jacob adds, moving slowly away from me.

Sage, however, shakes his head. "Two points, Jacob. One, Raven is here."

I grin toothily at Jacob at this point to indicate my feelings about those who abandon me in battle, even if I do not need them in it.

"Two," Sage continues, "given that I have no supposition as to why Quantas are not attacked by Grays normally, I do not have sufficient reason to believe that Saxe's wishes might not override, on special occasion, such a circumstance."

"So you mean we're still buggered," says Jacob. "I suppose we'll all be joining Lady Hocquard soon, then."

He's wrong. I just do not know how yet.

And that's when we hear the knocking. Knocking on the door to the roof.

I turn to face the sound and I ready myself for the Grays.

28

Drain It All

It is frustrating for those of us who wish to study such things that just as modern methods of reasonminds and knowledgecrafters with regards to the effects of blood absorption began to advance quickly around 400 AL, the outcome of the Twin War left instances of vampires ingesting large amounts of wolfblood at a time, and therefore the study of their effects, very thin on the ground. One almost hopes for another war.

Quantas Quintide, *The Blood of the Wolfkind*

Sage

We've all heard the knocking now, too, and a voice behind it as well, just loud enough to be heard over the wind whipping across the roof. There is a moment when we look at one another, confused, and we say it at almost the same time. "Is that . . . Sam?"

I rush to the door, realizing as I do so that I have let reason, logic, and caution slip away for a second in my haste to see her.

"Hold on," Jacob says, grabbing me just before I open it. "How do we know it's her? Why in Light's name would she be here? It's a trick."

"Unless a Gray has found a way to smell exactly like her, I think not," says Raven.

"Fine," Jacob replies, reluctantly letting me go, "but *he* didn't know that."

I pull the bolts back and open the door, and Sam stumbles onto the roof.

"Shut it!" she cries as a Gray appears on the turn of the stairs behind her, weapon raised. I do so just as a bullet slams into the wood of the closing door.

Sam collapses on the floor, panting heavily. Her eyes are a dark shade of red, and it's clear even from my rudimentary knowledge of bloods and blood-taking that she's on some of the more potent variety. It seems to be a habit with her these days.

"So," says Raven quietly, "that was . . . unexpected."

I help Sam off the floor and hold her for a little longer than I should have. I do not believe she notices. She studies each of us carefully, then laughs slightly manically. "I'm here."

"But . . . how did you get past the Grays?" I ask, fascinated.

"There's a tunnel system that runs under First Gods. From when the bloodgod priests weren't the only religion in town and needed safe passage from their enemies. Takes you right into a room behind the altar. Kinet Lastassion, *On the Prayhalls of First Light*. A good read." Then her face creases up in confusion. "Where's Lady Hocquard? And Alanna?"

"Sam, I'm so sorry, but . . ." I begin.

"The Lady is dead, or at least soon to be, and Alanna escaped with her," interrupts Raven. I stare at her. She shrugs. "We do not have time to break it to her gently."

Sam sits down and stares at the floor a while. "How did she—"

"A Gray bullet," says Jacob. "She'll be a little smaller when you next see her."

"By the Five, Jacob, shut your damn mouth just this once!" I say, a rage suddenly taking me, and immediately regret it; he is using his humor as a defense because he is scared and I should know better.

He bows his head instead. "I'm sorry. I . . . I really don't know why I said that."

I see Sam fighting the tears now, choking them back, keeping her head, and I marvel at her bravery, so untrained. "None of this is right. Even for the Lords, it's—"

"It's what they do," starts Raven, "it's what they've always done, since we went from beasts to folk and you Bloods started to arrange yourselves into classes of status. It's never been right."

"Sam," I say, unwilling to point out that the wolves have not been completely innocent in all this, "we don't have time to explain everything. So I'm going to explain some things very quickly. It's . . . quite a lot to take in."

"That's okay," says Sam, "I thought it might be."

I explain, and she follows my words carefully. She doesn't seem too surprised. I don't think I've ever met someone who adapts to her circumstances so quickly. It is fascinating. The shock and the sadness and the hysterics that the normal mind would encounter just aren't there. I am finding that she is remarkable, and I wish . . . I wish I had encountered her earlier.

Just because there's no hysterics, it does not mean she's fine, though. She goes quiet. It's a lot to take in. Sometimes your entire life changes in a few seconds, more so for her than the rest of us.

"All the people killed in Grayfall," she says eventually.

"I know," I say.

"An entire city destroyed."

"I know."

"Why?"

"I don't know. But I think we're all quite keen to find out."

"Never a truer word said, mage," says Raven. "And now it's time to put our plan into action."

"What plan?" Jacob says, looking one step behind as usual. "I thought we were trapped?"

"Not anymore," says Raven, staring hard at Sam.

I bow my head. "Oh, Sam, I'm sorry. I wish you hadn't come."

"I don't," Sam says. "I thought this might be the solution when I realized you were trapped. I was hoping Alanna might step up, but—"

"Sorry," Jacob says, "this is yet another of those moments that are happening with increasing frequency today when everyone's had a secret meeting about a plan and not invited me. This time it would be really nice if someone could say words instead of meaningful bloody looks, if that's not too much to ask."

Sam grins at him, and there's something wild about her now, teary eyes mixed with a smile, and for a moment I put my analyzing aside and I choose to fix on that expression, fix it into my memory. Just for a moment. What harm can it do?

"Why tell you when I can show you, Jacob?" she says eventually. Then she walks over to Raven. "How does this work?"

Raven shrugs. "Bite me. Drink up."

"How do I know how much to take?"

"Take as much as you can. You'll need bulletproof skin as well as wings."

Sam thinks on this. "How will I know when that's enough?"

Raven grins. "I think you'll know."

"What if I drink too much and hurt you?"

"I won't let that happen, trust me."

Sam goes for another question, but Raven grabs her arm. "We don't have time. You've come this far, Sam. This part's easy."

I don't know what I was expecting, but the next part is something I know will stay with me, lingering in the corners of my mind forever. I've seen vampires drink from other immortals before, it not being the most unusual thing in this world, especially during war, but I've never watched the process closely, and I have definitely never seen anything like this: Sam's slow, long stare at Raven, almost amorous, except then you realize that she's not staring at Raven's face, but at her neck, eyeing her jugular. There's a strange silent pause. Sam's mouth is open, her head leaned back, her fangs extended. Then she bites down—swift, forceful. Next moment she is sucking the blood, no, not sucking, *inhaling* it into her body, her neck moving like a pump, draining Raven like she's a wet rag being squeezed of water. Raven's body goes limp. She's completely subjugated herself to Sam, her eyes half closed in a trance. I can't tell if she's in pain or ecstasy.

And, as if it couldn't get any stranger, I watch Sam's body as it fills with the blood of the wolfkind. Her skin starts to glow softly. Then it seems to harden and darken, as if she's becoming a statue. Her eyes are so red it is as if they're burning themselves into the very color. Her fangs are growing now, as are her fingernails. She even seems taller. And all throughout, all the time as she sucks Raven's lifeblood out of her, all the time she is *smiling*.

I never saw a grin so wide.

Sam

I thought I was ready for the wolfblood. I was a godsdamn fool. I had a little when I fled from Rufous. Now I've had a lot. So much coursing through me. I see Raven's body fall to the floor, still breathing; I didn't kill her, so there's that. Then everything is rushing in so fast and with such clarity that I . . .

My sister. We were just young wild street urchins, me and her, but we owned the city in all the ways that matter. We had such plans. And she let me down . . . except she didn't, did she? She saw my rage and my determination, and she knew where it was headed: to a sunburned cross like my father. So she chose a different way. It wasn't her failure, but mine, that led to the palace and her death. I see it now, clear as a raindrop against my eyeball.

My mother, dead-eyed and listless, mourning my father. All I wanted was for her to be angry, but she faded away instead, and my frustration surely only quickened her fall into despair. No wonder she wanted out of this life, with her partner gone and her daughters blinding her with their rage. I'm sure she couldn't wait to face the sun.

Sam?

Beth, the friend I let down. She was a sideshow to my life—important when I felt like it, but annoying when I didn't. I didn't see her true courage until it was too late. She was only ever going to die having a friend like me. If you see who you really are and the extent of your failures, can you start again? Or is it wiser to accept that your path is too broken to carry on walking over, and your feet too stuck with the bloody shards of everything you've smashed to pieces?

Sam, come back to us.

I can't, I won't. So many people I've disappointed. To have such high hopes for myself only to let everyone down? What a jest is this thing we call life. Why would anyone put themselves through it?

Sam, don't.

I see life as it is now, empty and bottomless in its cruelty. There's only one logical way out. The Grays down below. They can end my pain. I don't ever have to let anyone down again.

Samantha!

I . . . I don't know how, but I follow my own voice back. Or is it Sage's? I'm not really sure. I look down and I see myself standing on the edge of the roof. I step back quickly, my breath dying in my throat.

"Are you okay?" asks Sage, his face close to mine, but scared, ready to jump back. I don't blame him. I'm glowing and I'm supercharged; I could kill him with a single punch to the neck.

I smile. "I am for the moment, I think. Things just went a little dark. As in *really* dark. How do the Lords cope on this?"

"Well, I doubt any of them have had as much as you since the Twin War, or at least the last time a vampire killed one of the wolfkind and drained half their blood. What did you feel?"

"Guilt. Self-loathing. Shame."

"Well, there you go. Do you think those are ever emotions that would come within ten miles of a Lord, no matter how much wolfblood was coursing through him?"

"No." I laugh. "I suppose not." I look at Jacob, who is staring at me cautiously. "How do I look?"

"Like I want to run away from you screaming and shitting myself, join the Cloaks of Kluzillion, and promise never to touch a drop in vain again."

"I think he means that as a compliment," says Sage. "It is fascinating, though. I've not seen such a reaction since the war. Your voice is . . ."—he searches for the word—"ethereal."

I glance at Raven. She's still on the floor, passed out. Her neck wound has already started to heal, though.

"You didn't drain her completely," says Sage. "I'll expect she'll be okay."

"She will be," I reply.

"How do you know?" Sage asks.

"I don't know . . . I can smell she will be."

"Like a wolf?"

"No. How . . . I don't know. How vampires are meant to be, I suppose. Operating at full capacity, if you like." I grimace then as a coursing pain shoots through my back. For a second I panic, and then I realize. Of course. I'm surprised it took so long. My wings are coming. And that's when I know what I have to do next.

"Sage, I . . ." I'm interrupted by the hammering of the door to the roof. The wooden frame bursts open, and a slight figure covered in tight gray cloth jumps through, moving so quick I can hardly process him, but then my mind adjusts, and I see the small weapon in his hand being raised and everything seems to slow. I have time to inspect the strange metallic surface of the weapon, painted in gray of course, and the weapon's underside, where a series of capsules are lodged in its underbelly, all different colors. Red for vampire, green for sorcerer, and blue for wolf, if I remember from my Grayfall reading. I have time to stare into the barrel of this weapon, and then more time to duck and feel the bullet pass over my head. Then my body takes over and I barrel myself forward into the Gray's chest, the weapon falling out of his hand; as it falls I catch it even as I go tumbling to the ground with the Gray. Then I point it to his head and I start to press the trigger, but then instead I drop the weapon and I punch him, punch him in the head repeatedly until he isn't moving anymore. Then I pick him up and go to throw him down the stairwell, only to see another Gray there at the turn of the stairs, almost identical to the last one. Our eyes lock for a second, and then he raises his weapon. But as he does so, I launch the Gray in my arms toward him, through the door and down the stairs, and though he almost jumps out of the way, the airborne body catches his leg and he falls with it, clattering down the stairs. Finally I shut what remains of the roof door, and I turn to Sage.

"Well," says Sage, "that was . . . ripe for analysis." He tries to smile, but his voice is faint. He looks nervous. If I was being unkind, and who's to say I'm not on this blood, I would say he preferred me as the impressionable maid finding my way, not the full-blooded warrior who's already found it.

"Most of that was instinct," I say.

"I imagine it was," he replies. "You know, I always wondered about the plan to store wolfblood to defeat the Grays. It seemed a little hopeful. But after what I just saw, I think it might just have worked. Not that it was ever needed, of course."

"You didn't kill him, though," says Jacob. "I saw it . . . At least I think I did, I was quite busy with an attack of the heart tremors at the time, but you were going to shoot him and then you just knocked the piss out of him instead!"

"Yes." I nod.

"Why?" asks Sage, and he's careful to avoid judgment, but I can smell it a little on him. Bloods. I'm beginning to sound like Raven.

"They've been tortured, yes?" I reply. "According to Sinassion at least. Driven mad, until Saxe could control them like animals. If that's true . . . I'm just killing victims, aren't I?"

"More like soldiers," says Jacob.

I turn back to Sage. "I'm not doing what a Lord would do on this blood. That's not how we'll beat them."

"But you're going to have to kill some if we're ever going to get off this shading roof," pleads Jacob behind me.

"No." Sage smiles, noticing my new wings edging their way from my back. "She isn't."

29

Stagecraft

I almost pity the Worns, they who never know the joy of flight. It is a pure thing, a wondrous thing, a gift of birthright. I say almost, but really could they ever grasp the thrill of feeling so much closer to the Bloodhalls when they are barely deserving of passage into them? Better not to experience that which you are not built for; this is the route to contentment—both theirs and ours. A contract of happiness, if you will.

Garnetia Marinara, *The Finer Things*

First Lord Azzuri

Lord Saxe is speaking, but I am not listening. I am not focused on his speech to the First Council, his long rambling explanation of the events unfolding to the Lords gathered around the long table of the council chambers. I already know its contents. Redgrave told me before the meeting, having learned only shortly before himself. The shock I see on their faces is the shock I have already been through.

Instead, I am focused on the sky, which I can see through the stained glass of the window, red or blue depending on which pane I look through.

Out of the corner of my eye I can see Redgrave staring at me concerned, trying to monitor me. Lord Saxe, too, keeps glancing my way, not nervously, because he is not capable of nerves I think, but cautiously, nonetheless. But I do not care. I am skyborne now; I am imagining myself flying through the air, a feat I have not done for so long I can only just remember the feeling of the wind running under my wings as I make a turn, and the cold night air on my face as I soar upward. Upward I soar in my mind, away from all this, away from the twin hells unraveling before me.

There was not always stained glass before me; the ostentatious, gaudy monstrosity that is the emblem of the Azzuris, the drop of blood outlined in royal blue, with the panes behind it in soft pastel blue. There used to be no glass at all. The Dome Room, the highest room, was open to the elements when this was a castle, not a palace, and in the days before the Twin War, when wolfblood flowed almost as freely as wine for a select few, the Lords of First Light would make their entrance to the castle by swooping in here. But the wolfblood dried up with the war and the truce, and the next time I visited First Light, only a few years before Grayfall, I saw the modern building that had replaced my ancestral home and the great window my uncle had installed. I smiled and appeared grateful while inwardly bemoaning the gaudiness of it, the pathetic attempts to ape the palace of Lightfall. But now this is my home, and everything I sneered at is all I have. And now all I have is something I need very badly to get away from, to break through this memory and break through this window, leaving this city and its Lords far behind. But rulers can never escape.

I am roused back to the room. Lord Saxe has finished his speech. The Lords look less shocked than they did before it, but some are still concerned. They turn to me, but I do not acknowledge them. I can get through this only if I do not speak. Saxe will do it all, I am sure. I am just along for the ride. Redgrave is still staring at me. Perhaps he expected a reaction, but honestly? I cannot even summon the anger.

Lord Beryl is speaking now. He has a ruddy face, a result of four centuries of excessive bloodwine and little exercise; it is a good job he does not age slowly like the Worns or it would be even worse than it is now. He is complimenting Saxe. Amazing how quickly people adapt. Next to him, leaning back in the velvet-backed chair, is Lord Sapphiri. He is tall and clean-shaven, with oddly boyish features. He is a troublemaker, a rabble-rouser. He is one of those who looked concerned before but is coming over to it; I see the fires of resistance dying when faced with the crowd. Lord Saxe knows all his secrets, after all. When faced with things so great and people who have such knowledge over them, even the freethinkers fall into obedience.

I turn again to the window, back to my night dreams, and I stare at a dot in the sky. There is something flying, but it is not any of my First Guard. An eagle soaring, perhaps. A particularly large eagle. I squint my eyes, and I wonder how much my dreams have bled into reality.

For it is a blond woman, and she is descending fast.

Sam

I was five years old the first time I saw a vampire fly. I'd heard about it, of course. The few times people around my streets spoke of Lightfall, the ones who saw it anyway. They would speak of how the skies would be full of Lords on wings, and even Midways. Wolfblood wasn't a dirty secret back then to be hoarded, it was something that when you got your hands on it—whether you smuggled it in or somehow managed to kill a wolf for it—you would let the city know, whether it be a blur in the night sky to be spotted in the moonlight by those down below or else swooping low over the streets, flaunting your power.

But in First Light, wings were rare, at least in Worntown, from which my five-year-old self would hardly ever stray. Until one day when I was at our local market with my mother, and a strange vehicle rode into view. "That's the First Lord's carriage," she whispered. Barely had she said the words when I heard the sounds of flight and looked up to see two of the First Guard flying above me, great leathery wings outstretched to catch the current as they readied to land. I'd seen pictures of vampire's wings in books before, but up close they looked different: more alive, fragile, and . . . real. I thought the tufts of hair on the tips of the wings were pretty revolting, and I started to say something, but my mother told me to shush. Their movements, though, they were beautiful, coordinated, graceful.

My movements aren't so beautiful. If some vampires were born to fly, then I was born to flap. Not even the wolfblood wiring my body to its best abilities can help me here. The fact I'm flying at all with no practice amazes me; every movement, every turn of the wing to realign myself is on instinct, like a thousand flying vampires calling out from years gone by, guiding me.

I look down the road toward the palace, its lights twinkling in the horizon. With my eyes the way they are at the moment, I can just about see the thick protective lines of bloodguards at the palace gates. I can also spy two of the First Lord's own First Guard circling around the building, slowly flapping their wings; much more graceful than my pisspoor attempts. Finally, I can see the Dome Room; its great white stone roof and the stained glass wrapping all around it. Bright light filters through the glass; I know it's occupied, and my senses, so combined now I can barely tell which ones, tell me that it's occupied by many. You don't have to be half a wolf down to work out who they will be at this time of emergency.

As I get closer, I suddenly realize the great honking flaw in my hasty plan. How do I get in? I look for any entrance, but there's nothing that I can see, and it's approaching so fast.

Then I see that one of the winged guards circling around the palace has spotted me, and he comes swooping through the night—big, slow flaps of his wings, in stark contrast to my hasty flutters; his red and gold First Guard tabard bright against the moonlight. He speeds toward me, and now I have to do something. I look down and see the Dome Room is nearer now, the stained glass winking in the soft moonlight, and I know that really there was only one way I was ever going to make my entrance.

I push my wings back and try and arch my body, and as I descend down toward the glass I become a bullet. I speed up and tuck my head beneath my wings and pray to the Blood Gods I doubt exist that my wolfblood skin is thick enough for the impact I'm about to make.

When I crash through the glass, I'm going at twice the speed I was flying, yet time seems to slow as it did when I was fighting the Gray. I see shards speed past me, touching my skin but not cutting it—no, not on this blood. I land on a cold marble floor, glass still falling around me, and for a second I see it not as glass but as falling timber, and I see my dying sister bathed in sunlight before me. But that's not who's there when the vision fades. Instead, I see a long redoak table and two dozen Lords sitting around it, watching in stunned silence as I stand up, unfurling my wings as I do so, as if answering the questions dancing in their eyes.

The silence continues. I smell the sweat of the Lords and their panic, growing stronger and more pungent with every moment. I lock eyes with First Lord Azzuri at the far end of the table. I could almost swear he is smiling, but when I look again his face is blank. Finally the moment is broken when a guard standing by the door rushes me, and I smell the wolfblood steaming off him, but he's on vials while I'm on a whole wolf, and when he runs into my suddenly outstretched fist, he's knocked cold. That's what you get for bringing a vial to a wolf fight.

Before any more can rush me, I drop what I've been carrying this whole flight; the centerpiece without which I'd be laughed out of the room. It makes a loud crash that echoes throughout the chamber, and its contents fall out and roll toward the Lords. A couple instinctively jump, which makes me smile, but most just stare as the bullets roll to their table and they reach down and pick them up, still confused.

Another guard has reached me now, but a voice comes from across the room. "Leave her be. She is mine." It's Rufous, of course. Who else would it be? He's sitting to the right of his father at the head of the table, and when he stands, I can see he's on the wolfblood, too; he unfurls his wings despite the confines of the room. He's wearing his First Guard uniform, the red and gold edged in commander blue. The shine on his boots tells me that he's not been in the thick of it today, though. He's saved all his violence for me. We lock eyes and he grins that half-sane grin, his lengthened fangs peeking over his bottom lip. Then he slowly advances on me.

"Little Samantha," he says, "you cannot help yourself, can you? It s a brave girl to fight again. I see you have more blood in you this time. You are positively glowing, my girl."

"Enough in me for you and your grin, you highborn prick," I say, letting all the anger in me surge, letting the blood have its way with me.

"You could drink a barrelful of wolves and still not have what it takes," he replies, closing the gap between us. "As I shall demonstrate now."

"No, Rufous." We both turn to see who's speaking now. It's not his father. It's the voice of the spymaster Saxe, who is standing in the shadows of the far corner, a little behind Azzuri. I've heard and seen him many times in the palace, and always with the same look he has now on his face: the look of someone who's just heard he's been complimented and wants you to know it pleased him. He's wearing a black velvet jacket, with silver buttons and silver cuff links; I can hear the worth of the silver and so I know it is solid. No, that's not right, I can't *hear* it. I'm still working out my new senses. I just . . . know. I can see the fine detail of the ring on his finger, too, the key engraved on the owl, but I knew it before I saw it, at least I think I did.

Saxe pushes some of his unruly blond mop out of his face as he speaks. "I must have words with her first, Rufous."

A scowl replaces Rufous's grin and his right eyelid flickers. "This is mine, Cinibar."

"I must have words with her," repeats Saxe calmly, and I smell the reaction from Rufous: a strong copper on the back of my throat, which

I somehow know is anger, but also a little bit of fruit, a little bit of bitterness. The blood tells me this is fear, just a little, but enough to hold
him back, enough to make him back away from me, right eye winking
furiously, unclenching and clenching his fists.

"Where did you get these?" says Saxe, indicating a bullet he has picked
up and is now inspecting in his hands. "How did you get these?"

He's interrupted by a Lord close to me, with thick sideburns and
a red, jowled face squashed between them. "By god, she looks like a
Worngirl!"

Saxe turns to him. "Thank you, Lord Teal, I have this, really." Then
he turns back to me, while the rest of the Lords' expressions go various
shades of even greater pale at the bullets they are inspecting in their
fingers, for while Rufous has been threatening me, the bloodcoin has
certainly dropped.

"Tell us your story, girl," says Saxe, committed to his act. "You have
the floor for a brief time."

I don't answer at first, but I look properly around the room at the
faces of the Lords, these masters of their domains and kings of the city.
Some of them have rooms at the palace, a couple live here, and the rest
visit regularly, but not a single one has ever spoken to me, and though
they've all seen me, they've never *looked* at me. Well, they're looking at
me now.

Nearest to me on the left side of the table is Lord Sapphiri, Lord of the
Blood Markets, chair of the Bloodshares Council, and down one wolfblood vial thanks to my ransacking of his room several days past. His
clean-shaven boyish features don't hide the stench of corruption. Literally, thanks to my new nose. A few seats down I see Lord Ceruli, tall,
gaunt, and with dead eyes. When he's not busy ruining lives he's Lord of
War and chair of the War Council, a slightly pointless role now that there
are no wars in the world of Grays, just the war against the Grays that
may one day come. Opposite him is Lord Teal, the ruddy-faced lardheap
who was so surprised at seeing a Worngirl crash this little party. I'm
amazed he has time at all to be Lord of Trading and Commerce with all
the objects he has his valet shove inside him while his maids are forced
to watch. I thank Alanna for telling me that. Finally I glance at Lord
Cobalti, overseer of the Blood Bank, a shriveled, wiry-bearded, mousy
man who has no doubt recently found out that his precious bank's been
robbed for the first time in its history. The vast stores he oversees could

stop all Worns from aging for a century, so I'd say he's probably earned the shock that's coming to him.

Having surveyed the Lords who rule over such cruelty and play their part in it, I try and savor the moment, but the wisdom of the wolfblood is in me and I know that these moments never live up to their name. So I stop trying to write memories and I just give them the plain truth of it instead.

Sage

The first Gray comes crashing through the door shortly after Sam has flown away.

Raven is still passed out, and the Light of Luce knows that I've tried to bring her back, so that leaves me and Jacob holding the fort. We sit there, watching and waiting, and when the first Shade wrapped in Gray pops out, I fire the weapon in my hand: the strange light weapon, like two metal cylinders jammed together in an L-shape, the one you hold filled with small colored bullets. All the bullets I have loaded are blue, for those are the ones that kill sorcerers, and two of them come flying out of the firing cylinder at the pull of my trigger finger. That's one more than I would really like, given that we only have half of what was in the chest; the other half is with Sam. Not so good for our odds if we are swarmed by Sinassion's old army.

Luckily, both the bullets that I fire hit their target square in the chest, and I marvel at how fear for my life has instilled a sense of aim in me. Worth looking into that effect further, if I ever get off this tiresome rooftop.

I have never seen a sorcerer die from a Gray bullet; I was not at Grayfall, after all. I have heard what happens, so different from vampires and yet the same end, but seeing it up close is another thing entirely. As he falls to the ground, his whole body flashes a yellow light, like some energy is passing through it. Then, lying on the ground, his figure begins to shrivel, as if all life is being expelled from it. Next there is a small flash, and what remains is just that—remains—more debris than sorcerer. It seems so quick, perhaps because my bullets hit his heart or maybe it is just that sorcerers go quicker than vampires. I try and feel the guilt of killing what Sam called a victim. I feel nothing. I am glad Sam is not here for me to disappoint.

"Do you think," Jacob says after a few moments, "that it would be too much to ask, just one time, *just one time,* if I could face the possibility of death with a shading woman by my side instead of you?"

I grin, but I don't reply. I think we both know the answer to that one.

Then two Grays come through the door, and more bullets are fired, but they are not enough.

Sam

There is silence. Everyone's turned to face Saxe. Everyone except the First Lord, who is staring at me—no, not at me; almost behind me, like he's busy watching the sky.

"It's a damn lie," says Saxe. "And quite why in the twin hells we would listen to the ravings of a *Wormmaid* whose life has very suddenly got an expiry date I haven't the faintest, I'm afraid."

"The bullets. Raven Ansbach and the sorcerers. Lady Hocquard. You don't have to believe a Worngirl," I say, looking at the rest of the Lords. "You just have to believe your own eyes."

"I . . ." Saxe turns to the Lords. "I . . . you don't." He begins to stammer, and a look of panic flashes across his face.

But then he stops.

And he starts to laugh.

"Ah, I am sorry." He guffaws, bending down and holding his sides, so great is his amusement. "I really am. I can't keep it up anymore."

A cold grip tightens around my heart, and the wolfblood hammering through my brain tells me what's happened a little before he does.

"You are right," he continued. "It was me. Me and a select few others, some of them here. We did indeed arm the Shades with the ammunition found under Lightfall, and yes, we did indeed construct the myth of the Grays. Grayfall was our strategy, and yes, you and your plucky little crew of erstwhile reprobates have forced me to lay my plan bare. For that, I suppose I should congratulate you, dear."

I look around at the Lords, and I see many of them grinning at me. A couple still look disgusted, though whether at me or Saxe's words I can't tell. First Lord Azzuri is not looking at me, though, and neither is his first man standing behind him to his right, who has concerned eyes only for his master.

"You admit it now?" I ask, struggling to keep up on this new, muddier ground which I'm up to my elbows in. "In front of all your . . . fellows?"

"Because they have already heard about it. I told them not but half a glass ago."

The old call of the wolfblood grabs me again, and I suddenly wish I'd taken that dive into the Grays.

"Oh, I'm sorry," Saxe continues. "What's that? I can't quite hear you. No, nothing? Oh. Anyone would think that was your entire plan. Oh . . . Was it? Oh dear. Oh dearie me. It looks like I've left you with less than a leg to stand on. What a good job it is you have two wings now, aha!"

"Really, Saxe, must we tolerate this Worn bitch any longer?" says Lord Teal, his face turning newly discovered shades of puce. "She has no right to hear any of our truths, for the purpose of her humiliation or otherwise."

"My dear Lord Teal," replies Saxe, a calm grin on his face but a little flicker in the eyes giving away his fury at being interrupted, "she has feigned to be like us, to drink the blood of all bloods. Let her see some truth of it, for sport if nothing else. Unless you think that we are so powerless as to ever allow her to speak of it to her own kind." He turns to First Lord Azzuri, seeking some form of agreement, but Azzuri just stares ahead; Saxe seems to take this as permission to carry on. In that moment, I see how power has shifted without anything formal happening, without any words being said. Almost invisibly, yet clear to see for anyone looking for it.

"You see, Samantha Ingle of Ashfall Lane, poor little orphan all alone in this world—oh yes, I know everything about you—the *why* is really a very simple thing. Lightfall was spiraling out of control. Your brothers and sisters, the Worns of the city, were multiplying like flearabbits, and worse than that, they were wielding influence with their growing numbers. Feigning to tell us how to control the city; they who would destroy it with their own chaos draped in egalitarian finery if they ever had real ownership of it. The very *gall* of it. And the wolfblood that gives our small number of Lords the strength to be sure we can stand against your hordes if such a day ever came? Well, it had become a resource hard to come by since the Twin War. After all, how do you bleed wolves when to do so could be to ignite a peace?"

Saxe looks around the assembled Lords, as if challenging them to interrupt him, then continues. "My plan gave us back our power in one stroke. We had an enemy to rein in your kind, to whip the ambition out of them and replace it with the sheer gratitude to be alive. And—and this, if you don't mind me saying, dear, was the masterstroke—we made a useful deal with the wolves: their blood for our promise to use it to win back the Centerlands one day. It's amazing what people will give up for a return to normality."

"But . . . you destroyed your own city," I say, beginning to feel like I'm arguing into the wind. "And many of your own kind. Your own *class.*"

"A few Lords had to go for the look of it, yes, though no one that anyone sitting here will have mourned. Troublemakers and weaklings alike, in the main. They were a small price to pay for the freedom to start again. And as for the destruction—oh, what's a brief cityfall when you're immortal? A temporary dip in our glorious cycle; a necessary evil to give us a kingdom of wolfblood for a thousand years. We'll carry on the charade until we have stored vast amounts, and your Wornkind's will has been sufficiently sapped. Then the Grays will vanish as mysteriously as they came, perhaps following a glorious yet unseen military victory or two on a wolfblood army. Then we will expand back into the Centerlands, renewed and repurposed, ready for Lightfall to rise again, a leviathan from the depths, but one that *we* control."

He takes a breath, and I also take one, just to keep myself steady. There hardly seems any air in the room now, just the suffocating talk of men with plans.

"Do you see now, Sam, do you see what I and my so-called conspirators did?" he continues. "I stole a century and gave the Lords millennia. A fair bargain, I daresay even a Worn like yourself would have to admit."

"You won't get away with it," I reply, realizing even as I say the words that I stand among people who have built their lives on constantly getting away with it.

"But we *did,* Sam. You're living in a world that is proof of that. And as plucky, courageous, and amusingly intelligent as you are, it will not change for all the bullets in the land. You see, I'm thinking in the arc of history, Samantha. Those who think in mere years and decades haven't really grasped what we are, we immortals. We best history. We own it. We *mold* it."

"If you stay alive that long."

"Oh, do not worry on that front, my dear. You see, Sam, any immortal who dies with just a few centuries under their belt is just . . . careless. And out of the two of us, I can guarantee it won't be me who gives up immortality today."

Maybe it's his jarring laugh or maybe it's the sheer reality of the tablecloth being pulled out from under me, but I feel the same fury I felt when Rufous was standing in front of me, the remains of Beth decorating his face. I edge toward the table, and the Lords seated nearest to me recoil slightly, staring at my lengthy talons. Rufous, this time free of Beth's brains, readies his own talons.

"This wolfblood you crave so much to kill so many," I say, milking all the deep new layers to my voice for all they're worth. "Should we see what it can really do? And how many I can cut through before I tire? I wager a whole tableful of piss-scared Lords at the very least."

Lord Saxe's expression doesn't falter. And he doesn't smell scared. He's a special kind of crazy, you don't need to be on wolfblood to see that. "Oh, you're not thinking, Sam," he replies. "It's true that you've got more strength perhaps than any vampire in this city right now. But even then you're not thinking. You're not thinking, for example, about your friends on the roof of First Gods. It's amazing what thoughts my Grays, my Shades, my trained Neuras can pick up. They can't properly read my mind from here, thank the Halls, but they can certainly sense a single word, constantly beamed out to them from a voice like mine they know well. A word like *kill*. How long do you think two powerless sorcerers and a half-drained wolf will last against a troop of Grays, Samantha? Really, my dear, I thought you cleverer than that."

He's right. I can think more clearly than him right now and I know he's right. I know I have no options. So that's what having all your wits increased to their fullest does to you. It steals your hope.

"Oh, don't look so crestfallen, my dear," continues Saxe. "It's not your fault your little plan has failed. Just the wolfblood isn't enough. It's the way you *wear* it. We've had centuries to wear it well. You've not even had an hourglass. Not enough time to even try and mimic us, Samantha. It knows, I'd wager. It knows you're not the real thing." He pauses, long enough to allow the reply he knows I don't have to make a loud noise in its absence.

"What, did you think this was your moment?" he continues. "Your grand finale? Did you think your brave stand meant something? You're not the hero, Sam, because there is no story. There is only *us*."

He turns to the assembled ring of bloodguards who have entered the chamber. "Take her away. She won't resist. She cares too much. She's drunk enough to be a goddess, but she forgot to dispel the woman from her first."

His reedy laughter rings in my ears as they take me, meek and placated, away from my stage.

30

Every Godsdamn Time

And then there was the great age of poison. That age is long gone, now the likes of ashcap and wolfsbane are vanishingly rare, but there was a span of years, from Lightfall's founding to the Twin War, when barely a meal or glass could be consumed by certain vampire nobles or wolf pack alphas without concerns over what little extra had been secreted within it.

Redtide Jarfast, *A Chronicell of Death*

Sam

So. I'm a prisoner once again. To be captured twice in two days seems a bit reckless. If I get out of this alive, which seems pretty unlikely now, I should probably do something about that. This time, I'm not alone, though. I have a wolf and two sorcerers with me. But I don't know if that will help the odds. Just like the dungeon room I was kept in last time while Rufous tortured me, this room has thick iron bars. But that's not the end of it. That's just a prison within a prison. Beyond the bars is the other half of the room, which ends in the thickest stone doors I have ever seen. It doesn't take a quickmind to work out that this room was designed for someone so high on wolfblood that they could smash thick stone with their fists if they tried hard enough. My fist-smashing days are over, though; it's been half a day since we were thrown in here. Lightfall has come and gone and now it's night again, and all the wolfblood in me that let me soar above the city for a few glorious moments has long since gone, leaving me with a dull throb in the head and a feeling that all the joy in the world has been sucked out of me. I try and remember the feeling I had, the certainty that everything I'd been doing wrong I would do right; but all I see is another failed way of thinking, more deceiving of the self, the image of myself all faded and twisted. It was still all about me, and I didn't help my friends at all.

If the wolfblood has sucked me dry of cheer, then my companions aren't exactly any better. At the moment, we're on the subject of death.

"If we die here . . ." begins Jacob.

"We're not going to die here," snaps Raven, who has been locked in a separate dungeon room from me, Jacob, and Sage, a mere ten feet away. This is presumably so I can't repeat my wolf-draining trick, but even with a whole wolf inside me I wouldn't be getting through the stone doors, so it's just a waste of a good dungeon.

Raven was given clothes by her jailers and is clearly not happy about it, scratching at her garments as if they have fleas. I don't see why she doesn't just take them off, but Raven's stubbornness rarely makes sense.

"At least *I'm* not going to die," Raven continues. "Not to these pathetic men of lavender and greed. You, on the other hand, are more than welcome to do so if you want it so badly, Jacob."

"As I was saying before Raven forgot she was locked up in a stone room surrounded by dozens of guards with wolfblood vials to hand," Jacob continues, "if we die here, do we all know where we go? Because it's something we should talk about. Might give us some cheer in our last few hours."

"*Your* last few hours, whiskey breath."

"Okay, fine, Raven. Let's imagine then that you find yourself in a much braver and more heroic situation where you were finally happy to die, then what I am *trying* to say is, where do you really believe you would end up? What about you, Sam?"

I turn to Jacob, who is sprawled across the floor of the cellar, his robe catching all the dirt on the floor but not really seeming to mind. "I don't know. I was raised to believe in the Bloodhalls and the Blood Gods, like most of this city, but it all seems . . . a bit too easy, I suppose."

"Easy?"

"Yes. I've always thought that. Even as a child, I always thought the vampire world beyond death seemed too simple. What do vampires love? Blood. What are you afraid of most if you are immortal? Surely it's dying, and losing all those potential centuries in the blink of an eye. So of course the afterlife is just drinking lots of blood and having life continue more or less as normal."

"I couldn't have said it better myself," says Sage, giving me another unearned compliment. He's been quiet these last few hours. I think the revelation that Lord Saxe turned the tables by simply admitting his plan to the rest of the council has got to him; he thinks he should have seen it coming. I told him that you can't predict the madness of the Lords, drunk on power and the thought of more of it. He just replied that there's no such thing as madness, it's just sanity from a different angle, which was such an expected response from him that it made me smile. I thought his annoyance at not getting everything right would itself get annoying. But the more I get to know him, the more I'm finding it a little bit endearing.

"So many of the afterlifes in the religions of the immortals are based on fear of something," Sage continues, "not the likelihood of what actually comes after. Take the Light of Luce, for example. The most common sorcerer religion is surely a result of the fact we don't know how we're born, or why, or what our magick is really for. So of course you die and follow the Light of Luce until you meet your maker, who gives you the real direction for your magick so you can start your life proper."

"So you live your life, then die, and then . . . start to live another life?" I ask.

"Yes, in a sense. Like this one is a trial run."

"What about wolves, then?" asks Raven. "Where is the fear in our life after death?"

"Ah yes, I know about this," says Jacob, clearly not having taken the hint earlier, "you turn into a tree, don't you?"

"What?"

"You turn into a tree."

"We do not turn into a fucking tree."

"I think," says Sage hastily, "that what Jacob is trying to say with astonishing ineptitude is that you believe, if I am correct, that upon the death of your body, your spirit dissipates among the land or nature, becomes part of it."

"Yes," says Raven, still glancing darkly at Jacob. "That is a fitting description. We lose ourselves to the forest, you might say. You are not aware of your own existence, merely that of the forest you are part of."

"It's very poetic," says Sage. "But I'm not sure I would like it myself. The awareness that I exist, self-consciousness, seems to be the most central thing to who I am. To not be aware of yourself at all, to just be part of something with no awareness of your part in it, I can hardly imagine it. I'm not sure I would like it at all."

Raven thinks on this awhile and then nods. "I know what you mean, sorcerer. You are not the first to put something like that to voice. But think on it like this: maybe you are so attached to your, as you say, sense of self only because you have never had anything else. In the same way that a fish in the sea can scarce imagine the desert, maybe you cannot understand it because it is not understandable the way you are. Maybe if you had always been in the form I speak of, then the idea of having a self and being aware of it would seem equally impossible."

"Not that they would think on it, because they wouldn't have a *they* to think," adds Jacob helpfully.

"A good point, mage," says Raven. "You are not always so stupid."

"Compliments don't sit right with you, Raven." Jacob grins back. "I think I prefer it when you're threatening to eat me."

There is silence then, the conversation on death having run itself out, same as our lives appear to have. I turn to my own thoughts, and I start to tick off my own life achievements.

My slightly disappointing list is interrupted by Jacob, who sighs loudly. "We're really going to die, aren't we?"

Sage looks at him. "Have you only just noticed? That last conversation didn't give you any hints, did it?"

"I'm serious, Sage. This is it, isn't it?" I wait for some wit, but none comes. "I wish . . . I wish I'd been a little less . . . a little less *me*. My life . . . what have I done? Shading nothing."

"You were my friend when I could have been alone," says Sage, his hood up so his eyes are hidden in its shade. "That isn't nothing. It was a lot, in fact, to me." Jacob looks at him, and then he grabs his hand, and I see his eyes are framed with tears. Raven and I find the grace to look away.

"It's funny," I say when enough time has passed, "I always had the certain feeling my story was a special one, that I was going to play a role in something big. But I was wrong."

"It's still not a bad story you've had," says Raven. "Better than most who come from Worntown."

"That's true. But it doesn't help. Not at all. That's bad, isn't it? I still want more. I thought I was . . ."

"Special?" says Sage.

"Yes. Pathetic as that sounds."

"Everyone's special to someone," says Sage, holding my glance. "I'm just as guilty," he says, quickly moving the moment on. "I thought I was going to change everything. Find out everything. The truth of it all. I'm a rational man, and I know I should believe in chance, not destiny, but I succumbed. Maybe humility is the final gift that life gives you. Everyone thinks they are the special one, don't they? The master of their own narrative. And when we're proved wrong, we wonder how we ever thought ourselves capable of such powers."

"What does that even mean?" asks Jacob.

"Well, I . . ." Sage begins. And then he laughs, loud and long. "I have no idea." And suddenly we're all laughing, laughing in the face of our end like we don't care at all.

Our hysteria is broken by a sudden high-pitched noise. I can't tell what it is, but I see Raven stiffening, her guard up, and that's when I realize why, because the whine is the noise of the stone doors slowly being levered open. We all stand then, ready for whoever or whatever is bringing our end. I'm expecting a whole regiment of guards to be behind that door; a whole regiment to march us to wherever we will be killed, ready to spear us if we make a move. In my mind's eye, I see it happening. Our deaths, again and again. Wolf and sorcerer and vampire together; it would be quickest to blow us up with firepowder. Or perhaps we'll be at the center of a nest of spears, stabbed and stabbed until no amount of blood or time or magick can heal the severed body parts. I always had a good imagination, and I'm imagining it all now.

But it isn't a regiment. It's a man. One man.

He's a bloodguard, and the three blood droplets stitched into his tabard tell me he's a captain. He's blond, with thin, neatly trimmed sideburns and notable creases on his forehead that shows he's a good century old, and not much of that time on good blood. He's sweating a lot, and he's armed not with a spear or sword, but simply a dagger sheathed in his belt. He approaches our bars cautiously, something in his hand, and stops still a good three feet from us.

"You're going to need a bigger blade," says Raven.

He doesn't reply, but opens his hand, to reveal something small and cylindrical wrapped in a piece of paper. Then he laughs, the laugh of a man who doesn't really care anymore, and he growls in a broad Southwestfall accent, "I fuckin' hope one of yous can catch." Then he throws the object through the bars and promptly turns away.

Raven sticks out her hand and grabs it from the air, and then when I turn my head again, I see the captain is running away, out the stone doors and down the corridor, quickly lost in the shadows—shadows that are dark but not so dark that I can't see the obvious lack of guards outside.

While Raven inspects the item and the piece of paper, I wait for the doors to swing shut again, even though there's no one there to operate the pulleys. After a few moments, I realize they're staying open.

"What in Light's name is this?" asks Jacob.

"It's how it begins," says Raven, and then turns to me, handing me what I see now is a vial of blood, wrapped in a note. "I think it's for you."

I take the blood and I read the note out aloud.

Thank you for devoting yourselves to the murder of my son. No one else did. As a token of my gratitude, your way out is clear. The rest of the guards whom I did not trust to obey my commands will be distracted by other events in the palace by the time you read this. I enclose some wolfblood for Samantha, in case you do need to fight. I trust the rest of you can look after yourselves. Yours, First Lord Vermillion Azzuri.

We look at one another and then at the open door beyond. "This is surely a trick," notes Jacob.

"How could this be a trick?" asks Raven.

"Simple. They convince us to escape, which gives them an excuse to execute us. Looks a little better for Ashen Ansbach and the Archmage— and anyone else who might take it badly if we're killed—if they pretend that we were only meant to be held for a while, but then things went a little awry in the escape."

"It's a very convoluted trick."

"But it's a possibility, right?"

"Potentially." He turns to me. "You were there in the council meeting. How did Azzuri look?"

I think on this. "He looked . . . haunted. Like he didn't want to be there. Like he wasn't there, in a way."

Sage nods. "That's good enough for me."

Jacob rolls his eyes. "Of course it is. So we're going to risk our lives because the First Lord looked a little peaky."

"It is a bigger risk if we stay here and wait to be killed, you would have to agree, mage?" says Raven.

"I'm just saying let's think about this."

As they continue to argue, I open the vial and down its contents. I wait a few seconds for the blood to hit. I feel its power, the tingle

I immediately get in the back of my throat and the pulsing sensation within me. It is stronger than a simple vial's worth. I feel it wake up the blood still in me, Raven's blood, and I realize it isn't all gone. It's still there, waiting to be revived.

Then I pull my fist back and let it loose on the bars. One goes, then the other, the bars snapping outwards like twigs against a strong gust of wind. I look at my fists in amazement. I wonder if you ever get used to this.

"Oh," says Jacob, staring at the gap in our prison. "So that's decided, then."

"Such strength. It's incredible," says Sage.

"Yes. And how many wolves have had to die to sustain it?" says Raven quietly.

"I'm fairly sure you killed some vampires in the process," I reply, with the fearlessness my new meal has given me. Before she can reply, I do the same to her bars, then step out and walk toward the doors. "That was quite loud," I say. "But no one has come. Azzuri has told the truth, so far."

"So far," says Sage.

"So what now?" asks Jacob.

I stare down the tunnel, leading to the Rose Garden and whatever else lies outside.

"We run."

First Lord Azzuri

I breathe in the bloodwine as if it's my last. I inhale its fumes, its sweetness, the metallic tang, the hint of wood underneath. I do not take a sip, though. Not yet.

Instead, I reflect on a memory of my son. It is strange how all these memories come out of the stonework when a loved one dies. Afraid to reflect on it, I buried this one in various places, and now, with the aroma of the blood hanging in the air, I take it in properly.

It is a memory from Grayfall. Not a time to be thinking of ever, but a fitting time to turn to now. I am running, running through my palace, desperately looking for my son, my youngest. My carriage awaits outside. We must go now, Redgrave says. Anything less will be our end. I am not flying, I say. I will not take wolfblood. I will not have my people, my desperate, fleeing people, see me and my kin airborne, speeding away from their ground flight, abandoning them in their time of fear. It would be the end of me and my family. It would do just as much harm to them as the Grays, in a way.

So instead my carriage awaits, but I cannot go because my son, the young Azzuri, Red, as he has taken to calling himself in what I can only assume is pure spite, a common tongue jestname to mock our class . . . my son is missing.

I race through the kitchens where he liked to be so often, talking with the blood servers. I race through the gardens where he spent so much time literally smelling the roses. I race to all his haunts, but he is gone. Then almost as an afterthought, I go to check to the cellars. There I find him coming up the stairway toward me, holding a cat in his hands. My sister's cat. My fury is incandescent. I tell him in no uncertain circumstances what I think of him for risking our entire family's safety for an animal, for an animal whose blood is barely ranked higher than cow. I let all my anger out on him and almost strike him; I have to hold myself back from throwing him down the stairs with his rescued beast. He doesn't reply; he just looks at me. He looks at me with that expression I could never understand, and we never speak of it again.

But now that I think on it, I remember the sheer joy of my sister when she was handed the cat. The tears that came, and the way she thanked him, like he'd saved her life ten times over. And when I think on it some more, I remember now why that cat meant so much to her. How my wife had procured it for her on a whim, part curious, I imagine, to see if she would drink it or care for it. How, when her betrothal was abandoned in such terrible circumstances, and she cried and cried for days in that room, how the only one she would talk to was the cat, her company for weeks until she came out of her gloom. Funny how I had never dwelled on it like this and thought on my son's actions. Except, of course, it is not so funny. Not at all.

My memory ends when I hear steps from outside my study. A knock on the door.

"Come in," I say. In walks Lord Saxe, his unruly hair even more askance than usual, the look on his face of a man juggling a thousand urns at once.

"You wanted to see me, First Lord?" he asks, with the not-so-subtle undertone implied: *You wanted to see me when I am busy fixing this city. How annoying.* He must think himself the center of everything now. I hope he enjoys the feeling while it lasts.

"Yes, I did, Cinibar. Thank you for taking time out of your preparations. I imagine there is a lot to be done before lightfall."

"Yes, indeed, First Lord. Several loose ends."

"Loose ends that you allowed to come untied," I say, swirling the wine coolly in the glass.

"I allowed it to get this far, yes," says Saxe, taking this attack fairly calmly, "but I will let it get no further."

It is funny how in such a time of emergency, certain men rise and others fall. I have been a ghost since I was told of the truth that my son waded into, by accident they say, and I have been allowed to become one. Now I haunt the corridors of my own palace, watching men of the hour come into their own.

"Have a glass of wine with me, Cinibar. It is a very good blood vintage. Magicked bear, twenty years old. When it comes to wine, I find that bear is better than stag. It ages more delicately. Less potent, of course, but more subtle."

"I . . . I would love to, First Lord, but there are matters—"

I cut him off. "I am still First Lord, am I not? I have not been abrogated my title in some additional plot of which I know not?"

Saxe recoils slightly at my directness, and for a rare moment he is lost for words. Alas, it does not last. "Of course," he says, his small beady eyes carefully watching me. "It would be an honor."

I pour him a glass and hand it to him. "A toast," I say. "To secrets laid bare, and the new world they have given us."

Saxe raises his glass with mine, and we drink. I savor the taste, let it swirl in my mouth: the acidity, the metal, the fruit, all hitting my tongue at different moments, and then the long finish when I finally swallow. I shall remember this, I have no doubt.

"You know, First Lord," says Saxe, "I feared you would struggle to see past the lies, and the, ah, violence it took initially for the plan to come to fruition. I want you to know that everything that has been said to you by Redgrave and by me is true about your son. It was an accident. But his sacrifice will not be in vain. Because of him, the leader of the Leeches is now dead, and we are now in control of the city even more than before. Enough to begin to think about the final stage and our return to the Centerlands, but with wolfblood for decades and a more pliant Worn population. If you think that's the right move, of course," he adds hurriedly. I can see he is tired. He would normally make his pretense to care about my wishes more convincing.

"Speaking of freedom," I say, ignoring his weasel words, "it is a feeling that comes with so many side effects. You realize what you are happy to give up, to defend what you really care about."

Saxe's expression is neutral. He is waiting until I reveal myself. He won't have to wait long.

"Do you know where I went while you've been running around cleaning up after your mess and trying to hold on to your secret? I went to Westfall. To one of my son's abodes. I found something you did not, some letters that confirm that my son and a bank clerk called Keepsake were . . . intimate. And that my son was wanting to know what was in the vault he was responsible for. Your vault."

Saxe's eyes narrow. He already suspects where this is heading. He really is very quick.

"You will know Keepsake, of course. The one viciously dispatched by Raven Ansbach to get the vault key prior to her raid on the bank. Well, in these letters was one that really stood out."

I reach into my undershirt and pull out a small collection of parchments tied together with string.

"Do you know what it said?"

"I do not, First Lord," says Saxe, carefully watching me, his smile replaced by a wary glare, his real visage shining through at last.

"It was a warning. A warning to my son."

Lord Saxe's face is fixed now, unmoving, his eyes barely blinking.

"You're going to make me spell it out, aren't you, Cinibar? Well, here it is. In a moment of weakness, Keepsake sent word to you that my son knew of the vault and the packages. That he was going over the wall to see for himself. He instantly regretted it, knowing what you would do. But he sent it nonetheless. And then he sent a letter to my son, warning him of his betrayal. That you were aware. But my son, my brave son, such bravery as I am only just realizing, *he went anyway.*"

I move slightly closer to Saxe. "An accident, you said. The Gray just happened to be there as my son went to inspect the package. That's what you said. Well, let us call it now for what it was. A plan. An order given by you. The girl was right. I waited all this time for someone to solve my son's murder. And now I have the proof myself."

I see Saxe consider this for a long time. Then something in his expression changes, and I can tell he is resigned to what is coming. It is like a shadow has passed over his face and left in its wake his real underbelly.

"He would have ruined us all," he begins. "You know now how close he was to the Worns. He would have spread word through the city and brought the bloody world down around us. It wasn't ideal, I know, but he was hardly one of your own. He hadn't been for decades. You don't have to be the spymaster to know that; *everyone* knows that. I mean, really, Vermillion, aren't you glad he was gone? He brought shame to the family. Consorting with coinboys and the like. Some of this I've kept from you, but you should have seen some of the people he fraternized with. *Sordid* doesn't even begin to describe it."

I stare at him and then at his wine.

"What would you have had me do?" he continues, to fill the silence I have gifted him. "Destroy us all to save your son?"

"Do you recall I spoke of freedom?" I reply, ignoring his question. "With freedom comes clarity. Clarity to see."

"To see what?" asks Saxe, who has begun to rub his right leg a little, as if in pain.

"To see the depths I failed my son."

"My legs . . ." says Saxe, sitting down suddenly. "They feel . . ." I see him thinking, I see that sharp brain thinking, and I know *what* he is thinking. He is thinking *What would I have done?* And suddenly he knows. And the knowing, even amid my personal agony—watching the knowing is delicious.

"Why?" he asks, trying to stand up but failing, rubbing his arms now.

"What you should really be asking, Cinibar, is *how*. How did I get ashcap? They got rid of most of it after the Twin War, just like the wolf-kind got rid of wolfsbane. But I kept some. Just as Ashen Ansbach kept some wolfsbane. We leaders need a method of last resort, I am sure you'll agree. There are ways to mask its scent, even for one on wolfblood, even from a wolf's nose."

During my speech, Saxe has attempted to get off his chair, but ashcap works fast and he finds himself now a cripple. He touches his face, which is slowly succumbing, too. He manages to speak, to move his lips even as his expression becomes fixed.

"But the city," he says hopelessly.

"Are you going to pretend this is for First Light? We're not Worns. We're the same, remember. We're nobility. I know who this was really all for."

"You doom yourself by doing this." Every word is slurred now.

I shrug. "Oh, I'm already doomed." I point to my wineglass. "We're on the same vintage today, Cinibar. I put a heavier amount in yours so it would act quicker, of course. I'm sure you wouldn't deny me my final dramatic speech."

"Why?"

"You would not understand. I don't think you are built for it. There are words for what you are, but I am not sure they have been invented yet. You are power and pain, and all the rest of it. I am not perfect myself, I see that far too late, but I do not think we can even have a conversation that would make us understand each other. So just go ahead and die, and let everything you have done unwind itself."

He tries to reach out, but he cannot move now, and as he sits there and breathes his final breaths, I slowly walk over to him and lean down until my mouth is next to his ear. "To answer your question from earlier. Would I destroy us all for my late son? *Every godsdamn time.*"

Then my spymaster's breath stops completely, his organs and skin hardened as wood, and he lies there as a puppet lies on its master's chair.

I can feel my legs starting now. Funny how it always starts with the legs. I take a seat at the end of the table opposite Saxe. How funny the scene will be when Redgrave walks in. Two rag doll wooden corpses sitting as if at dinemeal. That is my revenge for my first man, for failing me when I needed him. To find his old friend like this. Redgrave is not Saxe. His guilt will follow him through the centuries.

I drink the rest of the wine. No point in wasting it. Then I close my eyes and wait. In my mind's eye, I can see my son already, see him in the Bloodhalls waiting for me. There is no barrier between us now, no words left unspoken or said in anger. We can talk with nothing around us, we can talk like men, and then when we find that ridiculous, we can talk as people, seeing the truth of each other. We can talk and talk, and let the others say what they will.

I have so many questions to ask him.

I open my eyes to the sensation of someone trying to force liquid down my throat. I cannot move the rest of my body.

I am not entirely sure this is the Bloodhalls.

As my eyesight focuses, I see Redgrave, tipping a vial of a greenish substance into my mouth. It is not blood; aside from the color, it tastes of bitter leaf and dewed grass.

"Thank the gods," he says, red-faced, more lustered than I have ever seen. "This was a foolish move, Vermillion, if you don't mind me saying so. Very unlike you."

"No," I say weakly, trying to grab him, but as I slightly tip my hardening head, I see my limbs are still rigid. Something in me acquiesces and I let the liquid fall down my throat.

"I must die, Redgrave. You do not understand. I am just as responsible as Saxe. I must . . ." The last few words crumble into the air as my tongue hardens, too. Whatever this potion is being forced down my throat, it is surely too late.

Redgrave sees me lose my voice and grimaces.

"You cannot speak, my lord, so let me speak for you. You do not want to die. You think you do, because you feel guilt. Who in our long lives of centuries has not felt such guilt for someone? But you will come around, Vermillion, and you will be grateful I saved you. Because we did not survive the war, we did not survive Grayfall, we did not keep the whole city from tipping over into revolution just to see it burn now. And mark my words, old friend, Saxe's companions and his converts will see it burn. They will overplay their hand, and the Worns will rise up, and then the whole city will bleed. I followed you because you were good at maintaining balance, and I have seen to my cost what a lack of balance brings. And I will continue to follow you. I will certainly not follow them."

If I could speak, I would tell Redgrave that this is the most emotion I have seen in him for centuries. But for the moment he unquestionably has the floor.

"If you still want to die in a year, I will not stop you. But you do not die today. This salve will take effect—you can thank my time in Dawn Death for that, they have cures for all ailments there, or they *had*—and we will flee before they discover what you did, and we will find those of your class and . . . others . . . who do not want madness and chaos and we will wait and we will regroup, Vermillion."

Something else I would say, I think, my head groggy and my thoughts awhirl, is that he has not called me my choicename for centuries.

"And another thing. You won't be First Lord anymore," he says, reading my thoughts, "so I will be a lot more forthright in saying what I think." He pauses and suddenly grabs at his top lip. "And I might shave off this buggering moustache."

I want to smile at that, even in my half death, but my face is still rigid, so I wait stiff as a plank with my friend for my life to return to me.

31

You May as Well Do Something

Unlike the Flight Guard, the only other vampires in First Light regularly allowed wolfblood these days, the First Guard train with wolfblood in them constantly, not just in flight. They are used to its ways—not just the strength and speed and the rest it gives you, but the other effects that some feel on it, too—the sense of time slowing, the sense of battle tactics of fights only watched, not fought previous, and of course, the sense of fatality it bestows upon you.

Redflash Quickchange, *The Guard After Grayfall*

Sage

The bells begin shortly after our escape. Azzuri was true to his word; our path is clear. No guards in the catacombs. No guards in the Rose Garden, where the catacombs end. No guards when we jump the palace wall, Sam springing me and Jacob over in one leap. No guards as we cross the road into the woods; just the far-off shouts of commotion as Azzuri's distraction works its magick.

As we flee through the woods, imagining half of First Light on our tail, I think on our route. It's a simple, unbroken path that snakes from the north side of the palace eastward, all the way to Northeastfall. We can get almost to the northeastern border without having to break the tree cover. Beyond that lies the relative safety of the Borderlands, with thicker forest and routes that Raven knows, routes that cross Extinction Valley and into the Wolflands. Once we're there, we really are safe.

I calculate the odds of us making it. They are poor. Even with the distraction, the bloodguards must be on our trail by now. And while the border is a full hour away at a quick run, it occurs to me that Sam on her wolfblood and Raven at her full wolf pace could make it quicker, and that we are slowing us down. It must have occurred to them too. But no one says a word about it, and I realize that I am not among mere conspirators anymore. I might just be among friends. Jacob will be pleased. He always says I should get more than one.

Somehow, despite my reservations, we get within a quarter glass of the thick forest lining the edge of Northeastfall, where the woods end and the Borderlands begin. We reach a small clearing and take a brief rest before the final rush to the forest. Clouds have scuttled in front of the moon and I can barely see in front of me. The air here is crisp and I breathe it, slow and calm, trying to still the panic humors surging through my veins. Beyond the clearing to the south are the fields that lead to the Lords' houses of Northeastfall. If I were to follow that route we would end up at Lady Hocquard's within half a glass.

"Almost there now," says Raven, who has stayed in person form to run with us, no doubt hardly worth the bother of changing into wolf at our pace. Her nudity is not unusual now; even Jacob has stopped look-ing. Most of the time. "Once we hit the border properly," she continues, "we will be almost completely safe. Any bloodguards or Lords chasing us will have no chance of success. I know the forests there better than anyone alive."

"Being half drained of your blood has not dented your confidence, I see," says Jacob.

"No. It's not dented my appetite either," she snarls at Jacob, although her heart's not in it. She is more tired than she is letting on from the running, her brow covered in a light patina of sweat.

I start to ask her if she's okay, but I'm distracted by Sam, who has turned back the way we came and is staring at the sky.

"Sam, what are you . . ."

"Oh, crikes," she says, and then turns back to us and mouths just one word.

"*Wings.*"

I stare at the patch of sky where she is looking, but I can't see anything at first. But then I'm not on wolfblood. A few moments later, though, I see winged figures in the sky, flying low over the woods about a mile away. For a second I hope they might just be eagles, flown over from the mountains, but from the look on Sam's face, I realize we're not going to be that lucky. Moments later I see what she does: flying toward us, in a perfect V-formation of leather wings and full-blooded armor, is the entirety of the palace First Guard, all twenty of them, their red-and-gold tabards outlined in blue, their wings a deeper black against the night sky.

"Well, what are we waiting for?" cries Jacob. "Let's shitting run for it."

"We wouldn't make it to the forest," says Raven. "They're coming in fast. Besides, I have never run from a fight and I am not running now. There are twenty of them. I have fought much larger numbers of bloods and won."

"These are First Guard, Raven," I point out. "The most well trained in the city. The First Lord's own. Furthermore, they'll be on a considerable amount of wolfblood to have flown this far after us. You're still weak."

"Which will ensure it is not over too soon, like all good fights," she replies, but I spy a flash of concern on her face. "Besides," she continues, "I will have Sam with me. She is a fighter like me, I fancy, with the wolfblood still in her." She turns to Sam and gives her a toothy smile. "What do you say, Samantha Ingle, do you want to stand with a wolf against your own kind?"

Sam grins. "I thought you'd never ask," and I see with a tight spasm of despair that wolfblood is giving her courage over wisdom.

I turn to Jacob, who is looking pale. "What do we do?" he asks.

For a second I want to volunteer to stand with them, to fight to protect Sam, even with literally no tricks up my sleeve and no hope of physically matching them. But I've always found that line of thinking as embarrassing as it would be offensive to Sam. "Jacob, old friend, we stay the Light out of their way."

"I was really hoping you'd say that."

The winged vampires land at the edge of the clearing, fast and hard; they fold their wings in almost at once, coordinated. I marvel that they can stop in time at that speed. The dynamics of the movement of vampires in flight is fascinating, almost impossible, and I make a mental note to write on this a little, and then I remember that it's still odds-on that I might have done my last scribing.

"Stand away from me, Sam," says Raven, cracking her knuckles. "If you get a chance, hit them."

"How?" asks Sam.

"You fought Rufous for a while, did you not? And you got a couple of hits in. Do that again. This time without the losing."

"Right. Thanks for that."

Then as the guards approach, Raven transforms, giving me another taste of the demented shadow play of fur and flesh that I don't think I can ever get used to, and I stand back and mouth a prayer to any gods listening, whether or not I believe in them.

Sam

The First Guard go straight for Raven. She was right. I am nothing to them. They circle the Midnight Assassin, in a crouch, talons at the ready. Two step forward. Two more circle behind her. I wonder that they don't rush at her at once, but when I see the looks on their faces, I understand why. Cocksure. The alphas of the pack. They want the glory of taking down a legend.

Raven growls at the front two, then turns her head a little to look at the others. She stands taller than any of them and wider than all four put together. I honestly don't know how this will go.

It goes like this. Raven ducks just as the two to her rear thrust their talons her way. They lose their footing a little, and Raven extends one huge paw, knocking them off their feet with a mighty swipe. The two to her front attack as she does so, raking claws aiming for her face, but Raven, restoring the balance after her attack, leaps nimbly to the side, as if she's made of air, not two hundred pounds of wolf. Landing on her front two paws, she spins round and leaps again, this time on the two who've just gained their footing; one of their jaws ends up in her jaw and she bites down quick and hard. There's a muffled scream and I hear, with all the clarity of my better wolfblood hearing, his nose and ears slough off with her teeth. She moves to do the same to his comrade, but the two with the talons have now recovered from their miss and have stuck their claws in her side. I see those small yellow wolf eyes of hers narrow, and I know it's more in anger than pain, and as she shakes off the now-faceless guard, she barrels into the others, knocking them to the ground. She swipes one massive paw at one of their faces and takes off their jaw, knocking it into the face of the other. While the jawless one stays frozen in shock, tongue lolling helplessly in the new space where the lower half of his face used to be, Raven uses the brief moment of pause to focus on the other, the one who couldn't help but turn and stare at the arc of his comrade's jaw through the air. He regrets this im-mediately as Raven barrels him to the ground and rips out his throat.

And that is when the rest of the guards decide that their strategy needs more refining, and six more rush at her. She leaps in one bound over them, swiping her paw at the side of the face of one as she does so. One is quick, however, and when she lands, he twists round and in one fluid motion shoots his fist into her solar plexus and extends his claws as he does so, raking a deep gash in her side. The other four, minus the one trying to stick the side of his cheek back on, join in the attack, and for a brief moment it seems as if they will all descend on her at once, but she bounds to the side, and circles back once more, backing off and eyeing them with new murder in her eyes.

She's going to lose.

The thought comes to me then, clear as night. A wolfblood thought. I see the fight play out, see all the moves. For a second I feel a shift in my perception of time—is this the wolfblood, is this how I think now?—and I see myself at the end of the fight, a wolf before me, corpse on the ground.

I spy the remaining eight guards circling Raven, wondering when to join in, trying to calculate the danger of confusing the fight for their comrades against giving them enough support.

What if they all rush me? I can't fight. The defeat by Rufous proved that.

You've taken more wolfblood than them and their vials. You still have half of Raven inside you. You just don't know how to use it. Stop thinking, Sam. You know your problem? You're always thinking.

Shut it, me.

I'll shut up. If you start up.

Oh well, I reason. I wanted a better life. I wanted my destiny. Time to see what I am made of, literally. I close my eyes. I try and feel the blood within me, deep in my veins. I breathe out. I refine my senses. The tang of the forest air. The fear and sweat, tasting . . . is that lemons? Focus. Calm. Nothing matters, the wolfblood tells me. That's the truth of it. Nothing matters. So you may as well do something.

I run, screaming, a throaty yell that comes out in two pitches, tenor and soprano all at once. The vampires not fighting Raven turn to look at me, noticing me properly for the first time. The nearest one smiles. He has short dark hair and a small, groomed beard, and I note that the color matches the dark streaks of fur among the leathered skin on his folded wings. The one next to him is tall, surely six foot seven at least, and he sports high cheekbones, a little goatee, and dark, mousy blond hair tied back in a ponytail.

When I get to them, their look of amusement showing no sign of washing off, I feint to the left, and I connect an uppercut to the jaw of the dark-haired one, giving it all my force. He grunts and falls back a little, and then as the other one reaches for me, I chop a hand at his throat.

That's it, says the voice in me, my voice, but also that of the wolf-blood. *You remember how a maid defended herself once. Hit the windpipe. Run away. Use everything you've ever seen. Let the blood do the rest.*

I chop again harder, and he falls to the floor gasping for air. I turn to face them once more, bidding them to try again.

More have noticed me now, and one says, voice poisoned honey-soft, "A little Worngirl with the blood of wolves. How fucking sweet." Then he runs at me, extending his talons. I wait and I wait and I see him running, but slower, and I realize that time is my plaything now. I stop and stare up at the sky and I admire the moon, coming out of the clouds, and for a brief moment the moon tells me that all things shall pass, all will die one day, but the moon will still be there.

Then he reaches me and I step to the right at the last second, and I thrust my arm into his side and feel around for what's in there, all the soft things of his life and his organs, and I squeeze, and he screams and falls to the floor.

I turn to the others. Ten are circling me now. The one whose throat I gave a good working over has recovered and joined them. He scowls at me, a little hoarse. "And what do you make of these odds then? How are you going to take us all on, girl?"

"This girl doesn't have to," I reply, wiping some blood off my lips that isn't mine. "She just has to keep you distracted long enough." Then he turns and sees Raven. She's finished with the others and she's still standing. She has several wounds in her side and she's slower now, but she still has the element of surprise. She grabs his torso and rips longways, rips until it comes apart, the meat and tubes of either end falling onto the ground as the guard looks on in shock at both his halves.

I take that as my cue and I charge at the one next to him. I hammer my fist into his solar plexus, but it's harder than I thought, whether he's on more wolfblood than the rest I don't know, and he smiles and sticks one taloned fist straight into my shoulder. I choke, blood flying out of my mouth as I bite my tongue in shock. I don't feel pain, not that much anyway, but my arm goes numb for a second, and the reality of the battle and what it will do to me hits home.

Everything comes to an end, says the doom of the wolfblood. *All things die. It was a good effort.*

Shut up, me. Not the time for this. But as he raises his fist again, I know the wolfblood speaks true, because I can't move my right arm anymore, and I stare at the large hole his claws have made. But as his next blow comes, I find the wherewithal to duck, and I roll into him, taking him to the ground with me. I punch and I punch with my left arm as he rakes his claws down my side. I can't feel it but I can hear the blood, smell my blood, sense the arc of its droplets to the ground. So I punch harder, punch his nose, put all my fist into it, and I smash it into a different shape and he roars with pain. Aha, I think, you've not taken enough. You still feel it. And I laugh, a sort of crazy laugh, and I tell him how nice the moon is tonight, and didn't he know he was going to die?

But then two of his friends launch themselves at me and it doesn't seem so funny anymore.

Sage

They are fading, any fool could see that. I'm a little less than a fool, so I watch their movements more closely. I see Raven reacting a little more slowly to each attack. I see Sam working miracles, her untrained self against the finest of the guards. But her fights are to maim, not to kill. I turn to Jacob and come to the only logical conclusion.

"They're going to lose," I say.

"So we help them," replies my deputy, who has ventured from his hiding place behind a bush to offer his tactical acumen.

"With what?" I ask.

"You know well," says Jacob. "I know you have it. Have one of them, anyway."

I am quiet for a moment. "If I did," I say slowly, "do you not think I would have used it on the roof, when our lives were in danger?"

"At the last moment, maybe. But only if death was certain. I know you. Your self-control."

I inhale sharply, preparing for the spar to come.

"You know that's not a serious proposition."

Jacob snorts. "I know that the wolf who saved my life and the girl you're so fond of, even though you won't admit it, are about to be killed."

"Yes. Which is why we must run now."

"You. Are. Not. Shading. Serious," says Jacob, an octave lower and finding some gravel to go in there, too.

"It's the only logical choice, Jacob. We can't save them. There is no point being captured or killed and having everything go to waste."

"Yes, exactly, you massive prickard, which is why we use the third option, where you ruin their shading day."

I sigh. "What don't you understand about this, Jacob? If I do what you're suggesting, everything we've been trying to do is ruined. Gone."

"It might not be. They might not notice."

I stare at him.

"Okay," he says. "They might notice."

"You don't think I want to help?" I continue. "You don't think this is going to haunt me for the rest of my days? But there are other things that will haunt me more. The world burning. The world burning because of *us*."

Jacob bats my words away with his hand as if they're flies. "So? It's going to happen anyway. The Lords found the weapons under Lightfall. Don't you think they already suspect? They can't all think it's some gift from the Blood Gods or whatever. Once their plans are furthered, they'll come for the other things. They'll put two and two together and our temple will be done four."

Despite myself I grin at the pun, so esconced in gallows humor that I can't tell if I'm smiling or gurning, and then I turn back to the fight, which cuts my grin off at the waist. One of the guards has caught Sam in a headlock and is beating her in the ribs. She uppercuts him, and then Raven comes in and slices his head open. There are only seven guards left, but Raven half stumbles when she lands, her movement difficult, and Sam is bleeding. Sam is bleeding quite a lot.

Then I turn back to him. "A war, Jacob. If we reveal ourselves. There'll be a war with the kind of things that don't leave the place the same when the war's over."

"You don't know that."

"I do. As do you."

Jacob scowls. "Well, at least don't pretend this is you being noble. I know you too well. You just want to work out all the secrets yourself. You've always been bad at sharing. Classic only child."

"All sorcerers are only children, Jacob, and my motivation doesn't change the outcome."

There is a brief silence. Sam has blood running all down her legs now. I can't look away.

"What's the point," says Jacob, lapsing into wolf cursing for the first time in a long while, "of saving the fucking world if you can't save your fucking friends?"

I don't reply. Sam is jumping back from a guard now, every step painful. Raven is distracted by the rest who are circling her, sensing her end, grinning.

"She's going to die, Sage."

"She might not."

"She's going to die, and it'll be your fault."

Nothing.

"She's going to die on this hill, and all that's good and remarkable will die with her, and I'll never forgive you, and you'll never forgive yourself."

It was there, for a second. Heat, in my brain. The death of reason. The start of something more.

"By the Light of Luce, she's going to *die.*"

Ah. There it is.

I throw my cloak to the ground, leaving me in my undershirt, but not before I reach into a hidden fold in the cloak and take out a small black metal cube.

I turn to Jacob. "You're a very bad influence on me, have I ever mentioned that? Everything that happens from here on in, I blame on you."

Jacob sticks his tongue out. "Oh, by the five magicks, just get on with it already."

I grimace and stare at the cube. If you were never going to use it, I think . . . why did you bring it with you? You gave one of these to Sam. Yes, but that wasn't . . . this one. Ah, Sage, I finish, tired of my inner dialogue. Don't pretend you haven't wanted this for as long as you can remember.

Then I throw the cube into the air, and I click my fingers.

Nothing happens.

"It doesn't always work the first time," says Jacob from behind me.

"You haven't tried it. Only I have," I say, narrowing my eyes at him.

Jacob thinks on this. "If I had to guess, from definitely never having tried it behind your back, then I would guess that it doesn't always work the first time."

I pick the cube up and try again.

This time, on the click, it happens. A stream of metal, solid but flowing, shoots out from it and envelops me like a second skin. It's black and glistening, and when it hits my skin, the cold leaves me breathless. I am covered in it, head to toe, skin to skin, entombed. For one horrible, claustrophobic moment I wonder if something has gone wrong.

But then I feel it loosen from its grip on my skin and harden and thicken; I feel the gaps form between it and my skin, and soon it has solidified into a hard metal casing covering my entire body. My blindness is cured by a small rectangular window of light in what is now, I suppose, my helmet, and I move forward in my new armor, feeling how effortlessly light it is, yet hearing the heavy steps on the ground as I move forward. Dimly, I hear Jacob in the background, laughing, I think, maybe whooping, but all I am focused on is Sam, surrounded now, bathed in blood.

I clench my fist, my metal fist. And then I break into a run.

Sam

I hear it first, my senses keen; then I feel the vibrations along the ground. I pause in the arc of my fist, and the bloodguard stops as well. I turn to see where the vibrations are coming from, and my mouth drops open in shock, my fangs retreating a little in sheer awe at the sight. A figure is running my way, encased in black armor—smooth metal, but I can't see any joins. The metal covers his head, all except for a small rectangle of glass that I can't see through. I look beyond him at where he came from, and I see Jacob back beyond the trees, smiling. And then my wolfblood kicks in, giving me a wolf's nose, and I know it's Sage in that metal man. And he's not coming to parley.

He hits the first bloodguard like a wolf against a hutwall. The guard's skin must be fairly hardened, not as tough as mine but still strong, but when the armor hits him at full pelt, he falls like all his bones are broken, and then Sagebeast simply walks over him. A great metal foot comes down on his head and crushes it like a distended grape.

The next of the First Guard closest to Sagebeast stares at him for a moment, with the look of a man who's having to come to terms with something whose terms have never been introduced to him before. Then he does something clever, and he leaps nimbly over the metal man, landing behind him and extending his claws out to the maximum the wolfblood gives him, which is very long indeed. Then he claws at

Sagebeast's back, and I understand his plan: he seeks to get under this armor and at the precious skin underneath.

But there aren't any gaps in this armor, and there are no rivets to take apart or seams to make short work of. The back's as smooth as the front, and slowly, inexorably, Sagebeast turns to face the guard as he hopelessly claws at the metal. There's a moment then, perhaps drawn out, or perhaps it's the strange time of the wolfblood making it seem to me like it's drawn out, but it goes on for an age, it seems like. *This is a possible future,* says the wolfblood in my head, *confronting the past.* Whatever that means. But then the moment ends, and I reckon that's a look of resignation on the First Guard's face as Sagebeast's fist comes crashing into it, smashing into the bone like a hammer into a grape. The faceless guard falls to the floor, head hanging half off his neck.

All the remaining guards have turned to face Sage now, the six with Raven and the remaining one with me. They exchange glances, looking for a clue on one another's faces as to how to take on an enemy they've never seen before, and they do exactly what I would do; they leap simultaneously up into the air, wings carrying them high in an instant, soaring in formation. Their intent is obvious. Dive down, all at once. Aim for the helmet, if that's what it is. Hope it's weak.

There's a sound of hard wing and hard flesh hitting metal, and I've never heard such a sound before so I can't describe it, and I can't describe the sight, either, because it's just a blur of leather and flesh and red and gold and black sheen. But when everything comes to a halt, I see the guards lying around Sagebeast, stunned, and the beast itself, though staggered a little, is completely unharmed, the armor catching a little of the moonlight and winking at me.

To their credit, though, they don't remain floored for long, and they quickly return to the sky, back to their formation. My wolfblood tells me that repeating a failed plan is not the best of strategies, but they don't have as much of it in them as me, so I won't judge them too harshly.

But as the First Guard descend once more, I see the Sagebeast's metal head look up to gaze at them. Then he raises a hand, and for a second it looks like he's pointing to the guards—an old giant in a new world, seeing the sights.

Then small holes open up in his fists and the bullets pour out of them, aimed straight at the winged guard, whistling through the air. Some puncture the wings of the guards on their descent down, some shoot straight into their heads, and some nestle themselves in their limbs. But none miss their target. And when the guards land, it's not in the deadly dive they'd planned, but with speed. They hit the ground in a radius around Sagebeast with a sickening thump and lie there, panting, broken, purple lines shooting out from where the bullets have hit, whether wing or face or eye or arm, just like the bullets of the Grays.

"Shoot them again, Sage," I say. "Or whatever you are now. Shoot them again."

I mean it as a mercy. No matter the intent of the vampires smoldering away before us, they don't deserve the final minutes of torture as the poison prepares their body for ash.

Sagebeast strides toward them and raises his fist again at the mound of near corpses, and he pumps more bullets into them, and at some point in the thunder of metal their bodies get the message and a great explosion of ash mushrooms up into the air before falling gently to the floor.

Then Sagebeast steps back, and the metal slips away, river-like, retracting itself from his skin and shooting itself, like a stream sucked into a tiny hole, into a cube that has detached itself and now hangs in the air. The cube falls to the floor and Sage, normal Sage, notably less metal Sage, stands there, panting.

"Well," says Raven, who at some point during the fight noticed she was not needed anymore and shifted back to human, "that's just cheating."

"I realize you may have some questions," Sage begins, but he stops and looks at my wounds: the deep cut in my arm, a gash across my cheek, my likely broken jaw, the wounds on my side where I think half my ribs are broken. "You're hurt, Sam," he says, reaching out to touch me, but stopping when I flinch away, still unsure of it all.

"I am," I reply. "But I won't be soon. Wolfblood heals very fast."

"Good." Sage nods. "Because we need to go soon. It will take the normal guard longer to get here, but we don't know how many will take wings, too, so we may not have as long as we think. More important, I am out of, uh, bullets in my, um, armor."

"We go when you explain, Sage." It comes out colder than I intended, with all the timbre of the wolfblood, and he backs away a little, seeing something older in my eyes, maybe.

"For Shade's sake, tell them," says Jacob, who has walked over now, keeping a close eye on the pile of ash as if it might re-form. "No point hiding anymore."

Sage sighs. "What's that old saying? The weight of a secret is heavier than gold."

"You just made that up now."

"This," says Sage, ignoring Jacob and holding the cube outstretched in his palm, "is mortal technology. A weapon of the mortals."

"You don't say," says Raven. "Well, I didn't think that was fucking vampire armor you had on."

Sage looks at her. "What?"

Raven shrugs. "The Grays fire impossible weapons. It makes sense that there is more of the impossible out there. May as well be the mortals of myth."

He turns to me. "How about you, Sam?"

I think on it. "That cube you gave me. In the bank. Mortal as well?"

"Yes."

"And do you have many of these?"

"We have thousands. Some of these. Some of the other. And other weapons still."

There is a silence at that. My wolfblood ears hear a fox cry a half mile away, perhaps escaping a bleeding.

"What about when we were imprisoned, awaiting likely execution?" I ask eventually. "A destructive suit of armor might have been useful then."

"Our death wasn't assured. I thought we still had a chance. And I turned out to be right." He winces even as he says this, realizing that this is not the time to be promoting his predictive skills.

I stare at Sage, this liar before me. He smells . . . scared. He smells ashamed of his lie to me. Shame, I discover, is meaty, savory.

"Should I be . . . afraid . . . of you?" I ask.

"Sam, listen to me. I have lied. No question of that. I have lied to many." He looks away from me and focuses on the trees. "But it was worse lying to you."

That makes me feel better. I don't show that it does, though.

"The Cult of Humanis," he continues. "We're not just pastcrafters. We're protectors, in a way. We protect the world against these things that would destroy it. There are caches under all the cities of old. Underneath Shadowfall, Dawn Death, Lightfall, Luce . . . We've found as many as we could. Not enough, as you see from the plans of Saxe. But we've kept them. To explore, yes. To study. But to hide as well." Sage sweeps his arms out, taking in all of First Light, at least what we can see from the hill we're on. "You've seen the chaos that Saxe has caused with his bullets and guns that must surely be mortal, too. Can you imagine what he would do with impenetrable armor and the weapons within it? Thousands of these? Or how about a pissed-off wolfpack?" He bows his head. "If it makes you feel better, you're the first outside the cult to be told. It's an honor, really."

"Honored, eh?" I say.

"I mean . . . uh . . ."

"Light of Luce, he's a moron," mutters Jacob behind him.

"It's okay," I say, allowing myself a small conciliatory grin. "This is me making a jest. You're still very gullible, I see."

"I am sorry, Sam. If I'd known we'd be in such danger—"

"You still would've waited until the last possible moment, and that is just your nature," I reply.

"I . . . suppose," says Sage, wearing his glumness well.

"But you saved my life," I add, and I punch his arm playfully.

"Uh . . . ow."

"Sorry. Forgot how strong I am on wolfblood."

"This is lovely," says Raven. "It warms my heart. But we should definitely go now."

"Oh, don't be going on my account," says a voice behind me, and as the words ring out, I remember something that should've been obvious . . . we just killed the First Guard, but their leader wasn't there.

"In fact, what say you never go anywhere again?" says Rufous, walking out from the trees behind us with the widest grin you ever did see.

32

Rumspringa

Every person has a choice to make at some point: Are they special or not? Are they the author of their own story or do they just wish they were? Much happiness and contentment of yourself and others depends on such a choice. Make it well.

Kinet Kandarillion,
Of Existence and the Self

Sam

I feel my whole body go tense when Rufous Azzuri walks out of the tree line into the clearing to face us. People talk of hair standing on end; well, I can feel my damn veins standing on end, like the remains of the wolfblood within me are trying to burst their way out. He's dressed the same as when he killed Beth just three days ago: the same red and gold tabard with the extra blue; the same black velvet gloves. Even his shoes are the same and I smell tiny spots of Beth's blood still on them, a gift from the wolfblood, a reminder of my rage. His hair is untied and flowing around that golden face of his. His wings are half folded behind his back, but I can see the long streak of blond fur that runs down them. Most of all, he still has that look on his face: the look of a man who walks through life, taking from it like a feast. A man born into his role who's never had to take it off for a second.

I imagine I also look no different to him from when he last saw me. But I'm not. I'm not at all. Last time the wolfblood added to my rage and my grief, the image of Beth's mangled face and bones dancing through my skull. But I have it tamed now, or at least I've fought a little with it in me and spent a little time in its care, and just like it told me how self-absorbed I was, it's now telling me that my anger will get me nowhere. But what do you have when you give up your anger? What am I, without my rage?

"Little maid, little maid," Rufous says, chewing over his words, enjoying them. "It seems we are destined to meet over and over again. I could not kill you last time, as you had information. But now you have nothing to offer me. Nothing in the world. Now, I fear, we fight for your life."

"Fine by me," I say, letting the wolfblood have its way with me.

"You see, Samantha, little Samantha from Ashfall Lane, I know you yearn to be more. You are different from most of them, I see that now just as I did on that day I first met you. You are different from most of your poor pathetic kind, scrabbling around in the dirt, growing wrinkles while we pass centuries unchanged. You want to take your life in your own hands and not accept your fate. I can respect that a little. But ultimately, I am afraid, it is pointless. Is it not more noble, in the end, to accept who you are? More noble to accept the comfort of never having to make anything of yourself?"

"Well, look at that," I reply. "You have a philosophy. And there's me just thinking you were a cunt."

He laughs at this and extends his claws farther. "I can be that as well, if you like, little maid."

I see Sage and Jacob behind me, hesitant, wondering what to do. Raven tries to stand up, but she is still shaky.

"No," I call to them. "This is me and him."

"That's the wolfblood talking, Sam," calls Sage.

"No. No, it's not. It's me."

Rufous circles me, stretching out his wings and his claws, smiling. Then, just as in our fight before, I run toward him and pull back a fist and aim it at his rib cage. And, just like before, he isn't standing there; he's leapt back in anticipation and awaits my next move, his grin unchanging. I go to punch him again, and once again he leaps out of the way.

"Experience," he murmurs. He's playing the game, too. His point is as obvious as it is boring. Our fight will never change, and neither will I. I play along, because why not? I extend my nails to talons and slice them through the air hesitantly. Am I a claw fighter? Or do I use my fists? I've not had enough time to work it out. I advance and go to feint, knowing he will remember this from last time, but I sashay to the right, a side step, but he has anticipated this, too, reaching out to grab me and flip me to the ground, then hammering his fist into my chest. I can't breathe, but I still roll away in time to avoid the razor-sharp edges of his wing, which come slicing down where I was a moment ago.

"She has learned a little," he says, his tone of admiration cutting into me more than his claws ever could. I think on my next move, but as I do so, he launches himself at me, pirouetting as he moves, each spin accompanied by a slice of his wings, a tornado of razor-edged leather. I'm surprised by the speed, and I back away in time, but the edges of the wings catch me as they go past and gash me in my left arm. Even on my strong wolfblood skin, the cut is deep. The wings must be that sharp. I try and lash out at him as he storms past, but he's too quick.

And that's when I realize that although I'm better than the last time I fought—more wolfblood, less nerves—I'm still not him. He has training. We are not in a stagetale where the underbeast wins. I don't have an edge; I don't have time to get one.

I listen to the voice telling me all this, the wolfblood truth putting doom into my veins. Then I tell it to calm itself. I try and think without its brutal honesty in my head. I look at my skin; then I look at Rufous. He clearly drank a lot of wolfblood before this fight, more so than the rest of the First Guard. But not as much as me. He didn't drink half a wolf a day ago. My skin looks stronger; it glows more, faintly yellow, like the sun itself is trying to burst out. Not as much as when I drained Raven originally. But enough. It means I can take more damage.

So I do. I go to uppercut his chin, but he grabs my arm with his right hand, and with his left he sinks his talons into my upper shoulder. I look; the wound is shallow. I was right. I am weaker. But I am still strong.

I headbutt his chest and he recoils a little, mainly out of surprise. Then he retracts his claws from my shoulder and punches me in the gut, so hard I lift off and land heavily on my back. He leaps into the air then, using his wings to give him extra lift, and he launches himself at me with both claws outstretched, aiming for my neck. I roll aside in time, but not enough to avoid the sideward slice of his wing, which cuts into my back. I feel that a little more; I smell the strong iron and know that I'm bleeding worse.

I consider sprouting my own wings, but it seems pointless; this is a man who is used to using wings in combat, and I can't challenge him that way. So I attempt a clumsy run at him, talons extended as long as I can make them, swishing through the air in threatening arcs, then attempt at the last minute to slide under him. He's seen the feint coming, of course, and he grabs me as I fly between his legs and lifts me back up to his face. "Nobility," he murmurs, and plunges his left fist into my side, goring a hole into me. I feel that. I squirm and then I spit at him, gobs of mucus landing on his regal features. He drops me, more in disgust than anything else, and I lie on the ground, trying to ignore the hole in me and the blood pumping out. It will heal, I think, but not in time for this fight. I don't have long. Suns, I don't have long.

He glances at me and grins, and I know the end is coming. I crawl backward away from him, and I press both my arms to cover my wound, as if to stem the blood. He stoops over me then, claws extended for the killing blow, with his wings poised to follow through and slice me in two. I look at him, eyes filled with pure terror, both hands still covering my wound, and I start to murmur: "No . . ."

Then his arms come down gradually, the wolfblood giving me a slower view of time. I whip my hands from my wound, drenched in my blood, and wipe my playacting look of terror from my face, and I launch my fists into his chest as I leap up. I strike as hard as I can as his arms close around me, and I see his look of surprise at the move. Then he does what everyone does when they're surprised. His jaw drops open, and in that split moment, drawn out as long as I need with my drip-feed view of time now, I shove my right fist into his mouth. We topple back together, so I land on top of him, my fist now halfway down his throat. His eyes burn with rage as he starts to choke on my arm, and his fists punch my sides, great strong blows, and I feel a rib bend, and then break, and then another one go. But I keep my hand there, feeling the damp moist warmth of his gullet, and his fangs closed around my arm where it enters his mouth. I close his nostrils with my other hand.

As his blows increase, I see the panic slip into his eyes, a frightened insect on his back. Each blow feels like it's breaking something new inside me, and I daren't look down at my chest. I feel the tip of the wings that can just about reach my back start to slice deep into me, razor-like, and I feel proper pain, so I know how deep they must be going. My chest and back on fire, I stare hard into his eyes as his eyelids start to droop. I give him the best of me, and as pure agony starts to join the simple pain of the cuts, I think about my sister, her life given away cheaply, and my mother and father, footnotes to history. I think about Beth, and how we could've gone to Last Light, and how I was wrong for ever thinking it foolish. I hold her there tight; I hold all the ways in which I failed her close to me and I use them as armor against the man who broke her.

Then I realize I'm screaming, right in his face, but even as I scream, I realize that the blows have stopped and his eyes are closed.

I keep my hand down his throat and my fingers on his nostrils for another tenth of the glass to be sure, and I stop only when I start to feel faint from my own blood loss.

Then I get up, rolling off his unconscious body, and I turn to Sage and Jacob, who are looking stunned at me like they've never seen a Worn defeat a Lord on wolfblood before. Which I suppose they haven't.

"You can't kill a vampire by taking away their air," I say, "but you can knock them out. *Anatomie of the Vampire* by Cloak Kuscantion." I smile. Some blood dribbles out my mouth.

"Libraries save lives," I add, and then the world goes black.

I come to with Sage above me, a vial at my lips.

"He had three on him," he says. "An emergency stash, I suppose. You need to drink them all." His face looks serious, even for him. "You're really badly wounded, Sam, even for all the wolfblood in you."

I look down at the hole in my chest, which is smaller but still leaking a lot of blood. I feel the pain now, as some of the wolfblood wears off— the beginnings of a throb in my side and the growing waves of pain from the deep gashes in my back.

"How long have I been out?" I ask as I down all three vials, gasping as they hit me all at once.

"Barely a twelfth of a glass," says Sage, a little admiration in his eyes. "I see everything is quicker on wolfblood."

I laugh, coughing up a goop of what I hope is just blood and not organ. "You have no idea."

I look beyond Sage, at a still-pale Jacob and beyond him at Raven, lying down, panting hard, slowly recovering. Then I turn to Rufous, panicked, and see him still out cold.

"He's dead to the world," says Sage. "Your tactics were . . . incredible."

"It was the wolfblood."

"Wolfblood only realizes your potential. In terms of the mind anyway. From what I've read on the subject."

I let that one go; I'm too tired for a lecture on blood. "We need to move soon. I don't know how long he'll be out. I couldn't fight him again."

"Wait . . . are we not going to finish him?" asks Jacob.

I stand up slowly, wincing at the slowly closing wound in my side, and watch him carefully. My nails form talons. I have enough strength still in me on the wolfblood to end him. Cut his throat, hold him down while he bleeds out fully, beyond any healing. Maybe even take his head off just to be sure, so no amount of wolfblood can bring him back. I try and summon some courage to do this, try and keep the images of my mother and father in my head to fuel my vengeance. But there's no fuel and there's no fire. I'm just . . . tired.

I drop my arm and my talons recede. I turn away from him, my Great White Wolf, and I let him lie.

"You are going to kill him, aren't you?" asks Jacob. "You know, the coldhearted prickard who spends most of his day torturing your kind. And who killed your friend."

"He did." I nod. "But I'm done with doing things I think I have to do as part of a narrative that never made any sense."

"Um," says Jacob. "I don't really know what that means, but I can get a rock if you like, and you could drop it on his head."

I shake my head. "He's better alive. Dead, he's a martyr, and an excuse for the Lords to rain down punishment on the rest of the city. But alive, he'll be angrier than ever, and he'll make mistakes. Better him in charge of the city than a more careful Lord."

"I see," says Sage. "But you know, Sam, while he's making these mistakes, a lot of people might get hurt in the meantime."

"Well," I reply, "I'll just have to be there to help them."

"What?" asks Sage, alarmed.

"I'm not coming with you to the border."

"What?" asks Sage, a genius reduced to repeating his words. That's some effect I'm having on him.

"I'm not leaving my city. Not now. Not now when everything might turn on the smallest of things. When the truth has a chance to come out."

"Sam," says Sage, "this is the wolfblood talking. The bloodrush."

"No, it isn't. It's me. The real me, finally. It's . . . it's hard to explain. All my life I've been fueled by two things. My need for revenge against Rufous and the Lords like him, and my feeling that I'm special, and I'm going to prove it one day. And where has this got me? A dead friend. A dead mentor. Almost dying myself more times than I care to count. It's time to stop thinking I'm the center of my own story. It's not the blood that's the problem. It's *me*. Which is exactly why I need to stay, because I can be a part of something small here. The Lords are going to try and keep everything the same. I can't let that be an easy task for them. Not in a big way. But a small cog in whatever happens next."

"I don't think you could ever be a small cog, Sam," says Sage.

"No," I say firmly, certainly. "This was . . . this was a test. A taster of a life I thought I wanted. It hasn't gone that well. I'm happy with being a person of small consequence, doing their best, little by little."

"This is all very inspiring," says Jacob. "But pointless if you're caught."

"But I won't be. They'll follow your trail and hardly notice mine. As Raven said, they don't have pure wolf noses, even on wolfblood. I'll carry on south now, down through Eastfall and then into Southeastfall; once I'm there in my old childhood streets of Worntown, they won't have a chance of finding me."

"Are you sure?" asks Sage.

"Yes, I really am."

He stares at me. He is uncharacteristically speechstruck.

"Sam," says Jacob, holding out his hand, "you're the bravest lass I ever came across. Shade that, you're the bravest person. Let's have a proper drink the next time we meet. The kind where you check all your limbs are still there when you wake up."

I ignore his hand and hug him instead. "No offense, Jacob, but for the sake of my liver I hope that's a little while off."

Sage goes to say something but stops. A little silence. Maybe something there, but the moment passes, as they always do outside of stage-tales.

"Right," I say. "I'll be going now. How's Raven?"

"I think she can run again," replies Sage. "She's just . . . getting some sustenance."

"You mean she's eating those guards, don't you?"

"Ah, yes. She really is."

"Can't say they don't deserve—" I start to say, but my words are stopped by Sage, who does the strangest thing. He wipes away the bubble of blood around my lips and then he kisses me and holds me, and though it's not the best kiss I've ever had, probably not the second-best, either, in that moment it feels pretty close.

"Hmm," I say after it's finally ended, the taste of him lingering. "I wasn't sure you were the type to do that."

"I'm not sure I am," he replies. "I think at some point in the last day or so I've lost my mind."

"Well, it's not the end of the world if you don't find it again."

We stare at each other a little more then, two people forgetting they have half the Blood Guard on their tail.

"Stay alive, Sam. I'll see you soon," he says, and I like that, because we both know we'll never see each other again. He seems to read my thoughts, because he adds, "You have a habit of things happening around you."

I smile. "Not very logical of you there, Sage. I think maybe just a lot of things have started to happen."

His next reply I don't hear, because I've turned away and started running. No one likes goodbyes, after all.

After a while I dare to turn around, and all I see in the distance behind me is an empty clearing.

33

The Threat of the Real

I have not been able to establish quite how the Cult of Humanis was formed, or the persons who populated its immediate founding. Like much of what we know about the cult, that much is shrouded in mystery.

Neuras Sondallion,
A Storied Overview of the Many Cults, volume 2

Sage

We emerge from the tree line into a clearing, with a cliff edge beyond it. Raven comes to a rapid halt and we half climb, half shoot off her. Then I watch the transformation from fur and claws to skin and nails, the rippling kaleidoscope of flesh and bone and everything else in between. It never gets old, and it never gets any less disturbing.

Beyond the cliff edge I see a valley spread before me, vast and wide and verdant, and on the other side of the valley I see thick, dense forest; the real thing, not the scattered woods we've been running through so far.

"Extinction Valley. Beyond that, home," says Raven, watching my gaze.

"Not our home," notes Jacob, who is busy rubbing his legs, the grimace on his face giving a fairly good indication of how much he enjoys traveling by wolf.

"Ours for a while," I say. "With the news Raven is bringing home, she will need some corroboration from others who were there. We owe her that much for her assistance. Not to mention we are still technically representing the Archmage, so if there is any talk of war we will need to be there. Isn't that right, Raven?"

"Oh, he's welcome to leave if he wants," Raven says, smiling toothily at Jacob. "Though it may take him a little longer with less limbs than he started."

"Right," replies Jacob, "the Wolflands it is. I just hope you have a hot bath ready when I get there."

"And why would we not?" asks Raven slowly.

"Well, you're wolves. I just assumed you lived in the forest and did . . . forest things."

"Forest things? What do you mean, 'forest things'? We can do both, you know. We are civilized and we are wolves. What, did you think we just bathed in fucking rivers all the time?"

"The thought had crossed my mind."

"I bet it has."

"Why would I have to imagine it? I've seen you naked more than I've seen myself, I reckon."

"Yes I know, you stare enough."

"Now that's just mean."

As my new and hopefully temporary traveling companions bicker away, I stare across the valley and ruminate on why I'm really so keen to escape to the Wolflands for a while. To do so, I have to examine myself objectively, a tough skill at best and one that few have and I am struggling to hold on to. Do I not want to go back to my cold, quiet, sometimes sad temple just yet because I can still feel Sam's lips on my face, all warmth and stirrings of feelings I thought I'd put aside? Or is that the tale I want to spin, knowing that the truth is colder and deeper and more real? Put simply, if the vampires found the weapons, then they must suspect the mortals were real, and I am no longer the only one hiding the secrets of a long-gone race. Everything has changed, or to put it more accurately, everything had already changed, and I'm only just spying the extent of it.

My thoughts exactly, Brother Bailey. I'm glad we see eye to eye on this.

I freeze. That sensation in my head again, that dull throb; that tiny needle picking its way around my head.

Please don't alert the others. Unless you would like me to explain how we really met, and what followed from it. I'm not sure Jacob would appreciate that. Just think your replies in your head to me. I know it's been a long time since you've done that, but I'm sure you can pick it up. Old habits never really die, after all.

I give it a go. *Why you here?* I try again. It requires more concentration than you might think. *Why are you here?*

I have a final message for you. I didn't think it very appropriate to give it back in First Light. You had more pressing matters at hand. Staying alive, I believe, was the main one.

What's the message? I think, scanning the valley all around me. *And where are you?* Far enough away so that Raven cannot smell you . . . but *you read my mind so easily? Sinassion, just how much have your powers grown?*

Always the curious one. Always the deducer. I never quite had your patience for the smaller details, did I? Maybe that's why I gave up on the Cult of Humanis, back in its founding, back in those wild early days of ours. As much as it would be nice to tell you what I have been up to, I'm afraid that will have to wait. I just want you to know. I want you to know that I'm sure this time.

Oh, not this again. Time has not made you rational, I see.

But it's not opened your mind, either.

Fine. What is your proof? How you can be sure this time?

He tells me the proof he has, and it is everything I can do not to speak out loud.

If you are lying to me . . .

Ah, old friend, I never lied to you. Not even once. I never have and I never will. People always mistake this of me. I do not lie. I just choose my time to tell people what I know. And I know this for sure. They are coming back.

He pauses for a few seconds, savoring the moment. He always was a drama mage.

Our mortals, Sage. The ones we've devoted our lives to in one way or another. They're alive and they're coming.

And then I feel him going out of my head; and of all the questions I still have to ask him I pick one that is less important overall but of great importance to me.

Wait. I have to know. Your Shades wouldn't touch us. Me and Jacob, they let us travel freely on our way to First Light. It's my thesis that they've done this for all Quantas since Grayfall. Why would Saxe instruct them so?

He didn't. That wasn't Saxe. Those were my instructions. No Shade has ever harmed a Quantas. You probably didn't notice in the war, since none of you were really involved in it, were you? It is nice to hear they have not forgotten everything I taught them.

I think back to the roof. When they attacked. They were after Raven, I see now—not us.

But why? Why would you tell them so? What's so special about us?

Go where I lead on what is to come, old friend, and I might tell you.

That's not good enough! I think angrily, but he is gone, gone out of my head, and I know better than to speak into the winds of the valley searching for him again. Instead, I have to resume my conversation with my companions, and act like my life hasn't changed; transformed in an instant, my future forever altered in one direction even as the world feels the same. Then again, if the mortals are returning, then it won't be the same for long.

I remember once talking to a Cloak in Luce, a philosopher. Cloaks are always the philosophers of the sorcerer world. Something about the power of illusion starts them thinking about reality and all the rest of it. He asked me to imagine I was a brain in a jar, imagining my life, and how I would prove such a thing, or rather how I could disprove it. Following my flawed attempts to answer him definitively, I was left feeling completely adrift; completely set apart from reality. Now, staring across to the Wolflands, I feel that same feeling.

There are worlds beyond mine and things I have only dreamed to touch.

But those things are coming, and my dreams threaten to be real.

34

Just When I Thought I Was Out

Oh and I must tell you of how I met Lady Hocquard's daughter. What a treasure! Wit and intelligence, though I do spy some willful independence even at her young age . . . What a woman she will become— though I fear she will be the death of her mother!

> Sinopia Azzuri, in a letter to her cousin,
> dated 498 AL, two years before Grayfall

Sam

The inn is busy tonight. It's Hallsday, and you're meant to drink more blood than any other day of the week, not that anyone in here needs telling. I sip my oxbloodwine carefully, savoring every drop, not because it tastes good—the events of the previous month have made my palate much too choosy to be satisfied with this—but because I don't have much coin for any more. And I don't exactly have a Lord's room I can sneak into to top up my supply. I don't, in fact, have anywhere, save a worn clump of blankets in a small room I sleep in with three other girls in a tall, rambling house on the western edge of Westfall that I share with dozens of others, mostly actors in the stagetales. I clean the taleboards and serve blood and do other assorted things for the cast. It's little better than what I used to do at the palace, but it's half a city away from there and a whole city away from the streets where I grew up, so it's a place they aren't likely to come looking for me. Not that they'd recognize me; I cut my hair to just above my shoulders, as short as I could bear it, and colored it blond with a mixture of fastberry and whale fat; the smell isn't great, but it surely does the job.

I look around the inn and see no faces I recognize. That's good. For the first couple of weeks I ventured nowhere but the stagehall and my lodgings. But I won't hide forever. Not from them. The Lords that seek me—if they still do so and do not think me fled—don't know their city well enough to find me here. Especially now that their spymaster is dead.

I stare into my blood. I feel like my life has been reset; like my time at the palace was another path from another Sam, and someone somewhere has clicked their fingers and put me back right where I was, except properly alone this time, not even with a sister slowly falling away from me.

Except the city is not the same. It's been an entire month since we solved the murder of Azzuri the younger. Everything appears to have gone back to normal; Rufous is now First Lord, his father's funeral a great procession from the palace through to Centerfall, the noise of the crowd so loud I could hear it in Westfall. The story is that he died during the attack by Grays, which people seemed to have swallowed easily. The invasion of the Grays rallied the city to a great state of mourning. No one ever shows so much love for their overlords as they do when they think their lives have been threatened. The bloodguards who defended the city against the aborted attempt by the Grays are heroes, though the ones who actually saw the illusions that day know something's not right; you can see it in their eyes if you pass one in the street. They look distracted, like they haven't quite woken from a dream but been thrown into the world anyway. Certainly, no one can explain how the Grays breached the wall. Rumors spread that a couple of Grays somehow broke through the lines and breached the Blood Bank, but that hopeful piece of cover seems to be falling apart: the rumor I heard yesterday was that the surviving guards swear it was a wolf that jumped them, not a Gray. *Oh yes,* I think. *And what a wolf.*

So everything is normal, yet everything is not. The city is still ruled by Lords, busy in their continuation of the great lie that a small cabal of them began. But the city doesn't feel right, like the lie itself is stretched, holding up the city like the worn rope that holds the well bucket. I can feel it in the air, feel the strands fraying. A lie is always greatest just before its exposure. Sage said that, soon after we found out the truth. Sooner or later the rope will snap, but it won't be me that pulls its last threads apart. Not anymore. I'll do what I can to tell people of the truth without getting sunburst for it, but my time on the stage is surely over.

"Well, this is a depressin' sight for my disbelievin' eyes if ever I saw one," says a voice behind me.

I turn around so fast I drop a good portion of my pint on the floor, and I see Alanna grinning at me, letting her whole face smile for once. Her clothes are a little more ragged than usual and her face is even more dirt-covered, but other than that she's the same tight-ponytailed manic-eyed demon that first drew a blade on me in a mansion far away.

"I thinks you've spilled some, Sammy girl. Always were a bit careless with the blood, weren't you?"

"Alanna!" I cry, and then seeing the frown on her face, I whisper, "Sorry."

"That's better, Sammy, my girl. The king of ears and secrets may be dead, but there are still a bunch of smaller prickhearts begging to hear the words o' a Leech girl."

"I don't . . . I don't understand. They told me you'd fled. Gone."

"Ha!" laughs Alanna, that memorable laugh from deep within her that I never thought I'd hear again. "They may call it fleein', but I call it survival. Survivin' another day. Leeches are worth more than a couple of lives, Sammy girl. That's a truth you can take to the twin hells and back."

I reach out to touch Alanna, but I think better of it, and try and put my feelings in my voice instead. "I don't know what to say about Lady . . . about Daphnée. I'm so sorry, Alanna."

Alanna's expression doesn't change, but one eye twitches a little. "I know you're sorry, Sammy girl. But she wouldn't want no reminiscin' or teardroppin'."

"And what would she want?" I say, feeling the start of something again, slow but sure.

"Like I say, I'm following her instructions. One of which was to give you this." She pulls out a small brown rolled-up piece of parchment from her petticoats, tied with both a red and a white ribbon.

"What is it?" I ask.

"Why you ask when you can read is a mystery to me, Sammy," replies Alanna. "Meet me outside when you're done."

As Alanna leaves, I inspect the parchment, and then for no real reason I smell it. It smells of roselily, and for a split second I'm transported back to the Lady herself, sitting on the end of my bed and holding my hand. Then I untie the ribbons and unfurl the parchment.

Dearest Sam,
Do follow Alanna now, there's a dear.
                                        With fond regards,
                                        Daphnée

I gawp at these words for a good few moments, and then I do as the letter says, draining the oxblood before leaving the inn.

Alanna is waiting around the back alley, idling against a wall and grinning. "I trust you had a good ogle of the words, Sammy?"

"Alanna, I don't . . ."

And then I see her, standing in the shadows. She's dressed like a Worn now, her hair tied back and half covered in a cap, her face shorn of makeup, her rough linen dress more rags than riches. But the sharpness of those eyes, the breeding of that face, the smile that speaks of more—those can never be hidden. And poking half out of the cap is one of the small white flowers that were always in her hair, like a memory of a dream I thought I had.

"I thought you were dead," I say quietly. "You were shot."

"I was, Sam, my dear. And then this remarkable creature saved me." She nods to Alanna. "And now here we are, reunited."

"How did she save you, Lady Hocquard?" I ask, the shock of seeing her and my need for knowledge keeping my relief at bay, for now.

"Daphnée, Sam. And this time you actually have to call me that. I have lost my house and my standing; my title may remain, but after what we've learned, I'm not sure I want it. As for Alanna, she won't tell me how she saved my life. Much like she won't tell me who she was in Last Light, or why that strangest of cities fell. The more I learn about her, the more questions I have." She flicks a mischievous smile at Alanna, who looks away. "A little like you, Sam," she adds, moving closer to me. Her defining smell of roselily is gone, replaced by the mud of the streets, but I see she still has her fox pendant around her neck, only tucked into her street clothes. Sign of a life now burned to ash.

"Except," she continues, "the question for you, Sam, is how I could have so cruelly sidelined at the death someone who is so remarkable."

I look away. I find anger still there, despite my relief. The two fight it out.

"Let me see if I can explain," says Daphnée. "You are special, Sam. I know this because I have met you before, in a way, in another time. I told you of my daughter. I did not tell you that she died shortly after Grayfall, not during it. Such bitter irony to survive that event but succumb soon after. The Leeches were her idea, her child. Her initial plans laid the foundations for what Alanna and I built on. She was gutsy and brave, but also fiercely intelligent and kind, and a little bit driven—perhaps too much, perhaps too keen to grasp whatever the future had for her. All things I see in you, Sam. It is like a reflection cast across the years." She turns away from me now, and stares into the shadows of the alley, whether steeling herself to continue or falling into the memories, I can't be sure.

"My daughter was killed for her fire, however. The third Lord she blackmailed—herself, with no help—took a madness upon him that is normally held in check by common sense and the desire for a quiet life. He broke into our home and he sliced my daughter's neck from ear to ear, making sure that enough blood had drained from her that even the finest wolfblood would not resuscitate my girl, and making sure it took hours for her to die. I know this because he told it to me later, in his death throes. I was away at a ball as my daughter was dying, flirting with some blooddrunk Lords, the desperate widow. I came home and found her ashes on the floor amid all the bloodstains. I didn't even get to see her face one last time. I wanted to die right there, die with her and see if she and I could survive the passing of our bodies."

Maybe it's the tiny remains of half a wolf I consumed a month ago or maybe my senses are heightened from the shock, but I can smell the salt of her tears as they run down her face even as she remains turned away from me.

"But I didn't die, Sam. Instead, I found the strength to be a tenth of what she was, and I became hard and capable, and when I met Alanna soon after, I became cunning, too. We had our revenge on that Lord—never has any revenge been fiercer—and then we built upon what my Lucretia had begun."

She turns back to me now, wiping away the tears, firmness replacing sadness so quickly I can tell she's done this trick before.

"I tell you this, Sam, so you can understand that when I met you, when I met my daughter, in a different form, but that spirit, that quiet determined drive to learn and to gorge on a new life, I am afraid I did not know how to react. I was encouraging at first, but no doubt seemed cold later as I drew away, remembering how it felt to hold my dying daughter in my arms. I recklessly put you in harm's way in the bank, then retreated, shocked at my feelings, and left you out of the final placing of our puzzle piece, for which I am sorry, my darling, so sorry. You were like a fire I had helped set alight, and now I was afraid to touch its flames. Or something like that. I am sure Alanna would it put a lot better."

"I'd put it exactly like that," says Alanna, quiet, looking rapt at Daph-née with what I now see is pure love, the kind I should have spotted long before.

"But I will never disrespect you like that again, Sam, if you forgive me and choose to stay with us. The Lords may know of us, our home may be gone, but we will continue as we ever have, and we will make this city know the truth and give such consequences to the Lords that they will fear the day they ever underestimated us. And you will play a key role in that."

She stands before me then, down but not out, and I find with a little annoyance that my anger has gone and all I have is the thrill. Sam, you are verging on the predictable.

"Do we have lodgings, Daphnée?"

"We do."

"Will we be okay?"

"We'll give it a good try. I still fancy burning it down, don't you?"

"As long as the right ones fall in the flames," I say, smiling.

Daphnée laughs, sharp and loud, then turns to Alanna.

"What do you think, then, Alanna of Last Light. Shall we take her to them? Is she ready?"

Alanna grins her snaptail grin. "If she ain't ready now, then I know not when she'll ever be."

"Take me to who?" I ask.

"Oh, Sam, dear," Daphnée replies, barely containing her amusement. "You're never going to guess."

I don't know how the inn the Five Cuts got its name. No one does, far as I can tell.

My favorite story tells of a time before the towns and cities of the continent, not long after the Great Intelligence, when vampires were still barely past the feral age, still wild in many ways and living in tribes. It tells of how one tribe came across one of the wolfkind for the first time. They couldn't believe what they were seeing. A large wolf that could turn into a man. The wolf asked them permission to be on its way. The vampires said yes, if they could take a sip of its blood, just to see what it tasted like. The wolf made a cut with its paw and let them taste a few drops. The blood tasted better than any animals they had ever had before. It made them feel strong. They asked for another taste. Just one more, they said. But wolves heal quickly, so it had to make another cut. But this second taste of blood made the vampires feel even stronger. One more cut, they said. And another. After the fifth cut, the wolf said, *You must let me go now. You promised.* But the vampires had started to grow wings, and liked this new development very much, so they fell upon the wolf and drained it dry. The very spot where the wolf died was where the Five Cuts was first built.

Though it's obviously a story with its foundations firmly in cow shit, I've always thought it tells you a lot about vampires.

I don't recognize the area the tavern is in much. It's the southwest of the city. I'm from Southeastfall. Still Worntown, but a little less intense than here. Southwestfall has always had a harder feel than its sister district. Not that the streets are much different. All mud and wood and fluids and barely concealed chaos. The tavern itself looks different from the ramshackle inns around my way, though. You can still read the words on the sign, for a start. The Worns around here must take a little pride in their pisseries.

I enter the inn behind Alanna and the woman I'm trying to get used to calling Daphnée, and I feel a little fear run through me. I don't know who we're about to meet, but what I do know is that together we are the three most wanted people in the city, and despite our clothes and our caps and different appearances, someone could still recognize us.

Daphnée seems to sense my hesitancy. "Now now, Sam, my dear. This is not the time for nerves. Even if someone did recognize one of us, I can assure you that of all the places in the city, this would be the least likely for word to get back to a Lord of our presence."

"And I would kill them anyway," adds Alanna helpfully.

"Yes, that, too."

We go up to the bar, me wrinkling my nose at the stench that lies heavy in the air: bloodwine fumes, the unwashed whiff of blood-drainers and bloodtraders alike, and a mysterious hint of something I never want to get to the bottom of if I live ten centuries. You'd think I'd be used to this, with what I do all day. *Did* all day. But this is something different from a Lord's chambers. A wider variety of drinks, for a start.

The barman is a tall thin blond with the faint start of wrinkles around the eyes and mouth that a century or so on cow gets you. Beneath his blood-spattered red apron, he wears a light gray tunic and gray breeches. He also wears a necklace; it's tucked into his tunic, so I just see the string, but I wager it's in the shape of a small bloodvial. The Vials are the main street gang round here, and their necklaces signal this to anyone unwise enough to provoke them. I'm not in the genteel world of Northfall anymore, that's for sure.

I order plain oxblood, neat. No alcohol, but a better kick than cow. Daphnée has a blood orange, an unhelpful name because it's infused with berry juice instead of orange, although the blood is certainly correct. Alanna is the only one who orders alcohol in her drink. She asks for an ashchaser and I don't recognize it when it comes, a small glass shot full of something black bobbling in a pint of blood, but I'm not sure that I want to know, so I don't press it.

Drinks in hand, Daphnée leads us past the splintered malderwood tables and various floor stains and inhabitants in the shadows, who I see are adding to the stains in various ways, through to a door at the back. It leads to some warped and faded stairs, though made of better wood than you see in Worntown these days. The Five Cuts has history, and though it may have seen better times, its foundations are stronger than I realize.

At the top of the stairs, on a corridor lit by desertmold lamps, giving it a strangely intense glow, there are three doors. Daphnée chooses the one on the far end and knocks five times, the first three normal, then a pause, then the last two rapid-fire. It's the first time I've seen a secret knock, and it's as artful as it sounds.

"In you come, me dears!" shouts a female voice from inside, with one of the strongest Southwestfall accents I've ever heard. A much friendlier tone than I expected from what I'm wagering is a secret meeting.

We enter, and I'm a little taken back by the normality of the scene. I expected to find a shadowy figure hidden by hood or cloak, whispering at us from a dark alcove. Instead it's a fairly large oblong of a room well lit by several oil lamps in sconces on the whitewashed oak walls. In the middle are two women seated around a nice-looking, if a little faded, redoak table, which is covered in various blooddrinks and scattered with playing cards. It even has a window at the far end, through which I can see some of the midevening stars, but there are thick sun-blind curtains around it, too, so this is a room for all occasions. There is another door right of the window, which I assume to be a cupboard.

Hanging on one of the oak walls is a large oil painting depicting a large group of vampires dressed in Worn clothing all crowded together in what looks like a square, with the huge columns of some imposing building behind them, like the Blood Bank but twice the size.

"That, Sam my love, is a gathering of the Worns in Lightfall who managed to get the deal with the Lords that got us some of the good blood at better prices. We opened up the markets, by the Gods we did. Smugglers, all of us, but we made it work with the nobility an' we changed that city, for a short while at least."

I turn to the woman saying all this to me with such familiarity, the same one who hollered at us from inside. She has a jolly, round face, the kind you'd want to see at a market stall or on your deathbed. Curly shortish blond hair rings her face, or at least it was blond at one time but almost all of it's gray now. This and her deep, wrinkled face means she can't be much younger than two centuries. Definite old age for a Worn.

"Probably what made Saxe and his ilk do that dirty plan with the Grays you stumbled on," she continues. "We got too high up in the world for 'em, and so they brought the whole city down and the bloody Centerlands all along with it. But I ain't blamin' no one but them for that one, you can be chuffin' sure of that."

I'm speechless. She knows my name, she knows who I am. Daphnée must have told her everything.

She senses my confusion and grins even wider. "Sorry, Sam, I can be a bit much at first. I'm Molly Threetimes."

I don't bother to hide my shock. "*The* Molly Threetimes?"

"No, girl, the other Molly Threetimes. There's loads of that name around." She grins at Daphnée. "Bloods, Dee, what did she get at the bar?"

"Oh, Sam is sharper than the best of us, Molly. I think she's just not been out of the palace much in the last few years."

I recover myself enough to know that I want to make a good first impression. "I'm sharp enough to know that you were behind the Worn uprising of 430, soon after the war. And that you supplied noble blood to the Dawn Death Patriots of 475. That you founded the Smugglers' Confederacy in 487. The one that led to the deal shown in that painting."

"Ha!" says Molly. "Well, there we have it. I can see why she almost brought the whole city down around her, Dee."

Before I can get over someone calling the woman formerly known as Lady Hocquard *Dee*, Molly continues, "You probably won't know this one, though." She nods to the other woman seated opposite her across the table, still looking at the playing cards in her hand with a slightly vacant gaze. She looks up finally and holds her eyes with mine, and a light chill runs down my spine. There's no emotion in those eyes; they are cold, bereft, dead. Her lank dark brown hair falls around her face, her cheeks sunken, her lips a tiny colorless smudge on a blank canvas. She makes Alanna look like a woman to keep your children entertained with.

"This is Hands Parker. Probably just Hands to you. She leads the Vials."

I nod. The Vials. The main gang in these parts. My observation of the barman was correct. Sage would have liked that, I think, and immediately feel a little sad.

"Hands is not my real name," she adds, her dead stare capturing me again. Her voice is dry, like a breeze through an urnchamber. I can't tell if she's being deadpan or helpful, or something else, but I just nod. I definitely don't want to know how a gang leader got the nickname Hands.

"So we have the best smuggler in Lightfall," I say, my courage a little returned, "and the leader of the biggest gang in First Light. I suppose we're not here for a gossip."

"No. We're here because Dee vouched for you," says Molly, gesturing at Daphnée, who has sat down opposite Molly and taken her hairnet off, carefully rearranging the sole flower in her locks. Alanna remains in the shadows, as is her wont. "And said that you should be involved in what is to come."

"And what is that?" I ask, feeling that shiver of anticipation you get when a room starts to become more than the sum of its parts and history starts to move around you. Or something. Sage would have put it better.

"People think there ain't no rebels left in First Light," says Molly, pouring herself some more bloodwine from the carafe next to her. "No organized ones, at least. But that's plain old nonsense. Nonsense we like people to think. You see, that's how you take on the Lords, Sam. You play like them. Patient. Waiting centuries. But thanks to you, we don't need to be so patient anymore."

"For this next bit, Sam," says Daphnée, "I need you to trust me. Do you trust me?"

"I do," I reply, meaning it.

"Well, you'll need all of that faith in me for this part."

Molly turns to the other door in the room, the one by the window I thought was a cupboard. "Come in then, lads, if you're coming. May as well meet her."

The door opens and a short, unremarkable man shuffles in, dressed in standard Midway clothes: a good-quality red-beige jacket over a soft linen shirt. There's nothing notable about his thin face, short brown hair, and clean-shaven cheeks other than a sense of calm, a feeling of intelligence. I immediately recognize him. He's shaved his moustache off, but how could I not?

"Redgrave," I open with.

"Samantha Ingle," he replies, touching his upper lip in honor of his fallen facial hair. "The one who almost took down Saxe. Remarkable. I'm sorry you had to live in that place. Someone of your intelligence, you deserved more."

"We all deserved more."

He smiles. "Fairly put."

I turn to Molly, who winks at me. "He's been one of ours for centuries, even before he was Azzuri's first man. Speaking of which," she finishes, signaling again to the door, "Redgrave's newest recruit is here, too." I turn to stare as a second, taller man with a wide-brimmed hat steps through. He has a large coal-black unkempt beard and seems to be dressed as a Westfall artisan Midway would be: a frilly shirt tucked underneath a long coat, soft cloth breeches, and dainty buckled shoes. But there is no mistaking those high cheekbones or that aquiline nose or the shrewd eyes or the perfect skin of decades on the finest red.

First Lord Azzuri gives me a smile that could mean anything.

I turn again to Molly, and then to Daphnée, the woman who changed my life forevermore.

"That, dear," Daphnée says, "is how you light a fire."

Alanna whispers from behind me, a voice in the dark.

"An' burn it all down."

END OF BOOK 1

ACKNOWLEDGMENTS

At the risk of being flippant and true, I am and have ever been a bad person surrounded by good people, and I will now thank them in tedious monotony.

First the Yorkshire Hitman—my agent, Harry Illingworth—a good tall lad who always has my back and eats book deals for breakfast. Second (yes, I'm counting), my foreign rights agent, Helen Edwards, for whom no territory is too far (Mars deal just landed). Third, my legendary editor, Pete Wolverton, who very rightfully saved the lives of several characters in this book (for now, ha ha). Thanks for reading my manuscript instead of going shopping, Pete. Fourth, Claire Cheek, the most patient editor in New York. Fifth, all the rest at St. Martin's Press whose industry has created the tome you have before you, including the art department team, who patiently crafted my wonderful cover, especially Ervin Serrano. Sixth, Lamia N. Bayen, the genius polymath who crafted my beloved map and went above and beyond for me.

Seventh (I began a new paragraph for the hell of it), my original Book 1 draft beta readers and old, constant friends, Josh, Jane, Katrina, Laura "Hands," Gen, Mark "Sage," Mike "F Tall" and Caroline, Olly, Jonny, Oli, Dr. Film, and Daphnée (Hocquard, ahem). You may recognize some of their names from the pages of *Lightfall* (yeah, I'm that guy). Eighth, Sam Ingle for the small kindness years ago that gave him main character naming rights. Ninth, Illers Killers, the mighty Discord of my agent sibling authors who keep one another sane. Good people and good friends, I owe them much. Tenth, the CBC crew—Team Henrietta—from which I'll also call out my old podcast chum Julia Boggio for somehow pulling off my author photo. Eleventh, the Notorious Richard Swan, who has consistently helped me in many ways, presumably to one day cash in a horrific debt. Twelfth, the endlessly brilliant FanFiAddict crew, Feet = Meat. Thirteenth, the Fear For All horror crew = best horror reviewers in the business, but avoid them at night. Fourteenth, Antonia: Go Team Orchid! Fifteenth, Eleni, who will never read this, sadly, so I can say anything here—oh, the possibilities.

Sixteenth, my family: Nana; Mum and Nick; Dad and Roz. I've made a lot of weird choices in life and it took me a while to get here, so thanks for never giving up the faith (even if you did privately, I won't judge). My feelings on my Grandad I think I've already made clear in the dedication. Seventeenth, Ceri. Last but hardly least, Jake, for the oddness of the tree's welfare, and for Writers Eponymous and what that's meant.

Don't know how I accrued such a good army. I struggle a lot (most?) of the time to be serious, so let me say for the immediately deniable record: I owe you a debt that can never be repaid. Thank you.

ABOUT THE AUTHOR

Julia Boggio

Ed Crocker was born in Manchester, United Kingdom, and has managed to stay there ever since. By day he edits books—his clients include *Sunday Times* bestselling authors, award-winning indie authors, and acclaimed small presses. By night, or sometimes also by day (freelancer rules), he reviews books and interviews authors for various publications, watches horror films, and plays video games. He did his best to make the above sound impressive, but seriously, what a nerd.

You can find him on most socials as @edcrockerbooks and at ed-crocker .com, where you can sign up for his newsletter for your sins.